ANGELA CAMERON PAGE

A FLEETING TRICK OF THE LIGHT

Copyright © 2025 by Angela Cameron Page.
All rights reserved.

This is work of fiction. Characters, names, places and events are products of the author's imagination. Any similarity to events or places, or real persons, living or dead, is purely coincidental.

No part of this book may be reproduced in any form or by any electronic or mechanical means, including information storage and retrieval systems, without written permission from the author, except for the use of brief quotations in articles or reviews.

Cover art and interior design by Louise Page at Lobster! Lobster! Graphic Design.
Set in Bliss 11/14pt

ISBN: 978-1-0683125-0-2

Author's Note

This book contains references to death, suicide, and brief descriptions of sexual assault.

For Tom, of course

1

'Is there anybody there?'

Silence.

I wait for a beat.

'Will you join us here in the circle tonight?'

Another pause. For dramatic effect.

'Will you communicate with us?'

My eyes are closed. It makes me look as though I'm somewhere else, off in some sort of trance, which adds another little touch of drama. But I don't need to look to be able to picture the scene around me.

Except for a single, foot-high altar candle burning on a brass dish in the centre of the round drop-leaf table I picked up for a steal at the PDSA shop, the room is devoid of any other source of light. I tell my customers that it helps to create the optimum conditions for a successful session, which is partially true. The more relaxed I am, the better reception I tend to get from The Other Side, and a quiet, dim room helps chill me out. But the chances of an *actual* supernatural presence deigning to show up tonight are roughly seventy-thirty against, so in reality it's more about creating an atmosphere of suggestibility, just in case I end up having to fall back on using the non-supernatural alternative to earn my tips.

'We're waiting to receive your message.'

This whole production relies on whoever I'm hosting round the table being immersed enough to really buy into it, and every element of the room is designed to play its part. The eerie shadows cast across my patrons' expectant faces every time the candle flickers; the gentle *thunk* upstairs which is just loud enough and happens at odd enough intervals to make them jump; the occasional tinkle from the bell chimes in the window hinting that something not quite of this world might actually be floating about. In reality, the candle is positioned in exactly the right spot to catch the draft from the broken chimney seal in the fireplace that our landlord can't be arsed to fix; the *thunk* is just the noise the pipes make when the heating's getting ready to come on, set on a conveniently specific timer; the chimes behind the curtain jostle just enough to sound like an angel getting their wings every time a car drives past the house, the front of which sits about three feet from the particularly well-used Erdington side road my housemate and I live in. Throw in some strategic set dressing with occult props and a few crystals and you've got yourself a regular old circus sideshow.

'I'm getting something…'

Even my outfit – the layers of thin scarves hanging around my neck, the floaty gypsy skirt ensemble, the plethora of silver rings dripping from my fingers – is designed to evoke a particular image, one they're already familiar with from every trope of film and TV. *'The Medium.'* Trust me, I wouldn't be seen dead in any of this get-up outside of this room. Pardon the pun.

My eyes flutter open, my gaze directed just slightly towards my right shoulder, as though something might be going on back there that only I can see.

'There's someone with me.'

The aforementioned chimney draft chooses that exact moment to violently flicker the flame before us, and one of the three girls sat around the table makes an audible gasp. It's the first time in a few minutes that I've heard anyone breathe but me.

I tip my head and frown, hard in concentration, like I'm straining to hear. The spirits do tend to get themselves a touch of lazyitis when I have a group in.

'I see an elderly gentleman. He would've passed in the last few years.'

I make a slightly theatrical show of tensing up my whole body, my hand on my chest as I take in a heavy deep breath and let it out noisily.

'Problems with his heart, maybe his lungs?'

The gasper's eyes widen almost imperceptibly – what I said struck a nerve. Which isn't a huge surprise. When customers first rock up, I give them a few minutes to themselves in the front room to soak up the well-crafted ambience while I disappear to 'prepare'. This lot spent their time talking about last months' Freshers shenanigans, which puts them around eighteen or nineteen. The sad odds are that at least one of them will have lost at least one grandparent by now, men die younger so the chances are greater it's that one, and elderly men in the UK die most often either from some form of heart disease, pneumonia or flu.

'Does the letter J mean something to one of you?'

My wide-eyed gasper jumps straight on it. 'My granddad Jim. It might be him.'

I never said that the J related to a first name. If nobody picks it up that way, I can spin it off as a surname, a place, a pet, a profession, almost anything really. But James, John, Joe and Jack are some of the most common male names, especially in the older generation, so it's often a good place to start. Plus, sometimes I just get lucky. Cold reading – technical term for 'making stuff up' – is about as far removed from anything genuinely supernatural as you could possibly hope to get. It's all about statistics, body language and a dash of amateur psychology. Derren Brown's made a fortune from it, although of course he's more than upfront about the fact that he doesn't really, *actually* see dead people.

Me, not so much.

There are plenty of charlatans out there advertising themselves as mediums, psychics, tarot and crystal ball readers, whatever, and they'll happily use every cold reading technique in the book to tell you everything you want to hear and part you from your cash. If I'm having a bad night – work's been stressful, I'm knackered, or the dead folk just aren't up for chatting – then on occasion I do end up being one of them.

'Before the end, before he got sick, did he have a problem with his back?'

With me, the difference is that sometimes, I really, actually *do* see dead people.

'He walked bent, like he was hunching over?'

It turns out, this is one of those times.

'He's telling me it's— what?' I frown as I try to focus. 'Ketosis?'

Grandad Jim – the man himself, or a cloudy, spectral version of the man he was when he was on this side of the curtain – is beside me, hovering behind my right shoulder. I can see the hunch at the top of his back, plain as day. It definitely affected his breathing too, because his voice in my ear is shallow and raspy. In fact, I can barely hear a bloody word he's saying.

'Not ketosis.' I shake my head as I just about make it out, catching myself before an instinctive, mildly irritated eyeroll kicks in. Of course it's not *ketosis* – anyone who's spent half their adult life bouncing on and off the Atkins diet like I have knows exactly what that is.

I don't have the first clue what this word means, but it's what he keeps yammering at me. *'Kyphosis.'*

Now the girl across from me is *really* gasping. Her two mates are looking at each other with mild scepticism, frowning back at her as if to say: *'Don't take the mick. We only came here for a cheap giggle. We all know this is bullshit.'* Then they meet each other's eyes again, silently questioning: *'Isn't it?'*

I can feel that raspy tickle against my ear again.

'Oh, he says it's not really Jim.' This is interesting. 'He went by that, but it wasn't his real name. Was it…'

More shallow whispering, the hairs on the back of my neck prickling.

'What?' Sure I must've heard wrong, I turn sharply to look directly at him. They often tend to up and disappear when you do that.

'Like the engine?'

He smiles and nods.

Now I'm the sceptical one, wondering if he's just messing with me. 'Was his real name *Ivor?*'

'Oh my god,' wide-eyes blusters, incredulous as she looks back between the other two for support. 'That's him. It's really him!'

'You couldn't say it when you were little, you had trouble with your V's,' I hear myself start to explain. I really can't begin to adequately describe how utterly weird and creepy it feels to hear somebody else's thoughts come out of your mouth. Nearly forty years I've been doing this sort of stuff, since I was at junior school, and I've still never really got completely used to it. 'So he used Jim instead, because it was easier for you.'

I'm telling her things she already knows, but it hits different when you hear details about a part of your life you'd mostly forgotten come out of the mouth of a total stranger. She looks on the verge of tears now. That's another thing I've never got comfortable with, even though it happens a lot. At least her reaction is based on an actual, genuine visit from someone she loves, which makes it slightly less awkward than the guilt-provoking alternative. The Dearly Departed don't always turn up exactly when you happen to call, and I can hardly blame them. If I'd just been granted the gift of infinite knowledge and wisdom and access to all the answers to all the questions I'd ever had in my life, I certainly wouldn't be popping back to the physical plane for a casual chinwag any time soon. But bloody hell, do I feel like the crappiest, lowest form of life on earth if customers get teary on the days where I *do* have to fake it.

But today is not that day. Grandad's back in my ear again, and he wants me to look at something.

I frown, confused. 'He's showing me a tin of custard.'

Sometimes the dead can be so random.

'Did he… was it his signature dish or something?'

She wipes tears away with a finger and nods. 'He could never cook. Grandma does all the cooking. But it was his job to heat up the custard when I stayed with them. It was the only thing he could do.'

A lot of stuff I hear from folks in the beyond only makes sense once someone on this side puts it into context. Also, sometimes it's hard to tell what messages are even worth sharing. I have a theory that some people develop a deeply skewed sense of mischief when they shuffle off this mortal coil, as a lot of them spout the most ridiculous bunch of crap. I had one who wanted me to tell her poor grieving husband that their cat was being especially vocal at night because it was possessed by the soul of a Bee Gee. Never mind that the poor guy was sat here bawling his eyes out, missing the woman he'd shared thirty years of his life with and desperate for some sort of reassurance that she was still around. She couldn't have cared less. I guess if you're an arsehole in life, nothing much changes in death.

'He wants you to know that when you think of that memory,

he'll be around if you need him.' He's chattering away like the clappers now, and I'm fighting to keep up. 'He's very proud of you, he says you're the first one in the family to get into Uni?'

All three of them look pretty thunderstruck at this point.

She nods again, slowly. 'That's right.'

'He says he was there when you graduated, when you finished your A levels, I mean. Did you win some sort of prize?'

If she nods much harder, her head might just pop right off.

'He says he was there when you collected it, and he was proud as punch. He always knew you could do it. And don't worry about tripping up the step onto the stage at school, nobody thought any less of you for it.'

A sudden giggle breaks through her tears. Poor kid. It's nice to see a smile.

'He says you worry too much about what other people think, and he wants you to pack it in.' He's quite animated now beside me. 'He keeps saying it again and again, and he's being very specific about those words: 'pack it in'. Does that make sense to you?'

She smiles wryly. 'It does.'

Probably something he used to say a lot.

'Tell Flora, Joey's just the same.' Well, that one came out of my mouth from nowhere.

Another laugh from her in response. 'Oh my god.' She's shedding happy tears now, though. The difference in her whole demeanour is screamingly obvious.

'I think Flora's your grandma, his wife?'

'Grandma Florence. He's the only one who called her Flora.'

Now he's brought me a gorgeous, bouncing red setter. 'Was Joey their – dog?'

She's loving this now, glowing as she looks back and forth between her friends, all smiles and contentment. 'He was.'

'He had a little patch of blonde fur...' I have to look down a bit to see it on him as he sits by my feet, panting enthusiastically. 'Over his—' I mix up left and right sometimes, and look back and forth between my own hands for a second to make sure I'm not back to front. '—his *right* eye. Where he had a tumour removed.'

Specificity is the holy grail of mediumship. The more detail you can give, and the more obscure that detail is, the less room there is for doubt. I'd say I've covered that particular base pretty well this evening.

'Uh huh.' My star customer is grinning away at this point, shrugging casually now with every new snippet, as though all of this is perfectly normal and she's been hearing about her grandparents' dead dog's health conditions from strange middle-aged women since she was knee high to a grasshopper. But I'm pleased she's pleased. It always feels good to pass on something real, to give someone some genuine comfort. That's why I do it.

I'm lying, of course. I do it for the twenty quid cash in hand. But the other thing can be pretty satisfying too, when it happens. Back when I started this racket – sorry, 'side hustle' – as a way of making extra cash, I only planned doing it long enough to get out of the debt I built up living on credit cards back in my poorly paid twenties. But after more than two decades living with housemates, I'm desperate for my own place. Not to buy, of course; I could afford the mortgage payments, but saving up a big enough deposit on my salary to satisfy a bank? I'd have more chance of getting a pet unicorn. No, I'll rent till I die; but that's okay. I just want somewhere that's mine. A little one-bed flat, maybe with a balcony and some sort of view, decent heating and landlords that aren't dodgy, and no roommates. I don't think that's a lot to ask.

The raging success of Grandad Jim's appearance does mean that the other two who came along for the ride get short shrift, unfortunately. Group sittings are fiddly that way; just getting one bona fide visitation from beyond is pretty good going; there's not a chance in hell anyone else is going to turn up now to natter with the others. Which, to be honest, is all well and good. I guarantee you, none of these lot booked in a week before Halloween expecting anything more than a mildly amusing spectacle – some spooky atmosphere, a couple of calculated guesses about their lives, some fortune teller bullshit about what handsome guys, gorgeous girls or foxy fluids they're destined to meet. And if that's all I can manage, I'm more than happy to deliver – it's a mutually beneficial delusion. My customers tend to be an even split between the ones who really want to believe, and those who are just up for something different to do, and the first lot usually book a one-to-one. Uni groups don't visit because they're looking for proof of life after death, they just want something interesting to do in this one. It's like a reverse escape room – you escape *into* it to forget dull old reality for an hour, and the ones who don't get a genuine reading are still entertained. I never tell them anything negative, I always try and make them smile, and when you take into account the cost of taxis and drinks, I still work out cheaper than a night out at Reflex.

As the voice of our visitor finally fades away back into the ether, I switch my attention to give the remaining audience members what they came for and chill things back out a bit for the fifteen minutes of time they have left. Amongst other nuggets, I throw in a couple of the old fortune telling standards. One of them gets a vision of a half-packed suitcase indicating some upcoming travel and is told she needs to have more faith in her studying abilities; the other an image of opening doors, signifying opportunities, and advice to stop looking back to the past as what's done is done. I also throw in one of my personal favourites as a general catch all for the whole group: *'beware of a red-headed woman'*. A medium I once visited imparted that little gem of advice to me once and I always found it mildly amusing. Mostly because, in my considered, professional opinion, the supposed medium in question had all the supernatural ability of a garden gnome.

The evening draws to a close and I lead them back to the hall, where they each part enthusiastically with their cash. I never take payment upfront, and I always tell people on arrival that if they're not satisfied at the end of the session, they don't have to pay me a penny. In the fifteen years since I started doing sittings like these, I've only had a couple of refusals, and those were when I was still back in my heavy drinking days, often useless, and therefore completely fair enough. The hangovers disrupted even my most basic attempts at cold reading, and actively prevented getting anything remotely resembling a genuine connection with anyone on the Other Side. Of course, those drinking days started in the first place as a way of blocking the whole thing out, so I don't know why I was ever surprised.

I shut the door on the chilly Birmingham evening as the Uni group excitedly chatter their way down the road towards an exceptionally shiny VW, showing up my knackered old Fiesta three cars down. Locking up behind them but leaving the chain off – Lisa comes in from her night shift at some ungodly hour of the AM, and the last thing I need is an early wakeup call from a locked out, hacked off housemate – I head back into the front room, clear away my props, and blow out the candle.

2

Hosting visitors – whether in corporeal form or not – always takes it out of me, so I slept like the dead last night. Always with the puns, sorry. Despite the solid sleep, I still struggle to drag my lazy arse out of bed on Friday morning. If I'm honest, that's not just a today issue. It's becoming more and more of a challenge pretty much every working day of the week.

My bare foot whacks something hard as I wander dozily onto the landing and I crouch down beside it with a frown. I'm greeted by an empty jar of Lisa's super fancy Bushido coffee that she spends an absolute fortune on, with a passive-aggressive sticky note attached.

If you must drink the last of it, please at least have the decency to replace it.

If I rolled my eyes any harder, they'd pop right out of my head. The joys of housemates. Honestly, still having to live in a share in my forties is just embarrassing. Lisa needs to take it up with her girlfriend, who knocks back that bougie overpriced swill every time she's over like she's drinking my cheap Aldi stuff. Shuffling back into my room to grab a pen from my bedside drawer, I scribble on the back of the note – *NOT me! Talk to Penny!* – before I stick it inside the empty jar and dump the lot outside her closed bedroom door at the other end of the landing.

By the time I'm showered and ready and walking towards the train station, it's already faded to the back of my mind. The occasional passive-aggressive note aside, Lisa's a decent housemate, and I've worked my way through every variation of bad ones in the decades I've lived in shares. She doesn't leave piles of dishes in the sink, doesn't bring a crowd of strangers back high from the club at three in the morning and doesn't attempt to force her way into my bedroom when she's drunk and horny. Plus, sometimes she leaves me leftover veggie lasagne. She's also a member of a select group of people in my life who didn't look at me funny on finding out what I do in my spare time. An exceptionally select group, in fact, made up of just her. My doing it for extra cash in our shared living room doesn't bother her either, because it's only two, maybe three times a month that it happens, and I'm careful to schedule bookings only on evenings when I know she's on shift. It probably helps that she suspects I fake the whole thing.

Snagging a seat on the train – miracle of miracles – improves my morning mood some, but I still need a caffeine hit before I can fully deal with the bullshit that is Work. Friday is Treat Day – the one day a week I allow myself to shell out for breakfast outside of the house on my limited budget – so as I exit with the rest of the throng out through the back of New Street, bundling up against the developing cold, I turn in the direction of the closest coffee shop, with the promise of a massive caffeine hit and a cheese and Marmite ciabatta dancing before my eyes.

'Dot!'

I'm so deep in my own world I barely register the sound of my own name.

'Dot, wait!'

The light ring of Mags' voice breaks through my haze as I reach the door. 'Morning, Mags.'

'Hey you,' she beams, far too perky for this time of the morning. 'Friday breakfast?'

'Oh yeah.'

We head on in together and join the queue.

'Excited for tonight?'

Hmm. Excited isn't exactly the word I'd use. Mags is talking about the annual Halloween party that Rebecca, our Big Boss – so named for her status in the team as the Partner who all of the other Partners and fee earners report to – is throwing. She's been hosting it for years, and while nobody's technically obliged to show up, it's very much noticed around the firm if you give it a pass. I'm not a fan of parties – almost all social situations involving the living make me intensely uncomfortable, in fact – but in the few years I've been going, I've managed to carve out a cushy position as designated driver. If I can just grit my teeth through the first hour, I can get away with grazing at the food table all night while everyone else gets silly. Also, I tend to keep a watchful eye out in case anyone too drunk to look after themselves needs rescuing from any overly affectionate senior partners. It's a valuable service that's been needed before.

'Thrilled.'

My voice drips with sarcasm, but Mags either doesn't hear it or is choosing to ignore it.

'I've got all the bits of my costume done finally.'

Oh yeah. There's also fancy dress. Terrific.

We edge closer to the till and I grab my breakfast from the chiller. 'You're still doing Wonder Woman?'

'Of course,' she nods back enthusiastically. 'I was up till two sewing the last few stars onto my hotpants.'

When Big Boss first started these parties, there was an expectation to show up as a zombie, or a vampire, or Pennywise the Dancing Clown. You know, something at least vaguely spooky, scary, horror-y. Appropriate to the Halloween theme. Now it's all just cosplay.

I shake my head, weary at the thought of it. 'Mate, you're gonna be *freezing*.'

She grins back at me. 'Yeah, but I'll *look* hot.'

We both laugh. Mags is slim, tall, gorgeous, legs for days. There's not a question she won't look hot.

'What do you think he'll come as?'

'Oh god,' I groan. Not this again. Mags has been nursing a crush on one of the Senior Associates. So far of the unrequited variety, which I personally think is no bad thing, considering his nickname is Dickhead Scumbag. At least, that's what I call him.

'Patrick Bateman, probably.'

'Who?'

I sigh disappointedly. 'Never mind.' Sometimes I forget that a twenty-two-year-old is technically young enough to be my daughter. We don't always get the same cultural references.

'Maybe he'll shed his human skin and turn up in his natural lizard form.'

Mags is *definitely* too young to remember guinea-pig scoffing Diana from 'V' in the eighties, but I think the picture I'm painting is clear enough.

'Dot,' Mags frowns back. 'He's not that bad.'

'Oh, so you admit he *is* bad?'

'He's sweet when you get to know him.'

'So was Ted Bundy.' I know she gets *that* reference. She binge-watches half of Netflix every other weekend.

'Well, I like him.'

'I'm aware.' We're next to be served. 'Just watch yourself with him.'

'Yes, Mom.'

I give up. Although I do appreciate her adoption of the colloquial Midlands' dialect preference over the vastly inferior *'Mum'* instilled during her southern upbringing.

'Please at least promise me you'll bring a coat?'

'*Yes*, Mom.'

I reach the counter and hand my ciabatta to the server. 'This to take away please, with a Venti americano.' I nod in Mags' direction. 'And a Venti caramel macchiato for this one as well, please.'

'Aw, thanks Mom,' she gives me an affectionate side cuddle as I flash my card at the reader and we squeeze into the inadequately-sized hovering spot to wait for our drinks.

I love Mags to bits. She's not a local product – she came up here to Brum for Uni and joined us fresh after graduation last year. The few mates she made while she was studying all scattered back to their home towns, but from what Mags has told me, her folks weren't thrilled at the idea of having their only child back in the house after three years of having it to themselves, not that they ever seemed that interested even before that. So, she found the job with us, was plonked in the spare desk next to me, and promptly got herself semi-adopted by my moody, middle-aged childish self, and by extension Lisa and Penny. And she's an absolute sweetheart of a person, but still young and green enough that the ugly realities of life haven't yet beaten all light and hope from her soul, like they have with the rest of us secretaries. Dickhead Scumbag – sorry, Nathan Kenway – was allocated to me when he started two years ago, and in the six months I put up with his bullshit before going to HR in desperation, he earned the nickname in a million ways. From the relatively banal, demanding I arrange his personal car repairs (not part of my job, thanks); to the increasing annoying, constantly pointing out what he found attractive or not about all of our looks (not remotely interested in your opinion, tosser); to the far more deeply concerning, having me field personal calls to his work number from a number of increasingly distressed and confused sounding young women (if you can't keep it in your pants, keep it away from work, slimeball). The final straw for me was the day I opened the door to the stationery cupboard and caught him getting a blowjob from one of the work experience students. Under the circumstances, I'd hoped HR's promise to 'do something about him' would translate to 'kicking him out of the business on his arse', but it turned out to be 'moving him to the other side of the open plan office'. My challenges around getting up for work started right around then. Turns out realising that your employers, who claim to value employee welfare so much they've won awards for it, actually couldn't give a shit about you is a bit demotivating.

Mags knows all of this about Nathan. I spelled it out super clearly for her the first time she hinted about thinking he was cute. Her take on it is that the car thing was a misunderstanding, the comments about my weight (amongst others) were social awkwardness and I'm reading too much into the phone calls. Plus, technically the work experience girl was old enough to be legally consenting therefore it's condescending of me to assume she wasn't fully in control of her own sexual autonomy that day and was in any way coerced into it. *Please*. A side-effect of the whole medium thing is that sometimes my bullshit detector twitches more accurately than most, but I don't need psychic powers to tell me the guy's a predator.

Liquid sanity in hand, we head up towards the office. Just as we turn onto Colmore Row, I spot a familiar figure in the distance walking down from the opposite direction, and yank Mags back out of sight.

'What?'

'Pat's in early.'

Mags' face says it all. 'Oh, no.'

'Must be catching up on her pile of fuck all to do,' I murmur dryly.

Pat is our Team Leader, which allegedly makes her responsible for the day-to-day management of our secretarial team, as well as supposedly being admin support for Big Boss and a couple of other fee earners. Only, she delegates all her daily work amongst the rest of us, she couldn't organise a bunfight in a bakery, and she never seems to actually *do* much of anything. Actually, I take that back – she invests masses of time in brown-nosing, shit-stirring and pretending she's working when she's actually browsing Reddit. Okay, we all do that one.

'I didn't think she was coming in today,' Mags shakes her head as we wait for Pat to disappear out of sight into the building. 'She's been going on and on *alllllll* week about how Rebecca needed her to help with the party, that she'd be at Rebecca's *alllllll* day.'

The irritation is clear in Mags' voice, which shows just how truly disliked Pat is. Mags is niceness personified; butter wouldn't melt. I told you, she's young and naïve yet, she'll learn in time, bless her. But she never normally has a bad word to say about anyone. Not the idiot who dented her hybrid Yaris a week after she picked it up from the dealership, not the friend who screwed her out of money for some hen do nonsense, not her fee earners when they expect her to stay back till seven at night. When even *she* dislikes someone, you know they've really earned it.

'Rebecca must've changed her plans,' I suggest sarcastically.

The idea that Big Boss Rebecca would ever in a million years ask Pat to play a role in her big 'do' is beyond laughable. This is a woman who had professional planners for her daughter's infant school graduation party. As a boss, she's actually decent – I looked after her for a couple of years, before her Big Boss promotion came along – and she was always respectful, considerate and generally not a massive twatwaffle, which seems to be a key recruitment requirement for most of the lawyers. But as a human, she needs everything in her life to be super-duper totally perfect, down to the tiniest detail, all of the time, every second of every minute of every day. The annual Halloween do isn't the only party she throws on a regular basis, but it's the only one us plebs get an invite for, and is still an immaculately designed extravaganza of a military operation. There's food, drink, games and entertainment, changing every year. I can barely imagine what delights might be had at the parties we *don't* attend, and I have a pretty vivid imagination. Guessing the plans for the evening's festivities has become something of a tradition in the office, and the weird and wonderful ideas have been circulating around the communal kitchen for the last couple of weeks. Themes I've heard suggested so far range from 'murder mystery' (not a bad shout), to 'Crystal Maze' (fun but probably not very practical) and 'Dinosaurs!' (what on earth would that even look like?). In previous years we've had magicians, circus acts and my personal favourite, giant games, although Nathan and his cronies hogged all of the Giant Connect Four grids for the rest of the night after Postroom Phil beat him three times in a row.

There's no sign of Pat in the lobby as we reach the glass entrance doors. 'I think the coast's clear.'

On our way through Reception, Jackie waves me down whilst politely sticking her caller on hold on the switchboard. 'Still okay for tonight?'

'Pick you up at seven,' I smile and nod as Mags and I swipe through the barriers.

'Is it just me and Jackie you're giving a lift to tonight?'

'And Sue from the post room.'

She nods as she calls the lift. 'Hey, what are you going as?'

I shrug. 'Same as last year.'

Outside of the requirements of my side gig, fancy dress is really not my thing. One year, I did think about actually going dressed as a fortune teller as a private joke with myself, but it felt just a bit too much on the nose. Plus, I convinced myself someone might magically twig the truth behind the costume and the secret I've worked so hard to keep hidden from everyone in my 'normal' life for all these years would be rumbled. It's not like I'm the only one who moonlights – a couple of the secretaries do waitressing at the weekends, I've spotted Terry from the canteen behind the bar at the Nightingale and the collective Etsy crafters even have their own WhatsApp group. As long as work's your priority when you're in the office and you don't use the post room to send out your eBay parcels, nobody cares. But as far as I'm aware, nobody else tops up their salary talking to The Other Side and I'm paranoid it'd take HR all of about three seconds to issue my P45 if it ever came out. Dickhead Scumbag brings in clients so he can get away with all manner of scuzzy behaviour, but the rules are different for people like me. Besides, it's not as though I could provide an industrial tribunal with any tangible proof that my choice of side gig isn't reason enough to dismiss me on the grounds of mental health concerns.

Even Mags doesn't know what I do when I'm not here. When people find out that you profess an ability to speak to the dead, they tend to back away slowly in case you've forgotten to take your medication.

We step into the lift and Mags sighs as she presses the button for our floor. 'Really?'

'I don't know why you sound so disappointed. You haven't even seen my costume.'

'Haven't you been wearing it for years? You could at least make an effort.'

I feign offence. 'It is an effort.'

'Jeans and a t-shirt?'

'Don't forget the rucksack,' I tell her pointedly. 'That's a key part of the outfit.'

I started going as Ellie from The Last of Us games when I realised that I could basically get away with wearing normal clothes, as long as I stuck a brick and a bottle in a rucksack and carried it round all night.

'It's still just jeans and a t-shirt.'

'It's a perfectly valid costume choice.'

She rolls her eyes as we step out onto the landing. 'You're such a grinch.'

'It's not a Christmas party. You go on,' I smile back, 'I need to pop my lunch in the fridge.'

We head off in opposite directions. Setting my precious breakfast on the worktop as I walk into the kitchen and dumping the rest of my stuff temporarily on the floor, I try not to be too overwhelmed by food envy as I look for a handy gap amongst the Pret salads and Waitrose wraps for my sad little chicken paste sandwich.

'In early again, I see?'

Pat's enquiring voice appears behind me. I stand up and push the fridge door shut.

'Just clearing the decks before the big do tonight,' I smile with as much politeness as I can bear to muster. Which isn't an awful lot, if I'm honest, as I still haven't drunk my coffee yet.

She frowns back at me. 'Oh. Are you a bit too stretched with your workload?'

That's a trick question.

Pat took over the Team Leader role six months ago after Priya, her much-beloved predecessor, departed to bigger and better things. She'd been coveting the job forever – she first applied years ago, back before Priya's predecessor started – didn't get it. Applied again when they left – *still* didn't get it. This time, she was the only internal applicant, so she landed it by default. I realise that sounds mean, but the reality is that they would likely have given it to almost *anyone* else from the team if they'd bothered applying. Rebecca even asked *me* to put my hat in, and I'm not exactly known for my attitude of sunshine and rainbows. I thought about it – for two seconds – but the tiny salary bump didn't feel like it was worth the extra hassle of managing the team. Although I suppose I could've taken Pat's approach and taken the cash whilst abandoning the team to their own devices. Her appointment finally opened the door to the position of status she'd spent the last ten years craving, but the reality is, a different job title doesn't take her out of the same crappy boat the rest of us are in. Hers might be an even crappier one, as getting promoted despite having a long-held reputation in the team as a two faced, condescending, workshy suck-up didn't exactly endear her further to her already exasperated colleagues. She thrives on gossip, any information she might be able to twist to her advantage to try and get cosy with the fee earners, and asking me about my workload is her clumsy attempt at fishing. But this isn't my first rodeo. If I say yes, she'll hold it over me come appraisal time, spinning it that I can't manage my work and deny me a pay rise. If I say no, she'll twist that as I don't have enough to do, and dump on me whatever she currently has on her *own* plate that she doesn't want to do herself.

'Just sorting the filing while it's quiet.'

Pat puts a hand on my shoulder, fixing me with her most well-practiced look of empathy. It has all the sincerity of a velociraptor eyeing up its next meal.

'Dorothy, I don't want you covering for your fee earners if they're causing problems. If there's an issue and you don't tell me, how can I help?'

I fight the urge to laugh in her face. Just a *hint* of criticism of a fee earner, and she'll immediately run to them with a vastly exaggerated version of anything I'm daft enough to blab about.

'Come on, Pat.' I turn to grab my belongings, sidling out of her intrusive grasp before I give into the compulsion to break her fingers. 'You know if I had any problems, you're the first person I'd come to.'

We both know that if I happened to be randomly engulfed by a blazing fireball in the middle of typing a dictation, she's the last person I'd ask for a glass of water, but heigh-ho.

'I hope that's true.'

She knows damn well it isn't.

'Well, don't overdo it,' she relents, backing off in disappointment. 'Too many early starts and we might have to rebalance that workload for you. Maybe change your fee earners.'

Bollocks will you, I think to myself as I toss her a casual shrug.

'Whatever's best for the team, Pat.'

I'm sure she can detect the sarcasm in my voice as I turn away, my best efforts to bury it notwithstanding, but she'd never call me out on it directly. I think she sees herself as some sort of Machiavellian schemer, that now that she's finally bagged the role she's been after all this time, she can pull all of our strings and run some kind of elaborate puppet show for her own entertainment. But she's not actually that smart, and the job doesn't hold the level of prestige she imagines. It's all about making up for what's lacking in the rest of her life – she's a sad little person, desperate to feel like a powerful one, and there's one of them in every office. It's a shame really, and under different circumstances, I'd probably feel sorry for her. As it is, though, she's a lazy, deluded, annoying pain in all of our arses, so I struggle to be the bigger person.

'Where did you get to?' Mags is checking her emails as I reach our desk pod and drop into my seat.

'Her highness.'

She flinches like she's been shot. 'Oh *nooooo*.'

'Doesn't matter,' I shrug as I sip my drink, unwrapping my food and breathing in the comforting aroma of dripping cheese and yeasty spread. 'It's Friday breakfast. Not even Poison Pat can ruin that.'

I frown in the direction of my already bulging in-tray, which I'd completely cleared out before I left the office half an hour later than scheduled last night. 'Seriously, when did they have chance to dump all this in here? None of them are even in yet.'

'Stephen was still dictating when I left at six,' she shrugs back.

'Sad bastard.'

Mags flashes me a wry smile. 'Why're you still here after eight years if you hate it so much?'

'It pays better than waitressing and I'm qualified for nothing else.'

'There are at least six more law firms within about a ten second walk of here, you know.'

'All of which would be full of exactly the same bullshit as this one. At least here I know exactly what bullshit to expect.'

Before I landed this job, I had temp gigs at four of those six firms she's talking about, and each one was a carbon copy of the one before. Mags always thinks I'm exaggerating about not being able to do anything else, but the truth is, with no degree and a CV of bouncing from job to job every couple of years, this is the best paid thing I *can* do. The downside is, compared to everything else I've done – call centres, warehouses, retail, serving – the legal profession really does seem to attract a much higher than normal proportion of arrogant, entitled, narcissistic idiots. Maybe that's why our job is better paid than other admin roles: we get asshole tax.

'Besides, I can't leave now,' I remind her. 'Not until we've sorted you out with your dream job.'

Mags wants to cross over to the dark side, become a lawyer,

but the firm's graduate roles are super competitive, and her First in Humanities from a non-Oxbridge university didn't stand a chance. Landing this gig was her foot in the door while she studies for her SQE on the side, which gives her a leg up on next years' grad openings. She's bright, talented and capable, and deserves so much more than to be wasting her considerable abilities slogging away next to me. I've made it my personal mission in life to help get her where she ought to be.

'I take it all back,' she pleads across the desk, 'please don't leave. I don't know what I'd do without you.'

She's only half joking.

'Don't worry,' I reassure her through a mouthful of Marmite. 'I'm not going anywhere.'

More's the pity.

3

Wonder Woman navigates from the passenger seat whilst Annie Wilkes and the purple Teletubbie natter in the back. Now there's a sentence I never thought I'd say. My old Fiesta's from the era before built-in satnavs were a thing, so Mags has been assigned Apple Maps duty. Big Boss moved last month from a fancy old place in Harborne to an even fancier, older one out in the sticks near Lichfield, and I have no idea where I'm going. Currently, we're on a single-track country lane, no lights anywhere, and a strong possibility of no 4G. In fact, I suspect Mags' phone signal dropped out a while back and she doesn't have the heart to tell me.

'Is that it?'

I squint through the dark in the direction Mags is pointing. 'That's a farm.'

'Well, it must be down here somewhere.'

I'm dubious. 'Should go back to that pub we passed and ask?'

'I'm *sure* it's down here somewhere…'

If only I had actual *psychic* powers, as opposed to just chatting with the dead, I could easily figure out where we're supposed to be going. 'Let's carry on down this way,' I nod encouragingly, 'see where we end up.'

Possibly in a ditch all night waiting for the RAC.

'Are we lost?' Jackie pipes up from the back seat.

'Of course not. Get back to your gossiping.'

She pulls a shocked face at me in the rearview mirror. 'As if we'd ever!'

'Of *course* not,' I sing her words back at her. They *are* gossiping, of course. Anyone who's ever worked in an office will tell you, the Reception folk are always the ones with their ears closest to the ground. They know everyone, everyone talks to them, and they see and hear about everything that happens in the building, not to mention plenty people get up to outside of it. They're the central repository of all office rumour, and other than with those in their trusted inner circles, they're also exceptionally discreet, so even the Senior Partners have been known to court their opinions. I guarantee, you ever want to know what's *really* going on beneath the façade of any seemingly respectable organisation, make friends with the Receptionists. They can tell you stories from the office that'll make your hair curl, the have inside info on everyone from the cleaners to the Managing Directors, and woe betide anyone who's daft enough to make them an enemy.

'Are those lights?'

Mags is pointing again, this time farther ahead. It's faint, but there's definitely something twinkling down there.

'Is that it?' Sue leans forward from the back seat, Tinky Winky's antenna nearly taking my eye out. 'I heard it's massive.'

Jackie nods. 'Two mill, Becs said they paid for it.'

I told you Jackie knows everything. She's also on good enough terms with Rebecca to get away with calling her Becs.

Sue's eyes grow wide. The pair of them have been necking miniatures of Malibu on the drive over, and the effects are kicking in. '*Wow.* I did like the old place though, that was nice.'

'I never saw it,' Mags muses. Tonight's her first Big Boss party – she joined us too late last year for the Halloween season.

'It was definitely easier to find,' I murmur to nobody in particular.

The lights grow closer now as the narrow, rough road starts to widen, and the faint slam of car doors and hum of people floats toward us through the night.

'We can't be far.'

I nod ahead. 'There.'

Now the lights are just ahead on the left, illuminating a wall, a sign and what looks like the entrance to a grand, tree-lined gravel drive.

'Lea Hall House, yep,' Mags grins happily at me, satisfied with her efforts. 'That's it. Told you it was down here.'

'Never doubted you for a minute, mate,' I pat her shoulder reassuringly.

Turning the car through the open double gates, I drive us slowly up towards the house, raised spotlights embedded along the treeline guiding our way. It's not long before the trees fall away, the drive widens and we find ourselves in front of an imposing pile with insane kerb appeal. While the others stare open-mouthed through the windows, I manoeuvre carefully into a space between the rows of Audis and Teslas and turn off the engine. It's quite a sight: three floors of Georgian grandeur swathed in fairy lights. Elegant white pillars support the porch outside a large central front door, there's hints of perfectly landscaped grounds peeking all around through the dark, and a stunning room of glass on one side of the house which is definitely *not* your nan's conservatory. It's all quite beautiful, and we haven't even seen the inside yet. The others' expressions are a picture, a mixture of reverent awe tinged with slightly sickened jealousy.

'You want to sit in my crappy Fiesta and stare all night, or shall we go in?'

Sue sighs dreamily. 'It's *gorgeous*.'

I don't disagree – the house looks stunning, and knowing Rebecca's taste and style, it'll likely be a feast for the eyes on the inside too – but I've been saving my afternoon appetite to take full advantage of the annual hog roast she puts on, and it's been nearly eight hours since my pathetic excuse for a sandwich. 'You lot can stay here if you like, but I need my dinner.'

The others follow suit as I open my door, quickly collecting bags and props. Mags hands me my trusty backpack and bundles up in her massive puffer coat as she climbs out of the passenger side, and I smile to myself – at least she listened to my Work Mom advice and brought a coat – as the four of us make our way through the maze of cars and head towards the front door.

I'm at the back of the group as we reach the threshold, the sound of music and laughter and clatter of glasses just a few short feet away. With my foot on the bottom step of the porch, I suddenly stop short.

Mags feels my absence and turns back. 'You okay, Dot?'

I can't reply to her. I can't move, I can't speak, I can't do anything.

I'm *stuck*.

'Dot?'

Or, more accurately, something's *made* me stuck.

Suddenly, two things happen simultaneously. First, I feel overwhelmingly, utterly nauseous, and second, something *yanks* me, holding me back, not letting me complete my next step. This isn't like someone's grabbed my arm – this is *inside* my body, a massive *pull*, like something else has rocked up in there and is using its full force to stop me moving.

'Are you okay?'

I can barely hear her. She seems far, far away, in another place, surrounded by fog. What I do hear, though, is a voice inside my head. Commanding, authoritative, but kind.

I know this Voice. I've heard it before.

It just says: DON'T.

'Dot?'

I should listen to it.

I *should* listen to it.

Mags grabs my arm, shaking me roughly. The fog's gone, if it was really ever there in the first place, and I'm back at the porch step, her worried face inches from mine.

'Dot, come on, you're scaring me.'

I shake it off. 'It's okay,' I tell her quickly. 'I'm okay.'

'What on earth happened?'

'Nothing, sorry, I'm fine. It's fine.'

I'm not sure which of the two of us I'm trying harder to convince.

'I just… spaced out for a minute.'

'Spaced *out?* Jesus, Dot, I thought you were having a fucking stroke or something.'

Wow, it must really have scared her. She almost never uses the big swears.

'I'm fine,' I shrug back at her. 'Probably just hangry or something.'

'*Dot.*'

'Give me a hot pork bap and I'll be sweet,' I tell her firmly. 'Honestly mate, it's nothing. I promise.'

Liar, liar.

'You sure?'

'Absolutely.'

Pants on fire.

'Come on, let's get in there,' I chivvy her forward. 'You could clearly use a drink.'

Mags looks unsure, but heads inside. This time, as my foot hits the step, there's no pull, no fog, and I shrug off the memory as I follow. Crossing the threshold, I tense, half expecting something else to happen – but nothing does.

Sue and Jackie are nowhere to be seen amongst the groups milling about the palatial hall. Uniformed waiting staff expertly navigate their way across the immaculate marble floor carrying trays of drinks and canapés, winding seamlessly through the gaps between a devil, a zombie and a couple of people in those massive T-Rex costumes. Mags is approached politely by a man in a suit offering to check in her coat. My olive-green parka is part of my fancy dress, so I decline to give it up, asking a proffering waiter if there's a non-alcoholic option. Drinking wasn't on the agenda for me tonight anyway, but I might have allowed myself half a shandy to smooth out that awkward first hour. After what happened at the door, though, I'm still a little on edge.

'Wow.' Mags turns to me, wide-eyed. 'I knew it was going to be fancy, but...'

'I know. It's *super* fancy.'

'Where do we start?'

I look around, taking in the various doors leading off from the opulent hall to the music and voices beyond, the grand oak staircase rising to the shadowy upper floors.

'Well, upstairs is always off limits.'

'Really? How come?'

'Kids,' I gesture in the direction of the first floor landing, where I can just about make out two little pairs of legs poking out of the darkness, dangling through the banister side by side. 'But there'll be a bar somewhere. Plus there'll be food, and the hog roast. I'm personally super keen on finding out where *that* is.'

'Will there be veggie options?'

'Don't worry,' I reassure her, 'everyone gets catered for, I promise. You won't just end up with some soggy mushroom quiche.'

'And the entertainment?'

'Always a high point,' I grin. 'Last year they laid it out in the garden, but with the size of this place, who knows.'

Mags grabs a glass of something fizzy from a nearby moving

tray. 'Okay. Shall we look for the others first?'

I nod, gesturing a doorway off the hall to our left, where most of the noise seems to be. 'Door number one? They seem to be taking the trays that way.'

She necks the contents of her glass. 'Let's go.'

'Jesus Mags, pace yourself.'

She grins back. 'Yes Mom.'

I roll my eyes and take the lead through the open doorway. Greeting us on the other side is the stuff of surrealist nightmares: the Grim Reaper is deep in animated conversation with a couple of Super Marios and a fairly impressive Gandalf; in the far corner, some sort of zombie nurse who I vaguely recognise as a Partner from the Tax team is dancing with Ghostface to the music piping through from an invisible DJ; and on one of the sofas, Pinhead, Candyman and Ezio Auditore sit in a bizarre pastiche of the three wise monkeys.

'I can see Annie Wilkes at the bar over there.'

I follow Mags' gaze, but my five-foot arse is a lot shorter than hers, and there's a Freddy Krueger between here and there with a really big hat.

'There,' she points. 'Talking to the guy dressed as a priest.'

Now I spot Jackie.

Mags nudges me, nodding back in her direction. 'He's your type, isn't he?'

'Who?' I frown back, baffled.

'The one in the priest costume.'

I look back over properly. Hmm. Tall without being too tall, broad but not overly muscly, a mop of wavy brown hair that's just begging to be played with. She's not wrong, but I hate parties, I'm crap at flirting, and being already unsettled, I'm far from in the mood for that level of effort. I've always wondered if part of the reason I do so well talking to the dead is simply because

I find it so much easier than most conversations with the living, especially one you might try to strike up with a random cute stranger at a party. I shrug back at her, feigning disinterest.

'Meh.'

'Spoilsport. Ooh, which reminds me…' she starts scanning the room, searching the crowd.

'He's not in here,' I tell her, knowing exactly who she's looking for.

'How do you know? He could be one of the T-rexes.'

Two more of them are padding in our direction.

'Bloody hell, how many of those *are* there?'

'Seriously,' Mags frowns unhappily, 'how do you know he's not in here somewhere under a load of face paint?'

'Didn't you hear Jackie in the car? He told her he was coming as Don Draper.' Of course he'd dress up as one of the most misogynistic, egotistical male characters ever committed to celluloid. 'I'm amazed your Nathan radar didn't explode when she mentioned it.'

'Ooh, he looks nice in a suit.'

'Bit low effort, isn't it?' I tease.

'Hah! You can talk.'

'Exactly my point. When I do it, I'm a grinch. When he does it, *'ooh, he looks nice in a suit'*,' I mimic her with an exaggerated squeak.

'Shut *up*,' she laughs back.

I flash her a heads-up as I spot Holly Golightly making a beeline for us from the opposite side of the room. It's Big Boss.

'Hi Rebecca,' I smile as she approaches, the iconic look she's chosen absolutely flawless, right down to every last pearl. 'You look great.'

'Thanks,' Rebecca shrugs, twiddling with a long, slim cigarette holder, not a single perfect hair out of place. 'I've got a Tiffany's bag in the kitchen just in case anyone doesn't get it. You two look fantastic.' She gives Mags an encouraging hand squeeze and looks at me with amusement. 'Always nice to see Ellie. Where's your brick?'

'In the rucksack.'

'Of course.'

'So is Rob wandering around dressed like Hannibal from The A-Team?'

They always do a couples costume, every year without fail. Their Morticia and Gomez last year was exceptional.

'Somewhere,' she shrugs. 'Last I saw him he was with one of the T-rexes. I'm not sure which one.'

'We've seen four already,' Mags chimes in, amused.

'There are a few about,' Rebecca nods gracefully. 'Anyway, enjoy yourselves. Dot, the hog roast is in the Orangery,' she points back towards the door she just came in through. 'Left from the sitting room back there.'

I sigh gratefully. 'You know me so well.'

Rebecca smiles. 'The entertainment is in the drawing room. That's to the *right* from the sitting room. I think some of them have moved into the library next door.'

'What have you laid on this year?'

'What's the good money on?' She knows it's a subject of much speculation around the office.

'Most guesses I've heard were a casino.'

Rebecca scoffs. 'Yeah, with me putting up the cash for everyone to bet with, no doubt. What about you? You have a guess?'

I've been spot on with them more than once in the past. Just lucky like that.

'Well, I was *hoping* for a big gaming arcade.'

'But you don't think it is,' she replies matter-of-factly.

'No, I think it's—'

My mind clears, and I'm suddenly struck with the oddest image of a dainty, old-fashioned china cup and saucer.

'Afternoon tea?' I fumble doubtfully.

Rebecca's eyes light up. 'Oh, so close. I can almost never surprise you; you always guess. I can't wait for you to see.'

'I can't wait to see the hog roast,' I shrug honestly.

'Off you go then,' she gives us both a light nudge. 'I know how much you love your crackling. Have fun, you two.'

Mags turns back to me as Rebecca works the crowd. 'I might go check out the entertainment.'

I raise my eyebrows. 'Look for Dickhead Scumbag, you mean.'

'Can't I do both?'

I sigh deeply. She's a grown woman after all. She can do what she wants. I can't police her all night. 'Fine. Go have fun.'

She beams back at me. 'Thanks Mom.'

'I'll come find you after I've eaten.'

'You're the best,' she hugs me and skips away happily.

I follow Rebecca's directions to the Orangery, otherwise known as the posh person's conservatory. After winding my way through the throng, I'm rewarded with a sight that seems like heaven. Tables are set along the length of the curved, floor to ceiling windows, waves of fairy lights reflecting on the glass, with a sumptuous selection of food spread as far as the eye can see. There's pork, there's crackling, there's gravy and apple sauce and huge, fluffy white buns to stuff it all in, and everything seems right with the world. Further along, there are signs for veggie options, vegan, gluten-free and more, but Mags can sort herself out thanks. There's only one thing I want right now, and it's at the front of the queue I join, trying not to drool as I wait for my turn to be served.

A few seconds in, a low, unfamiliar voice pipes up behind me.

'That crackling looks amazing.'

I turn and find myself face to face with the guy from the bar in the priest costume. Close up, he looks pretty amazing himself: big brown puppy dog eyes, nice bit of facial scruff, cute dimples smiling down at me.

'It *all* looks amazing,' I reply, not entirely meaning the food. Reminding myself that he's a total stranger – and just because he looks even tastier than the crackling, doesn't guarantee that he's not a complete dick – I turn back to the queue before I embarrass myself.

'They certainly know how to throw a party.'

'They really do.' It occurs to me I haven't seen him at one of their Halloween things before. Trust me, I'd remember. Unless he was dressed as a T-rex. 'I don't remember seeing you last year?'

'No, I've not long known them,' he smiles crookedly as a couple of stray curls fall across his forehead and I have to fight the urge to brush them back. 'I only met them after they moved here. You come to this every year?'

'Uh-huh. Rebecca's my boss. Well, one of them.'

'Oh, okay.' He pauses, not taking the opportunity to ask about work. Rules him out as another lawyer, at least. 'Nice costume, by the way. Are you Ellie?'

Oh wow. He gets my costume. Nobody *ever* gets my costume. It must be fate.

'Well spotted.' I can't resist smiling back, looking him up and down, the urge to make an arse of myself apparently irresistible. 'Hasn't the sexy priest thing been a bit done to death?"

He laughs heartily and easily as we move along in the queue. The most adorable creases crinkle around the corners of his eyes as he grins, blushing slightly, and I find myself instinctively checking for a wedding ring and really, really hoping he doesn't have a partner. His dark brown eyes twinkle back at me, catching the lights. 'Thanks for the compliment. But it's just plain old priest. Well, technically it's Vicar.'

Ohhhhh… *shit*.

'Father Theo Gregory,' he puts out a hand.

I stare at it for a second like a deer in headlights.

'You mean…' I gesture to his extremely simple yet convincing outfit.

He nods. 'Yep. *Not* a costume.'

Oh god, I just hit on a *priest*.

'Oops.' This is why I don't socialise with humans. Live ones, anyway. 'Sorry about that.'

'Don't be,' he withdraws his hand as he realises that I'm clearly far too traumatised to shake it. 'I'm extremely flattered.'

'What's a priest even doing at a Halloween party?' I muse aloud. 'Isn't it sacrilegious or something?'

'Community outreach. Great night for recruiting.'

I think he's joking, but it's hard to tell.

'Besides,' he goes on, smiling crookedly, 'where else am I supposed to meet interesting women, in church?'

Is he flirting with *me* now? I've never been very good at figuring that stuff out.

'Why do you even want to? You're a priest.'

'Vicar,' he wags a playful finger at me in correction. 'And I'm not Catholic.'

'Hmm. Well, there's certainly plenty of interesting women here,' I shrug back. 'Take your pick.'

A slightly puzzled frown lines his handsome face. 'I thought I just did?'

Oh yeah, he's definitely *flirting* with me. Ah, if only it *was* just a costume. But I know exactly what people in the Church – almost *any* church – think of people with my sort of 'gifts'. I've had plenty of past experience.

'I'm not Christian.'

'I'm not suggesting you convert.'

'I'm about as far removed from Christian as you can get.'

'Ooh, are you a Satanist?' his eyes light up as he teases me gleefully. 'I don't think I've ever met a real one before.'

I roll my eyes pointedly.

'Maybe we could have a nice chat over our pork sandwiches.'

I'm not sure he even meant that one to be suggestive, but that's straight where my mind went. And he's distracted me so much that I hadn't realised we've reached the front of the queue.

'One with everything, please,' I ask the server.

Father Gregory leans over my shoulder. 'Make that two.'

I laugh at his gentle persistence despite myself. What a pity. If only he weren't a real, honest-to-god Vicar.

'Sorry, but you're just not my type.'

Total lie. Mags was right; he's *exactly* my type.

'I thought you said I was cute?'

Actually, the word I used was sexy. And I wasn't wrong.

'That was before I knew you were really a priest.'

'Vicar.'

'Same difference.'

'You'd prefer a Rabbi?'

'I'd prefer an atheist.'

He feigns a theatrical sigh of disappointment. Or maybe he really is disappointed. 'Shame.'

I agree with him, but I'm not volunteering that.

The server hands me two paper-plated pork baps, filled to bursting and wrapped in paper napkins, and I pass one to him, trying desperately to curb every impulse I have to make a pork-based joke. 'Here you go, Father. Enjoy your evening.'

I turn away from him by sheer force of will, leaving the fancy conservatory and landing back in the sitting room, where I spot

Postroom Phil with Terry and Paul from IT. They're dressed as a group, each one of them a different Tetrimino. Easily my favourite outfit of the night. 'Hey guys. You seen Jackie?'

Phil points towards the next room along. 'Taking in the entertainment.'

There's a disparaging note in his voice.

'You don't sound impressed.'

'Load of bollocks,' he shrugs back over the music as he swigs from a plastic pint glass.

Rebecca's entertainment, a load of bollocks? That'd certainly be a first.

Wondering what could possibly have put his back so far up, I make my way across the room and poke my head through the door. As I clock sight of Jackie, I realise what's going on around her, and for the slightest of seconds, I'm certain my heart actually stops.

It's mediums.

The entertainment is *mediums*. Well, sort of.

I see tables of psychics, crystal balls, tarot cards and people reading tea leaves. My initial, visceral gut reaction – oh shit, this is me, *I'm* the entertainment – passes after I spend a couple of seconds rooted to the spot in a panic. But it passes when it hits me that it *is* just entertainment; none of these people are the real thing. Okay, sometimes neither am I, but mine's at least rooted in something genuine. This bunch are most definitely not. If they were, I'd feel it in a second. We'd trigger each other's radar.

Jackie's having her palm read, and I wave to try and get her attention, Sue giggling over tarot cards at the next table. As Jackie spots me, I mouth Mags' name as a question, and she nods over at the door to the last room, the one Rebecca called the library, which is just ajar. No doubt more of the same fun and games in there.

As I approach the library door and reach to push it all the way open, out of nowhere, that queasy, overwhelming feeling suddenly rushes back through me, like the bottom's just fallen out of my stomach.

DON'T.

The Voice is back. That horrible, sickening *pull*.

I fight it off quickly this time, before the fog has chance to descend. What the hell is on the other side of the door?

I push it open.

It's more of a large snug with books than a library. Three sofas make up three sides of a rectangle, with a couple of high-backed chairs completing the fourth edge. The bookcases themselves are set back into alcoves in the walls. I see another crystal ball, more tarot cards spilled around on side tables, but no armchair psychics plying their trade; this seems to be more of a do-it-yourself room. Every seat is occupied, with more people perched on sofa arms and cabinet edges, maybe a dozen or so in all. Mags is sat on one end of the main sofa beside Dickhead Scumbag, and there's someone on the other side of his who I don't recognise dressed as Beetlejuice. Pat's hovering behind an occupied chair, a couple of other faces vaguely familiar beneath makeup which, under the dimmed lights in the room, makes them look faintly demonic.

But all my attention is on the coffee table in the middle, directly in front of where Mags and the others sit, each one with an arm outstretched towards it.

Their fingers are on a planchette.

They're messing with a Ouija board.

Oh *shit*.

4

All my instincts want to scream at them to stop.

Instead, I'm frozen in the doorway, watching with a growing feeling of slowly creeping dread. How can I tell them to stop? What reason could I possibly give? I'll sound like a crazy person. To them, it's a harmless parlour game, at a Halloween party no less. I can hardly tell them to pack it in just because it's cliché.

'Bit cliché, isn't it?'

Guess who's hovering over my shoulder, peering at the scene. I can't even produce a sarky response, I'm so stricken. And it must show, because his tone abruptly changes to one of concern.

'Are you okay? You look like you've seen a ghost.'

If only he knew.

'And not just that one,' he jokes lightly, pointing to the occupier one of the high-backed chairs, wearing a sheet with two cut out eyeholes.

I force a weak nod.

'Okay…' he frowns, unconvinced.

He probably thinks I'm blowing him off again, which I kind of am, but not intentionally. I'm just sort of… lost.

'You going in?' he asks.

I shake my head quickly, remembering the Voice's warning.

'Then please can I?'

He gestures to the gap between me and the doorframe, not quite wide enough for him to get past. Priest – sorry, Vicar – thing aside, first impressions suggest he seems a decent enough bloke, and I really want to tell him that if they're about to play with a

Ouija board, going in there is a very bad idea. 'Should you?'

That smile again. 'I like to check out the competition.'

Against my better judgement, I move aside to let him through. What's the alternative?

There are different schools of thought about Ouija boards. Do they *really* do what they advertise? Are they just harmless nonsense? Sceptics dismiss them as bunk, scientists explain them away with the ideomotor effect – where your unconscious mind influences microscopic muscle movements, in turn moving the planchette to spell out the letters – and Catholics would like to burn every one of them, probably on the same fiery pyre they'd stick me on for maximum efficiency. From my perspective, all camps have something of a valid point. Depending on the situation they're used in, and the people involved, different outcomes can happen. Yes, they absolutely *can* be a load of old bollocks, as Postroom Phil suggested. And yes, your subconscious absolutely *can* make them move, theoretically spelling out things only you could possibly know, because they're lifted from your own psyche. But they have a darker side, and not just the Catholic terror of invoking a cloven-hoofed demon.

They *can* open a door.

The board itself doesn't really do it; that's just a tool. It's the collective belief sitting around it, the accumulated energy of a bunch of people willing open their minds, *wanting* something interesting to happen. What you end up with after that is a crap shoot, depending on the people and the circumstances. With a group of spiritually-minded individuals, some of whom with experience like mine, you might get lucky and have a pleasant chat with a friendly, genuinely supernatural entity about the nature of spiritual consciousness. If you and a mate sit down for a go in a dark room, either of you already have issues with your mental health and you're hoping for reassurance from the great beyond, the ideomotor effect is likely to kick in – giving you nothing but echo chamber responses from your already troubled mind, potentially sending you into a downward spiral.

And if you're sat at a party with a bunch of half-cut idiots blundering along like it's all some stupid game, you risk getting a lot more than you bargained for.

Pockets of the assembled group are muttering amongst themselves. I see Nathan lean over to Mags, whispering something that makes her giggle. The music isn't so loud in here, just a vague background hum; someone makes shushing noises and in front of me, a guy from Accounts dressed as Kermit comes over to close the door.

'In or out?'

I hesitate. Probably nothing'll happen. Probably it'll all be fine.

But something *might*.

At least if I'm in there with them, I can intervene if it goes bad.

'In.' I make my choice and cross the threshold, closing the door behind me.

Nathan clears his throat. So, he's the ringleader of this foolish little party game. Shocker. 'Is there anybody there?'

Someone snickers from elsewhere in the room and is promptly shushed. I glance briefly across the room at my new friend, leaning against a bookcase in the opposite corner, casually munching away on his pork bap. He chooses that exact moment to look in my direction, giving me a lopsided smile which simultaneously says 'I'm still up for that chat, if you fancy it later' and 'this lot are barking if they think this'll work'.

Nathan tries again. 'Is there anybody *there?*'

Beside him, fingers touching his on the planchette, Mags is in her happy place. The board in front of her doesn't matter, she's just thrilled that not only is she finally this close to him, not only is he whispering god knows what slimy bullshit in her all too eager ears, but he's actively including her in his chicanery. With the lights low, she hasn't even realised I'm in the room with them, albeit staying as far away from the action as I can physically accomplish without leaving altogether.

'It's moving!'

I don't know who said it. Not Mags, not Nathan, not Beetlejuice, whose fingers are lined up on next to theirs. A collective murmur rises through the room, and over by the bookcase, the Vicar pauses mid-mouthful, frowning dubiously.

The planchette is in full view from where I'm standing. It's slow, and staggered, but whoever spoke up was right. It's moving. Clear as day.

Why it's moving at this point is anybody's guess. But my hearing the Voice at the threshold of the door suggests it's not just muscle spasms.

'It's really moving!'

Gasps echo through the room, followed by cries of 'what?', '*they're* doing it, right?' as the tool begins to pick up speed. It swirls across the wooden board in gentle circular motions – three, four, five times – before finally coming to a stop over the word 'HELLO', printed on the surface in neat black letters.

'Oh *shit*.' I can't tell who said that either, but I'm inclined to agree.

Mags, Nathan and Beetlejuice exchange glances, frowning.

'Are you doing it?'

'Is it you?'

'*I'm* not doing it.'

Someone shouts out from one of the other sofas. 'Who are you?'

More shushing, a 'don't encourage it!', then silence. For a second, nothing happens; I can just make out the relief on Mags' face as she starts to believe Nathan's just been mucking about.

Then it moves again. *Fast*.

It hits a letter. 'W!' someone says.

'E.'

'A.'

'R.'

'Maybe it's come giving us fashion advice,' someone jokes, only to be met with an annoyed bark telling them to shut up, the clamours for quiet now urgent and demanding.

'E.'

'H.'

The Vicar's ignoring his food completely now as he leans forward, brows furrowed, pork bap forgotten on the shelf beside him. He looks uneasy, and he's right to be.

'E.'

'R.'

'E.'

Then it stops, making another theatrical twirl around the board before it comes to rest in the centre.

'What was that?'

'What did it say?'

'Did anyone get it?'

I did.

Sam, another secretary from our team, looks up from her phone where she's been tapping in the letters. 'It said WE ARE HERE.'

More gasps, more murmurs. Some unease.

'Who's 'we'?'

'Come on, it's not real.'

'It's just the three of *them* doing it.'

'It's not—'

'*Shush*, I want to hear!'

'Fuck *this*.' One of the Grads from Planning jumps up abruptly out of her prime sofa spot, right in the middle of it all. 'No,' she responds as a friend beside her protests, 'I'm out of here.' Lightning fast, she strides for the exit, and I have to press myself right back against the wall so that she doesn't take me out on her way, slamming the door again behind her. Smart girl.

Back in the room, another hush falls, but it feels different now. There's a tension that wasn't there before, along with a dash of confusion and a fair amount of disbelief.

Beetlejuice turns to Sam. 'Can you take notes?'

Sam nods, phone back at the ready. Pat, who I'd forgotten was even there, chooses this exact moment to volunteer her services. First time for everything, I suppose.

'I'll do it.'

Sam looks up. 'I'm already doing it.'

Nathan looks irritated. 'Who cares who does it.'

'But she—'

'Tell you what,' Beetlejuice interrupts diplomatically, 'why don't you both do it. Just in case.'

Pat's face is smugness personified as Sam glowers in her seat.

Mags doesn't look so sure as she leans forward. 'Maybe we should stop.'

'No,' Nathan snaps back sharply. 'Why would we?'

She hesitates. 'I— I don't—'

'It's just getting interesting.'

'But—'

'Go if you want then,' he snaps dismissively, and she sits back quietly. I want to punch him in his self-satisfied face.

'Don't carry on if you're not comfortable,' Beetlejuice leans across to reassure her.

Mags shakes her head with a shrug, a thin, forced smile across her face. Dammit, Mags, ignore him. Just *go*.

But she doesn't.

Beetlejuice turns back to face the board. They at least seem like they're approaching the situation with some consideration, unlike Dickhead Scumbag, whose smirking face has been verging on laughter almost the entire time. 'Who are you?'

A pause, then more letters in quick succession, before Sam repeats the words back.

YOU MAY CALL US WHAT YOU WISH.

Legion, maybe?

'Will you speak to us?'

I roll my eyes at that one. They already are, idiot.

More letters.

WE ALREADY ARE.

That gets my attention. It's a logical enough answer, and I'm likely not the only one in the room who had that thought cross their mind. But I'm hyper-conscious of every possibility behind this little performance, and the unsettling idea that it might have been plucked directly out of my head isn't lost on me.

'Do you have a message for us?'

The small plastic wheels on the bottom of the planchette squeak faintly as they shoot across the wooden surface beneath.

'MANY…' Sam starts.

Pat cuts her off. 'MESSAGES.'

My default Pat response – extreme, immediate annoyance – threatens to kick in, and I force it away. Big if, but *if* this is real, any negativity in the room could influence its direction, and between Pat, Sam and Dickhead Scumbag, there's plenty of that floating around already. In the meantime, I start trying to focus. Back to the big if again, but *if* it's real, maybe I can use my own channels to find out what it is.

The group mutter uneasily.

'What messages?'

'For who?'

The Voice will know what it is. I assume it must – why else would it try to warn me on my way into the room, on my way into the *house*, that something wasn't right? I need to open a door of my own. I need to ask it.

I should probably explain what the Voice is. Open mind now, please.

The whole talking to the dead thing works differently for different people. Some see dead people, walking around like regular people, if you'll forgive the obvious reference. Some hear voices outside of themselves, like a spectral whisper of sweet nothings into their ear. Some don't see ghosts, but they get visual 'impressions' of things, like footage from an old film running inside their heads, like a waking dream. And I do freely acknowledge that all of these also sound like potential symptoms of severe mental health issues.

Me – I'm just super-*duper* lucky, because at one time or another in my life, I've had all of these happen. Sometimes all at once. For me, it's the gift that keeps on giving. And if my sarcasm isn't dripping heavily enough, let me clarify that in no way at all do I consider myself remotely lucky, and if it's gift, I wish I could find the receipt. It's no wonder I spent half my teens and twenties in an alcohol-induced haze. Sometimes it was the only way to shut the fuckers up.

Anyway, the one thing every genuine medium has in common, is at least one Guide – someone from the Other Side who connects to you, helping you through the process. They literally 'guide' other spirits to you so that you can hear what they have to say and pass those messages on, if they can't reach you themselves. I have a couple – they've changed a bit over the years – and if I need help, I can always ask. Unlike a recent paying customer's dear departed Grandad, neither of them appears by fluke, and will usually come if I call.

But the Voice is *different*. Also, it's been a good long while since it rocked up into my head uninvited, which is why it threw me off so badly. It first appeared in my early teens, and although I have little memory of that time – it's always been a bit of a blur – I do know it was around. In the years since, it's appeared occasionally – it usually shows if I'm very stressed, or in a proper bout of depression, and those times, it's been a reassuring, soothing presence. Other times, though, it's come out of nowhere, bringing that 'pull' with it, but accompanied with an overwhelming feeling that there's something I need to be doing, someone I need to help, but I never know what or who. When that's happened, it's left me feeling desperately upset and powerless, like there's something I'm missing, something I should know. But I can never quite put my finger on it.

The Voice is *not* a Guide. It's something more, something different, something *other*. Exactly what, I don't know – for a long time, I wondered if it was my own internal voice, my subconscious, and part of me still wonders about that. But whatever it is, it's always felt *powerful*. If it's here, it's here to help me, and as rubbish as I am at asking for that in real life, with supernatural bods it's less of a problem for my ego.

Sam's voice rings out across the room. 'MESSAGES OF JOY, MESSAGES OF PEACE.'

Then Pat. 'MESSAGES FOR ALL.'

If this *is* real, it's the cheesiest spirit I've ever heard of.

I quickly check to make sure I'm still well in the shadows and out of sight. The Vicar's focused on the board like everyone else, and by now has probably forgotten that I ever existed, thankfully. Then I lean into the corner of the wall for a bit of support, close my eyes, clear my mind, breathe deeply, and focus.

Focus.

Focus.

The fog descends, but this time, I'm wrapped up completely within it. The room disappears around me, the group's expectant murmurs and the noise of the rest of the party beyond falling far, far away, down towards the other end of a long, bright tunnel. Time disappears, and my mind is free, elsewhere, in a place of pure consciousness.

YOU MUST STOP IT.

There it is. The Voice. It's neither male nor female nor anything in between – not recognisably anything, in fact.

'What is it?'

My Guides have names. They had family once, physical forms I can recognise and connect to. Not this Voice.

TRICKSTER.

I wish I knew what it was. I've always wished I knew.

'What do you mean?'

LIAR. DECEIVER.

I know what a trickster is, you patronising git.

The Voice hesitates. I forget that *it* always seems to be able to hear what's inside *my* head, just as well as *I* can hear *it*.

IMPOSTOR.

It draws the word out for extra emphasis.

EVIL.

That's not good.

YOU MUST STOP IT.

'Stop them using the board? How?'

USE YOUR STRENGTH.

Oh, that's a big help. Anything more specific? Grab the board and smash it over Nathan's head? Use the Force? I'm open to suggestions.

USE OUR STRENGTH.

Wait. Since when is the Voice an *us?*

YOU MUST STOP IT.

It's not a suggestion.

And just like that, no more fog. I'm back in the room.

'MESSAGES FOR THOSE WHO ARE LOST.' I hear Pat's voice again. I haven't missed much; maybe half a minute. Time isn't the same where I just was.

'MESSAGES FOR THOSE WHO ARE GRIEVING.'

But how do I make them stop?

I jump as a low, newly familiar voice murmurs softly in my ear. 'Where did *you* go?'

'Jesus,' I hiss.

'Not quite,' Father Theo whispers with a smile, avoiding drawing attention from the others. 'You sure you're okay?'

'I would be,' I lean back to him, shaking off the tingle developing along the back of my neck from feeling his breath against my skin. 'If you'd stop sneaking up on me like that.'

Pat's still talking. 'MESSAGES OF COMFORT AND UNDERSTANDING. WE ARE TEACHERS, WE ARE HERE TO GUIDE.'

What *is* this shit? And how the hell do I *stop* it?

'WE ARE HERE TO SHARE OUR WISDOM FROM THE ASTRAL PLANE.'

A trickster, the Voice said. You must *stop* it. Use our strength to *stop it*.

How to stop it, stop it, stop it.

'STOP IT.'

I look up. What?

That was Sam's voice.

'STOP IT,' she repeats.

Now I hear Mags. 'It's getting faster again.'

'STOP IT.' Sam and Pat, in chorus now. 'STOP IT, STOP IT.'

The planchette's whirling around the board in a frenzy, all over the place, picking up an alarming amount of speed.

Stop it.

'STOP IT.'

I'm trying not to completely freak out.

Stop it.

'S, T, P, X,' Sam reads. 'A, T, W… it's just gibberish.'

But it's still moving.

Stop it.

Then a *whoosh*.

The speeding planchette flies suddenly from beneath their fingers, followed immediately by the board itself, over their heads and through the air, smashing right into the bookshelf where the Vicar left his half-eaten pork bap. The board breaks apart in two with incredible force as stunned silence fills the room.

Father Theo stares shellshocked back at the spot he just left. I feel bad for him. Had he still been stood there, it wouldn't have been pretty. And he's *so* pretty.

'Are *you* okay?' I ask him tentatively.

He nods slowly. I don't believe him.

'You think I can get another sandwich?'

Then again, maybe he's just fine.

5

The rest of the party passed in a blur. The massive thud attracted immediate attention, and the moment Jackie and half a dozen others from the next room burst through the door in curiosity, the sudden intrusion of the lights shattered the collective reverie of the group with a *pop*. In the confusion which followed, I grabbed Mags, nudging her through to the Orangery with little protest, although not before she managed to notice I was standing by the door with the Vicar ('I *knew* he was your type!'). Nothing else happened – no more Voice, either – but we spent the rest of the evening on edge, despite studiously avoiding any conversation about what had happened. I was hyper alert to the slightest hint of anything else untoward, and Mags put on her best party face dancing with Jackie and Sue, but spent most of the time messing about on her phone and I could tell her heart wasn't really in it. Thankfully, Jackie and Sue are both even older than I am, so didn't object when I started dropping hints about making it an earlier night than planned, and we slipped out well before there was any chance of turning into a pumpkin.

All I could think about was how it ended. Hearing the words from my own mind spoken aloud as they were spelled out on the board – to say it was unsettling would be the understatement of the century. The Voice had already confirmed whatever was communicating was definitely real, but what ultimately happened just made it hit home. Whatever actually caused it to end so abruptly, I didn't really care; I was just grateful it stopped. But even so, I couldn't stop myself from hashing it over and over in my head. When Lisa came in late off her shift on Saturday morning, she found me stewing in the living room and immediately knew something was up. I skipped the details, but she was determined to get me out of my funk and wouldn't take no for an answer. So after a nap and an early pizza, she and Pen dragged me out, starting at the pub around the corner and ending up in town, where my only memory is dancing with a beautiful, wavy-haired, brunette woman in some club – what can I say, my type is my type, whatever the flavour – and getting extremely upset when I remembered that the original Mr Egg was no more and that if I wanted a bacon and egg sandwich at two in the morning I'd have to go and make it at home.

The girls were up for a repeat on Sunday, but they're not forty-two, and I don't bounce back like I used to. Having obliterated my brain on Saturday night, I surfaced only for water, paracetamol, more water, and eventually the aforementioned bacon and egg sandwich, which I realised was a bad idea about thirty seconds later when it came rushing back up. By the time I'd finally slept it all off and my Monday morning alarm kicked me rudely back into touch, I'd put just enough distance – and vodka – between me and Friday night's festivities that I could almost put the whole thing down to some weird, Halloween fuelled hallucination. And by the time I got to work, sipping on the generic office coffee and hoping for a long dictation so I could plug in my earphones and zone out for the morning, I'd almost managed to convince myself that maybe none of it was real.

Just as I start to wonder if Mags has missed her train, checking my phone for a text, Pat suddenly appears out of nowhere with a stack of files in her arms.

'Morning, Dorothy,' she leans down gleefully, angling for any possible gossip. 'Interesting party, wasn't it?'

I ignore the opening. 'It was all right.'

'I don't think anyone expected *that* to happen.'

I shrug. 'Food was nice.'

'The food? Never mind the *food*,' she replies choppily. 'Who cares about the food? I'm talking about—'

'Ooh,' I murmur over her as a notification pops up on my screen. 'Dictation from Stephen. A big one.' I smile back at her innocently. 'Better crack on, eh?'

Pat frowns, irritated at my lack of interest. 'Fine. Margaret has called in sick,' she nods towards Mags' desk beside me, huffing with contempt. 'You're covering Paula and Josiah's work.'

I'm immediately concerned. Mags hasn't taken a sick day since she joined, even when she's actually been ill. 'Oh, okay.'

Pat dumps the files on the edge of my desk with an unceremonious thud, smirking with satisfaction as she knocks my shorthand pad on the floor. 'The top two are urgent, finish them by ten.'

I nod blithely, her demand washing over me. I just want her to leave so I can text Mags. She turns on her heel and slopes back off the way she came.

'Please and thanks cost nothing,' I mutter, leaning down to grab the pad, together with my phone out of my bag under the desk. It's on silent, so I double check every app known to humankind, but there's no word from Mags. I didn't hear from her over the weekend either, and we often text nonsense outside of work, but after Friday night I wasn't surprised; I figured she just wanted to forget it all and start fresh today. But if she was sick, I'd expect her to let me know what's up. There's no texts, no missed calls, no WhatsApp, nothing.

I shoot her a quick message.

Hey mate, you ok? Let me know how you're doing. Big hugs xx

Then with one eye darting back to the phone screen every few minutes, I crack on with the jobs that need doing for Mags' fee earners. As I'm rifling through instructions, checking what's what, I finally see movement.

Three dots. Mags is typing.

I watch with bated breath, waiting to see what appears.

Nothing. The dots vanish as she changes her mind.

I *hate* that. But maybe she just feels rough and tired and can't be arsed right now. Or maybe after the trauma of calling in sick to Pat, who no doubt did her damnedest to make Mags feel guilty as shite for not coming in, she's gone back to bed to recover and stupid me went and woke her back up. Leaving it alone, I plug in my earphones and start on Paula's most urgent dictation. If I haven't heard from her by the time I get home, I'll call her after tea.

Time flies when you're wading through a crapton of work, and that's how my morning vanished, in a haze of typing and coffee. Every document, every new file, every set of property searches brought me back closer to reality, the mundanity and repetition of it all numbing me like clockwork. Whenever I topped up my caffeine supply, the kitchen was rumbling with constant murmurs – *'did you hear what happened?'*, *'Sam said it was unbelievable'*, *'hmph, unbelievable sounds about right'* – but Friday night's theatrics gradually faded farther and farther away, like a vivid fever dream.

It wasn't until lunchtime that it all came crashing down.

At first it seemed like nothing much. I was heading out for some fresh air, desperate for a break from my screen, thinking if it wasn't too cold, I might try and claim a bench in Pigeon Park to eat my lunch. As I walked out through Reception, a couple of suits were coming back into the building, people I didn't know. But there was something familiar in one of their faces. The moment we passed each other, I heard them say 'no, Rebecca's not in today', I realised it was Beetlejuice, then everything went dark.

As I come to, it's like I've been transported right back there.

I'm inside Rebecca's house, and I immediately know something's *wrong*.

Everything is dim, silent, oppressive – I can feel it all around me, the air thick with it, something off, something *not good*. Amidst the suffocating darkness, a tiny fleck of light from above draws my gaze, and I walk slowly from where I've landed in the echoing hall towards the large, curved staircase. As my right foot meets the first step, I feel a rumble, a low vibration running through the house, reacting to my approach. Reaching for the ornate banister, when my hand touches the wood, the rumble evolves into a low, guttural sound, almost a growl – the sound of something hidden, or something *hiding* – some ancient thing of nightmares lurking in the shadows. With nowhere else to go, I make my way up the stairs, all the while becoming more and more enveloped by the vacuum of gloom.

On the first-floor landing are five doors, all closed, each humming with their own gentle tremor, faint shadows dancing in the sliver of a gap between it and the floor. The light I saw comes from here, behind these doors, glowing with menacing purpose. I move carefully towards the closest one, hitching my breath as the shapes beneath it flicker in response with increasing urgency. As I reach towards the doorknob, the noise around me builds, the snarling cacophony almost deafening, the force of it shaking the door in front of me, the wood rattling against its frame, thundering louder and louder as I grip the handle and begin to turn, feeling the latch release as the door bursts suddenly open, the blinding light within engulfing me as I step across the threshold and find myself—

—lying on the floor of Reception, concerned faces hovering over me.

'She's waking up.' A vaguely familiar voice.

'No ambulance for at least a couple of hours,' I hear Jackie say from the front desk, phone to her ear. 'Not unless she's got a serious head injury.'

'Can you hear me?' My eyes slowly come back into focus, and I see Beetlejuice leaning down beside me, searching my face carefully for signs of recognition. 'Do you know where you are?'

I make a gentle nodding motion and realise there's a cushion under my head.

'At work.'

I start to sit up.

'Woah,' Beetlejuice stops me, shaking their head. 'Not too fast.'

'I'm fine.'

'Be careful,' they warn firmly as I push upright, hunching forward, the marble floor cold under my arse. Thank god I wore trousers today. 'Did you hit your head? You might have a concussion.'

I reach back gingerly to check but my head feels fine. Well, fine in the sense that it doesn't hurt and there's no bump and my brains don't appear to be leaking all over the floor, but *less* fine in the sense that I'm completely freaked out by what I just saw and fighting desperately to keep my composure.

'We should really get you checked out.'

'I'm okay, really,' I shake my head, lying through my teeth. Reaching for a nearby table for leverage, I push myself awkwardly onto my feet.

They look unconvinced. 'I don't know…'

Jackie shakes her head. 'Jesus, mate, you went down like a sack of potatoes. Are you sure you're okay?'

'I'm fine,' I shrug weakly.

Beetlejuice turns to her. 'Who's her line manager?'

'I'm right here, you know,' I glare, mildly irritated at being talked about like I'm not.

'Rebecca Hudson-Hicks. But—'

'She's out today, I know.'

My ears prickle. I thought that was what I heard them say as we passed each other, right before my subconscious went flying off to Rebecca's house. Coincidence?

'Well, let's say I'm her line manager today.'

They turn back to me.

'I want a First Aider to look at you.'

'I'm a First Aider,' Jackie replies happily. 'I can do it.'

'Perfect. Once you've checked her over and you're happy she's okay, order her a taxi home. Charge it to my cost centre.'

Jackie and I exchange glances. I don't know who Beetlejuice is, but I already like them.

'Who's your Team Leader?'

'Pat Gage.'

'Fine. I'll let her know she'll have to do without you this afternoon.'

Pat won't like that. 'I'm already covering for someone else today.'

'Then she'll have to cover you both, won't she.'

Oh, I *really* like them.

'Any comeback, tell her to take it up with me,' they instruct firmly. 'You go home and get some rest.'

'I'll do that. Thanks.'

They nod, and turn back to Jackie. 'I'll leave her in your capable hands, Jack.'

As they carry on their way, Jackie leads me over to sit on the sofa while she gives me a once over.

'I like them,' I tell her.

Jackie laughs, studying me carefully. 'Yeah, they're a good

one. Anything hurt?'

'Only my pride.'

'Never knew you had any.'

'Funny.'

She holds a hand up to my face. 'How many fingers?'

'Twelve.'

'Har har. Follow them please.'

I move my eyes in time with her movements, back and forth, up and down.

'Who were you covering?'

'Mags.'

Jackie frowns. 'She's off sick? That's not like her.'

'Surprised you didn't already know, you usually do.' I wonder if she knows what's up with Rebecca. 'What about Rebecca? Do you know why she's off?'

She frowns, messing with my neck and shoulders, checking for who knows what. 'Not exactly.

Hmm. *That's* curious. 'Not like you not to know the goss.'

'I don't know specifics,' she shrugs. 'Just that she's planning on being out for the next few days.'

Next few *days?* At no notice? With client appointments to keep and deals to negotiate? That's so wildly out of character for Rebecca I can barely believe it.

'Not like her either,' Jackie goes on. 'Outside of maternity and Christmas, HR usually have to force her to use most of her leave. I'm not sure I've ever known her to just take a random week off out of nowhere.'

I try not to show on my face how much this is disturbing me after the vision I just saw. 'Aw, mate, what's the world coming to when *you* don't know everything that's going on in this place. You must be losing your touch.'

'Had to happen sometime.' She pats my shoulder affectionately.

'Okay. I'll call you a taxi. But any headaches, blurred vision, anything like that—'

'Straight to A & E, I swear.' I give her a Guide's honour salute as she heads back to the reception desk to use the phone.

'Good. And Dot?'

'Hmm?'

'Try not to worry about Mags. I'm sure it's nothing serious.'

'Hmm.' I hope not.

'You want me to wait with you till the taxi gets here? Phil can cover the desk.'

'Thanks, Jack.'

Jackie nods, making her calls efficiently before trotting back to sit beside me. 'Ten minutes. Hell of a way to get a half day, matey,' she shakes her head.

I laugh ruefully. 'Yeah. I like my new Line Manager though.'

'Izzy?' Jackie grins. 'Pretty badass, aren't they.'

Ah, so Beetlejuice is Izzy Ramsay. I've heard about them. 'The new Partner, right?'

'*Senior* Partner,' she corrects me.

'The one who's been taking scalps in Technology?'

Technology: super toxic division, populated by a vocal minority of juvenile but high-ranking bigoted idiots. Kitchen gossip is that since Izzy joined the team as Senior Partner – and a member of the Board of Directors – a couple of months ago, they'd made it their personal mission to correct their collective unpleasant behaviours. Within the first six weeks, they'd put the main offenders in official performance measures with HR, had them unceremoniously turfed out on their arses on 'garden leave' for any minor infractions since, and all but a couple of the diehard stalwarts had already chosen to quit. Since these people were all well known around the office for proudly sharing their pathetic prejudices under the guise of thinly veiled 'jokes', I have zero sympathy for them, and nothing but admiration for the person who finally had the balls to sort their nonsense out.

'That's the one.'

'Wish they could do the same with a few other scumbags in this place.'

Jackie understands exactly which particular Scumbag I mean. She's the one who coined the nickname in the first place, after all. 'Hope springs eternal, matey.'

'Yeah. I won't hold my breath.'

She smiles back sadly. Jackie's been with the firm – god, nearly forty years, I think it is; she joined straight out of school when she was 16 – and believe me, she's seen *everything*. She knows very well just how much shitty stuff some people at this place have got away with. And it winds her up as much as it does me; I don't know how she's had the patience to put up with it for all this time. I suppose at this point in her life, it's better the devil you know.

'Taxi's here,' Phil shouts from the desk.

'That was fast.'

'We spend a bomb with them,' Jackie shrugs. 'They like to keep me sweet.'

'Doesn't everyone?'

Jackie laughs, turning to hug me quickly as we both stand. 'Go on, get your arse off home. If I hear Pat's head's exploded, I'll let you know.'

'Now there's a mental picture,' I smile back. 'See you tomorrow.'

'Look after yourself,' she tells me sternly as I head out.

After the taxi drops me home about half two, the temptation is to take full advantage of the bonus half-day and spend what's left of the afternoon vegging out with a couple of DVDs and a massive pile of chocolate – for medicinal purposes – but I know

I can't. What I saw – what I *felt* – before I hit the deck in Reception unnerved the bejesus out of me. Whatever's up in Rebecca's house is about more than just what happened on Friday night, and as much as I'd hoped to just forget the whole thing, my pesky conscience is pricking at me to at least check into it a bit more closely.

As for that pesky vision – well, it's been a while, but I *used* to get premonitions, for want of a better word, back when I was a kid. At first, they were just silly stuff – like seeing that my mom left her house keys on the counter at the Post Office, or that Louise from Primary School was going to end up with her arm in plaster if she kept swinging on the monkey bars like she thought she was Indiana Jones, or who'd win what on Bullseye before it aired, back in the days of four TV channels and no internet. Even now, I tend to have an instinct for early-stage pregnancies and surprise breakup announcements. But like all the other trappings of my unwanted gift, my teens sent it into overdrive, plaguing my *conscious* mind with scenes of horror I could do nothing about – car wrecks, fires, accidents – twisted bodies, faces contorted in fear and pain, scenes nobody should have to witness play out in their head, let alone a terrified thirteen-year-old kid. Another contributor to my precocious drinking habit. This particular vision seemed more like a general warning of something, rather than any specific thing which might actually happen. If I'd found myself in that situation in reality, I'd never have actually opened that upstairs door, not with that glow coming from underneath it. Everyone knows you should never, *ever* go into the light. But this lingering disturbance in the force was pushing me to try and suss out if there really *was* anything to worry about behind all the smoke and mirrors of Friday night's theatrics, and try and find some earthly way that I could subtly warn Big Boss about it. Preferably without getting myself the sack in the process.

As I find myself driving back along the single-track lane, the last clouds of daylight stretching out across the fields around me, I try to figure out what the hell I'm going to say when I get there. 'Hi Rebecca, I think some sort of malevolent spirit might have taken up residence inside your lovely new house. Mind if I check it out?' Hmm. Maybe not. How about: 'I heard you were off sick and thought I'd come over to check everything was okay.' A bit of a boundary stomp – I get on with the woman, but we're not besties outside of the office or anything. Maybe I can say there's some sort of issue at work I need to talk to her about? But if there were, surely I'd just text or call to let her know; her mobile is work-issued after all, every fee earner has one, and the number's on her email so it's hardly a state secret.

When I reach the turn for the gates – so much easier to find with the benefit of some crisp autumn sunshine to guide me, albeit low in the sky – I'm mildly surprised to find them already open. At least I don't need to announce myself over an intercom just to make it up the driveway, and that buys me ten extra seconds to figure out how to explain my presence there in the first place. Without the rows of cars and clamour from the party in the background, the wide drive beside the house feels oddly lifeless and desolate. Rebecca's Jag is parked in one corner beside a slightly muddy Bentley, probably Rob's, and a dinky, older model Peugeot. The smaller car almost makes my heap of crap look like it belongs, so I pull up beside it and kill the engine, still drawing a complete blank for what to say once I get through the front door, assuming anyone will open it for me. I do one final quick check of my phone – still no word from Mags, so I resolve to call her after I get back home – and climb out.

Standing here in the cold light of day, looking at the beautiful building in front of me, the perfectly manicured lawns surrounding it, it's hard not to feel a little bit ridiculous.

It's just a *house*, after all. I see no bleeding walls, no ghostly apparitions at the windows, and given that we're smack in the centre of the Midlands, I highly doubt it's been built on top of any ancient Indian burial grounds. I send a quick message out to my Guides, hoping they might have some insight, but they're both unresponsive, and the Voice is eerily quiet as well. Because of course, now that I could actually *do* with an otherworldly pep talk, the sneaky little buggers are absolutely nowhere to be found. Crossing the gravel, I'm acutely aware of the sound of my own footsteps as they crunch against each tiny individual stone, echoing through the Autumn chill around me.

This time, I reach the door without any interruptions. No pull, no sixth sense, nothing but the light draught of the low October wind. I still don't know what I'm going to say as I reach up from the front steps and draw down on the old brass bell pull fixed to the wall. A few long seconds later, the sound of footsteps approaches from the other side of the door and my breath catches in my chest as I beg for some sort of divine inspiration to guide me.

Then the door opens, and it kind of does.

'Oh. It's you.'

6

I find myself looking into the twinkling, deep brown eyes of a certain flirty Vicar. Does that count as divine inspiration?

The surprise in his voice at finding me stood at the bottom of the steps is, I suspect, a pretty close equivalent to the shock on my own face at seeing him in the doorway above me. He eyes me suspiciously.

'What are you doing here?'

I raise my eyebrows. 'What are *you* doing here?'

Father Theo flashes that smile. 'I'm here in a professional capacity.'

'More recruitment?'

'You're funny. Did you forget something on Friday night? Apart from my number, I mean.' He blushes and coughs suddenly, like he's just remembered why he's actually here and that it's not to stand on a doorstep flirting with me. 'There's a pile of stuff people left behind.'

Damn. Why didn't I think of that? What a perfect excuse to turn back up here.

'Erm…'

My head wants to say yes – my brick, a scarf or something, anything just to get me in the door – but there's something else telling me no, don't lie to him. No Voice – just good old-fashioned instinct. And maybe a teensy bit of extremely ill-judged attraction. Maybe.

'Well?' He shrugs, trying to hurry me along. 'There's a box in the hall if you want to check. You'll have to be quick though.'

Father Theo glances nervously back behind the door, towards the front room where I first saw him at the bar the other night, like there's something pressing going on back in that direction which he really needs to deal with.

It's possible I'm going to regret this, but I decide to trust my gut, for now at least. It's not often it leads me astray. Although this is an attractive bloke we're talking about, so it might not even be my gut that's talking. 'Actually, I need to see Rebecca.'

He shakes his head. 'Sorry. It's not a good time.'

'It's important.'

'Rebecca's… the family, are…' he searches awkwardly for the words. 'Otherwise engaged.'

'With a priest in the house?' Now it's my turn to be suspicious of him. 'Did someone die?'

His eyes widen. 'No, of course not.'

'Then what?'

'Look,' Father Theo gestures toward me, a slightly lost puppy dog expression on his face. I realise I never told him my name before.

'Dot.'

He nods. 'Look, Dot, whatever it is, I'm really sorry but I'm afraid it's going to have to wait. Rebecca's really—'

Good old divine inspiration finally hits me.

'Wait. Are you here because of what happened on Friday?'

That gets his attention.

'In that room? With the Ouija board?'

He flashes another brief look beyond the door again, uncertain.

That's it. That's why he's here.

'Did something else happen?'

His eyes dart back uncertainly to mine. A sudden thought pops into my head unbidden – from somewhere else entirely, I suspect – that the bedroom door I saw in my vision belongs to one of the kids, that it's something to do with them, and I decide to take a leap of faith. Out of character, I admit, but given my current conversation partner, it seems fitting.

'Something happened to one of the kids?'

His mouth drops open and he tries to hide it, but not quite quickly enough.

Another image in my mind. 'The younger one? The boy?'

Father Theo stammers slightly as he speaks this time, something I don't think is normally an issue for him. 'How could you *possibly* know that?'

Oh no. *Not* good. I do hope nobody was daft enough to go into the light.

'That's why I'm here,' I shrug.

The conflict in his face is clear. Conflict, coupled with an expression which says: 'remind me never to flirt with some random crazy woman at a party ever again'.

'I *need* to talk to her,' I tell him again, willing him desperately to take me at my word. Mind control is sadly not part of my supernatural repertoire.

He takes a couple more seconds to think about it then lets out a deep breath, shaking his head, before pulling the door all the way open and stepping back into the hall to let me through. 'Please don't make me regret this.'

'No more than *I'm* about to,' I reply wearily.

With the cold air shut firmly outside, he turns to lead me back through the house. I cast a wary glance up towards the landing as we pass the bottom of the staircase before I turn and follow him.

The cleaners must've been in over the weekend, as there's no sign in the front room that a party ever took place here at all. The bar, the lights and the music are all long gone, replaced by the sofas and coffee tables, back in their natural positions, supporting a couple of half-drunk mugs of tea nestled on coasters in between remote controls, somebody's phone and iPad and a random scattered pile of Lego. As we walk through into the sitting room at the back, I can hear raised voices further on, coming from the drawing room where Jackie gleefully had her tea leaves told less than seventy-two hours before.

The voices are unmistakeably Rebecca's and Rob's.

'I don't care.' Her. 'I already told you—'

'I know what you said. We're not—'

Father Theo turns and stops me just short of the door. 'Look, before we go in there…'

Surely he's not about to carry on flirting again *now*?

'Everyone in the house is very tense at the moment.'

Oh. That's a no then.

'So whatever it is you have to say…'

I slap away a silly, minor stab of disappointment. Of course he's not about to flirt again now, it would be *completely* inappropriate, given the circumstances. Besides, it's not like I even *want* him to.

'Please be careful how you say it.'

I nod back at him. 'I'm not a complete idiot. Just call me Little Miss Sensitivity.'

'So I *can* call you then?'

Aha, *there* it is. I flash him a disapproving look, whilst not being entirely successful in suppressing my own smile. 'Is this really the time?'

'You're right, of course not.' He looks down with a quick shrug, seemingly chastened, but I can tell from the lopsided smirk he's desperately trying to hide that he's having a similar issue. As he straightens his face and opens the door, the crescendo of the quarrel evaporates as he walks into the room ahead of me.

'Father Gregory, I really don't think…'

Rebecca's gaze turns immediately to one of utter confusion as I step out from behind him.

'*Dot*? What are *you* doing here? Is something wrong at the office?'

I can see in her face that she's searching for any logical reason as to why in the world I'd turn up randomly at her house, now of all times.

'I called this morning,' she goes on quickly. 'I'm out for the week.'

'I know,' I nod back calmly. Before I can say anything else, Rob, Rebecca's husband, steps in.

'Dot, it's really not a great time,' he says firmly.

I can tell he's trying to be polite, but I can hear the strain in his voice telling me that the situation – whatever it is – is balanced on the edge of a knife. I've met him a few times before, mostly at the parties, but he's occasionally come along for a drink after a Christmas 'do or two as well – decent guy, some sort of doctor, as driven and committed as Rebecca is. A well-matched pair by all accounts, a proper little power couple.

'I understand,' I tell him, keeping my voice as level and composed as possible, trying not to add to the tension already flooding the room. 'This isn't a social call.'

They share a dubious glance, whatever argument they were having before we walked in temporarily forgotten. Their questioning eyes search Father Theo's for some sort of explanation, and he looks back to me with a silent nod to go ahead.

God, this is awkward.

'Okay. Well.' I breathe out slowly. 'This is going to sound a little…'

I hesitate, and find myself reflexively looking towards Father Theo for support, although I have no idea why as I don't know the man.

'A little *weird*.'

Rob laughs abruptly, but the sound has no joy. 'After the weekend we've had—'

'*Rob!*' Rebecca hisses at him. I suspect her reaction is more about not wanting him to spill the details of whatever weekend they've had, rather than rebuking him for the interruption.

I raise my eyes to the heavens and nod up towards the ceiling. 'Something happened, right? With your son?'

Another look passes between them, this time of complete incredulity.

'Father, did you—'

'Not me,' he raises his hands, not guilty. 'She already knew when she turned up at the door.'

'But how could you *possibly*—'

'Know that?' I finish for her, sensing the pressure of time. It'll be dark soon, and I'd like to be long gone out of here when that happens, thanks very much. Things can sometimes get much creepier in the dark. 'Yeah. Look, never mind how I know, it doesn't really matter.'

'It matters to us.'

'What matters,' I walk towards them slightly, some urgency in my step, 'is *what* I know.'

'Which is?' Rob frowns.

I turn to see Father Theo looking back at me, concern etched across his face.

Deep breath. 'There's something in this house. Something not good.'

From the expressions on their collective faces, I sense that this news is not quite the big reveal I expected.

Rebecca scoffs. 'This is *ridiculous*.'

'What do you mean,' Rob takes a step in my direction, '*not good*?'

Behind him, Rebecca is pacing furiously, grabbing at a bunch of papers strewn across the large coffee table in the centre of the room. 'Don't tell me *this* is not good,' she says, waving the loose bundle in the air at nobody in particular.

'Look, Dot,' Father Theo steps in. 'There's been some odd things going on over the last couple of days. Rebecca believes—'

'I *know*,' she fumes.

He carries on, not acknowledging the interruption. 'She believes that whatever's causing it,' he looks at me pointedly, holding my gaze, 'is something *positive*.'

'Of course it is!' Rebecca yells. 'Did you even read the messages?'

'Messages?' I don't like the sound of that. 'What messages?'

She moves to thrust her handful of papers in my direction, but Rob cuts her off with a frustrated, angry sigh and snatches them away. '*Fuck* your damn messages, what about *Adam*?'

A sudden stab inside my head, alerting me to something. Wait – what I saw in my vision, the stairs, the landing, the light – if that bedroom door *was* Adam's…

'Something up there hurt him,' I hear myself say.

They all look at me. Believe me, I'm as shocked as they are. I have no idea where this is coming from. Well, I sort of do, really, but the method is new to me. Words don't usually just pop out of my mouth without me at least being aware of them first.

'He saw something in the light.'

Seriously, you should really, never, *ever* go into the light, not unless you're already dead, or you really want to be. I *cannot* stress this enough.

'It scared him. It didn't want him to tell.'

It's scaring *me*, is what it's doing. I can feel the hairs on the back of my neck prickle, and I don't like it. '*Enough*,' I snap quickly, reclaiming my voice for myself, fully back into the present moment. The weirdness lifts from me as quickly as it appeared.

Across the room, Rebecca is leaning over as she sits on one of the sofas, rifling back frantically through her precious papers.

'Rebecca?' I frown over at her hunched figure, unnerved by her out of character behaviour.

She ignores me.

'*Rebecca*,' I repeat firmly.

Her head snaps up, a strange expression across her face. She looks shifty, almost panicked, like… like she's just been caught doing something she shouldn't be. It changes in an instant as her eyes meet mine and she suddenly breaks into a broad smile, but there's something not quite right about it. Something… *off*.

'Yes, dear girl?'

My heart catches in my chest. What a weird thing to call me. And why does it sound so… *familiar*? Like I've heard it before somewhere?

I gesture toward her papers. 'Where did the messages come from?'

Her smile broadens to a point well beyond creepy. 'From *them*, of course.'

'Them?'

Rebecca looks up, eyes on the ceiling. 'Them.'

She blinks slowly, returning her attention to the mess in front of her. Rob and Father Theo are both staring, incredulous. I ignore their expressions and turn to Rob as I decide to focus on the practical.

'Is Adam still here?'

'What?'

'Adam. Is he still in the house?' I keep a watchful eye on Rebecca as I talk.

'Against my better judgement,' Rob nods dully. 'He's up in his room.'

'He's in some sort of catatonic state, yes?' I'm asking from previous, long forgotten, nauseating experience.

'Y-yeah,' another nod, his eyes wide now with growing disquiet. 'We couldn't wake him up after everything else happened. I tried to call an ambulance but Becs went mad about it, that's why I called Father Gregory, that's all she'd agree to.'

Rob looks scared to death of me. I glance at his wife, frantically murmuring to herself, utterly oblivious to the rest of us, and on the face of it, potentially in the midst of some sort of mental health crisis. I'm not the one he should be worried about.

'Okay. First priority is to get him out of the house. Your daughter too.'

'What?'

'You have relatives? Friends? Anyone who can come and get them?'

He shakes his head. 'Not locally, not that we'd— not who could—'

Father Theo steps in. 'I could take them, for a bit. If that'd help.'

I shake my head and open my mouth to explain, but Rob doesn't give me the chance. 'I'll take them myself, we can just go—'

'You'll do no such thing,' Rebecca suddenly storms out of nowhere, up on her feet, away from her spot on the sofa and raging towards us.

'They're my kids too, Becs,' Rob dives straight back into the argument.

I know I promised to be sensitive, but the situation feels like it's slipping away, out of control. Behind them, through the massive bay window which looks out onto the back part of the garden, I can see the final slivers of afternoon sun beginning to turn to pink and orange. Not much longer now before it's full dark, even with the best part of the week still left before the clocks change.

'Pack it in, both of you. There's really nobody else who could pick them up?'

'I can take them,' Father Theo suggests again.

I shake my head. 'No, you can't, it's not just—'

'Nobody's taking my kids anywhere!' Rebecca yells furiously, pushing past all of us and storming out of the room, slamming the door behind her. Heading straight upstairs to the kids, no doubt.

The room finally falls silent and I let out a sigh, rubbing my head as it threatens to start aching. What am I getting myself into?

'Dot,' Father Theo asks cautiously. 'What were you going to say? Why can't I take them?'

'Because,' I look back up at him awkwardly, nodding towards the door and the whirlwind that just closed it. 'The house might not be the only thing that's a problem.'

7

'What do you mean?'

Since my lunchtime detour to Never Never Land, the back of my brain has been trying to figure out exactly what I'd seen there. But the extra little breadcrumbs of detail I'd witnessed during the short time I'd been back in the house for real changed my perspective. Rebecca having called in sick so unusually was already an indicator that something wasn't right, but coupled with the way she'd acted just now – the frantic, out of character demeanour, her desperate defence of these 'messages', which I wanted a nosy at – did suggest she could be having some sort of urgent mental health crisis.

On the other hand, it could be something else. Something creepier.

'What do you *mean*,' Rob repeats insistently.

How the hell do I explain this?

'Okay. So, it's possible that whatever's behind… whatever odd things you've had happen this weekend…'

I search for the best way to come out with it without sounding like I'm completely delusional. Then it occurs to me that there probably isn't one.

'It's possible Rebecca could be… affected by it as well.'

Rob snorts. 'What? Are you trying to say she's *possessed*?'

'No,' I shake my head quickly. 'No, I'm not saying that at all.'

Possession – in the way most people imagine it – is really just not a thing. I love a good horror film, but they have a lot to answer for on that count. Ghosts can't just up and possess people, that doesn't happen in real life. The amount of physical energy they'd need to force their spirit or soul or whatever you want to call it into a living person's body is just not something any of them are capable of. The closest you usually get is when they want to pop into someone on this side to use them as a channel, to actually speak or write messages directly through their body, which is possible. But that's a two-way process, requiring a skilled, strong trance medium who's a willing participant. They can't just jump inside you and take over at random. You'd be talking about something phenomenally powerful, and spirits like that aren't exactly ten a penny. I certainly don't recall ever having come across one.

'Is her head going to start spinning next?' Rob goes on scornfully.

But, if somebody's mentally vulnerable, they *can* exert influence on that mental state.

'That's not what I'm—'

'You're a fucking crazy person,' he practically spits as he storms across the room, flinging the door back open and charging after Rebecca.

I sigh, shaking my head. I knew when I decided to come here that none of this was likely to be a fun conversation, but at that point it hadn't occurred to me my boss might be under the influence of evil spirits. Being called names comes with the territory in this sort of side gig, but it still stings when it happens.

Father Theo pipes up gently behind me. 'I think that went well.'

I flash him a glare. 'Look, Father—'

'Theo, please.'

'Father,' I repeat pointedly, trying to keep things professional. 'Look, possession's mostly bullshit. You work for the church, you know that, right?'

He shrugs. 'So?'

'Possession's mostly bullshit. Influence isn't.'

'What do you mean, influence?'

I try to explain. 'Like somebody's whispering over her shoulder. She can't hear them exactly, but whatever they're saying, some part of it still gets into her head.'

He raises his eyebrows. 'Influence, huh.'

I shrug. 'Possibly. I'm not absolutely sure, but – Rob said other things happened. Do you know what they were?'

'I only know what he told me,' Father Theo shrugs. 'It started on Saturday evening. Banging, noises, doors opening and closing. Then yesterday, little things moving around the house, being in different places than they should be.'

Hmm. Those can be explained away, if they have old pipes, creaky floorboards and a few draughts. Even things moving can have a rational explanation. A lot of the time, what people think are signs of being haunted – seeing a ghost, leaving something in one place only to find it later in a completely different room and there's nobody else who could've touched it – are chemically induced. Taking the wrong dose of your meds, using someone else's, other drugs in general. I once heard of someone who kept finding random sticky notes around his flat, filled with bizarre and increasingly threatening messages in unfamiliar handwriting, despite the fact that he lived alone. He was convinced there was a supernatural explanation, that something was 'there' with him and wanted to murder him. Turned out he had the first stages of carbon monoxide poisoning and he'd written them all himself.

'Then Rebecca started writing all this stuff,' he gestures back to the papers on the table. 'And this morning Adam wouldn't wake up. He's alive, he's breathing, but it's like he's just stuck asleep.'

'And she wouldn't let Rob call an ambulance? For Adam?'

Father Theo shakes his head. 'He said she got so agitated when he tried, like she was having a panic attack. He didn't want to make things even worse. She begged him to call me instead.'

That surprises me. 'Calling you was her idea?'

He shrugs. 'She's the one who joined the church when they moved here. I get the impression he only does it to make her happy. Of the two of them, she's definitely the believer. Him, not so much.'

Interesting. Rebecca's belief – in anything, it doesn't have to be in ghosts or the afterlife – her lack of scepticism, could be what made her an easier target. But it still feels like all of this has to be connected – Rebecca's behaviour, the Ouija board, my own little episode earlier, Adam's deep sleep. But if there *is* something in the housing causing all this, if it really is influencing Rebecca, why on earth would it want her to invite a priest into the house, of all people?

Then again... there was that thing where the Ouija board aimed itself right at the spot where the very same priest had been standing. Maybe it wants another crack at him.

'Not sure how she thought I could help,' he mutters sadly.

Aww. I want to hug him. In a reassuring, platonic way. Honest.

'Look,' he goes on quickly, 'you suggested getting the kids out of the house. I think that's a great idea. Maybe if I can convince them to let me do that, I can get Adam to hospital. Then Rob might be able to talk Rebecca down, get her to accept she needs some help.'

I grimace. 'I already said you can't do that.'

Father Theo frowns back at me suspiciously, arms crossed. He looks hot when he's being all serious. 'You did say that. Why is that, exactly?'

If I'm right – big if, of course – and this is all connected to Friday night... well, he was smack in the middle of all that. So was I, and look what happened to me at lunchtime. Rebecca might not be the only one who's been... touched. I take a deep breath, readying myself for a barrage of scepticism.

'Okay. I suspect whatever's going on here, all the mucking about with the Ouija board on Friday night is what kicked it off.'

He looks like he's at least trying to keep an open mind, his reply slow and measured. 'Okay.'

How do I also explain my own weird connection to that particular incident?

'Something… odd happened to me when that was happening as well.'

'I saw you,' he interrupts quickly. 'You looked… *gone*. Like you were somewhere else. That's why I came over, to check that you were okay.'

And missed taking a direct headshot with a big wooden board by seconds, but that was probably just a coincidence. Probably.

'If I'm right, once they opened that door, something took the chance to sneak in.'

'And influence Rebecca.'

'It would explain her odd behaviour. Nothing else happened during the party, and if anything *had* been around the rest of the night, I would've felt it,' I explain matter-of-factly. 'But if other things started happening here on Saturday, if it's been hanging about for a couple of days, then it's possible it might not only be Rebecca.'

'Rob too? You really think so?'

'It's *possible*,' I reply. 'But possible's a hell of a risk to take with those kids.'

Father Theo frowns darkly. 'You still haven't answered my question.'

Oh dear. I was coming to that. I don't think he's going to like it.

He answers half of it for me. 'You think I might be affected too.'

I hope not, but… 'It's possible.'

'There were a hundred people at that party,' he huffs tightly, obviously offended. 'You included.'

'I know that, but—'

'Are they all affected too?'

'They weren't all as close to ground zero.'

'All right, so all the people in the library then. That must be,' he looks up, mentally recalling the haphazard seating arrangements before he glares angrily back at me. 'Fifteen, twenty people? Are all of them about to start speaking in tongues and spider crawling up the stairs?'

I wonder if he watched The Exorcist for business or pleasure.

'And what about you?' he rumbles, voice low and wavering. 'If anyone's under some sort of influence, wouldn't it make more sense to be the nutjob who's turned up on the doorstep with mysterious inside information?'

Ouch. I appreciate being told you might be suffering side effects from a run-in with an evil entity isn't the cosiest idea, but I didn't say it because I wanted to upset him. 'Okay,' I raise my hands in a gesture of peace, hoping to pivot the conversation back on course. 'Do you remember what happened on Friday night *after* you came over to check on me?'

'Yeah, the Ouija board went berserk and all hell broke loose.' He shakes his head, irritation abruptly displaced by his bewilderment at the memory. 'I'm still not really sure what that was all about.'

He breathes out slowly, calming himself.

'Then you snuck off before I could talk to you again and spent the rest of the night hiding from me.'

That gorgeous smile of his is back. I have to fight to ignore its effect on me. 'You saw the Ouija board hit the bookcase?'

'And smash into about a zillion pieces,' he nods blithely, 'yeah.'

'And nothing about that struck you as odd?'

'What, an inanimate object throwing itself across a room after spelling out messages from beyond the grave? Seemed like a normal Friday night to me.'

He's maddening, but I can't deny how much I'm enjoying the dry sense of humour. And the pretty eyes. I mentally slap myself round the face with a wet flannel. Pack it in, Dot.

'You didn't notice where it landed when it smashed into a zillion pieces?'

Father Theo shrugs, oblivious.

'Right where your head would've been.'

A look of bleak realisation comes into his eyes and he pales. 'If I hadn't just moved to get a better look at you.'

'Exactly.'

There's a moment of awkward silence as he processes the implications.

'It's probably just a coincidence,' I suggest unconvincingly.

'I'm a priest. I don't believe in coincidence.'

'Vicar,' I remind him. 'And of course you don't.'

'Do you?'

'Generally? Of course.'

'I wasn't asking generally.'

'I know.'

'And?'

'Probably not.' Sometimes my honesty pops its head out faster than I can sugar coat it.

Father Theo sighs wearily. 'Terrific.'

I try to soften the blow. 'I might've, if Rebecca hadn't specifically asked for you to come back and deal with this, instead of doing the sensible thing of taking her kid to the hospital and getting the hell out of Amityville.'

He frowns back at me again. 'If you really think it's as bad as all that, why on earth did you come back?'

Do I take a chance and tell him the truth?

All my instincts scream yes.

'Something else happened to me a couple of hours ago, at work. It was definitely connected—'

'What happened?' He's suddenly back on high alert, concern in his voice, and the sweetness of it isn't lost on me. 'Are you okay?'

'I'm fine,' I try and shrug him off. 'Look, it's not that big of a deal.'

'Tell me.'

I sigh, knowing I'm about to throw more fuel on the fire that already makes me look like a lunatic. 'I had a little... episode.'

'An episode?'

'A... well... sort of... a vision.'

'A vision?'

'Of this place. Of stuff happening here.'

'You had a vision of here? Of stuff happening here?'

'I passed out at work, and—'

'You passed out?'

I round on him, a little irritably. 'Are you just going to keep repeating everything I say?'

'I don't know, what else are you going to say?'

Funny.

Father Theo smiles ruefully. 'For a second there I actually thought you were going to say you came back for me.'

'I didn't know you were here.'

'Crystal ball needs a clean, does it?'

I roll my eyes. 'Never heard that one before.'

He sighs as he tries to process everything he's learned in the last ten minutes. 'All this... knowledge you have, about this stuff. You're a medium, right?'

Bingo. 'If that's what you want to call it.'

'What do you call it? Gifted?'

I snort. 'Cursed would be more accurate.'

'You know the Church doesn't recognise mediumship,' Father Theo says carefully.

'That's putting it mildly.'

He shakes his head. 'Look, I don't really understand what's going on here. This isn't the sort of thing that's part of my job description.'

'Shocker.'

'But,' he pointedly ignores the sarcasm, '*you* seem to.' He holds my gaze for a second, and I find myself thinking again what a shame it is that he's what he is, which is so very, very much the opposite of what I am, and so religiously – *literally* – opposed to it. 'So what do we do?'

'*We?*'

'You came here to help, right?'

'I came here to warn them.'

He looks back at me, shocked. 'What, just tell them their house is haunted and oh, by the way, you *might* also be possessed by some kind of evil spirit as well—'

'I told you, possession's not—'

'—and then you were going to just up and leave them to it?'

Honestly, I hadn't even thought the whole thing through any further than getting over here and passing on the message. What *did* I expect to happen after that? I shrug awkwardly back at him. 'I didn't exactly have a plan.'

We stand in awkward silence. Not quite wanting to look him directly in the eye, my gaze drifts to the bay window and the panorama beyond. I hadn't realised the time. 'It's dark.'

Father Theo looks up at the tension in my voice. 'So?'

I shrug. 'Sometimes it makes things worse.'

'I thought that was only in films?'

I realise I'm chewing absent mindedly on the nail of my left thumb, and yank it out of my mouth. I haven't bitten my nails since I was a kid. 'Depends on the circumstances. Some people can be more susceptible. More *suggestible*.'

He rolls his eyes. 'Terrific. Look, I should go and check on them up there. Will you at least stay here until I get back?'

I'd rather do a cowardly runner, in all honesty. But I can't stop thinking about the way that Ouija board smashed into pieces against the bookcase in the other room, and the thought it might have been intentional is making me start to feel oddly protective of him. I want to make sure it can't happen again. I nod back at him. 'Okay.'

'You promise?'

'What are you, twelve? I said I'd stay. I'll stay.'

Father Theo gives me one final troubled look before he heads out of the room. Surrounded by silence, I head over to the bay window and pull the heavy curtains closed against the approaching night. With nobody else in the room, the house being as big as it is, it doesn't take long for me to feel completely isolated, as though everyone else has disappeared completely and left me in the middle of this creepy situation to fend for myself. I steal an uneasy glance in the direction of the library, suddenly acutely aware how close I'm standing to the epicentre of Friday's night's action. As my nerves get the better of me, I walk quickly to the door and flick the panel of switches beside it to turn on every single light in the room. Just in case.

Talk about suggestible.

8

Despite my trepidation, the longer I wait for Father Theo, the more my curiosity gets the better of me. By the time he finally reappears, I'm sat on the sofa, engrossed in Rebecca's scribbled scraps strewn across the coffee table.

'Sorry I was so long,' he makes a placating gesture as he sits down beside me.

'How are they?'

He grimaces. 'Not great. Rebecca's taken Hannah with her into Adam's room and locked herself in. I don't think she's going to hurt them or anything,' he adds quickly as he sees the look of concern on my face, 'she just seems to be really upset and doesn't want to let them out of her sight. She's convinced Rob wants to take them away from her.'

'Is there any – is it worth trying to get a doctor or something in there to talk to her, maybe?'

Father Theo shakes his head. 'Neither of them wants anyone else – anyone from outside, I mean – to get involved. The way it looks...'

'Like everyone in the house has gone batshit crazy,' I finish for him. Probably not the exact words he would've chosen. 'Social Services would have a field day.'

'Exactly.'

'What about Adam? How's he?'

'As far as I could tell from the other side of a locked door—'

'Smartarse.'

'The same,' he concedes with a smile. 'I think.'

'Did you see him when you got here this morning?'

He nods.

'And? I need to know what you saw, how he was, was he hurt…'

'Just catatonic. Isn't that enough?'

'No, actually,' his mildly snarky tone is getting to me. 'How do you expect me to help without all the details?'

Father Theo looks back up at me, sudden hope in his big brown eyes. 'So you will help?'

I roll my eyes, wondering how big of a mistake this is. 'As much as I can.'

That killer smile breaks out across his face again, dimples and all, and it feels as though the sun just lit up the room. 'Okay. Okay, that's…' he breathes a sigh of relief. 'Thank you.'

'Yeah, well. I'm only doing this because you guilted me into it.'

'I'm a Vicar, that's my speciality.'

'And don't get too excited. I don't think I can even do much myself, but…'

'But?'

A vague sort of plan – ish – is forming as I skim through the papers. 'But there's people I can contact who could probably deal with it.'

People I'd rather avoid, truth be told, but he doesn't need to know that.

Father Theo's expression turns wary. 'I just told you; they don't want anyone else involved. I had to argue with Rob just to stop him from kicking you out as it is.'

'They don't really have a choice, do they,' I point out. 'Look, it's not like I'm talking about calling the police. People who clear out haunted houses aren't exactly keen on official channels themselves.'

'What about you?'

'What about me?'

'Can't you do it?'

'What, clear the house, you mean?'

'Yeah,' he shrugs. 'You're a medium. Can't you just…'

'What? What in the world do you imagine I'd do?'

'I don't know. Say some magic words, burn some sage or something.'

'If you think it's that simple, why don't you just chuck about some holy water and say the Lord's Prayer three times? Then I can go home and order a pizza.'

'Would that work?'

I laugh, not sure if he's being serious or sarcastic. 'By all means,' I gesture to the room, 'be my guest.'

He backs off with a frown. 'All right. Not that simple then.'

'No.'

'So you can't do it?'

'Not bloody likely. You need mediums, *plural*, to clear out something that's strong enough to interfere with people. I'm just… me.'

'So what do we do?'

'What I already said. Give me details, so I have the full picture. We also need to rule out any alternatives, they'll want to know that we've checked—'

'*Alternatives?*' The look of utter disbelief on his face is a picture.

'Look,' I explain, 'most of what goes bump in the night has less to do with visits from the other side and more to do with dry rot, dodgy plumbing and wood pigeons nesting in the eaves. I mean, if you're convinced the stubborn cold spot in your spare room is the ghostly manifestation of your Great Aunt Elsa, anything's *possible*. But the boring truth is you probably just need to have someone take a look at the seals on your double glazing or invest in some better insulation.'

I watch him as he contemplates the idea.

'Especially in a big old house like this. It's just best to check, okay? They'll want to know before they agree to do anything anyway.'

Father Theo nods. 'Fair enough.'

'Good.'

I can see he wants to say something else, but he's hesitating.

'What?'

'What you said before,' he starts carefully. 'About… the board. When it… you know.'

I raise my eyebrows. 'When it almost hit you in the head, you mean?'

He grimaces. 'Yeah. You really think it might've been… deliberate?'

'Well, Father…'

'I wish you'd stop calling me that.'

'I wish never gets.'

'Shame.' His eyes twinkle, full of mischief, and I have to force myself not to rise to his very attractive bait.

'It's a possibility,' I bring him back down to earth.

'But *why*,' he looks desperately around the room, as though something in it might provide him with some sort of explanation. 'Why would it even— is it— am I—'

'Look, I shouldn't have said anything. It's really probably just coinci—'

'Coincidence,' he finishes irritably. 'Yeah. You said.'

'Not my fault you don't believe in coincidence,' I shrug.

'There must be a reason—'

I sigh resignedly. 'Sometimes they don't like priests, okay?'

'Vicars.'

'Whatever. Religious people in general. There's power in that, you know?'

'In being religious?'

'In having *faith*,' I tell him, hoping it sounds reassuring, because it's actually true. 'They see it as a threat.'

He frowns uncomfortably.

'That's a thought,' I go on with a suddenly realisation, 'if it was on purpose, maybe it hasn't been trying to influence you at all. If it thought it could, it wouldn't—'

'Try and kill me?' he suggests helpfully.

'I was going to say maim.'

'That makes me feel so much better.'

'Look, I don't know for sure. I just thought you should know there's a chance it was intentional. Just in case.'

He groans unhappily. 'In case of what?'

Oh dear. I think I've upset him again. 'I don't want to say.'

'*Dot*—'

'In case it has another go.'

Father Theo leans forward, elbows on his knees as he sighs, rubbing his forehead. 'Terrific.'

'Let's go with coincidence for now, okay?'

'This just gets better and better.'

I try to lighten the mood. 'Maybe it saw your outfit and thought you might try and exorcise it.'

He rolls his eyes as he turns sideways to look at me. 'Again, just the Catholics.'

'I'm sure that distinction will make all the difference.'

'What about you?' He straightens back up, holding my gaze steadily, and the couple of inches between us on the sofa suddenly seems considerably smaller.

'What about me?'

'Well, it sounds as though if anyone in this place is any sort of threat to it, it's you. Why hasn't it thrown anything at *your* head?'

'I told you,' I dismiss the suggestion, 'I can't hurt it. You need multiple mediums to kick it out.'

Except… except I sort of did, didn't I? I went into myself, I heard the Voice, I stopped the session. Somehow.

'You really don't think *you* might've been…'

'What?'

'Influenced.'

I brush him off. That much I *am* certain of. 'Positive.'

'How can you know? You were here in the middle of it all on Friday just as much as I was. And then you had this… episode, today. Surely if you were, you wouldn't be aware of it?'

I shake my head at him with a tut. 'Oh ye of little faith.'

'It's a valid point.'

He's not wrong about that. 'Fair enough,' I shrug back. 'I'm sure because I've doing this stuff since I was a kid—'

'Flirting with Vicars?' he feigns shock.

'You're the one who's been flirting.'

'Not *just* me,' he smiles, raising a crooked eyebrow.

'Seeing dead people,' I steer us back gently. 'Since I was a kid I've been seeing and talking to dead people—'

'Walking around like regular people.'

I love that he knows the reference.

'I know how to deal with anything that might… try and get into my head. I'm well protected on that score, I promise you.'

'You going to tell me how?'

'That's a long conversation.'

'I've got time.'

'Do *they*?' I gesture above our heads. 'Remember why we both came here in the first place.'

He nods quickly, chastised. 'Of course. Sorry.'

'So, Adam. Rob called you this morning?'

'Yeah, early. Phone rang, I thought it was my alarm at first, I was still in bed.'

I fight the barrage of mental images that conjures up. I'll bet he looked nice. 'What did he say?'

'Not much, at first. Just that Adam was in a bad way and they needed my help. I asked if he was sick, should they take him to A & E, he just kept asking me to come over. I thought they were just panicking and when I got here I could call the doctor for them or something.'

Father Theo goes on to explain more about what he'd been told had happened over the weekend. Rob had heard about the incident in the library on Friday night but wrote it off as nothing – booze, scary costumes and Halloween atmosphere. Saturday morning, the pre-booked cleaning crew came in as planned, clearing out the leftovers, dismantling the trestle tables, taking down all of the pretty lights. Rebecca slept in later than usual, but it had been a very late night, after all. Rob spent the day hovering around downstairs, one eye on the cleanup, the other on the kids, pottering about doing normal mundane weekend stuff – telly, papers, toast, lots of tea. When Rebecca still hadn't come down by the afternoon, he took her up some food, thinking she might fancy a walk into town with the kids, maybe feed the ducks at Beacon Park. But she was already wide awake, sat up in bed, scribbling away furiously away on a notepad.

I look at the pages spread out across the table. 'The messages.'

'Yep.'

'Have you read them?'

'Only a glance. Bit flowery for my taste.'

I muse over the pages I'd looked over earlier. 'Lots of stuff about pathways, lessons, guidance. You remember what the board was spelling out?'

'Not in detail. Something about messages of love and peace.'

'Love and peace my arse,' I murmur, checking myself as he raises his eyebrows. 'Sorry. What I'm getting at is that it sounds like the same schtick.'

'Lots of happy clappy stuff.'

'Yeah,' I can't hold back a gentle laugh. 'Bit like this big book I read once.'

'You've read the Bible?' he teases.

'Glad you recognise your own material.'

'Last time I checked, there was more brimstone.'

'Try the apocrypha. That's very colourful.'

'You really *do* know your bible,' he smiles, possibly impressed, definitely surprised.

'I always enjoyed the story about the dragon. Nice for them to include a Lord of the Rings reference.'

'I think the dragon was in The Hobbit.'

He's got me there.

'Anyway. Similar flouncy language to the board.' I pick up a couple of sheets and scan quickly. 'We are here to share our wisdom, we are here to guide. Those are lifted almost exactly from Friday night's script.'

'Meaning?'

'Proves a connection, between what happened then and what's happened since.' I take a second to consider. 'It's positioning itself as a teacher of sorts. Offering what though, enlightenment? Reassurance?'

'You don't buy it.'

I shake my head. 'I've never met a dead person who talked like that.'

'That's the weirdest sentence I think I've ever heard.'

'Welcome to my life,' I sigh resignedly. 'I've heard of – higher beings, I suppose you'd call them, sharing their knowledge. But it's insanely rare. And they don't tend to do their thing at parties. Rob definitely said Rebecca was awake when he found her writing this stuff?'

'Wide awake, he said. Why?'

I shrug. 'If she wasn't aware, it could've been automatic writing. But I've never heard of anyone doing that who wasn't already a practising medium.'

'That's when someone does it unconsciously, right? Like they're in a trance.'

Now *I'm* impressed. 'Now how would a local parish Vicar know about a thing like that?'

'Ah, know thine enemy.' Father Theo winks teasingly at me, cheeky smile twinkling. It's a good job I'm sitting down.

'Inspired writing then, maybe,' I suggest, 'but not automatic.'

'Something whispering in her ear,' he echoes my words from before. 'And it couldn't just really be what it says it is?'

'What, messages of peace and love, you mean?' I look back at him like he's got a screw loose. 'You think peace and love knocked their kid unconscious?'

A frown. 'I suppose not.'

I can appreciate the hope. It'd be nicer to think it was really as warm and fluffy as it purported to be. But Father Theo didn't see everything I saw on Friday night when peace and love first started spouting. Time to fess up properly.

'Look, on Friday night. When I… when it happened. You said earlier it looked like I'd gone somewhere else. Well, you weren't entirely wrong,' I admit awkwardly.

His eyes are wide. 'Where did you go?'

It's hard to explain to anyone who hasn't done it themselves. 'Somewhere else.'

'Heaven?'

I roll my eyes.

'Joking,' he smiles apologetically. 'So where then, the other side?'

'Not exactly. There's more than just here and there,' I try to explain. 'There are places kind of... in between.'

'In between,' he repeats slowly. 'Hmm.'

'I know it sounds ridiculous.'

'Hey,' he shakes his head quickly, 'I'm not judging. How do you think I sound having have to sell the whole virgin birth thing every Christmas?'

That stumps me. I stare back at him wide-eyed. 'You don't believe in the virgin birth?'

'Do you?'

'Of course not.'

'Well then.'

'But you're a *Vicar*.'

'I'm not an idiot.'

My sudden giggle bursts out as an unflattering snort.

'Hot,' he laughs back gently. 'Look, I don't doubt the basic story. But you can't argue with biology.'

I'm not sure I've ever been this speechless in my entire life. A Vicar who doesn't believe that? Maybe he's not as much of a lost cause as I thought.

'I also don't believe people who work on Sundays should be put to death, and my favourite food is shellfish. Don't tell anyone.'

I raise my eyebrows. 'Shellfish?'

'Leviticus 11:10,' he shrugs simply. 'Never mind. Finish what you were telling me.'

I'll have to look that one up.

'Okay, well, in this place,' I go on carefully, 'there's a Voice. I've known it for years and I trust it completely, with as much faith as you have in your God. It told me that I had to stop it. It called it a trickster, a liar, an impostor.'

'A trickster,' he muses quietly. 'Like – like the devil?'

I pull a face. 'I've seen a lot of weird shit in forty-two years. Not once have I seen anything that backs up the existence of that old chestnut.'

Father Theo raises his eyebrows. 'I could say the same about the afterlife your lot bang on about.'

'I don't have a *'lot'*,' I reply, sharper than I intend. 'Look, I'm just saying. I know from personal experience there's more things in heaven and earth and all that. But that's because I've actually seen and heard them.'

'So what do you think it is? What does it want?'

'Who knows. Could be it's linked to the house somehow, a real person who died here, I mean, and they're not properly at rest. Or someone to do with the family, maybe. But with what's in this writing,' I look back down at the table, 'and the general tone of bullshit it came out with on Friday, my money's on some random troublemaker that felt the pull of that session and grabbed the opportunity to come through and cause some mischief.'

'Sounds harmless enough.'

'No,' I whip back quickly to face him, a warning in my eyes. 'Don't make that mistake. Spirits – whatever you want to call them – that turn up here intending to cause trouble are rare, which can make them a handful. Your bog-standard dead bod who's passed before they were ready, or doesn't realise they're dead, they usually just need a helping hand to guide them the rest of the way to where they should be. If I thought that was all it was, I could deal with it myself. This thing is *dark*.'

Father Theo looks unnerved at my clarification.

I take a breath. 'There's one other thing as well. About Friday night.'

He groans. 'Do I *really* want to know?'

'You should.'

'Something else trying to throw things at my head?'

'*Theo…*'

He lights up suddenly. 'That's the first time you've called me that.'

'So it is.'

'I like how it sounds.'

'Good for you. Friday night?'

He pretends to put on a serious face.

'Remember towards the end, how it kept spelling out 'stop it'?'

'Right before it all came to a screeching halt. What about it?'

'Well…' I shift uncomfortably in my seat. 'I don't think that bit was… *it*.'

'What?' He looks confused. 'That wasn't the evil demon, you mean?'

I roll my eyes at the trope. 'Whatever it is.'

'What was it then?'

I smile back at him innocently, hoping I don't have to spell it out.

'That was *you*?' he exclaims.

'The Voice told me to stop the session,' I explain. 'So I stopped it. I think.'

'You think?'

'I stood there thinking about how I could stop it,' I recall. 'I wasn't really sure what to actually do. But I just kept thinking that, over and over, stop it, and then…'

'And then it started spelling out what you were thinking,' he murmurs nervously. 'Okay. That's… I mean… thanks for stopping it, I suppose.'

I can't look at him. 'I know how it sounds.'

'It sounds…' Theo sighs. 'I was there, remember. It sounds… yeah, not normal. But I don't think any of what happened in there was normal.'

The silence settles between us until Theo raises his head, a question on his face. 'Wait a second.'

'What?'

'If that was you at the end, if you're the one that made it stop – doesn't that mean *you're* the one who threw the thing at my head?'

'That bit wasn't me!' I exclaim. Well, I don't think it was.

'I mean, I know you spent all night trying to get rid of me, but…'

'I *didn't*,' I protest, wondering why I even care. 'I was just trying to stop the session, to break the connection…'

'Break my head, you mean…'

'Theo, no,' I lean toward him, pleading, 'it wasn't like that, I would *never* –'

I break off as I catch the corners of a smile that he's trying to hide. He sees he's caught and bursts out laughing. It's a beautiful sound.

'Bastard.'

'Hey, I'm a man of the cloth,' he needles me primly. 'You can't call me things like that.'

'*Fucking* bastard.'

'So shy and retiring,' he shakes his head, feigning disapproval. 'You should really work on that.'

'Can you focus? For a *minute*?'

'Okay,' Theo holds up his hands in surrender. 'Okay. Just trying to lighten the mood.'

I'll give him a mood. 'So, Friday night happens, Saturday Rebecca sleeps in and starts scribbling this nonsense, then the disturbances start Saturday night and run through yesterday, then Adam this morning.'

'Yeah. Nothing else has happened today. Not until you showed up.'

I wince. 'Nothing's happened *here* all day.'

'Ah yes,' he remembers. 'Your vision.'

I cringe inwardly. It sounds so stupid out loud.

'So was a vision of something that's going to happen?'

'I'm not sure,' I answer honestly. 'Maybe.'

His eyes widen. 'You often have visions of things that are going to happen?'

'Not often. Not for a long, long time.'

'But you did?'

'When I was a kid.'

Theo starts to speak, then stops himself before the words escape.

'What?'

He shakes his head. 'I don't want to offend you.'

'I'm a big girl. I can take it.'

The briefest shadow of a smile passes across his lips and he fights it away. Not fast enough that I don't immediately see what filth he's thinking, though. There's no way this bloke was always a Vicar.

'All these… visions, and voices, and talking to things nobody else can see and hear.'

I know exactly where he's going with this. This is why I don't usually tell people. 'Mmm.'

'You don't ever think you might just be…'

'Delusional?'

He shrugs awkwardly. 'Sorry.'

'Don't be. And yes. I've wondered it often.'

'And how do you know you're not?'

'I don't.'

My response seems to surprise him. 'What?'

'I don't *know* I'm not. It's always possible. But I've been around this stuff my whole life, so… I *believe* I'm not.'

'And that's enough?'

I give him my smuggest smile. 'You know, *Father*, there's this little thing called faith. I'd expect a man of the cloth to know something about it.'

Theo laughs gently. 'Yeah, but I don't believe I can hear the literal voice of God.'

'That isn't part of your job description?'

God, that smile of his. I could stare at it all day and not get bored.

'You don't *sound* like a crazy person. Well, I mean,' he adds quickly, 'you actually do, but—'

'Hey!'

'What I mean is,' he starts to backpedal, 'the things you say, it seems like you must be. But you're so…'

Charming? Gorgeous? Sexy?

'…*grounded*. If you are delusional, you're the sanest crazy person I've ever met.'

As compliments go, it's not the best I've ever had. But given the circumstances, it's not bad either. 'I'll take that.'

'So what now? Check out the house?'

I nod. 'Make sure there's no rational explanations for the other stuff that's happened.'

'Then you'll get in touch with…' he searches for the words. 'Whoever they are. To help.'

The part of this I'm looking forward to the least.

'Yeah. It'll have to be tomorrow, though. Too late now.'

'You really think they can?'

'In theory,' I shrug blithely.

'In *theory*?!'

Maybe that was a poor choice of words. 'They've done things like this before.'

'But you're sure they can deal with this, right?'

I hesitate. Pretty sure. 'Look, one step at a time, okay? Let's just stick to the plan.'

'Okay.'
Theo doesn't look entirely convinced.
I don't blame him one bit.

9

Rebecca was still locked in with the kids when I rocked up on the first floor to check out the house for possible issues, supernatural or otherwise. It was evident from the look of thunder on Rob's face that he was less than thrilled to see me, so I kept out of his way and worked through the rest of the rooms, giving them all a quick once over. Father Theo came with me. He didn't need to, of course, and I made that abundantly clear – it wasn't as though he really knew what he was looking for, not to mention the possible risk of something else being thrown at his head – but he wouldn't hear of me wandering the halls alone. We found some dodgy pipes in the attic, damp spots in the cellar and more creaky floorboards than you could shake a stick at, but nothing out of the ordinary. And as far as spooky shenanigans, not so much as a cheesy jump scare.

Theo also insisted we exchanged numbers. Under the circumstances, how could I say no? And honestly, despite my misgivings, I really didn't want to. Say no, I mean. He also promised if anything changed or anything else happened, he'd let me know straightaway, and made *me* promise to stop in tomorrow before I went for reinforcements, jokily threatening to send missionaries after me if I didn't show up. It'd been so quiet since Rebecca's flutter of odd behaviour, it was possible that if overnight she calmed down and Adam woke up, that might signal an end to the whole thing. Hauntings can just suddenly stop, it's possible… but unlikely. I was already planning on calling in sick tomorrow so I could use the time to pass the situation over to the bods at the

Spiritualist church in Perry Barr for them to deal with, tie up my involvement in the whole business with a shiny neat bow, and get back to the regular old tedium of my normal, predictable week.

It wasn't until I got home – late, hungry, my meagre social battery well and truly wiped – that I saw three missed calls from Mags. One of them was accompanied by a voicemail: in it, she sounded fragile, sniffly, and asked me to call as soon as I picked up the message. But by the time I heard the thing, it was already after eleven and I didn't want to risk waking her. So, I texted her an apology for missing her and said I'd call first thing in the morning instead, hoping she was okay.

Sleep itself came easily enough, but it didn't stick. I was in and out through the night, vaguely conscious that I'd had bad dreams each time I woke, though I couldn't recall any details. All I knew was that each time I jolted awake, a leaden feeling of apprehensiveness followed me back into the space between wakefulness and dreams through the early hours, finally giving up and resigning myself to staring at the ceiling until my alarm was due to go off. When my phone vibrated early on the bedside table, I frowned, thinking I'd messed up my alarm, until I realised that it wasn't getting up time yet. It was a text from Mags.

Are you up yet? Call me ASAP x

She's keen. God, I hope she is okay. Maybe I should've called last night after all, never mind the hour. I tap the screen with a yawn, wondering if it's worth bothering to try and get another short round of kip in, not sure I've enough energy to deal with Pat's inevitable nonsense when I call in sick at ten to nine. My yawn isn't quite complete when Mags immediately answers, leaving me dissatisfied with the knowledge it'll come back later.

'Dot?'

I can hear it in her voice straightaway. She's not right.

But she's not sick, either.

'Hey. How're you feeling? I'm sorry I missed you last night—'
'Can you come over? Please?'
Something's *definitely* not right.
'Of course, mate. I just need—'
'I know you've got work,' she prattles quickly, nervously even, 'but I thought if I got hold of you early enough—'
'Mate,' I reply firmly, 'don't worry. Look, I just need to get ready. I can be at yours in less than an hour, okay?'
'I don't want to make you late.'
Bless her. 'Never mind that, I'm not going in today anyway—'
'What? How come?'
'Long story,' I sigh, rubbing my weary head. 'But it doesn't matter. Just stay put, I'll get there as soon as I can.'
'You sure?'
'Just fill the kettle up.'
It's about a twenty-minute drive to Coleshill, more if there's traffic. Before I leave, I text Theo to let him know I'm taking a detour but will be there in a couple of hours, and after a minute on the road I hear the familiar tone go off in my bag as he replies. Unable to silence it while I'm driving, the ding bugs me every couple of minutes – I know there's a setting somewhere to stop that, I really should find it one of these days – and I repeatedly tell nobody in particular that I heard it the first time until it eventually gives up and stops by itself. Once I pull up on the road by the development where Mags lives, I check it quickly in case there's anything important.

Glad you're still coming. Rebecca's asleep, Rob's stood down, kids fine, all quiet. Be good to see you again.

There's a smiley face at the end. No kiss though. Not that I'm disappointed. Honest.

It takes me a couple of minutes to reach the third floor of Mag's block of flats and as I alight at the top of the stairs trying not to gasp for breath, she's already hovering in her half open doorway at the end of the landing.

'Hey mate,' I pant, wishing I cared more about exercise.

'Hi, Dot,' she replies feebly, her voice cracking. Poor love, she looks awful – her face is red and blotchy, her eyes puffy like she's spent all weekend crying, her always-perfect locks in disarray, and she looks utterly exhausted, like it's been a good while since she's slept. She stands with her arms crossed tightly across her dressing gown, giving her an anxious, defensive air, and while my instincts are still saying that she's definitely not sick in the traditional sense of the word, it's plain to see that something is very, very wrong. God, I hope nobody's died.

Mags tries to force a smile as I reach the door, but it doesn't reach her eyes.

'Thanks for— for—' she breaks off, a loud, racking sob taking over.

I step forward quickly and wrap her in my best Work Mom hug. 'Hey, come on,' I try my best to soothe her, but she's weeping into my shoulder, trembling with the force of it. 'It can't be that bad.'

She gulps down air beside me, fighting to stifle her cries. When she pulls back, shaking her head sadly, she's calmed down to a low sniffle. 'It's bad.'

Closing the door behind us, I guide her gently towards the living room. 'Go on, you sit down. I'll put the kettle on, and then you can tell me what's up.'

'Are you sure—'

'Sit,' I order. There are snotty-looking tissues littered across the floor; a crumpled blanket strewn haphazardly amongst the cushions. I've never seen Mags – or her place, which usually looks like a show home – in a state like this, and I'm worried, although doing my best not to show it. 'Tea?'

She sniffs again. 'Please.'

Mags slopes into the room unhappily and I walk down the short passage to the kitchen. I know my way round her flat – I've been over for coffee and a chat more than once, and even kipped on the sofa a couple of times after nights out, for which my back has never forgiven me – so when I walk into the kitchen and see the mess in it, I have even more reason for concern. This is the first time I've seen even a single dish left in the sink, let alone a whole pile; there's a couple of barely touched bowls of cereal on the draining board, their contents soggy and congealing; the rubbish bin clearly needed changing a couple of days ago, but the overflow has just been dumped in a pile on the floor beside it. When I picked her up on Friday she met me downstairs in the car, and I wonder if this was building up then or has accumulated in the few days since. As the kettle boils, I root around under the sink for a fresh dustbin bag, clear up the mess, scrape the dishes and put everything in hot soapy water to soak. By the time I walk back through to the other room, mugs in hand, the screwed-up tissues have disappeared and the sofa looks a bit more like its usual smart, tasteful self.

'Thanks, Dot. I'm so sorry about the mess.'

'Come on. You've seen the state of my place.'

A sad shadow of a smile crosses her face.

I set the teas down on a pair of coasters she's already put out on the coffee table and sit beside her. 'So, what's going on?'

Mags sighs deeply. 'I… I didn't know who else to call.'

I wait for her to get comfortable.

'I don't know what to do, Dot.'

What the *hell* is wrong? 'It's okay,' I try to sound reassuring. 'Just take your time.'

She wraps her arms back around herself in a self-soothing gesture.

'You're not sick? *Sick* sick, I mean?'

Mags shakes her head quickly.

'Mags, mate, what's *happened*?'

'I...' she starts to cry again, quietly this time, hopeless tears of despair running down her face. 'Dot, I'm in trouble.'

'You're... pregnant?' That'd be my definition of trouble.

'Jesus, no,' she exclaims, a look of sheer horror across her face. 'At least, I don't think so. Oh god, I never even thought of that.'

Oh god, what the *hell* is wrong. 'Mags, love, you're scaring me.'

'I'm sorry, I just...' she reaches for her tea, picks it up hesitantly, then puts it back down and bursts into full on sobbing.

I reach across to hold her, tell her it's going to be okay, and wish desperately that I knew what to say to make it better. My mind immediately goes to the worst-case scenario I can think of and I hope with everything in me that's not what she's about to tell me has happened.

'I'm so sorry, I should've listened to you, I'm just so sorry...'

'Shh, stop apologising,' I soothe her gently. 'Whatever it is, it's not your fault.'

'I just feel so *stupid*,' she whimpers through her tears, pulling away from me as she wipes at her face with the sleeve of her dressing gown.

'I'm sure you've got nothing to feel stupid about.'

Mags shakes her head. 'I do. I really do. I just... Dot,' she looks back up at me, big eyes filled with tears, 'I don't know what to do.'

'Can you tell me what happened?'

She looks away again, and I can see shame in her face. 'I... Saturday night, I...'

She hesitates. 'I slept with Nathan.'

Oh. Okay. Well, I mean, she knows I think he's a colossal dick and everything, but... if that's all that happened, why is she so upset?

'We had such a good time together on Friday night,' she starts to explain, suddenly desperate to get the words out. 'He was all flirty, and sweet, and…'

Yeah. I saw exactly how sweet he was with her on Friday night, dismissing her opinion and telling her what to do.

'… we swapped numbers, and he texted on Saturday to invite me over for dinner. I was so pleased, Dot,' she tells me. 'You know how long I've wanted him to notice me.'

'He invited you to his?' I ask gently.

I notice she said 'over' for dinner rather than 'out'.

'Yeah. Which was fine,' she goes on quickly, 'I mean, I knew what he really meant. And that's… I was up for that, you know?'

Oh fuckity fuck. Where is this going?

'Mags…' now I hesitate. I don't want to ask the question; I'm scared to death of what the answer might be. 'Did he… I mean…'

'No,' she shakes her head.

Phew.

'Well…' she tails off, shifting uncomfortably. 'Not exactly.'

Oh no. Oh *no*. No no no no no *no*.

Out of nowhere, I start crying myself. 'Oh, Mags, love.' I reach out, but this time she shakes me off, determined to be brave, wanting to get the rest of it out.

'It was all right at first. I mean, it wasn't great, it wasn't how I'd pictured, but it was…' she shrugs. 'It was fine. Y'know.'

I do. We've all been there.

'Then after… he wanted to go again. I wasn't really… into it, I was thinking I'd rather go home to be honest, but I was just… you know, I was there, and we'd done it once already, so I just figured go along with it again and get it over with, no big deal.'

I nod understandingly. Lots of us have been there, too.

'Then he lost it, you know, he couldn't… he couldn't get it back up.'

There's a part of me desperately hoping she's going to say that she took the chance to get the hell out of there, but I don't think that's how this story goes.

'So I... I don't know why, I...' she shakes her head, confused and angry, looking for an answer she doesn't have. 'I didn't even *want* to do it again, so I don't know *why*, but...'

Mags hangs her head, feeling a shame that doesn't belong to her, that shouldn't have to. 'I... I went down on him. To get him... to help him... you know.'

'Mate, I—'

'Why did I *do* that?' she asks me plaintively. 'Why? I didn't *want* to do it again anyway; I don't understand why I *did* that—'

'Mags, sweetheart, it's not your fault.'

'Then whose fault is it?' she exclaims angrily. 'I was the only one there. Why did I do that when I didn't even *want* to?'

How can I distil an entire history on the utterly screwed up notion of that women have some sort of innate sexual obligation to others, and turn it into something I can say to Mags which could make her feel better, give her some kind of reassurance? How so many of us turn into people pleasers wanting to give someone we're with what they want, even if it's something we *don't*, even if going along with doing it makes us feel guilt and shame about ourselves? How insane is it that in this day and age, we still seem to carry these vestigial remains of the outdated notion that as women, we're supposed to always put what other people want before what we *do*, that we're somehow responsible for the sexual feelings of others, that it's *all our fault*? My heart breaks for her, that every good sexual experience she might have had before this – and all those which might present themselves in the future – could be forever tainted by this one moment.

Mags buries her head in her hands. 'If I just *hadn't done that*,' she groans desperately. 'If I'd just left it alone… then maybe he wouldn't have.'

Oh no. What she'd told me already was bad enough. There's more?

She looks back up at me, such pain on her face. 'He filmed me.'

What?

'*What?*'

'Once I'd got him…' she visibly gags at the memory, '…back to, you know. Ready. I looked up, and he'd been filming me on his phone.'

Motherfucker. I'll kill the fucking scumbag. I'll *actually* kill him.

'I stopped and I told him to delete it, but he just laughed,' she recalls bitterly. 'I even tried to grab his phone, but then…'

I daren't ask.

'He slapped me. Right across the face. Out of nowhere. I just – I just couldn't believe it, I just sat there on the bed, in shock.'

'Oh Mags. Oh, love.'

'Then he told me if I didn't… *do* other stuff, he'd post it online.'

She tells me this all of a sudden so matter-of-factly, like she's switched to talking about the weather, or asking if I want another cup of tea.

'He said he'd show it to people at work. That I'll never get the grad spot, he'd make sure of it.'

White hot rage rises through my throat like bile. I'll torture the fucker first, *then* I'll kill him. As slowly as I can fucking bear.

'So I…' she shrugs, empty. 'I let him.'

How many times can I kill him? 'You have to go to the police.'

'No.'

'I'll go with you, Mags—'

'*No.*'

'Love, you can't let him get away with this—'

'You *know* they'll never believe me,' she dismisses the idea. 'I went there willingly; I had sex with him— *initially*— willingly—'

'Coercive consent is a thing, especially if after that—'

'It's impossible to prove,' she replies sombrely. 'It'll be my word against his.'

'But—'

'*No*,' she repeats firmly. 'I'm not putting myself through that, that— *humiliation*— when there's no point. Nothing'll ever come of it, and my life'll still be ruined. You know that.'

I do. She's right. The statistics for rape convictions in our country are depressingly inadequate.

'So what *do* you want to do?'

Mags takes a deep breath. 'I need you to delete it.'

I frown, confused. 'Delete it? How?'

She shrugs. 'He only has the one phone.'

My eyes widen. 'He used his *work* phone?'

'He only has that one,' she tells me again. 'It's definitely the one he has with him at work, I recognised the case. Look, there's no way I can face going back there right now. I just can't.'

Understandable.

'But I can't call in sick forever. And he…'

Dammit. 'He *what*?'

'He texted me yesterday. When I didn't go in. Saying we should do it again.'

I feel sick to my stomach. I can't even begin to imagine how she must be feeling.

'Dot, I'm scared he's going to… keep expecting me to… as long as he has that video, he's going to keep holding it over me.'

That arrogant piece of shit. I mean, I always knew he was a loathsome little slimebag, but this? *Jesus*.

'He knows where I live, for god's sake.'

My panic radar kicks in at that. 'You worried he'll just turn up?'

Mags groans, sinking into her lap, then nods slowly as she eventually meets my eyes again. There's genuine fear in them.

'Okay,' I nod. My mind's racing, desperately trying to figure out what to do. I could go into work and snag the phone somehow – what then? It'll be locked, there's that. If he even puts the thing down. He's always been oddly attached to it – I remember when I worked for him thinking it was weird how he never let it out of his sight.

Suddenly, a tone rings inside my bag, breaking my train of thought. It takes me out of this nightmare and plunges me right back into another – Father Theo, the house, the Voice, Rebecca. *Dammit*.

'Okay. Look, mate,' I start to explain. 'Remember I said I wasn't going in today?'

'Yeah.'

'Well, there's… something I have to sort out,' I tell her, as vaguely as I dare. 'And I have to do it today. But once it's over with, we can fix this, okay?'

Mags looks panicked. 'But Dot, what if he—'

I instinctively know what she's going to say.

'You come and stay at mine,' I tell her quickly. 'Get some stuff together and I'll take you as soon as you're ready. Lisa'll be there all day so you won't be on your own, and I'll be home before she leaves for her shift tonight.'

'What about…'

What about the video, she means.

'Tomorrow I'll go back into work like I planned, and I'll get hold of his phone and delete it, okay?'

Although, how I'm going to pull that one off, I have absolutely no bloody clue. But one step at a time, right?

Mags looks back at me, unsure, chewing on her bottom lip.

'We'll figure this out,' I tell her encouragingly.

A flash of hope comes into her eyes, the first good thing I've seen this morning.

'You sure?'

I nod back firmly. 'I promise.'

10

While Mags packed a bag and got herself sorted, I checked the source of the ding, concerned something else might be kicking off at Rebecca's, and was surprised to see Jackie's number pop up instead.

Are you coming in? Pat's raging. Any word from Mags? x

Raging, eh. She should see *me* right now. I don't dare let Mags see just how livid I actually am with the state she's in, being so hard on herself for something so utterly horrific and not at all her fault – I'm worried she might take it the wrong way somehow, think I'm angry at her. But underneath, I'm *seething*, a tide of white-hot fury threatening to spill over and take control of me. In the moments right after Mags explained what happened, I started imagining ways I might get away with it if I really *did* go and murder Dickhead Scumbag with my own bare hands.

Noise from the shower confirms Mags will be out of earshot for at least a few minutes, so I go out onto the balcony and call Pat's direct line. I don't know about you, but when I call in sick in the past, I usually feel a need to *sound* sick, to assuage the weird ingrained guilt of letting people at work down by not showing up. So, I use my Sick Voice. My Sick Voice makes me sound like I'm unquestionably ill, so nobody doubts the veracity of whatever ailment is bothering me enough to stay home. Usually, it's some sort of miserable cold that feels bad enough to stay in bed, but not quite bad enough to justify not going in, despite the fact that keeping my germs to myself should always be the preferred option.

'Patricia Gage speaking.'

Screw it. I'm not using Sick Voice today.

'Hi Pat, it's Dot.'

She sucks in the air between her teeth. 'Dot, I hope you—'

'Just wanted to let you know I won't be in today. I'm still shaken up from that fall.'

A long, irritated sigh. 'I see. Well, Dot, that's not very convenient.'

I fail to suppress a snort. 'That's a shame.'

'We need you here today—'

'Well, too bad, because I'm not coming in. Also, I've been in touch with Mags. She's lost her voice so she can't call you herself, but she won't be in either.'

A huff of indignation. 'Is that so?'

'It is. And she's self-certing for the rest of the week.'

'Oh *is* she indeed?'

'Yep,' I trill happily. 'I'll be back tomorrow, though. Probably.'

'Look,' Pat snaps back, 'if Margaret isn't going to be in again, she has to call me herself.'

'No she doesn't.'

Pure outrage, now. How dare I question her authority. '*What did you say?*'

'I said, she doesn't. I told you, she's self-certifying for the rest of the week, Pat, for the same thing she was off with yesterday. And because she's self-certing for the same thing she already called in for, she doesn't need to call again.'

'She most certainly *does*—'

'I think you'll find she doesn't,' I reply pointedly. 'Company policy. Look it up in the HR handbook.'

If there's one thing at work I know, it's every single one of the firm's employee welfare policies. Backwards.

'But— how— what—'

'Bloody hell Pat, I'd have thought you'd know that of all people.' I can't resist a dig. 'All the time *you* have off sick.'

'You— how *dare*—'

'See you tomorrow!' I reply cheerily, still hearing her bluster through the speaker as I hang up. Sometimes just a little win is enough to keep you going.

After I get Mags settled at mine, tucking her up in my bed to get some much-needed sleep, I have a quick chat with Lisa, explaining why she's there but skipping the awful details. She and Pen dote on Mags anyway, so she's happy to keep an eye on her, and dismisses my efforts to give her cash for the chippy in case they're hungry later. Then I finally head back over to Lichfield. My plan is to catch up with Father Theo, talk to Rebecca and Rob some more if tensions allow, and check for myself what state the kid's in before I trek across to Perry Barr, fill the professionals in on the situation so they can swoop in and take over. Once I've washed my hands of it, I can use whatever time I've got left in the day to look after Mags and figure out a solution to *her* problem. The problem being how to separate that sickening excuse for a man from his phone, get it unlocked, and delete the footage of Mags. Maybe also put the feelers out for anyone who might be up for breaking his kneecaps on my behalf. If only.

Father Theo is halfway across the drive in my direction as I climb out of the car.

'Hi,' he beams.

Damn that smile again. I nod back, suppressing every natural instinct to melt into a soggy puddle on the floor. Today is about business, and it's a piece of business I want to get shot of as soon as humanly possible.

'Any more developments?'

'Nice to see you too,' he mutters, not quite under his breath. 'Nothing since I texted. It's been quiet—'

He stops suddenly as my eyes meet his.

'Are you okay?'

I blink at him. 'Me?'

'No, your evil twin over there.'

The sarcasm takes so long to register, my brain still distracted by Mags' predicament, that for a second, I actually look for one.

'Of course, *you*,' he frowns.

I shrug, confused. 'I'm fine.'

'You don't look fine,' he replies, crossing his arms. 'You look *pissed off*.'

And there I thought I was doing such a bang-up job hiding my incandescent murderous rage. Apparently not. 'It's nothing. Just… other stuff going on, that's all.' I start towards the front door as Father Theo crunches gravel beside me.

'To do with your detour this morning?'

'Mmm-hmm.'

'Want to talk about it?'

'Nope.'

'Maybe I can help?'

He's sweet. But not likely. 'You can't. Thanks though.'

He eyes me hopefully. 'A problem shared…'

'Not my problem to share,' I shake my head firmly and walk up the steps.

Father Theo follows me inside. 'Got it.'

'I do appreciate the offer,' I smile politely as he closes the door behind us.

'Which remains open if you change your mind.'

'Noted.' I glance up towards the landing. 'How is she?'

'Who, Rebecca?'

'No, her evil twin.'

'Touché. She seems…' he considers his words carefully. 'Normal, I think. Confused, mostly.'

'No more messages?'

'Not one. And she doesn't understand what they were about, either.'

'Hmm. Remember how we talked about influence?'

'Whispering in her ear,' he nods.

'Yep. If she's fuzzy about the messages, that lends more weight to the idea.'

'That's quite some influence,' he frowns, 'to affect her enough that she didn't know what she was doing.'

'Or wasn't fully in *control* of what she was doing.'

Theo's expression goes from dubious to horrified. 'It can… *do* that?'

'Depends what *it* is. If it's strong enough, it's possible.'

'Heard of it,' I shrug. 'When I was a kid.'

'You must've had an interesting childhood.'

'You have no idea.'

As we make our way up the stairs, I see a little girl sat on the landing, swinging her legs through the banister overlooking the hall. She's maybe eight or nine, the spit of her mom. She smiles briefly at Theo, then looks up at me curiously.

I search my memory for her name. 'Hannah, right?'

The kid nods.

I remember the legs swinging above Mags and me as we arrived at the party. 'You were sat up here on Friday night, right? Watching?'

Another nod.

I mirror her. 'You like looking at the costumes?'

'We were counting dinosaurs.'

All those T-rexes. 'You and Adam?'

This time Hannah looks down at her knees as she nods.

'He still sleeping?'

'Mmm-hmm,' she mutters quietly. Poor kid. God knows what

she must think is going on.

'Can I talk to your mom?' I nod towards the master bedroom, asking like it's up to her, and if she says no I'll just toddle back downstairs.

Hannah shrugs dully, slumped against the wooden rail. 'S'pose.'

'Thanks. How many dinosaurs were there, by the way?'

She leans back, holding the spindles for support. 'Seven.'

'Wow, really?' I widen my eyes in surprise. 'I only counted four. You're better at dinosaurs than I am.'

She swings herself from left to right, still holding on, smiling a little. 'Thanks.'

Theo gestures towards me from the centre of the landing and I leave her to join him. 'See you later.'

'Bye.'

He smiles sadly as I reach him. 'She's had a tough couple of days.'

'No shit.'

'Didn't take you for a kid person.'

'I'm really not.'

He shrugs, a nod towards Hannah. 'You're good with that one.'

'Happens once a year. Makes up for all the other ones I trap in my gingerbread house and fatten up for food.'

'That's pretty funny.' Theo smirks at me, dark eyes twinkling.

I stare him down, fighting the heat rising in my face. 'Can I talk to Rebecca now?'

Theo knocks on the door, his eyes still fixed on mine.

'Come in.'

He pushes it open, and I move under his arm to walk through. There's the briefest of seconds when my shoulder to brush his chest – he's a good eight inches taller than me – and my breath catches. Dammit. Pack it in, perimenopause hormones.

'Hi, Dot.' Rebecca waves half-heartedly at me from the other side of the huge room, reclining on a padded chaise, set back in a floor to ceiling bay window which looks out across the grounds. On the wall to my far left is a massive bed, framed by a pair of wooden bedside tables. A matching dressing table set sits beside full height built-in cupboards on the opposite wall. The furnishings are minimal but elegant, styled to suit the grandeur of the house, Rebecca all over. I've rented whole flat shares before that could fit in this one room.

I smile back, relieved to put some distance between me and the Vicar. 'How're you feeling?'

'Tired.'

She seems like herself. Nothing feels… *off*.

'I need to talk to you about it, if you feel up to it.'

She nods, turning to Theo behind me. 'Father Gregory, Rob's making breakfast downstairs. Would you mind giving him a hand? He's a bit out of sorts this morning.'

'I'll make myself scarce,' he replies, closer behind me than I expect. 'You want a drink?'

'Coffee'd be great, thanks. Just black.'

And then he's gone, a sudden silence hanging in the room as he gently closes the door. There's a small armchair in the bay across from Rebecca, and she gestures for me to sit as she adjusts herself, pushing a blanket down past her feet so she can move upright. 'I'm not sure what you want me to tell you.'

'Do you know what I'm doing here?'

'I think you… came to help? Yesterday.'

'Yep.' That's a start. 'Hopefully today I can help more. Can you tell me anything about these messages?'

'That's…' she looks down, avoiding my gaze. 'Hard to explain.'

I'm pretty sure she's definitely herself again. Gone is the urgency, the frantic, uncharacteristic mania from before. There's no guile in her words, no attempt to hide anything. Just… shame. And fear. Of being laughed at, of losing face, of being made to feel like there's something wrong with her. I have some experience with that.

'You're worried that if you tell me,' I start steadily, 'that you'll sound like an insane person. That I won't believe you, that I'll laugh at you. But remember, you're talking to someone who turned up on your doorstep to tell you your house was haunted. So…'

Rebecca lifts her head, finally meeting my eyes. 'First… I'd like to know how you knew.'

It's a very different Rebecca to the hysterical, chaotic mess I met yesterday. Her eyes are clear, her voice steady, she's succinct and to the point. This is Big Boss; the Rebecca I know. Which again suggests that the other one – yesterday's Rebecca – definitely wasn't.

I offer a tentative smile. 'You promise not to sack me?'

'That's what you're worried about?'

'It's not exactly normal employee behaviour.'

'Nothing about this situation is normal.'

'Fair point,' I shrug. 'Okay. So, sometimes I… hear things. That other people don't.'

'Like voices?'

'Basically.'

'Okay.' Rebecca folds her arms across her lap. There's no judgment in her eyes so far. Only calm curiosity.

'Sometimes I see things, sometimes I feel things. When I got here on Friday night, before I even got in the house, I was told something was wrong. Then the thing in the library happened—'

'Father Gregory told me there was a séance.'

'That wasn't a séance, it was a bunch of half-cut idiots messing with something they shouldn't have,' I roll my eyes. 'But when it happened, I got a... strong suggestion that whatever was communicating was bad, and that it needed to be stopped.'

'Father Gregory told me you stopped it.'

'Father Gregory's very informative.'

'You don't think you stopped it soon enough?'

'I think the genie was already out of the bottle by then,' I tell her, an apology in my voice.

Rebecca frowns. 'You didn't say anything about this on Friday night.'

'I wasn't sure then. Nothing else happened. And if had, what could I have said that you'd believe?'

She considers my response, accepting it with a quiet nod.

'Then I saw something else.'

'Here?'

I shake my head. 'At work. I had a... a vision, I suppose I have to call it. And believe me, I know how that sounds—'

'What did you see?'

Not a hint of scepticism, sarcasm or scorn in her voice. She just wants to know. I remember why I liked working for her so much when she started at the firm all those years ago – her straightforward, to the point, get-on-with-it attitude. I always knew where I stood with her, and it was a refreshing change.

So, I tell her what I saw – the dark house, enveloped in that creeping shadow, the rumbling and growling, the staircase, the landing, the doors, the light.

'What do you think it was?'

'Still not sure. A warning, a premonition maybe, of what might happen.' Another option occurs to me. 'Possibly showing me what already happened, to Adam.'

She looks surprised.

'The door I opened was his. Theo said there's no change?'

Rebecca raises a quizzical eyebrow, the faintest hint of

amusement across her face, grateful for a moment's distraction. 'Theo?'

'Sorry. Father Gregory.'

'First name terms, eh?' she smiles.

I roll my eyes. 'Don't you start.'

Her smile fades as she looks away again. 'What happened to me, Dot? What's happening to me?'

I breathe out slowly, even more certain after the last couple of minutes of conversation. 'Right now, nothing.'

'What do you mean?'

'That it's gone. From you, anyway. Probably not from the house.'

'But what *happened*?'

'I think whatever's here attached itself to you, somehow. The messages, the things you wrote—'

'Those awful pages,' Rebecca closes her eyes. 'I must've written them, it's my handwriting. But I don't remember, I don't remember doing it at all.' She shakes her head, grasping for anything that might help her make sense of it all. 'He doesn't understand how I can possibly not know what they are, he said I was going on about them all weekend.'

'Have you read any of them?'

She shudders visibly. 'Just a few lines. I couldn't stand any more. Seeing all of it, these words that weren't mine, but in my writing, it felt so...'

'Creepy?'

'*Invasive*. Like someone else was in my head, using me.' She looks back up at me. '*Is* that what it was?'

'That's my guess.'

'Is it a guess, though?' she asks plainly. 'You clearly know something about this kind of... situation. So, tell me. Is it a guess?'

It's hard to not constantly qualify everything I say with 'it's my guess', or 'it's possible', or any other caveat I've come up with over the years when implying that a situation might be of supernatural origin. It's a defence mechanism; I'm just so used to people thinking I'm delusional. I remember back at school, I must've been about seven, having one of my very few friends over for tea, and I don't even remember how the subject came up but it did, because back then I thought it was normal, that's how I was brought up, it was around me every day, like telly and Kellogg's Variety Packs and those awful warm orange squash things we had at breaktime. She must've gone straight home and told her parents, because suddenly she wasn't allowed to play with me anymore. Even later, in RE class not long before I left Junior School and asking so innocently why we never learned about Spiritualist Church, about life after death, and the look I got from the teacher, you'd think I'd asked why we weren't all praying to Satan. By the time I got to Secondary School I'd figured out I should keep it quiet, but whenever anyone bumped into my mom at the shops, she always *had* to find some way of bringing it up, she never could help herself, so bye-bye friendships and hello sniggers, whispering and people hiding my PE kit every week. After stuff like that, even now, it's hard for me not to assume everyone I meet is going to react to me the same way.

'No,' I finally tell her. 'It's not a guess.'

Rebecca nods. 'Why would that happen? Why would it do all… whatever it did, make me write those things, and just stop?'

A sudden light tap on the door makes us both jump, but it's just Theo with the drinks. He sees the relief on our faces when he appears through the door and pulls an awkward, sheepish grin. 'Sorry.'

'It's okay. Thanks.' Rebecca shakes it off as he hands her a mug of what looks more like milk than anything else.

I wince at the sight of it. 'God Rebecca, want some tea with your milk?'

'Rob made it,' Theo hands me my coffee with a broad smile, big brown eyes twinkling. 'I made yours.'

I smile back and look away as the blush rises again. Well, wasn't that nice of him.

Rebecca's less happy with her pasty-looking abomination. 'I can't drink that. He knows I won't touch it milky.'

'You said he was out of sorts this morning.'

'I'll say,' Theo sighs. 'He nearly bit my head off in the kitchen.'

Rebecca shakes her head. 'I was just telling Dot; he doesn't understand why I don't remember. It's frustrating for him, you know? Not understanding what's going on. He's a doctor, his whole life is about science and logic.'

'I'll talk to him,' Theo suggests.

'No,' she replies quickly, 'leave him for now. I'd like you to be here for this. Dot's started to explain, but I have more questions.' Rebecca turns, facing outwards on the chaise like it's a normal chair, pulling her feet away from the end to create space and gesturing for him to join us. Once he's settled, I start to try and answer her the best I can.

'You wanted to know why it stopped.'

'And why it happened in the first place,' she adds.

'Honestly, it could have just been to mess with you.'

Theo raises his eyebrows. 'Seriously?'

'Seriously. If it's some sort of – I hate to use the phrase, it sounds so cheesy, but – some sort of malevolent spirit, they're disruptive, it's the sort of thing they like to do. That's why they move stuff around, make noise, just generally be a pain in the arse. It can be quite mild, like an annoying, bratty toddler, but…'

'If it's not?'

I hesitate, not wanting to freak them out. 'If it's nastier, if it's genuinely malicious, those feed on negativity. The fear they create, the confusion. That's sort of how they draw their energy.'

'And that's what you think this is?'

It's a tough one. They've been hit with a lot of standard haunting tropes – noises, things moving – textbook playful, annoying spirit. But using Rebecca to write those messages… and my hearing the Voice… and having that vision. 'If it wasn't for you being weird, and me hearing things, I'd have probably said not. But this one seems to have a proper nasty streak, so I'm wary.'

'What about Adam?'

'My gut is he got a nasty scare and it put him out of commission. He's just been sleeping the whole time, right?'

'Well yeah, but—'

'Then there's probably nothing more to it.'

'But why won't he wake up?'

'If it scared him enough, his poor little mind probably couldn't deal with it, so it's taken him somewhere else for safekeeping. He just needs a bit of help to get back, that's all.'

'And you can do that?'

'People I know at the church can.'

Rebecca looks over at Theo, confused. 'But the Church doesn't deal with things like this, surely?'

'Different church. Their members are a bit more… well…'

'Like Dot,' Theo explains.

'Okay. But you didn't answer my other question.'

'Why it stopped?'

Rebecca nods.

'There's a couple of possibilities. It could've got bored.'

Theo starts to chuckle, checking himself at a look from Rebecca and clearing his throat instead. 'Sorry. But really? That happens?'

'It can. They're fickle buggers.'

Now Rebecca laughs lightly herself. 'Okay. What else?'

'It could've got what it wanted, and decided it was done. It could be that your subconscious fought it, and it decided you weren't worth the effort.'

A wry smile. 'I like the sound of that.'

Theo looks equally hopeful. 'So that could really be it? It could just be... gone? Over?'

I wish it were that straightforward. 'Not likely, I'm afraid. It's backed off from Rebecca, but once that stupid game on Friday night let it out...'

He nods. 'The genie's out of the bottle.'

'Right. It might go quiet for a few days, weeks, months even, but it won't just up and vanish back to where it come from, not now it's had some fun. Someone needs to put it away.'

'And these friends at this church of yours can do that?'

I bristle at Rebecca's choice of words. Not my friends, not my church, but now isn't the time to mention that.

'They've cleared houses before. They're your best bet.' I mean, what's the alternative? It's not like they can call the Ghostbusters.

A sudden interruption startles all three of us as we turn to see Rob glowering in the open doorway. 'Well now, don't *you* all look cosy.'

11

'*Jesus*, Rob,' Rebecca sighs, relieved, 'you scared us.'

'What are you busy little bees conspiring about?'

His tone is unnecessarily hostile, and I see immediately what Rebecca meant about him being out of sorts.

'Nothing, sweetie, we're just—'

'You're back on this *bullshit* again, is that it?'

'Rob, hon, come on. Be nice.'

'*Nice?*'

Oh great. This is going to be fun. I get to my feet and Theo starts to follow suit, but struggles to get leverage on the soft chaise to push himself up. I reach out a hand to help, and as our fingers lock, touching properly for the first time as I pull him up, a sudden, intense vision streaks through the centre of my brain with a harsh *crack*.

In the meantime, Rebecca tries to placate her surly husband. 'Just calm down—'

'Don't tell me to calm down. I know what you're up to in here, plotting your little schemes—'

In a split second, I see Theo standing where he is now beside the chaise, but it's not the scene in front of me, it's inside my own mind, like a tv screen inside my head. Something whistles through the air, something big and heavy – a lamp, I think – connecting directly with his head, and he's down on the floor, head bleeding, eyes closed, starting to convulse.

Rebecca's face is all confusion as she tries to figure out why Rob's being such a dick all of a sudden. 'What are you talking about?'

'Wasting your time scribbling *gibberish*,' Rob rages over her voice, 'and now you want to bring strangers into our house, into our *business*—'

I look at Rob, still yelling as he crosses the threshold into the room, and then I know.

I know why he's being such a dick.

I see it.

Behind him, hovering near his left shoulder is a shadow, a *darkness*. There's the vague shape of a figure, but it's unclear; it doesn't really look like anything to me.

'Sit, quick,' I tell Theo.

Theo frowns at me in confusion. 'What?'

Beside him, Rebecca's still making a pointless effort to calm Rob as he moves further into the room, thundering furiously. But it's not Rob.

Neither of them can see what I can see.

Rob suddenly breaks off his rant, stopping on the spot. As he turns to face me, a sickly, twisted smirk creeps across his face.

I hear my own voice before I know the words are coming. '*Sit!*'

I push Theo roughly down onto my chair, less than a second before a heavy brass lamp from one of the bedside tables yanks its power cord out of the socket and flies across the room, straight through the spot where Theo was standing, smashing the bay window and plummeting into the garden beyond. Rob throws up his head, cackling horrifically as Rebecca steps back, open-mouthed in shock, wondering what the hell is going on.

Theo looks up at me, stunned. 'Is he—'

Influenced.

'I'd say so.'

Or worse.

It looks at me again, grinning, raising Rob's hands slowly and theatrically from his sides until they're level with his shoulders, in a mockery of a meditative stance. As it does, I catch movement in the corner of my eye and the cord belonging to the matching lamp on the opposite bedside table starts jumping wildly, thrashing against the wall.

I lean toward Rebecca quickly, not taking my eyes from Rob's altered form. 'I'd move if I were you.'

Her eyes wide with disbelief, Rebecca looks around, lost.

'Behind me,' I beckon to her quickly and turn to Theo. 'You too.'

Rebecca darts towards me, closing the gap between us, shrinking her tall frame down behind mine just as the lamp strikes the wall directly behind the chaise, its glass shade shattering, the brass hitting hard enough to put a dent in the plaster. Rob – or at least, his shadowy passenger – looks back in my direction, eyes flaming with malignant glee. I glance over my shoulder at the others. 'Stay here.'

Neither of them is about to argue.

I turn back to Rob, cackling still as his eyes dart haphazardly around and back to me, and step into the middle of the room to face him head on, drawing his attention but still keeping a good bit of distance between us. 'Rob,' I start slowly, keeping my voice low and clear. There's a notion in my head that I know how to do this, that I've done something like it before, although it's a memory I can't quite reach. 'I need you to listen to me.'

He giggles eerily, the shadow cloud pulsating lightly behind him in time with the exclamation. 'Of course, *dear girl*.'

I flinch at the odd endearment; I'm sure I've heard it before but I can't place it.

'Just listen to me, okay? Listen to my voice, to the sound of my voice, to the words I'm saying.'

His head snaps back and forth, looking around manically as I talk. Probably picking out the next homeware to use as low-flying ammunition.

But I'm not talking to *that*. I'm talking to Rob. 'Listen to my voice, just my voice, there's only my voice, only *my* voice.'

'Dot…' Theo murmurs a low warning, gesturing past me to a slight movement on the left side of the room. On the wall is a large, ornate mirror, affixed parallel to the spot where I'm standing. Only now, it's not attached quite as firmly, rattling gently against its fixings, shifting enough to scrape audibly against the plaster, but not yet able to pull free. I've got a pretty good idea where it's heading if that happens.

'*Rob*,' I say his name firmly, not shouting, but commanding. His head snaps back towards me and I lock my eyes with his. 'Look at me. Focus on *me*.'

I can hear the jerky scratches of the mirror ten feet away as it fights to break its bonds.

'That's it,' I tell him. 'Stay right here. Keep listening to my voice. Remember, there's only *my* voice here. Nothing else, nobody else, just you and me.'

I think the shadow constricts slightly behind him.

'Now Rob,' I go on, my voice sounding a lot calmer and steadier than I feel, 'I need you to picture something for me. Just keep listening to my voice, and start making this picture in your head, okay?'

The scratching progresses into a rattle as the screws on the wall begin to edge their way loose.

'I want you to think of a brick. Nothing difficult, just a brick. Easiest thing in the world, right? Think of that brick, what it looks like, that long, rectangular shape. Think about the colour, is it red, is it brown, is it grey?'

His eyes stay with mine now, but the rattling doesn't stop.

'Now think about how it feels, imagine it in your hands. Run your fingers over it, feel that texture, feel the roughness of it, the edges, the corners, the weight.'

Rebecca and Theo are somewhere far away now, as all my energy focuses on Rob.

'Can you feel it in your hands?'

It's barely perceptible, but there's a flash of a nod in his eyes. He's there. Crouched in the back somewhere, not all the way at the controls, but he *is* in there.

'Good, Rob, that's good. Just keep listening to *my* voice, okay? Remember, just my voice, that's all you can hear.'

Has the rattling slowed down?

'Now, take that brick and plant it on the ground, inside your mind. But now you don't just have one brick, you have brick after brick after brick. Keep laying them over and over, one after another, again and again, use them to build a wall.'

The rattling drops down to a low, thrumming tap.

'Keep building that wall,' I instruct him as I create the same picture in my own mind, right there alongside him. 'Until there's nothing else, just you and my voice and your wall, surrounding you, protecting you, pushing anything else *out*.'

The rattling stops.

The shadow fades, disappears.

'Rob?'

He looks up, back at me, and it's all him. Rebecca takes a tentative step in his direction.

'Rob? Sweetie?'

He turns to her. 'Becs?'

'Is it— are you—'

'I think so,' he nods, dazed, then meets my eyes. 'Am I?'

The uncertainty in his eyes is what gives it away. 'You are. You're okay.'

Rebecca rushes over to him and envelops him in a desperate, overwhelming hug.

'Are *you* okay?' I only realise Theo's beside me again when

I hear his concerned voice low in my ear. As I turn to answer, I meet his gaze, his face leaning down so close to mine and it's almost as though I'm seeing him – *really* seeing him – properly for the first time. I'm suddenly conscious that all the emotions I can read in those beautiful, soulful brown eyes – worry, affection, confusion, fear and such an aching, longing *need* – are reflected completely back in my own. When I don't immediately respond, my heart tight in my mouth, he frowns, a concerned hand on my shoulder. 'Dot, are you okay?'

The edge of his thumb – a tiny fraction of it, less than a millimetre – is just touching my skin, along the neckline of my top, and as I feel the sudden rush of electricity course around my body, I realise that no, I'm not okay. I'm *really* not okay. But not for the reason he thinks.

'I'm fine,' I reply quickly, forcing myself to tear my eyes from his and feeling the sensation stab right through my heart.

'You sure?'

'Yeah. Look, now they're okay,' I nod toward the others, 'I should get across to the church. Before anything else happens.'

He nods. 'Yeah. Good idea.'

Ignoring the sad ache in my chest as I turn away from his touch, I cross the room towards Rebecca and Rob as he follows close behind me.

'Look, guys,' the pair break apart, teary eyed and shaken, and turn to face us as we reach them. 'I'm going to go while it's quiet, okay? Get some proper help over here.'

Rebecca shakes her head quickly. 'What? No. Absolutely not.'

Rob reaches for her. 'Becs—'

'What if something else happens while she's not here?' she blusters at him.

'Look, I have to go some time,' I tell her plainly. 'I can't get rid of this thing by myself.'

'But you just *did*.'

'I just got it to let go of Rob, and he did most of that himself,' I explain with a shake of my head. 'It's not gone. It should back off for a bit now, though, which is why now's the best chance there is.'

'Can't you just call them, for god's sake?'

'Listen to me,' I interrupt her firmly. 'That won't be enough. Look, with a normal disturbance, they'd come over first, check out the house, look for other explanations, do everything I did yesterday. They'd spend time talking to you guys, investigating, coming up with a strategy. All of that takes time. I have to convince them to skip all of that.'

'What? But we don't *have* time, this is—'

'Exactly. Most hauntings, genuine hauntings, are usually passive,' I go on. 'They might do things so you notice their presence, but they don't really target people directly, at least not on purpose. They're mostly just echoes, pictures left behind of things that have happened before. You might see something out of the corner of your eye, you might hear banging at 3AM every morning because that's when they died, they might chuck things about when they get excitable. But none of that can hurt you, not really.'

Theo frowns in concern. 'But this is different.'

'Yeah,' I turn back to him. 'The influencing thing was iffy, but could still be explained. If Rebecca was a bit stressed maybe, or a bit down, anything negative can make you vulnerable to that sort of energy. But what just happened with Rob, controlling him directly like that, with that sort of…'

'What?'

I recall the look in Rob's eyes as I faced off with him. 'Malevolence. That's rare. It's really, *really* rare. If all my favourite horror films are to be believed, it happens up and down your average suburban street every five minutes, but it just doesn't, and there's a good reason for that.'

Rebecca looks at me with uneasy curiosity. 'Which is?'

I turn back to her with a shrug. 'Normal ghosts, spirits, whatever you want to call them, they can't do that. It takes a huge amount of energy to connect with us on this side in the first place, let alone do much else. To directly work *through* Rob like that, to literally control him, that's...'

My words trail off as I see the increasingly worried expressions on their faces and search for the gentlest way I can explain.

'It's exceptionally unusual. Like, almost never happens, I mean. The amount of psychic energy it takes with someone who isn't a medium, who doesn't have their own supply already, is just insane. It would have to be something pretty powerful.'

Rebecca and Rob exchange panicked glances.

'Which is why I need to go over there and convince them to skip their normal procedure and get straight down to business,' I add quickly. 'Face to face, it'll...'

It'll be painfully like pulling teeth, I know it will. But it stands a better chance of working than an impersonal phone call. Face to face, they'll know immediately how serious I am, simply because I'm there.

Because there's nowhere else on earth I'd rather *not* be.

'There's more chance they'll agree. I don't know how much time we have before something else happens, or before it gets worse.'

Pained, Rebecca turns to Theo. 'Father, couldn't you go instead? So Dot can stay here with us?'

He shifts awkwardly. 'Well, I mean, I don't even know them, I'm not sure I'd know what to say.'

'Rebecca, it has to be me. In fact,' I look back at him again over my shoulder, 'it really ought to be both of us.'

'*What?!*'

Theo looks as shocked as Rebecca. I'm a little taken aback myself, truth be told.

'I know who to talk to, and what to say,' I explain, 'but if I turn up with someone in a dog collar backing me up, they'll *really* get how serious it is. Church of England vicars don't generally ask for help from the local Spiritualist church.'

Theo looks as though he doesn't quite know where to put himself.

Besides,' I add uneasily, 'that's the second time it's thrown something directly at your head. It doesn't seem to like you. Maybe getting you out of the way for a bit might help keep things calm here in the meantime.'

Rebecca looks anxiously to Rob, then Theo, then back to me. 'But, what about – what if something—'

'You were watching just then, right? You heard everything I said to Rob? What I told him to do?'

'The brick wall thing?'

'Yeah,' I nod urgently, conscious that the longer we spend, the more time we lose. 'That's how you protect yourself while I'm gone. Picture that brick wall – or concrete, titanium, imagine it's a castle if you like, whatever works for you. Just make it the strongest, most impenetrable structure you can imagine, like a steel trap around your mind that nothing can get through. Okay?'

Rob, having already had the benefit of putting one effective, sturdy barrier in place, nods steadily. 'Yeah. It definitely works, Becs. We can do this.'

Outnumbered, she sighs wearily, eyes closed. 'Okay.'

'Good. Get Hannah to do it as well.'

Worry floods back to both of their faces. 'What? You think it might—'

'Let's just be on the safe side, okay? Do it as a precaution.'
'What about Adam?'
'If he's still knocked out he's probably safer than you are.' It comes out of my mouth before I have chance to stop it. Oops.

The creak of the door again makes us all jump. But it's just Hannah, wandering in from the landing.

'Mom, can we go to McDonald's?'

She pushes the door all the way in until it folds all the way back. 'I really want a McFlurry.'

CRASH!

'What the—'

Loosened already, the force of the door as it brushes the wall is one knock too far as the heavy mirror comes crashing down. The others exchange uneasy glances as they take in the pile of shattered glass.

Good thing I'm not superstitious, eh.

12

I look in on Adam before we head out. As expected, he's tucked up tight in bed, to all appearances fast asleep. The others watch quietly from the doorway as I crouch down beside him, silently asking my Guides if they can show me anything: where he's gone or what had chased him there. But they're quiet, and all I see is fog. Were there more time, and no other risks to consider, I might try and to coax him back myself, use something similar to what I did with Rob. But wherever Adam slumbered, from a psychic perspective he really *was* likely safer than the remaining occupants of the house, at least for now. Better to leave him be and concentrate on getting the experts over to sort him and the rest of the family's problems out in one go.

'Stay together as much as you can,' I instruct, hovering with them on the edge of the landing as Theo heads downstairs. 'Hannah and Adam too. You're stronger that way. There's energy of your own there.'

'And if it throws something else?' Rob hugs the little girl to his side.

'Duck.'

'*Dot*,' Theo scolds sharply from the hall below.

'Sorry. Look, I don't think it will.'

'Why not?'

'So far, it's only been directly violent twice, right? When it came through on the Ouija board, and when it was… *using* you, Rob. It seems to need a tool.' I shrug. 'You protect yourselves using the wall, it won't have one.'

I don't think so, anyway.

'And don't forget, it just got a nasty scare of its own,' I encourage them. 'It'll retreat to lick its wounds, build its energy back up, and by the time that happens we'll be back with help, okay?'

Rob nods silently as Rebecca forces a warm but wary smile. 'Please be quick.'

'Quick as we can. I promise.'

I wait at the bottom of the stairs as Theo grabs his coat from the back of the living room sofa. Once we're outside, he closes the front door behind us and our feet crunch gravel side by side as we hurry to my car.

'You really think they'll be okay left alone?'

'What else can I do? A phone call won't be enough. I need to do this face to face.'

Assuming she's still there, I wonder silently. She's definitely still on this side, I know that much. If she'd shuffled off to the great beyond, I would've heard about it by now. Via an intrusively direct ghostly visit, most likely.

'I didn't mean it like that.' He looks at me apologetically over the top of the car as I unlock my side. 'Just— do you really think it's necessary for both of us to go?'

I can't resist a quick smile back as I open the door. 'Thought you'd appreciate me getting your head out of harm's way.'

I climb in, leaning across to open the passenger door.

'I do,' he crouches down, folding his tall frame awkwardly into my cramped Fiesta. 'Of course I do. But surely one of us ought to stay with them.'

Turning the key in the ignition, I pull on my seatbelt and adjust to face him. 'How much difference has it made so far, you being there? In practical terms, I mean?'

Theo frowns unhappily. 'Ouch. Bit harsh.'

'But fair.'

'I'm not useless,' he argues, hurt. 'I mean, I'm there for moral support—'

'Which is great, really,' I reply and I do mean it. 'But what can you actually *do*? To stop what's happening?'

He looks away sadly. 'Nothing.'

I know I shouldn't – it's stupid, and all I'll accomplish is to feed the very feeling I should fight – but I put a gentle hand on his arm anyway, wanting to reassure him, make him feel less bad about it.

'Which isn't your fault. But, as there's not much you can do anyway, never mind that your presence seems to really piss that thing off, for your own sake it's honestly better you're not there.'

The memory of my vision from the bedroom is still fresh in my mind.

'Not when *I'm* not there, anyway.'

Theo turns to face me properly, suddenly suspicious. 'Why?'

'Did you not notice the giant brass lamp flying in the direction of your head?'

'That was hard to miss. But why do I feel like there's more to it?'

I sigh. 'Okay. I had another vision. Just before the lamp thing.'

'What?' He looks shaken. 'What did you see?'

'You. On the floor, your head was bleeding…' I trail off, not wanting to recall the details.

'That's why you told me to sit,' he muses to himself.

'Yeah. Look, it seems to have it in for you—'

'So you *do* care.' Theo smiles at my hand on his arm, enjoying its warmth a little too much before he looks up to meet my gaze.

I roll my eyes and quickly move my hand to the gearstick.

'I *care*,' I reply crisply as I shift into reverse and back out, 'that it's apparently intelligent enough to target a specific person.'

'It threw a lamp at Rebecca, too.'

'But it went for you first.'

Theo clicks his seatbelt in as I switch into first gear.

'Coincidence?' he suggests hopefully.

'You don't believe in coincidence,' I remind him.

'I might have to reconsider some of my life choices,' he murmurs thoughtfully. 'Can I put the radio on?'

Clearly he wants to change the subject.

'Could if it worked. There's a tape in there though, some others in the glovebox if you want something else.'

'*Tape!*' Theo laughs heartily as he flicks it on and a blast of mid-90s Roachford blasts through the speakers. 'Oh wow. And I thought my car was a scrapheap.' He nods back towards the Peugeot disappearing into the distance behind us.

It's not a long drive to Perry Barr, and the time passes quickly. He takes the mick out of my musical taste, asks me more about working with Rebecca, about my fondness for black coffee and roast pork sandwiches and third person shooter games. I get the sense he wants to ask more about what happened earlier with Rob, what's going on in the house generally, how I can do what I can do, but he's pointedly steering the conversation elsewhere, maybe to give both of us some respite. He's easy to talk to – makes sense I suppose, given his line of work – and despite the charge I felt pass between us earlier, it's comfortable, almost effortlessly so, like we've known each other for years. Sitting how we are, all I can see is a smart, funny, easy-going man – an extremely attractive one, at that – and it's a little too easy to forget about that damned dog collar underneath the thick winter jacket.

As I pull the car into the street parking a way down from the church building, the mood shifts noticeably, both of our minds turning back to the task at hand.

I nod up the road. 'Here we are.'

Theo's look of surprise when he realises which building I mean is priceless. 'That's it? But that's… that's an actual church?'

'Yeah. Well, it was a chapel I think, before.'

'Like a *Church* church?'

His confusion that a Spiritualist church could also function in the same building which once belonged to his mainstream one amuses me. 'Yeah. Your Church sold it, their Church bought it.'

'But— I thought…' he trails off, not sure how to verbalise his thoughts.

I do it for him. 'You thought if a bunch of mediums and Spiritualists walked into an actual church they'd all spontaneously burst into flames?'

He looks embarrassed. 'Not exactly.'

'They don't sacrifice babies and use blood orgies to invoke Satan,' I point out sarcastically.

'I know that.'

'Do you? They're just people,' I reply, mildly irritably. 'They believe in God, same as you do, they even believe in Jesus, they just don't think he died purely to save our sorry pathetic arses.'

'All right, Dot.'

'Then understand something,' I turn abruptly to face him full on. 'This isn't a sideshow. I didn't bring you here for your own personal entertainment. I don't like them, but I spent my childhood in places like this, with people like this.' I take a breath, abruptly aware that my self-defence mechanism has fully kicked in and I'm bordering on having a go at him for something that isn't really his fault. A lifetime of being judged for something being part of you that you have no control over will do that to a person.

'Just don't ogle them like a bunch of circus freaks, all right?'

I get out of the car before he has chance to reply and shut the door behind me, waiting impatiently for him to follow so I can lock it. Father Theo rushes to catch up to me as I head down the road towards the open wrought iron gate, the 'Services' board on the brick wall beside it reporting afternoon and evening worship three times a week.

'Hey, wait.'

I hesitate, one foot already across the threshold on the small paved path. 'What?'

Father Theo stops beside me, searching my face. 'If they assume I'm judging them the same way you just did, will my being here really convince them to help?'

I stifle a chuckle. He's very perceptive. 'Possibly not.'

Although I'm very much looking forward to seeing the look on *her* face when she sees me rock up with a Vicar in tow.

He groans. 'Then what am I doing here, Dot?'

'I told you.'

'To get me out of the house? Bullshit.'

It's the first time I've heard him swear, and he sounds genuinely irritated, like I've put him on the spot for something he doesn't know how to deal with.

'You could've sent me to Asda for snacks or something.'

'Hmm,' I muse, wishing for Häagen-Dazs. 'Had you down as more of a Waitrose man.'

'*Dot.*'

Father Theo looks cross. He's thinking he could've stayed with the others, could've helped somehow. But he couldn't, and he really *might* have got hurt, and besides, I wanted him here with me. I do honestly think it'll help show how serious the situation is.

But mostly just because I need someone. Someone on my side.

I need him.

'Okay, okay. I wasn't completely lying about the convincing them thing,' I explain quickly. 'But I also brought you along for some of that moral support you claim to be so good at. All right?'

'Moral support?' His face is a picture of confusion. 'For who?'

I shrug awkwardly, suddenly finding lots of interesting things to look at that aren't his face.

'For *you?*' he twigs, incredulous. 'Come off it. I can't believe you've ever needed anyone else for moral support a day in your life.'

'Yeah, well,' I murmur sullenly. 'For this I do.'

'Why?'

I can't say it. Not out loud. Not just yet. The words won't come. 'You'll see in a minute.'

Turning away, I carry on down the path and through the open outside doors before he can push the subject any further.

The inside porch is exactly as I remember. A low wooden bench, faded from the sun, leaves collected around its feet where they've blown in from outside, waiting to be swept. The ugly aluminium noticeboard on the wall, dust in the ridges of its frame, leaflets pinned randomly against the blue felt, fluttering slightly with every light draught from outside. The big wooden door on the inside with its gothic ironwork, notches in the dark surface from decades of wear, slightly ajar. The silence from the chapel beyond is almost deafening as I push it gently open, the jarring squeak of it that lives in my memory long gone. After twenty years, somebody finally splashed out for some WD40 to shut it up.

I'm surprised how much smaller it looks. But then, I was smaller back then, when it seemed like the whole world. The cushions laid out on the rows of wooden pews came with the building when they bought it, a hangover from its Church of England roots. On the wall, the Seven Principles of Spiritualism, which I knew off by heart as a kid. And at the front of the hall, the platform. Raised up above the floor by a couple of feet, there it sits: a piano on one side, half a dozen small plastic chairs on the other, a cheap wooden lectern in the centre. A chill runs down my back as the tide of uncomfortable familiarity begins to rush in, a wave of unwanted, long-buried memories with it.

Theo's hand is suddenly on my shoulder, snapping me out of my reverie. I turn my head to face him and he nods towards the distant end of the platform. Two massive, ugly displays of cheap, plastic flowers sit on stands just in front of it, one at each end, and beside the far one stands a figure I hadn't noticed, bowed with a duster in hand.

It's her.

Older now, of course. Her blond hair's mostly white, up in its familiar bun, loose tendrils tucked tidily behind her ears. There's a slight hesitation in her gait that's new as she straightens up, the effort of age in her knees and hips, but otherwise she looks as sprightly as ever. She hasn't spotted us yet – if she's focused on something, the rest of the world might just as well not bother to exist, me included – but she will soon enough, and I need to be ready. Taking a deep breath, I remind myself why I'm here, that it won't be for long, and to just suck it up and do what needs to get done.

'Come on,' I gesture back to Theo and start down the aisle. Our footsteps echo in the almost empty space, finally drawing her attention as we reach the edge of the platform, and she turns around to meet the sound.

'Can I help you, dears?' All smiles and instant overfamiliarity. Sounds about right.

'Hello, Grace.'

She frowns for a second, bemused, then steps curiously forward, peering carefully for a closer look. Knowing Grace, my guess is that she's probably needed glasses for a good while by now but is just too vain to wear them.

'I'm sorry, dears, do I—'

Then there it is. The spark of recognition fires in those piercing blue eyes, so much like mine – about the only thing we share that's a dead giveaway, other than the whole communing with the dead thing – and she does a double take which is almost comedic.

'Sotty?'

I roll my eyes. It's so long since anyone but her has called me by that ridiculous name that sometimes I forget it's the one I was actually given at birth.

'*Soteria?* Is that really *you?*'

I sigh, my irritation reflex already kicking in. 'I've asked you repeatedly to call me Dot.'

'And I've asked you to call me Mom,' she shoots back icily.

Theo's outside my eyeline behind my right shoulder, but I don't need to see the look on his face to picture his reaction to this development.

'Just as soon as you earn it,' I counter.

'Sotty, don't be—'

'Difficult?' I suggest. Her favourite pet name for me from the age of about twelve.

'Oh, tsk,' she dismisses me with a flamboyant gesture and turns her attention to Theo, already bored with her only child despite not having seen me for more than a couple of decades. 'Aren't you going to introduce me to your friend?'

Grace beams, twinkling flirtatiously in his direction. Don't get me wrong, I'm all for ladies well over a certain age to take full advantage of any opportunity, and Theo's a fully grown man, but she's pushing her bloody luck.

'Father Gregory,' I announce quickly. His dog collar's hidden under the jacket, and I want it to make a point.

She hesitates, looking him up and down curiously. '*Father* Gregory?'

Then she turns back to me with a broad grin, and I immediately know that she sees it. The connection between Theo and I might as well be written all over my face. 'Really. You and a priest, eh.

How interesting.'

I can feel Theo about to correct her – we're not 'together', he's not a priest – so I shake my head quickly, indicating it's not worth the bother. She'll think about us what she likes, and call him what she likes. What the truth is, or what we might prefer, just doesn't matter to her.

'A pleasure.' She reaches an arm towards him and he shakes her hand awkwardly. As he goes to pull back, she holds on longer than necessary, continuing to examine him with that peculiar intensity, and a twinkle lights up her face as she finally lets go. 'My daughter's never brought a man home to meet me before.'

She just can't help herself, can she? Superficially, the comment is directed at him, but her eyes twitch towards me as though she's just stumbled upon some juicy secret.

Theo looks understandably flustered. 'Oh, well, erm—'

'This *isn't* home,' I hiss sharply and shift in front of him, placing myself between them. 'And I wouldn't bring you a hamster. He's here in a professional capacity.'

Grace straightens up primly. 'Is that right?'

'So am I.'

'Really?' Now her voice has a familiar edge. 'You need me to help you rip off your gullible clients?'

She's got some bloody nerve to judge me.

'Oh, but it's fine for you to tell bald faced lies to *your* precious parishioners—'

'Dot,' Theo steps in quickly as things threaten to spiral out of hand. So much for me sucking it up.

Grace scoffs at the mention of my name. My *chosen* name. 'That's not who you are. I gave you your name for a reason.'

I ignore her, my attention fixed on him. One reassuring look from those warm eyes and I instantly feel calmer, my simmering anger settling.

'Look,' I sigh deeply, annoyed at my own lack of self-control. It's always been a mission dealing with her. 'I didn't come here for a fight. There's a family who need help. Quickly.'

A switch flicks somewhere, and suddenly she's laser focused, all business. 'A clearance?'

I nod. 'A serious one.'

'How serious?'

I give her a look. 'I'm here, aren't I?'

Grace frowns down in thought for a moment, the implication of me showing my face after so long to ask for help not lost on her.

'Preferably now,' I add urgently.

'It takes time to lay the groundwork,' she reproaches dismissively, moving to sit on a pew. 'You know that.'

I take a seat on the opposite bench, far enough away from her to maintain my composure. There's a box of hymn books beside my feet, waiting to be laid out for the next service, and the blue covers with their tattered adhesive wrapping stirs some sad nostalgia in my heart. I always did love the hymns. Shame about the rest of it.

'They don't have time,' I tell her. 'There's already been at least one solid incident of possession—'

'*What?*'

'—and there's a little kid who's been scared into a coma.'

'But—' she hesitates. '*Possession?* You've seen this for yourself?'

Nodding, I gesture over to Theo, leaning on the edge of the platform. 'Him too.'

Grace eyes him cautiously as he nods in agreement, then turns back to me. 'You know how unusual that is?'

She knows damn well I do. 'Why do you think we're here.'

She shakes her head, troubled. 'Tell me as much as you can.'

And I do – the short version, we're in a hurry after all –

but making sure I include the stuff I *know* she needs to know. The Ouija board, the messages, my visions, the third hand details about the occurrences over the weekend, Rebecca's writings and odd behaviour, right up to what happened this morning. She asks some questions – who was present, who saw and heard what, have we considered other explanations – but mostly she just listens, nodding occasionally. Eventually, she heaves a deep, determined sigh.

'I'll need to convene the circle. It'll take a couple of hours to get hold of everyone, get them prepared.'

'So you'll do it?' Theo asks hopefully.

'Of course,' she replies brusquely. 'I don't know what my daughter's told you about me, Father Gregory…'

He smiles back, too friendly for his own good. 'Theo, please.'

'Ah. Theo. Theo— Gregory, yes, of course.' Grace stumbles for a second, something flashing oddly in her eyes, but she turns away before I can properly catch it. 'I promise you I'm not quite the ogre she's no doubt made me out to be.'

It doesn't occur to her that I haven't even told him she exists. It's nice to know there are still some things she can't see.

I stand back up beside Theo.

'Thanks, Grace.'

Pains me to say it, but better to keep the peace.

She nods smartly. 'I'll need to run it by Shaun.'

I bristle visibly at the mention of her partner's name. 'He's not dead yet, then.'

Grace looks up at me sadly. 'Sotty, I do wish you could just—'

'Run it by anyone you like,' I tell her briskly. 'But he doesn't take part. Got it?'

'He's head of the circle,' she reminds me, leaning forward indignantly from her seat. 'I can't just—'

'You keep him away from that house.'

I take a measured step towards her, standing directly above the spot where she's sitting, feeling the heat of rage start to build in my face.

'I'm not asking, Grace. There are kids there.'

She knows where I'm going with this, and sits back quietly.

'I mean it, Grace. I see him within a thousand feet, I get so much as one little voice in my head warning me he's in the car, I'll make sure you both regret it.'

Grace nods silently. It's nice to be able to shut her up for once.

I look back at Theo, my eyes pleading for that moral support I asked about earlier. 'Can you give her the address please? I'll see you in the car.'

As my chest starts to tighten with bubbling, molten fury, fighting to stop it before it boils over, I turn and walk out.

13

I don't have to wait long for him to join me.

'She said they should be there by three at the latest,' Theo announces as he opens the passenger door and drops into the seat. 'I gave her my number, in case they need to get in touch before then. She said she doesn't have yours.'

'Word of advice?' I suggest pointedly, reaching for the gearstick as I start the engine. 'Once this is all over, block her.'

Theo puts his hand gently over mine. 'Dot. Stop.'

Turning the ignition back off, I sit back in my seat with a deep sigh.

'Look at me.'

I don't want to. I'm scared I'll see pity looking back at me, and sorry, but bugger that. I don't need that, not from anyone, least of all from him.

'*Please*.'

Slowly, I drag my head kicking and screaming to meet Theo's eyes. His face is so serious, his gaze so intense, I can't even begin to read it.

'Who the *fuck* is Sotty?!'

I burst out laughing and all the tension, my fear, my defences evaporate, just like that. When I look back he's smiling – not the dazzling, lethally gorgeous, underwear-melting one from before – but one that says *yey, I did a good thing, I made her feel better*. I groan, rolling my eyes. 'Soteria, Greek goddess of safety and deliverance,' I recite by rote. 'That's what she named me for.'

'That's borderline child abuse.'

'Yeah. Good old Grace. She was the poster child for hippie tofu granola moms before granola was even a thing.' I let out a short laugh, but there's little humour in it. 'Always more interested in the hippie bit than the mom stuff.'

'Hmm. What about Dot, where did that come from?'

My smile fills again now, better memories warming a kernel of my otherwise mostly cold dead heart. 'Short for Dorothy, my middle name. Dorothy was Grace's mom, my gran. Anything good in me, that's her doing.'

'She's…gone?' he asks tentatively.

'Not that far,' I shrug. 'She's one of my Guides.'

'Guides?' he frowns.

'Sorry. Technical term for the voices in my head.'

Theo looks down at me, big brown eyes wide with curiosity. 'How many voices *are* there, exactly?'

'What, regular ones, you mean? The Guides?'

'There are irregular ones?'

I laugh lightly. I'm not used to anyone asking me questions like this, not when they seem to actually be genuinely interested rather than gathering ammunition to judge me with later.

'When I talk to spirits for a reading, it's a one-time thing. No need for repeat visits.'

I'm especially not used to this much genuine interest it from someone I'm attracted to.

'But the Guides have been around for years. They're sort of… part of my link to it.'

'They guide you to it? Hence the name?'

I'm really, definitely, not used to it from someone I'm *this* attracted to.

'Pretty much. They guide me to people who've gone and need help passing on a message, sometimes they guide those people to me. We all have them around us,' I explain, 'whether we know it or not. The only difference between me and you is you don't know how to tap into them.'

As he studies my face carefully, his expression earnest with warmth and concern, I suddenly find myself acutely aware of how small the car is, how few inches there are between us, and how much I'm enjoying the feeling of his large, warm hand over mine.

'They show me things, they help keep me safe if I'm... elsewhere.'

'They protect you?'

Theo's thumb idly strokes the back of my hand. I feel anything *but* protected right now. I feel completely, utterly exposed, like he can see straight through me, every thought in my mind, including all the vastly inappropriate ones I've been fighting so hard not to have about him.

It's overwhelming.

Turning away to start the car again – and hide the flush I feel heating up my face – I shuffle my hand slightly to shift out of neutral.

'We should get back,' I murmur quietly, refusing to meet his gaze.

There's reluctance in his hand as he finally lifts it away from mine, leaving me free to move the gearstick. He clicks his seatbelt into place, turning to look out of the window without another word as I pull out.

The atmosphere in the car on the way back is noticeably different from the easy, comfortable banter we'd settled into on the outward journey. He's so quiet it's painful, so I turn the music back on to fill the silence, but then that feels too loud, as though it's intruding. I don't know what to say to him, or if I should even say anything at all; we've got this nonsense to deal with, and I still have Mags and that issue in the back of my mind at the same time. And I don't know what he even wants, I mean, he's a bloody priest – sorry, Vicar – for crying out loud. It's not like we can *date*. What does he expect me to do? His lot don't even agree that people like me exist, which is a pretty fundamental difference of opinion. As we drive along, I feel my irritation start to build. We've got far bigger things to be bothered about at the minute than me rejecting his attempts at flirting – which, okay, maybe I have indulged bit too much up to now, maybe I should've shut it down sooner, that's my fault, I'll own that one – and yet there he is, sulking sullenly in the passenger seat like a mardy teenager who's just been turned down. I'm debating whether or not I ought to share any or all of those thoughts with him out loud when a chime rings out from my bag, tucked away on the floor beside his feet.

'It's yours,' he mutters quietly.

The road we're on is all double yellow lines so I can't pull over, and it's not like this old rust bucket has handsfree. 'Would you mind seeing who it is please?'

I use my politest voice. Father Theo glances across at me, but before I have chance to read his expression he's already leaning down, rummaging through my bag, the handset ringing loudly as he pulls it out.

'It says *Mags*.'

Damn. I can't ignore it.

'Could you answer it for me please?'

This time his look clearly asks if I'm serious, but he does as I ask. 'Hello?'

A pause. 'It is, she's driving at the moment.'

I can only hear his side.

'Just a second, let me ask her.'

Father Theo turns to me, lowering the handset. 'She says can I put her on speaker so she can talk to you.'

I nod quickly. 'Yeah, please.'

He does.

'Hey Mags, is everything okay?'

'Yeah,' she replies unconvincingly. 'Pat keeps trying to call me.'

'Don't you worry about her, all right?' I try to sound reassuring as I navigate a roundabout while Father Theo holds the phone towards me. 'I already told her you'd lost your voice, and you were self-certing for the rest of this week, remember?'

'She left a message saying she's speaking to HR, Dot, I don't—'

That bloody woman. 'Ignore her, love, she's full of it, I promise. You know I wouldn't do anything to put you at risk, right?'

A pause, followed by a sniffle. 'Yeah. I know.'

'Trust me. Block her if you have to, okay? Just until I can figure things out.'

Mags sighs deeply at the other end of the line. 'Okay. Are you coming back soon?'

She sounds so fragile, so desperately sad. It hurts my heart to hear her that way, and I'm immediately so filled with rage again, so angry at that piece of shit bastard for daring to do this to her. 'Later, sweetie. As soon as I can, okay?' I remember Father Theo telling me that Grace and her minions were aiming to be at the house by three, so hopefully not long after that. 'Teatime at the latest, I hope.'

'Oh. All right.' Her voice is disappointed, and I feel torn.

'Is Lisa still with you?'

'Yep, she's here. Do you want to talk to her?'

'Please.'

A shuffle in the background as she hands over the phone. Father Theo is still patiently holding mine so I can talk on speaker, and his expression has softened considerably since the last time I dared look.

'Hi, Dot.'

'Hey Lisa. I'm still so sorry about all this.'

'Don't be daft. We're having fun, aren't we?' I hear her turn at the other end of the line and picture them sat together on the sofa. 'She's kicking my ass at Exploding Kittens and we're gonna order lunch in a bit.'

'I'll cover it Lisa, I—'

'You'll do no such thing. Pen's coming over soon, I'm gonna leave the two of them to get up to mischief when I go to work.'

I don't know if Mags has filled her in on everything that happened – I'd doubt it very much – but I can hear the clear subtext in her voice. *Whatever's going on, don't worry if you can't get back soon, we won't leave her here alone.*

I sigh with relief. 'Thanks mate.'

'Don't thank me too soon. Knowing Pen, she'll probably make poor Mags spend all afternoon binge watching god knows what crap. Are you coming back tonight?'

'That's the plan.'

'Okay. Well, Pen's staying over, and I'm off shift after tonight, so we'll both be here if anything changes.' I don't trust many people – never have – but Lisa comes close, and she's good to have around in a crisis.

'Fingers crossed it doesn't. Look, I'm hoping to sort her… problem… tomorrow when I go back to work, but if by any chance I can't—'

Her voice interrupts me clear and firm. 'Mags can stay with us as long as she needs. You, on the other hand, well…' she jokes.

I breathe deeply, the tension in my chest easing slightly. 'You're a ledge, mate.'

'That's true,' she replies brightly.

'Love to Penny.'

'See you soon. Look after yourself.'

'Look after Mags.'
'Gotcha covered. Bye.'
'Bye.'

The signal cuts off as Lisa ends the call. I look awkwardly across to the passenger seat where Father Theo's quietly putting my phone back safely away in my bag. 'Thanks for doing that.'

'No problem.'

'I'm sorry,' I stumble on clumsily. 'I couldn't just ignore it—'

'It's okay, really,' he meets my eyes carefully, and there's no edge to his voice. 'Is that what you were dealing with this morning?'

I nod back. 'Yeah.'

'Mags is your…' Theo queries tentatively. 'Girlfriend?'

He's fishing. I know it, he knows it, and despite everything I was thinking to myself on the drive about how stupid it is, how pointless, how there's so much else to think about, I can't help but smile. The poor guy's a glutton for punishment. 'Just my friend.'

'Hmm.' He allows a second for that to sink in. 'Is she okay?'

'No,' I sigh sadly. 'She's not.'

'And you'd rather be fixing that than you would dealing with all this.'

How is he so good at reading me? I'm hardly an open book.

'I would, yeah.'

'So once Grace and her friends sort out Rebecca and Rob…'

'I can be done with it and sort out Mags.'

Father Theo nods understandingly as I turn into the driveway, passing along the now familiar tree lined route up to the front of the house. He stays quiet until I park up, passing my bag across to me as I kill the engine. Just as I reach for the door, though, he says something, but so quietly I can barely hear him.

'What?'

'I said, once this is all over, will you be done with me as well?'

An ache wrenches at my heart as I face him slowly. He's paying incredibly close attention to a little bobble in the knee of one of his trouser legs, concentrating on it like it's currently the focal point of his entire universe, refusing to meet my eyes. I don't understand why I feel such an incredible pull towards him – I mean, okay, he's certainly handsome, with that smile and those eyes and the broad shoulders and the big, soft hands and – damn, I'm already getting distracted. But it's not as though I've never met a good-looking bloke before. I suppose he did make me laugh from the start, that first time I met him at the party, and he *does* seem to genuinely care about what's happening to Rebecca and her family, and he's not been all preachy and judgy towards me which I honestly would've expected, given his profession. And he's put up with a lot of me giving him shit over the last couple of days too, so he must be pretty patient.

He's *good*.

He's a good man, is what I see in him, and the last thing in the world I want to do is hurt him. I think for a second about what's going to happen later when Grace gets here, about it all being over, and the thought that this afternoon might be the last time I see him makes my heart cry.

When he speaks again, I realise I've let the silence drift on far too long.

'I'm sorry,' he says softly. 'I really— I just— I thought you… y'know. I thought maybe you… *liked* me… that's all. I shouldn't have…'

He doesn't mean it quite how he says it, of course. What he means is that he thought I fancied him, and the idea he might genuinely believe I don't immediately *kills* me, destroying any logical instinct to avoid doing something stupid. I reach out, my hand on his upper arm, trying to ignore how the muscle under his jacket and shirt feels beneath my fingers, trying even harder not to think about how it might feel without them.

'I like you fine,' I tell him quickly. 'I do, really. It's *that* thing I'm having problems with.'

Finally, he looks up, following my gesture and brings his hand up to his neck, the tips of his fingers brushing the stiff, crisp white plastic of his dog collar. 'This old thing? It does come off, you know.'

'Hmm,' I murmur, raising my eyebrows, fighting the mental image he's just put in my head. 'Just because you're not wearing it, doesn't mean it isn't there.'

Those beautiful dark eyes meet mine steadily. 'It bothers you that much?'

I want to explain it so he can understand that it's really not about him, not about who he is as a person.

'Let me ask you something. If we… if something happened between us, and your bosses found out you were…' I search for a diplomatic word. '*Involved*. With a medium. How well do you think that would go down?'

Theo sighs dully. 'Probably not great. That whole life after death thing you're so keen on doesn't sit great with the concept of heaven and hell, you know.'

'I know.'

His eyes flash. 'I like you.'

I try to remember the last time an attractive man told me that – simply, directly, no messing about, no stupid games – and fail. 'I'm getting that.'

'I think you probably like me.' That cheeky, teasing spark from earlier is back in his voice again, and I realise I'd missed it while it was gone.

'I think you're probably right.'

He strokes his clerical collar again briefly, and I have to firmly direct brain to stop wondering how those fingers might feel stroking my skin. 'Seems like such a little thing to get in the way.'

'Seems like it.'

Theo nods. 'Hmm. No way around it?'

'Can you think of one?'

He tips his head to one side, looking at me steadily. 'Maybe if we both put our heads together, we could come up with something.'

I definitely must like him, otherwise his blind persistence would be annoying the hell out of me by now.

'Maybe,' I shrug as I open the door and climb out, leaning back down towards Theo as he stays put.

He looks briefly through the window, back towards the house. 'Suppose we should deal with this first, though. Maybe we can talk about it after?'

After is good.

I nod in agreement. 'After.'

14

Grace and her cohorts show up earlier than expected, a little after two, giving us all time to pick unenthusiastically at some lunch and sit around in a generally uncomfortable silence, which was fun. I spent most of it getting roundly beaten at Uno by Hannah, which I'd like to think was because whilst I was playing, I was also trying to figure out how I was going to fix the Dickhead Scumbag situation. Really it was because I'm just so rubbish at Uno that I'm easily trounced by a nine-year-old.

Father Theo made repeated attempts to talk to Rebecca and Rob in between their periodic checks on Adam, trying to take their mind off the situation at least a little, but with no success. Their replies grew shorter and more monosyllabic as time ticked on, and ultimately, they just weren't interested. I could hardly blame them under the circumstances, but I felt bad for him. He was just trying to help, in the only way he thought he could, but it wasn't enough.

He's the first to see Grace arrive from his seat near the window.

'They're here,' he announces, quickly on his feet.

The rest of us wander over to join him, watching as a mini fleet pulls onto the drive. There are four cars in all, and I wonder how many people Grace has brought to join the party. I sat in on clearances when I was a kid, helped on some once I hit my teens, and how many you need varies on what you're dealing with. In most cases it's simple enough that one or two can manage it easily, but trickier ones always had at least four mediums from the church – the bigger your circle, the more energy on hand to deal with the situation, just in case it all goes south. But this level of haunting isn't something I've ever seen, and from the number of people I see emerging, it looks as though Grace isn't taking any chances.

And there she is, the Grand Dame herself, climbing out of the driver's side of an old model Range Rover. I have to give her some credit – chuck a random family with a paranormal crisis in her path and she's all over it. Just a shame she never cared enough about being a mother to put the same effort in with me.

Suddenly, the blood drains out of my face as a familiar figure appears from the passenger side of Grace's car.

'Oh, *fuck*.' I catch myself and glance at Hannah.

The kid shrugs nonchalantly. 'I've heard it before.'

Rebecca frowns. 'Where?'

Leaving Hannah's parents to interrogate her about that one, Theo walks over to me. 'What's wrong?'

I shake my head slowly, my body tensing as anger rises quickly. 'I told her not to bring him.'

He follows my gaze to the stooping, white-haired figure on the drive, leaning on a cane as he navigates the gravelled surface, Grace supporting his other arm. 'Who is he?'

Now's not the time to explain, but I turn and meet his eyes, speaking as calmly and firmly as I can manage while all the veins in my head are threatening to explode. 'That man does *not* come into this house. Under any circumstances. Okay?'

Theo frowns. 'Is he the one you were talking about with her before? The one she said was the head of the circle?'

'Yeah. But listen to me,' I go on urgently, '*please*. He mustn't come in here.'

'But—'

'Theo, I mean it. I'm begging you.' Panic trembles in my voice as part of my brain regresses back to age twelve. He must hear it. 'Don't let him come in.'

I hesitate, casting a pained glimpse at little Hannah, highly amused by her parents' chagrin at her knowledge of big swears.

'Please.' I hold his gaze levelly, begging desperately with my eyes. 'I won't risk him near the kids. You understand?'

I don't want to have to spell it out to him.

Theo nods slowly. 'Okay.'

I sigh, relieved. 'You'll back me up?'

'Of course,' he replies quickly, frowning at that even being in question. 'He won't come in here.'

I take a deep breath as the doorbell chimes, so grateful that he's here. 'Okay. Thank you.'

Theo turns from the window as Rebecca and Rob exchange glances, unsure what to expect. 'Why don't you stay here,' he suggests, 'let us deal with them, okay? We'll let you know when we need you.'

They both look relieved, and sit back down with Hannah on the sofa.

He turns back to me, brown eyes serious. 'Ready?'

'Ready.' I steel myself as we head to the front door together, letting him lead. Before he reaches for it, he turns to check in with me again, I give him a firm nod, and he opens the door.

Grace is front and centre, of course. The old man cowers behind her like the utter coward he is, frail now, the hunched shoulders reducing his once considerable height. He looks so much smaller than I remember, shrivelled and diminished by the passage of the last thirty years, and I wonder briefly why I was ever as scared of him as I was back then. Of course, back then I was just a kid.

'Hello, Dorothy. It's been a long time.'

His voice is thin and reedy, as pathetic as the rest of him.

It's hard to imagine he's even capable of leading services the way he used to, all bombast and bullshit. I ignore him completely, my eyes on Grace.

'I told you not to bring him.'

'And I told you, he's head of the circle.' There's an annoyance in her voice, the suggestion that just because she commands it, I have to do as I'm told. Seriously, I'm twelve years old all over again.

Theo steps in quickly, putting himself between us. 'Well, there seem to be plenty of you here.' He glances at the group assembled on the drive a few feet behind them, talking amongst themselves as they take in the surroundings. 'I'm sure you can manage with one less.'

'Father, you don't understand how this works,' she dismisses him condescendingly. 'As the head of our circle, Shaun is essential to a successful outcome.'

'That's bullshit and you know it,' I hiss back.

'You need us to deal with this,' she shrugs simply, smug self-satisfaction dripping from her voice. 'Take it or leave it.'

Theo looks at me, worry in his eyes. He knows we can't afford for them to turn and leave. But *I* know Grace won't give up her chance to show off that easily, and although right now it might seem she's head cheerleader for her creep of a boyfriend, her loyalty is easily eclipsed by her ego. With the right encouragement.

'Okay then.' I look her squarely in the eyes and turn to the group behind her. 'Excuse me? Everyone?'

Heads turn in my direction.

Grace's eyes narrow. 'What are you doing?'

'You're so keen on keeping me honest,' I remind her with a shrug. 'I think your circle deserve the same consideration.'

And there's no way they've been told.

She frowns uncertainly at the group over her shoulder, a momentary chink in her armour, before scoffing back at me. 'You're bluffing.'

'Am I?' I turn my attention back to the bods shuffling up behind her, wondering what I'm about to say. 'That's it, come closer so you can all hear.'

'*Soteria...*'

The warning in her tone is clear, and the nerve of her *incenses* me.

I was twelve when it happened. The details are fuzzier now – after all, I've spent the last thirty years trying to bury the memory under a haze of booze and whatever other distractions were available. I do remember someone pulled him off me before he could fully go through with what he started. At the time I didn't report it – I was just a kid after all, and Mommie Dearest was adamant it was a mistake, it wasn't his fault. And of course she stayed with him. They didn't live together then, but he was around all the time, and the more he was around, the more I made sure I wasn't, choosing instead to hang about with whoever out of the house would have me, which is how the drinking started. Eventually I moved in with Grandma Dot, who was always my saving grace, pardon the unfunny pun. But when I was sixteen, she died, I had a breakdown, and *then* I reported it.

I shouldn't have wasted my time. It was the 90s, my word against his, and my own mother said I made the whole thing up because I was jealous of their relationship. Who were the coppers to disagree? They wrote me off as a silly, vindictive teenager, and no doubt I wasn't the only victim treated that way back then. Or since.

That's when I cut her off for good. I learned then that some people should not be allowed to have kids, and bad people get away with shitty stuff all the time.

I've spent all these years trying to let it go. But not now. Now I'm going to use it, to threaten her with the one thing she's more scared of than anything.

Losing face.

'Thank you all so much for coming,' I smile warmly at the assembled group. 'Before you get started, it's important you have the full picture.'

'You wouldn't dare,' Grace splutters.

I ignore her. 'I knew Grace and¬—'

I can't even bring myself to say his name aloud.

'—your leader, back when the circle first formed.'

Some frowns and confused glances at that. Probably because I look a little younger than my age, and they're doing the maths of that against how long they know the circle's been running and wondering why the hell a little kid would've been involved.

Scumbag Shaun – the OG Dickhead Scumbag, the one who started it all – shuffles uncomfortably behind her. 'Gracie…'

'She won't,' Grace bites. 'I told you; she's bluffing.'

'Do you mind, *Mom*? I'm trying to talk.' I glare down, fire in my eyes as I point straight toward him. 'When I was twelve, this man—'

'*Stop it.*'

I turn back to her angrily. 'Make me.'

I feel for poor Theo, caught literally in the middle as he stands in the doorway between Grace and me, watching the pair of them now with a burgeoning ire of his own as he finally puts two and two together. He turns back to Grace.

'He needs to leave,' he gestures forcefully at Shaun. '*Now.*'

'Father, really, I don't think you—'

'If you won't get him out of here,' he steps in Shaun's direction, practically spitting in his face, 'I will.'

Gratitude wells up in my throat as he stands beside me,

literally and figuratively. I don't think anyone's ever stood up for me like that.

'Well?'

Fuming, she turns to Shaun.

'I'll just go,' he mutters, shaking his head, carefully avoiding looking at either Theo or me.

Grace isn't happy, but she's realising she has no choice. Not if she wants to go on protecting her precious boyfriend – and their combined reputations – like she's been doing for the last thirty years.

'Fine,' she growls eventually, turning to the group and calling one of them over, a fresh-faced guy about Mags' age. 'Nelson, dear, would you take Shaun back? He's too under the weather for today.'

She scowls back at me as they turn away, young Nelson helping the devil over to another car. 'Satisfied?'

The circle members look puzzled, still waiting for my announcement. 'This man made my mom the happiest woman in the world.' The sarcasm and saccharine drip from my voice in equal measure.

She rolls her eyes. '*Can* we come in now?'

I shrug, stepping back to allow her through the door. 'You wanted me to call you Mom.'

I count twelve of them as they file through, piling up coats and opening bags to bring out various pieces of kit. Not a proton pack in sight – it's all crystals, Tingsha bells and ankhs. Theo nudges me gently as he eyes them going about their business. 'What's all that for?'

'Different things,' I explain. 'The bells are meant to clear a space of bad energy; the crystals and the ankhs are for protection. The crystals are supposed to be able to change energy from bad to good, as well.'

'Supposed to?' he frowns across at me.

I shrug back. 'If you believe it.'

'You don't?'

'I don't need to. I'm not using them.'

Theo straightens back up, watching them gather their tools, side-eyeing me with a less than confident expression.

Grace walks back up to us. 'Where was the most recent incident?'

I nod upstairs, recalling Rob's episode. 'Main bedroom, off the middle of the landing.'

She nods. 'Is the child still lost to the void?'

I roll my eyes. I play up the dramatics when I'm doing readings, but I'm not that over the top. She never could resist the theatrical side of things. Suits her narcissistic ego perfectly. 'He's still asleep, if that's what you mean. Also upstairs, first door on the left.'

She ignores the dig and turns to Theo. 'The parents?'

He gestures to the living room. 'In there.'

'We'll need them.' Back to me. 'We'll need to sit near the location.'

'Upstairs landing has plenty of space. You need chairs for all twelve of you, or will anyone sit out?'

'The whole circle.'

'Okay. Head up there, we'll grab the others and be up in a minute.'

All business now, Grace herds her group together and they start up the stairs.

I lean across to Theo, having to stretch up on tiptoes to reach his ear, enjoying the proximity to the bit of his neck not covered by the white collar. 'Now the fun *really* starts. Come on.'

With a quick yank of his sleeve, I pull him to follow me back into the living room, the others waiting expectantly as we walk back in.

'Okay. They'll start soon, but before we go up there, I want to run you through what to expect.'

Theo walks over and sits with them, automatically counting himself as part of the group needing a tutorial.

'They'll start with a meditation. They'll sit in a big circle – we'll need twelve chairs for that,' I add, 'so we should take some with us when we go up.'

Rob puts a hand up, like we're at school, and I smile back. 'We've still got the folding chairs from the party in the Orangery. They're being picked up next week with the tables.'

'Perfect,' I nod. 'I've told them to use the landing, as it's the closest big space to your bedroom.'

'Location of the most recent incident,' Theo adds.

'Yeah.'

'Why do they meditate?' Rebecca asks quietly.

'Gets them into the right state of mind,' I answer. 'They'll connect with their own spirit guides to ask for help and protection, then try to communicate with it.'

'With *it?* With that thing?' Rob looks troubled. 'Isn't that dangerous?'

'Only way to figure out what *it* is, is talk to it. Once they know what they're dealing with, they'll use their combined energy to get rid of it.'

Rebecca puts a protective hand over his. 'What about Adam?'

'One or two of them will probably sit with him, to protect him while the others try to connect.'

The couple exchange glances, Hannah between them, focused on her Switch. 'What about… how are *we* protected?'

'Well, use the wall I taught you, for a start. Do you have crosses in the house?'

'A few. Hannah and Adam both have necklaces, from when they were baptised.'

'They should wear them.'

'There's a crucifix in the kitchen,' Rob suggests.

'That'll work.'

'I have one in my jewellery box,' Rebecca looks up hopefully. 'But it's in the bedroom.'

I wince. 'Maybe leave that one.'

'Here.' Theo reaches behind his neck, fiddling beneath the collar, silver metal catching the light as it pulls free. 'Take mine.'

She looks back at him, wide-eyed. 'What about you?'

He turns, big brown eyes full of conviction, fixed on mine. 'You've kept me safe so far. And you haven't been wearing a cross.'

Oh great. No pressure. I shake my head. It's a sweet gesture, wanting to show me he believes so much in my abilities he'd rather rely on that than his own faith to look after him through this. I just hope neither of us end up regretting it.

'Fine,' I sigh eventually. 'You stay with me.'

Rebecca and Rob share another look, and she turns to me hopefully. 'Hannah too?'

'What?'

'After this morning…' she starts.

'What you did,' Rob jumps in, 'for me…'

'We talked about it while you were gone,' Rebecca goes on, 'and we agreed. We'd both feel better if she was with you. Just in case.'

Hannah looks up as she hears her name, glancing briefly at each of her parents, following their gaze until hers rests on me.

Oh, bloody hell. I can't look after everyone. But then again, if all goes to plan and Grace and Co do their thing, hopefully I shouldn't have to.

'Fine. Hannah stays with me too.'

The kid shrugs indifferently and turns back to Animal Crossing.

'But still get her that cross.'

'Thank you, Dot.' Rebecca smiles, reassured as she turns back to Rob. 'Shall we get the chairs? Hannah, pumpkin, you stay here with Dot, okay?'

'Mm-hmm.'

Theo walks back over to me as the two of them head out towards the sitting room.

'I've never met a Vicar with a death wish before,' I mutter quietly, conscious of Hannah's presence.

He smiles gently as he looks down at me, affection radiating from his face. 'I have complete faith in you.'

'Thanks for the vote of confidence.'

'Besides, if they can do what you say,' he gestures upstairs, 'I won't even need you.'

And then all this will be over.

My eyes follow his to the heavens. 'I hope we're both right.'

15

By the time we reach the landing, the party's already getting under way. The folding chairs Rebecca and Rob collected are set out in an almost-circle, a few random others pulled from elsewhere in the house scattered amongst them. I can hear the delicate tinkle of the Tingsha bells in the background as members of the group ring them in different rooms. Others lay out crystals around the outside of the circle, in front of the closed master bedroom and, from what I can see through Adam's now open door, over pretty much every available surface of his room.

In the middle of it all, Rebecca and Rob look like deer in headlights. As soon as they spot us, they catch my eye and wave us over.

'Remind me again what's going on?' Rebecca whispers urgently.

I can understand her trepidation. A bunch of strangers undertaking apparently random weirdness in the middle of your house would be unnerving under most circumstances, but with all they've gone through over the last couple of days, it must be spectacularly unsettling watching the scene unfold. It's a lot, and I say that as someone who finds all of the weirdness normal.

'They're just getting ready,' I reassure her. 'The crystals help with positive energy, which makes them stronger as a circle.'

'And the bells?' Rob frowns.

'Clear out negative energy.'

'They make a pretty sound,' Hannah smiles up at him.

Theo agrees, looking slightly dreamy at their gentle hum. 'I feel like I've heard them somewhere before.'

'They do chill you out, don't they,' I agree, 'which is sort of the point. They can also… open the door a crack, to help their spirit guides come through more easily.'

'And what do *they* do?'

I shrug. 'Help them get rid of it. Whatever it is.'

Hannah pipes up again, scrunching up her nose in confusion. 'They're all wearing funny crosses.'

'Yep,' I look down at her, 'those are called ankhs. They wear them for protection.'

She fiddles with the gold cross foisted on her by Rebecca, hanging from a chain she obviously outgrew several years ago. 'They look different to mine.'

'They are, a bit. Same basic principle though.'

A pointed cough interrupts us and I turn to find Grace stood behind me. 'We're ready to start.'

I cast a quick eye across to Adam's room where I see two of the mediums sat on the bed beside him. 'They're staying with him?'

'They're just as effective in there.'

Fair enough. 'You want me in the circle, or out?'

'You and the priest,' she replies commandingly.

I raise my eyebrows in surprise. That's nothing compared to Theo's reaction.

'Me? Why?!'

Grace looks straight up at him, her gaze piercing. 'You have exceptionally strong faith.'

He looks back at her, unsure. 'But I'm not—'

'One of us,' she finishes for him, smiling in what I imagine she thinks is a vaguely maternalistic way. Unfortunately, it just gives creepy cult leader vibes. 'That doesn't matter. Faith like yours is *powerful*.'

Theo looks to me anxiously, conflicted. 'Dot, I don't know about this. The Church—'

'Your church?' Grace scoffs. 'Really, Father, they don't have a clue.'

'Back off him, Grace,' I snap at her.

'He has strong faith, Soteria.'

'Tough. Leave him alone.'

'That power could help us, and *you* know it.'

'Not if he's unwilling,' I point out. 'All that'll do is risk helping a bunch of negative shit find its way through. And you know it.'

She can't argue with that. Negative energy in the space, people hostile to the process, anyone involved under duress – any of those things spell *bad idea* when you're dealing with the other side. They impact the 'vibes', and not in a good way. Once you've opened that door, you don't always know what's going to come through it. You have to do whatever you can to minimise the risk.

'Look, you've already got me as a bonus, and you shouldn't even need that. You don't need him as well.'

'Fine,' Grace sulks, shooting a piercing look at Theo and the others. 'They should stay close, but not interfere with the circle.'

'Positive vibes, Gracie,' I remind her sharply as she goes off to take a seat, the remaining circle members settling in on the other chairs around her.

Theo turns to me guiltily. 'Should I? I mean, if she's right, if it'll help…'

I shake my head. 'Don't worry about it. Ignore her.'

'It's just— the Church, I mean, it's one thing being here with all this going on, but actually sitting there and taking part, I—'

'Hey, no,' I soothe him gently, hearing the tension in his voice, the conflict between wanting to help but being bound by the rules of what he believes, what he *is*, and I curse Grace silently for making him feel even a bit bad about it. I reach up, intending to give his arm a reassuring squeeze, but as I look into those big, sad dark eyes my hand somehow finds its way to the side of his face, his light fuzz soft under my fingers. As his hand encases mine, the force of the connection between us is suddenly palpable, impossible to ignore. For a fleeting second, everything around us disappears as we stand in our own little world – no spooky goings on, no room full of people, never mind that I'm a medium and he's a Vicar – and never in my life have I wanted to kiss anyone more.

Of course, I don't do it. It's hardly the time or place, if either of those things might ever even exist together.

'Don't do that to yourself,' I tell him firmly.

'But—'

'*No*,' I shake my head. 'You're here, all right? That's plenty.'

He closes his eyes, basking quietly in the touch of my hand under his.

'Stay near me, just sit outside the circle, you and Hannah both. Okay?'

Theo nods, his fingers intertwining with mine for a too-brief second, squeezing them as we both let them drop, reassuring me as much as himself. 'Okay.'

'Stay where I can see you all,' I turn to Rebecca, who's looking at the two of us with undisguised astonishment. 'Use the wall, remember?'

She nods, pulling extra chairs away to the side.

'If anything kicks off,' I look back at Theo, 'I'm right here. Okay?'

Finally, a smile. Hesitant, but it's there. 'Okay.'

As they get settled, I take the last empty seat in the circle. Once the collective murmuring and shuffling dies down, Grace clears her throat.

'Are we all ready?'

She looks slowly around the circle, passing over each member as they nod back, towards the two in Adam's room, Theo, Rebecca and Rob.

Me.

'Then let's begin.'

The circle members close their eyes to meditate. I do the same.

Now it's quiet.

The gentle, steady breathing of the circle drifts around me. Their individual rhythms gradually converge as they slow, stilling the world around them, shutting it out to focus on the one within, silently asking their guides, their helpers, to join them, to join us.

Mine don't take long to show up. I never quite finished explaining to Theo, but at the moment, I have two. There's Grandma Dot – warm, gentle, quick to give me an encouraging word, basically exactly like when she was alive. The other is Norman – a calm, methodical, stoic Yorkshireman in his fifties – who's been with me on and off since I was five, and who I suspect died not too many years before that, if the beige seventies ensemble he appears in is any indication. Of course, there's the Voice as well, but that's a whole different kettle of fish I've never fully understood. I'm not calling it, not yet. The Voice isn't a guide in the normal way. Sometimes I think not knowing what it really is might be for the best.

Today, I *feel* rather than see the Guides gather around me. It's just a sense – the familiarity of recognising someone's presence, just like you would with a living person if they came and stood behind you. The others in the circle will be invoking their own companions however best works for them, to tap into their protection to keep them safe against spiritual danger, and use their energy to send whatever *it* is back on its merry way. As mine draw close, I silently request they have my back, but more importantly, they do whatever they can to protect Theo and the others. The unmistakeable feeling of two very different hands momentarily clasping each of mine tells me that they've heard me, they're with me, and they'll step in and do their thing if needed.

I hear Grace's voice as she checks with each circle member in turn to make sure they have their metaphysical ducks in a row. She comes to me last. 'Dot?'

At least she's taking this seriously. She knows using a name I hate in this moment, when we're about to invite some heinous thing to communicate, would be inviting a ton of that negative energy I mentioned. Just that one, tiny thing could be enough to skew the balance in the room, risking giving it more power, and that could work out badly for everyone.

I open my eyes to acknowledge her, glancing at Theo. His eyes are already watching me intently, and a steady, resolute smile breaks out across his face as I meet them. Reassured he's okay, I nod silently back at Grace. She then takes the lead for her group, focusing on a spot just above the centre of the circle. Two or three of the others follow her gaze, while the rest close their eyes again. It helps some mediums to do that, to stay connected to their guides and be open to whatever else is lingering at the border between here and there. For me it varies, but I prefer to keep them open. All the better to keep an eye on this side of the veil as well.

'We call upon the being within this house. We ask that you speak with us.'

Nothing.

I feel a slightly off sense of déjà vu, the scene oddly reminiscent of as the séance from the party, like a distant echo in a parallel universe. A couple of members of the circle shift in their seats, the cheap material squeaking under the movement, adding some comedic background noise. My Guides are hovering, watchful but quiet. I wonder briefly why I still haven't heard the Voice again since Friday night.

'We wish to help you complete your journey in spirit.'

Yeah, send you packing smack into the middle of the light where you belong.

It's quiet again on the landing, the air hanging heavy as the stillness of it drags, starting to feel alien and wrong somehow, as though time itself has ground to a sputtering halt. I feel my Guides gathering closer, the impression of protective hands circling my shoulders my first inkling that more might be happening than anyone can see.

A sudden crash breaks through the deafening silence, followed by a collective gasp as the group react. One of the folding chairs has fallen to the floor, its previous occupant having abruptly jumped up and staggered out of the circle. It's a woman about my age, maybe a few years older, and she's hunching over as she leans against the balustrade overlooking the hall, struggling to catch her breath. 'I'm sorry Grace', she sputters, 'I— I can't—'

My hackles are up, heightened by the sense of the Guides' grip tightening around me. This isn't right. Something's not right.

Then I hear it.

FIGHT.

A voice. *The* Voice. It's back.

I turn to Grace. 'Grace, we need to stop.'

She shakes her head dismissively. 'No, we're so close…'

A thud from the other side of the circle as a second chair falls, a younger guy this time, coughing desperately as he stumbles to lean against the nearest wall for support.

'Dot,' Theo's voice, worried. 'What's happening?'

I indicate for him to give me a second and turn back to Grace. 'Grace, tell your people to stop.'

She ignores me, pressing on, determined to do what she came here for, damn the consequences. I rise from my chair and cross to her, grabbing her roughly, forcing her to face me. 'It's going to pick your people off one by one, Grace, for god's sake tell them to—'

A scream rings out, small and high pitched. *Hannah*. As I turn, she's cowering, scrambling behind her parents, clutching at the cross against her neck, pointing towards the opposite side of the landing. I look around, my blood cold.

I see it.

Behind me, I hear Rebecca and Rob, all panicked bewilderment as they try desperately to soothe their daughter. They don't see what she sees.

But *I* see it.

Like with Rob earlier, it's just a dark shadow, a mist, hovering near the stairs. But the shape of it's changed since before; instead of what was an amorphous blob of nothing, a little, not-so-fluffy cloud, now it's grown, stretched out, taller. Almost…

…*almost* human-shaped.

It's still just a dark fog, fuzzy at the edges, nothing there of any real substance. But something in the way it's moulded – the slightly smaller ball at the top which could be a head, the long, spindly protrusions hanging at each side which mirror a pair of arms, the triangular gap in its lower half, suggesting the stance of widely-planted legs. Legs that are hovering six inches above the floor, but still. It's like a four-year-old scribbled their idea of what they thought a human might look like, and somehow invoked it into this floating, vaporous form.

FIGHT, I hear again.

The Guides are crowding me now, sharing their energy, their barrier. Someone else has already dropped out of the circle and as I glance quickly back at Grace, I see she's finally catching on. She looks past me, open-mouthed, eyes wide at the sight of the gestating form.

'Grace.'

It's like she can't even hear me.

'*Grace.*' I shake her roughly by the shoulder again and her head snaps up to look at me.

'We need to fight.'

'I'll—' She hesitates. 'I'll tell them to—'

Her eyes widen impossibly further, fixed over my shoulder. I look back anxiously.

It's advancing. *Not* good.

'Too late for that.' I turn back to my own people, ready to move to protect them, and get the jolt of my life when I see the look on Theo's face. It's not just blind fear and confusion like Rebecca and Rob, that helplessness of having no clue why chaos is suddenly unfolding in front of you. It's terror, cold white terror, as his eyes freeze on a point beyond me, past Grace.

He sees it too.

Shocked as I am – how can he? Why does he? What the *hell* is going on? – I don't have time to process that right now while all this floaty bullshit is kicking off.

I lean down to Grace, yanking her back to meet my eyes. 'Fight.'

It's not a request.

'*Fight!*' I yell at the remaining functioning mediums as I stride across towards Theo. 'If you can't, protect yourselves.'

The touch of my hand on his shoulder wrenches his terrified gaze back to me, and I grab Rebecca's arm with my other hand. 'Stay behind me and stay together.'

Theo grasps back at me desperately. 'I can see— Dot, I can *see—*'

'I know,' I hope there's reassurance in my voice as I smile down at the poor kid shivering in terror between her parents. 'Hannah can too.'

There's no time for much else. 'Remember the wall,' I remind them, and then I focus on Rebecca and Rob. 'Your love is your strength, the three of you. Believe that.'

It sounds cheesy, I know. But love is a damn powerful thing.

I need Theo to know he has something on his side too. 'Your faith is your strength.' I hold his gaze, *hard*. 'Mine too. Got it?'

He breathes slowly, steeling his nerve. 'Got it.'

I turn back round just as the mist reaches the opposite edge of the circle. 'Stay behind me.'

Others have dropped out from the circle, but there's still Grace, and I count five more, instinctively out of their seats and backing away from the thing they likely all see before them. The two in Adam's room across the way have thankfully stayed put, holding their posts uneasily. The others have scattered to the edges of the landing, doing whatever they can to protect themselves, building their own walls.

And then there's me.

I talk silently to Grandma, to Norman. To the Voice, in case it's accepting two-way calls today. *Help* me. *Guide* me. *Give me strength*.

And I feel it inside me: their warmth, their energy, their protection. Their *power*.

I feel something else too.

It starts as a tickle at the back of my neck, a tentative caress somewhere around the edges of my head, then—

—*prodding*. Fingers, probing, poking inside.

It's trying to get into my head. I shut a steel trap swiftly in my mind, clamping down on the invading, alien digits trying to worm their way through.

Did the mist recoil slightly?

Grace's eyes are closed now, but she felt the tremor somewhere, wherever she is in her mind with her own guides. 'That hurt it.'

She won't know what I did, but she felt a change, however slight.

Then there's another change, a less encouraging one. A noise.

A rumble, like a low, guttural growl. Above us, beneath us, around us.

Surrounding us.

The lights upstairs flicker and dim.

Another vision, courtesy of Grandma: the five of us, me and Theo and the others, standing together in our own circle, hands clasped.

'Quick,' I whisper urgently to him over my shoulder and hold my right hand out behind me. 'Take my hand.'

He doesn't hesitate.

'Join hands, guys, quickly. Hannah, next to me. Back-to-back.'

'What?' Rebecca now, unsure. 'But—'

'*Now.*'

I need to help protect them, help bolster their defences, help the Guides keep them safe. But I also need them connected to me, Theo and Hannah especially. Whatever's within those two allowing them see the thing across the landing, I *need* that. I need to use it.

As the lights drop still further, the space around us suddenly feels heavy and wrong, like the air pressure has dropped sharply by several hundred bars, and the temperature plummets with it. Hannah takes my hand, giving the other to her mom, who in turn holds Rob's, holding Theo's, his other hand already tight in mine. We stand there in our little group, facing out, holding on for what feels like it might be dear life.

'Grace,' I shout sharply. 'Have your people join hands.'

She doesn't argue, just pulls her remaining crew together. She must really be crapping herself.

The growl deepens and the shape shifts again, reforming, strengthening.

'Your love is your strength,' I say over my shoulder. 'Say it.'

Rebecca starts hesitantly. 'Our love…'

'… is our strength.' Hannah's voice is suddenly strong beside me, and I give her little hand a squeeze, oddly proud of her.

The shape changes further, as though it's trying to decide what it wants to be. There's still a vaguely humanoid impression, but then its head…

… are those *horns?*

'Our love is our strength,' Rob joins in, their chorus complete.

'Your love is your strength. Keep it going.'

'Our love is our strength. Our love is our strength.'

The chant swells behind me as they call out in unison. I cock my head towards Theo to pass on a similar instruction, but he's already way ahead of me, his eyes closed tightly in concentration.

'My faith is my strength. My faith is my strength.'

The man's a fast learner.

'May the angel Michael be at my right, and the angel Gabriel be at my left.' Voices echo across the floor as Grace and her group start their own refrain, a prayer of protection. 'In front of me, the angel Uriel. Behind me, the angel Raphael. Above my head, the Sh'khinah.'

My turn now.

'I will to will Thy will. I will to will Thy will.'

Mine's different from the others. It's not designed for protection as such.

Mine's an invite, a rallying call. To the Guides, to the Voice, to whatever other Powers That Be might be accessible in the great beyond. A call for them to tap into me.

Mine's *fighting* talk.

My gaze is resolute on the cloudy form as I recite. There are no eyes in the fog – I try to ignore that the armlike limbs seem have long, arrow claws forming at the tips – but if there were, they'd be right on mine, locked in a battle of psychic wills.

'Our love is our strength.'

'My faith is my strength.'

'May the angel Michael…'

'I will to will Thy will.'

This is me giving myself up to the universe, giving myself over to it, taking whatever power is shared between us, letting that work through me to shut this fucker *down*.

The unearthly rumbling swells, the walls almost vibrating with the force of it, and the shape presses forward, crossing the threshold of the dispersed circle.

Somewhere inside me, in another part of my mind, I feel the boundaries shift, stretching and pulling away to make space, let in something so much bigger than myself.

'Our love is our strength.'

'My faith is my strength.'

'… above my head, the Sh'khinah.'

'I will to will Thy will.'

The mist shifts again, pulsing and contracting until suddenly its outline blurs, the unsettling features it was developing slipping away, back to vague nothings, the whole vaporous entity returning to a shapeless cloud. At the same time, the will melding with my own is growing, filling my mind with light, with purpose, with *power*.

'I will to will Thy will.'

A picture forms inside me, a vision of the malevolent fog being pushed away, out of here, out of this house, out of our lives, back to where it came from. With everything in me, the collective will becomes my own as I breathe the thought into life, focusing on the shape as it kicks and claws and I stare it down and concentrate with everything in my being and in my mind's eye I throw myself behind it and *push*.

'I will to will Thy will.'

The rumbling stops.

The lights come back up.

Silence.

Hannah pulls on my hand. 'It's gone.'

I'm back to myself, whatever was with me vanishing in a flash.

She's right. It's gone.

I let go of her as she tumbles into her parents' arms, the three of them crumpling in a heap on the floor.

'That was...' Theo leans across to me uncertainly. 'Is it... over?'

He hasn't let go of my hand.

'I don't know,' I reply honestly.

I haven't let go of his either.

I look over at Grace and her group, shellshocked, in varying stages of confusion and disarray. 'Grace?'

She turns to me, her face haunted.

'Was that it? Is it over?'

Before she has chance to answer, the groggy, broken voice of a little boy calls out. 'Mom?'

Rebecca shoots up. 'Oh my god. Oh my *god*—'

Theo and I watch her rush desperately through the haphazard pattern of chairs to Adam's doorway.

'Rob, oh my god, oh he's back, he's *back*—'

Adam's awake.

16

Grace's expression is what tells me things aren't all sunshine and roses.

While the Hudson-Hicks clan enjoy a tearful reunion with their bemused, seemingly unaffected seven-year-old, she pulls me aside, roughly enough to yank my hand out of Theo's. That immediately puts my back up.

'What's your problem, Grace?'

She drags me out of everybody's earshot. 'It's not over,' she hisses quietly,

I sigh, annoyed at the confirmation. I'm not really surprised – it did all seem a little too easy, considering what the bothersome thing has achieved so far, exerting considerable influence in different ways on Rebecca, Rob, and now a bucketload of experienced mediums – but it's still a kick in the teeth to hear it aloud. 'Damn. Okay. So, what now?'

'You need to get out of here.'

That stuns me. 'What?'

'You and the priest both.'

'Have you lost your actual mind? I'm not just leaving them here—'

'*Listen* to me,' she spits back harshly, grabbing my other arm, loud enough that several heads turn in our direction, Theo's included. A concerned frown knots the lines in his forehead as he flashes me a look asking '*are you okay?*'. I shake my head quickly, one hand raised, telling him to stand down.

'You can't stay here.'

'Why?'

Grace searches hopelessly for a reply. 'This is beyond you. Beyond all of us.' She gestures to her people and meets a collection of scared, confused expressions as they try to make sense of what just happened.

It takes me a second to get where she's going. 'Wait a second. *You're* leaving?'

She lowers her head. 'I won't put my people at risk.'

'You're all just *leaving*?' My voice is rising with incredulity. 'You're just gonna abandon them?'

'It can't be helped.'

'What happened to helping a family in need?'

'It's unfortunate. I'm truly sorry.' Grace's words are clipped, her tone brusque. Oh yeah, that sounds a lot more like the Grace I remember. All cold, all business, all for herself. She's already walking away from me, but I'm right on her heels, fuming.

'What are they supposed to do, Grace?'

'They should leave too.'

'What?' I hear Rebecca's voice from Adam's room.

Then Rob's. 'What's going on?'

'And go where, Grace?'

She ignores me and instead starts giving instructions to members of her group. I refuse to let her off that easy.

'Where exactly are they supposed to go, Grace?'

The family wander up, clamoured together, Rebecca watching our interaction with concern. 'Dot, what's going on?'

'They're leaving,' I reply, exasperated.

'*What?!*'

'I'm sorry.' Grace gives her a curt nod. 'Really. We can't help you.'

'But if you can't help—'

'What the hell are we supposed to do—'

She dismisses them both with a wave. 'You should leave.'

'Leave?!'

'What?!'

Grace stops abruptly and I realise Theo's joined us his comforting hand rests on my back.

'Look,' she turns to face us. 'I'm sorry. But this… this is an exceptionally powerful entity. My people are simply not equipped to deal with it. Your house *cannot* be cleared.'

Rebecca and Rob start to protest, the kids hanging back from the fray, Grace's own people looking on with shame in their eyes.

To do a bunk so suddenly, either Grace must've learned an awful lot about the 'exceptionally powerful entity' in the span of our very short session, or something else is going on. I lean toward her suspiciously. 'What do you know about this, Grace?'

Grace gasps like she's been sucker punched. She tries to hide it, but the second she looks at me I see right through her. We do share DNA, after all.

So, she *does* know something.

'What aren't you telling us?'

Grace closes her eyes, taking a slow, deep breath before turning fully back to face me. When she opens them, there's something there I've never seen before.

Terror.

She's not just scared, she's terrified.

She *definitely* knows more than she's letting on.

'You know what it is, don't you.'

'Soteria—'

'Have you seen it before? Is that how—'

'Dot, for god's sake!'

The desperation in her voice coupled with her switch back to my chosen name startles me.

'*Trust* me,' she pleads.

Hmm. Unlikely.

'You can't win this fight. *We* can't. For your own sake, for his,' she gestures toward Theo. '*Take him* and get out of here.'

Seeing her team are ready, she strides purposefully towards the stairs, Rebecca following plaintively, trailing Rob and the kids. The other circle members form a deep enough barrier between them that her pleas barely register, not that it'd make any difference if they did. Once Grace has made her mind up, that's that, and never mind the effect on anyone else.

Theo faces me, astounded.

I shrug back at him, wishing I was more surprised. 'My mother, ladies and gentlemen.'

'What now?'

'I'm not sure.' I can't shake the feeling Grace is hiding something. 'I think she knows more than she's letting on.'

'So you do think she knows what it is,' he muses. 'I thought you were just winding her up.'

I feign offence. 'As if. Look, I'll let her cool off for now. If I push it she'll just dig her heels in. Let's give her a night to sleep on it.'

'Should we go see her again tomorrow?'

I'm pleased he's volunteering. More moral support. 'We a team now, are we?'

'She did say you should take me with you,' he smiles back.

Wait. She did say that.

Why did she say that? Specifically?

Not 'get the family out', not 'everybody out', but 'take him and leave'. I'll have to ask her tomorrow.

Oh shit. Tomorrow. Work. *Mags*.

But… oh Christ, how can I leave now, after all this? Grace and her lot turned out to be a big fat waste of time, and I'm the one who promised them it'd work. I really, honestly – grudgingly – believed it would. How can I leave them to it now, after they've witnessed a whirlwind rip across their landing and send a bunch of mediums packing in terror?

The simple answer, is that I *can't*.

But I promised Mags too, promised her I'd go home tonight to keep her safe, promised her I'd put things right.

'Dot?'

Theo frowns down at me, eyes swimming with concern. 'You okay?'

'Mmm.' I grimace. 'I still need to sort out that other thing.'

'For your friend?'

'Yeah. I promised I'd be home tonight to stay with her, but…' I rub my forehead, sighing at the scene before us, the aftermath of a disaster. 'God, what a mess.'

'Hey,' he soothes, warm hand back on my shoulder, 'you go if you need to. After today— my god, you've done so much already, and I'll be here, I can hold down the fort.'

'I'm not leaving.'

'You can.'

'But I'm not.'

'You *can*, really. I absolve you of any guilt. I can do that, professionally speaking.'

'You honestly think I'd just bugger off and leave you here by yourself after what just happened?' I scowl back at him. 'You must not think very much of me.'

My mind's racing with it all: the cloud, Grace, Mags, what to do, what should I do. Flashes of what just happened coupled with Grace's words: *he can see it, take him with you*.

'So you're really not leaving?'

'No.'

'Thank god,' he sighs, audibly relieved. 'Because I was lying about holding down the fort. I can't hold down anything. Right now I'm amazed I can hold down my lunch. Please don't go.'

I have to laugh. He keeps making me.

'I like making you laugh,' he smiles as though he's just read my thought.

'Don't flatter yourself,' I tease back, enjoying the lighter mood, a welcome shift away from the last half hour. 'I'm sure it's just a stress reaction.'

He leans in closer, the warmth in his smile becoming something more... intense. 'Of course it is,' he purrs in my ear, voice low and thick with want. I'm suddenly aware of how tall he is beside me, how I barely come up past his chest, the breadth of his shoulders, how close he is and is that a freckle on his neck just above his dog collar? Hmm, I wonder what his neck looks like without it and how many more freckles he has.

'Dot?'

Rebecca is back at the top of the stairs, Adam in her arms, the others coming up behind. 'What do we do now? I take it this isn't over with.'

'Grace didn't seem to think so.'

'Well, she's gone,' Rebecca replies curtly, trying to stay calm, 'and she made it clear she has no intention of coming back, so I don't really care what she thinks. I want to know what you think.'

'I think...' I shrug unhappily. 'It's not over.'

'Jesus.'

'Oh shit.'

'Rob, let's not panic.'

'But what the hell are we supposed to do now?'

'Guys,' I try to placate them, 'don't. Please.'

They break off abruptly.

'Look, I'm so, *so* sorry about Grace,' I start quickly. 'I really am. I honestly thought she was our best bet, I never thought in a million years she'd just leave like that. I mean, she wasn't much of a mom, but—'

'That woman—'

'Grace is—'

'Your *mother?*'

I forgot they missed the drama at the front door earlier. 'Her church has always been her whole world. She was never much use to me, but this stuff? That's the one thing she's never turned her back on.'

'Then why did she leave?'

Deep breaths. 'I was just telling Theo. I think she knows more about it.'

There's the slightest smile at the edges of Theo's mouth, and I realise I didn't call him Father Gregory. I used his first name. Openly, in front of other people.

'How do you mean?'

'Her reaction was just so extreme. What happened wasn't much like your usual house clearing, but we warned her about that going in. She knew to expect something more powerful than your average sheet-rattler. That's not what scared her.'

'So what did?'

Theo and I exchange glances. 'I wonder if she recognised it.'

'What?'

'Maybe she's seen it before, or something like it, or she's heard of it through the Church. I'm not sure. But she definitely knows more than she was telling.'

'So what now?'

I look at their tired, lost faces. 'Well, for a start, you all need some proper rest. Food, and sleep.'

'Oh, Dot,' Rebecca groans, gently dropping Adam down to stand with his sister. 'I don't know if any of us can possibly sleep.'

'You'd better,' I reply firmly. 'If we have to go another round with that thing, you'll need all the strength you can get, all of you. Now, I'm leaving Grace overnight to see if she grows a conscience, but I'll talk to her tomorrow back on her turf, so she can feel like she's in control. Hopefully she'll clue us in on what she's hiding.'

'You want to leave again?'

'We'll keep watch tonight,' I nod toward Theo, 'but yeah, I need to talk to her.'

'Then *call!*'

I shake my head. 'She'll just duck me. Look, you don't know my mother. If she wants to ignore something, you have to shove it under her nose to make her pay attention, and even then, it's a toss-up whether she'll give a shit. Sorry.' I flash a frown at the kids, who share a giggle. 'Besides, I need to go into work in the morning anyway.'

'*Work?!*' Rebecca's indignation rises in direct proportion to her volume. 'No, absolutely not, you'll call in, *I'll* call in and say you're not going, you can't.'

'I have to. Not all day, just—'

'You have to stay here with us.'

'Just first thing, just for a bit,' I try to explain, 'there's something I need to do and it's already waited too long as it is.'

'*No,*' Rebecca rages, her voice panicked. 'You can't, you *won't*, I'll sack you, you hear? You won't have a job to go *back* to—'

Rob steps in. 'Becs, that's enough.'

'She can't just leave us!'

Both of the kids have started sniffling beside them now, worried, and I motion for Rob to take them aside as I go up to her. She's angry and crying and red in the face, and I know she didn't mean it. She's just out of her mind with fear and exhaustion. I put my hands on her shoulders.

'Listen to me, Rebecca. I'm not leaving you.' I look around at each of them, lingering on Theo a second longer than I should.

'But if we're going to fight this thing— really fight it, I mean, and get rid of it for good— we need answers.'

'Now,' I go on gently, 'I understand why you want me here. I understand you're scared, for the kids, for Rob, for yourself. And you think you need me to protect you, right?'

She nods hastily through her tears.

I shake my head. 'Well, you're wrong.'

Rob frowns. 'What?'

'When all that was going on before, I did *help* protect you,' I explain. 'My Guides did too. But I— they— had to put too much energy into fighting to do much else. Mostly, you protected yourselves. In fact, you actually helped protect *me*, too.'

My gaze rests locks on Theo's. 'All of you did.'

'You mean— what we— when we—'

I turn back to her. 'I told you: love is incredibly powerful.' I nod towards Theo. 'Faith too.'

'We really did that?'

'It sounds crazy, I know.'

'So we can… if you go… we really can protect ourselves?'

I nod, smiling. 'You really can. Look, I'm not saying you can get rid of it, or even fight it, not alone. But if anything happens when I'm not around, you can stop it from hurting you. And,' I suggest, 'if you're not comfortable being here tomorrow without me, go out.'

'Out?'

'Yeah. Look, I know you can't do what Grace said,' I roll my eyes, 'you can't up and abandon a house you've just taken a mortgage on the size of a planet. But there's nothing to stop you leaving for a bit, not now Adam's awake, not now we know none of you are under the influence of that thing anymore.'

Rebecca looks at Rob, who shrugs back hopefully.

'I'll only be a few hours, if that. Just go out. It'd do you all good to do something normal for a bit anyway, not feel like you're looking over your shoulder the whole time.'

She breathes out the tension. 'Okay. I guess that's okay.'

'Good. In the meantime, you all need to eat, and you have to get some rest.' I frown at our current surroundings. 'I'd also suggest we stay downstairs tonight.'

'We can make up the sofas in the living room,' Rebecca nods.

'It'll be like camping,' Rob tousles Adam's hair, planting a kiss on the top of Hannah's head. 'An adventure. Right kids?'

Some adventure. Hannah forces a smile, Adam yawning as Rob shepherds them both towards the stairs. Rebecca hangs back.

'What about you two? Will you sleep?'

'Is there space in another room we can use? Separate from where you'll all be, I mean, but close by in case anything happens?'

Rebecca doesn't see Theo's raised eyebrows, but I do.

'Of course. There's the sitting room at the back.'

'That's perfect. Thanks.'

Rebecca shakes her head, her smile more relaxed. 'Thank *you*,' she replies, taking my hand and briefly squeezing it tight. 'I mean it.'

Her sudden affection takes me a little by surprise. I call after her as she turns to follow her family. 'Rebecca?'

She turns at the top of the stairs. 'Yeah?'

'Stay together, okay? In pairs, at least. Anyone needs the bathroom, to get up in the night for a drink, anything— each of you pick a kid and stick with them, got it?'

Rebecca nods back firmly. 'Got it.'

As she disappears from view, I head to the nearest wall for support, exhaling deeply as I lean against it and rest my head back, closing my eyes, exhausted.

'You must be exhausted.' Theo's voice is low and soothing, close in my ear as he reads my mind again. I could listen to him read the phonebook and it'd still sound like melted chocolate. Sexy melted chocolate.

'Mmm.' I keep my eyes closed. His proximity at the moment is too big a risk to my self-control.

'You need sleep.'

'I'm okay. Just… not looking forward to tomorrow.'

'You mean what you've got to sort out at work? Or talking to Grace?'

'Yeah.'

Both.

'Well, you still need to rest.' He pauses, and there's mischievous delight in his voice as he goes on. 'In our bedroom.'

'In *what?!*' My eyes are suddenly open again.

'Yeah, why did you ask her to give us in a private room, I wonder,' he teases.

I roll my eyes. 'Oh, come on—'

'All to ourselves…'

'Give it a rest.'

'Not that I'm complaining.'

'It's not like we're going to get much sleep anyway.'

Bad choice of words. He lifts one curious eyebrow, his smile lopsided, making him look like a cheeky, sexy…

Vicar, I remind myself, picturing a bucket of cold water over my head.

'Is that so?' he asks enthusiastically.

'I meant—' I stumble, flustered. 'I *mean*, we'll probably barely use it.'

He flounders. 'What?'

'We have to stay up and keep watch. In case anything happens.'

He looks disappointed. 'Oh. Right.'

'We don't want to disturb them by being up and down in the same room, do we?'

'Hmm. I suppose not.'

'I want them to get as much rest as they can. I wasn't joking when I said they'd need it.'

'And I wasn't joking when I said you do,' he replies adamantly. 'Come on, Dot. That whole thing has to have taken a chunk out of you.'

'I'll manage.'

'You'll *sleep*,' he replies. His tone is firm, the most commanding I've heard him, and I have to admit, it's… tempting. The suggestion of sleep, I mean. Not anything else. Honest.

'But—'

'I'll keep watch by myself. If anything happens, anything at all, I'll come get you.'

'But Theo—'

'I love when you call me that.'

I ignore the bait. 'You shouldn't be on your own, not after what you've just—'

'And you should?'

'I'm…' I search for the right word. 'Different.'

'I'll say.'

'You know what I mean.'

'I can protect myself now, remember?' Theo looks down at me, his eyes solemn and dark. 'I even helped protect you.'

I can't resist smiling back. 'I suppose you helped a bit,' I shrug nonchalantly.

'Please, sleep.' His face is so close to mine now. If I just reached up on tiptoes…

'We can take shifts,' I compromise, trying not to stare at his neck freckles.

'Deal,' he replies softly, his breath warm against my hair as

I feel the tension between us, in his chest beside me, in his arm around me.

He's barely fighting it, and I want him so badly it hurts. But… here? Now? In the midst of all this? *Careful*, Dot, I think to myself. A few hours ago it was not at all, remember? I force myself to pull back, to step slightly away from him, and I can see on his face that it hurts him, but I *have* to. I have to keep my head.

'We should probably…' I look towards the stairs, the words catching in my throat.

Theo smiles back. There's sadness in those extraordinary brown eyes, but understanding too. 'Probably.'

We head towards the staircase together, the silence so much more comfortable than in the car earlier, which might as well have been a million years ago.

It's only as we reach the hall below that I realise we've had our hands gently clasped together the whole way down.

17

I went to sleep feeling like the scum of the earth.

I had to call Mags to let her know I wasn't coming home after all, and when I spoke to her it was *brutal*. She cried, she begged, then she turned uncharacteristically angry, which is when things got ugly: she accused me of not really caring about her at all, of putting strangers ahead of our friendship and worst of all, of somehow *wanting* this awful thing to happen to her because I was jealous that she was young and pretty and everyone liked her and nobody liked me because I was a miserable, jaded, bitter old hag. Ouch. Thankfully, Penny stepped in at that point, took the phone away, reassured me she'd take good care of her and asked me to just check in tomorrow when I could. Making it abundantly clear to Pen that I was *definitely* going into the office first thing tomorrow no matter what, that I would *absolutely* get Mags' nightmare sorted out – I still didn't have a clue *how* yet, but I figured I'd jump off that bridge when I got to it – I begged her to pass that message on.

Hearing Mags say that stung, though, even though I knew – or at least hoped – she was just lashing out. I know how hard it is for her to trust people. It's not unusual for someone who looks the way she does to struggle with petty shit from other women – sadly, even in this day and age, plenty of us are still determined to drag each other down when we should be buoying each other up. At my advancing age, I can't be doing with that bullshit. Add to that, about eighty percent of blokes – straight ones, anyway – are only friendly to her because they want to get in her pants. So as open and friendly and lovely as she comes across, behind that she's wary: she's had so-called friends treat her like shit before. And feeling I've let her down is devastating.

Her words also hurt because there was an element of truth in them. Not the thing about wanting something bad to happen to her, god no; nor the bit about being jealous. But miserable, jaded, bitter old Billy No Mates? Yeah, I tick those boxes. They're all the parts of myself that I hate the most, and damn if Mags doesn't know that. For someone who I really *do* consider a good friend to turn and use my biggest insecurities against me feels like being punched in the stomach. I've never been great with people – partly my innate suspicious nature; partly the constant exhaustion of hiding this 'other' part of myself because any sane person would reject me for it; partly I'm just inherently antisocial – so friends have always been few and far between. And it's better that way, really, for them and for me. I don't have to expend a load of effort trying not to inadvertently out myself as a witch, and they don't have to worry if I can somehow read their minds. Which I can't, but that's what people think, and nobody wants to be friends with someone who they worry might be able to look into their subconscious and ferret out their deepest, darkest secrets.

What sleep I got after that was fitful, but bland, and I was grateful for once to have no dreams at all. When I wake, the house is silent, the dim light in the sitting room revealing no sign of Theo. I check my phone for the time – just after 1AM – and stick my head carefully through the door to the living room. Four sleeping heads – two big, two small – all present and accounted for.

No Vicar.

There's light coming from the Orangery though, and that's where I find him. He's sat on one of the cheap folding party chairs, leaning forward with an elbow on the end of a trestle table, propping his head on his hand, the splayed-out fingers of the other holding a book open flat on the surface. He's set up a small lamp further down the table, bathing him in a gentle glow. In side profile as I watch from the doorway, it's the first time I've seen him like this – alone, quiet, still with his own thoughts – and he looks so peaceful, so warm, so *inviting*. The little lines knotted across his brow as he reads; the way he plays with a stray curl as it falls across his face; the muscles across his back outlined taut against the black shirt as his broad frame leans over the book.

My god. He really is *beautiful*.

I step back into the shadows, not wanting to be caught gawking like a teenager with a crush, or to disturb him. But at the same time, all I can think is how much I want to be near him, feel the safety and comfort and warmth of his presence and attention. Detouring back, I tiptoe quietly through the drawing room and make my way to the kitchen, happy to find an already warm, half-drunk coffee pot waiting. Pouring out two drinks – black for me, milk for him – now I have an excuse in a mug. Not that I need a reason to go in there and sit with him, talk to him, of course I don't. So why do I suddenly feel so incredibly self-conscious about doing just that?

'Hey.'

Theo looks up, startled.

'Sorry,' I pull a face, holding up the mugs as a peace offering. 'Coffee?'

The smile breaks easily across his face, and the simple truth hits me like a thunderbolt.

I like him.

I *really* like him.

He's good, and kind, and sweet, and brave, and cheeky, and funny, and I feel better when I'm around him.

'Care to join me?'

I set down the coffees and pull up another chair, sitting at the long edge of the table to his right. As Theo leans back in his seat, stretching his arms back over his head with a deep sigh, my eyes catch a glimpse, a sliver of skin, and I realise he's not wearing his collar. That's his neck I can see. His actual neck. There are the freckles, so many of them dotted about, dancing across his collarbone, down to—

—his chest. Oh lord. I can see his chest.

Well, only a bit of course, it's not like he's taken his shirt off, not that I'm wondering what that'd be like, I'm not, I'm *not*… but he has undone the first couple of buttons, and there's a little triangle of skin, smooth and even more freckled, the tiniest hint of hair.

I'm not picturing what it would be like to kiss it. I'm *not*.

'Are you okay?'

'Hmm?'

'You're staring,' he points out, amused.

'Oh. Sorry. I just— you— erm…'

'Yes?' his eyes twinkle as he thoroughly enjoys watching me squirm.

'You're not wearing your collar.'

It's on the table beside the book, and he picks it up, twirling the stiff plastic deftly between his long fingers like a clerical fidget spinner. 'Off duty,' he smiles.

'Hmm.'

'If I'd realised taking it off would have such an effect on you,' he continues playfully, 'I would've done it sooner.'

'That's—' I rack my brains for a witty comeback, but they're empty. All I can think about are freckles. 'I— just—'

'Not seen you lost for words before. Does I really look that different?'

Up to now, the occasional passing thought about how cute

he was, or how lovely he might be didn't matter, because every time I looked at him, the first thing I saw was that collar, which said NO! OFF LIMITS! The C of E – most religions in general – are extremely anti-medium, hence their refusal to acknowledge the existence of abilities like mine. After all, if there really is proof of life after death, who needs the eternal salvation of heaven? The idea that I could be attracted to, much less want to be involved, with someone who not only follows their doctrine but actually preaches on their behalf is ridiculous. A passing fancy, fine; an amusing flirt, okay then, why not. But beyond that? Not a chance. The collar was my stern reminder of that.

Without it, he's just a man.

A biblically attractive one.

'Seeing you without it, it's just...'

Who I know likes me.

'Just what?'

He knows what I am, he's seen what I can do, and he *still* likes me.

I shrug lightly, finding it impossible not to smile. 'It suits you, that's all.'

Theo raises his eyebrows. 'Are you flirting with me?'

'There's only one flirt in this room,' I reply matter-of-factly, 'and I'm not it.'

He shakes his head teasingly. 'Hmm, nope. Don't buy it. That was definitely flirting.'

'How would you even know? They teach classes in it at seminary?'

Theo's smile is unnervingly suggestive. 'I wasn't *always* a priest, you know.'

I have no words. Redness inflames my face, a level of blushing I haven't experienced outside of perimenopausal flushes since secondary school.

'Vicar,' I remind him, my voice coming out like the croak of a strangled frog. Sexy.

'Touché,' he grins back broadly.

I sip at my coffee as a distraction. 'Do tell, though.'

'Tell what?' he looks confused.

'Before you were a Vicar. What did you do?'

'Oh.' He looks away, suddenly uncomfortable. 'Erm, bits and pieces. Different things.'

He hesitates. Damn, should I not have asked? 'If you don't want to talk about it…'

'No,' he shrugs me off, 'it's fine, really. I just – I don't often get asked.'

'Let me guess.'

Theo snorts. 'Oh, this should be good.'

'Mmm, let's see,' I tease gently, hoping to lighten the mood again, giving him a quick once over. 'Oh, I've got it.'

He eyes me cautiously as he sips from his mug. 'What?'

I flash him a knowing wink. 'Male stripper.'

He splutters out his coffee. '*What?*'

'In one of those troupes, hen parties throwing their knickers at you, all that stuff.'

'You're ridiculous,' he rolls his eyes, but he's smiling again. That's good.

'I bet you got the biggest tips.'

Now he laughs. Even better. 'There's something seriously wrong with you,' he shakes his head.

'Nothing a lap dance wouldn't fix.'

'Keep this up and you just might get one,' he threatens jokily.

'Promises, promises.'

'Okay, now you're definitely flirting.'

I look at him innocently over the top of my mug.

He falters slightly. 'Aren't you?'

Come on, Dot. Throw the guy a bone.

'Maybe a bit,' I admit tentatively. 'Hard to tell though, I've never been very good at it.'

'Me neither.'

'That why you became a Vicar?'

Theo laughs lightly, but there's an undercurrent in his voice. 'Not exactly.'

We both sip our drinks for a while.

'I was a teacher, for a bit,' he starts eventually.

Makes perfect sense. Patient, calm, understanding. That'd fit him perfectly. 'I could see that,' I nod back. 'What age?'

'Secondary.'

'Teenagers?'

'Yeah.'

I shiver. 'Scary. Teens are the worst.'

He smiles. 'They can be. *I* was.'

'Psh, I bet butter wouldn't have melted in your mouth,' I rebuke him gently. 'What did you teach?'

'English.'

'Ah, hence the book.' I nod toward the table at the copy of Grimm's Fairy Tales in front of him, open to partway through Hansel and Gretel. 'Interesting choice.'

He nods vaguely back towards where the others are fast asleep. 'They're a little light on grown up reading material.'

Another sip of coffee.

'So, did all the hormonal teenagers have crushes on the sexy English teacher and you had to leave for your own safety?'

'Not exactly.' He tenses again.

A horrific thought jumps into my head, and once it's there, I can't let it go. I'm certain it's wrong, but…

'You didn't…'

Sometimes words are hard.

'What?'

I shrug, squinting at him awkwardly. 'You know. With a student.'

'Jesus, Dot, *no*,' his eyes grow wide, pained at the suggestion. 'Of course not.'

He's right. Of course he would have never, and I know that, and now I've offended him because I'm an idiot who always says the wrong thing. I shake my head quickly. 'I'm so sorry. It was a stupid, thoughtless suggestion. I should never have said it, I don't even know why I asked.'

Of course you do, my brain calls me out immediately. You're looking for an out, some major flaw, a good reason to not like him, and if he'd said yes you could've cut off these scary feelings you're having about him without even a second thought.

Theo looks down at his coffee. 'It was nothing so… horrible. Well, it was horrible,' he concedes, 'but not like that.'

Horrible? What the hell happened?

'I had some issues,' he starts tentatively. 'With… drinking.'

You and me both, I think to myself.

'It got out of hand, caused me some problems.' He fiddles with the book, studiously avoiding my eyes. 'It was a bit of an issue when I was younger, but then it just sort of… spiralled.'

God, my heart hurts for him. My poor sweet man. I mean, not mine, he's not *my* poor sweet man, that's not what I meant, that's not what I was thinking.

'Lost the job, the fiancée, the flat—'

'You were *engaged*?' A stab of jealousy catches me very much off guard.

'Yeah. That was always a mistake, though. I think we both dodged a bullet when that fell apart. Her more than me, but… it was her place, where we lived. I crashed around with family for a while, with friends, but I couldn't work, the drinking was bad, I was a mess.'

I want to hold him, hug him, tell him it's all better now.

'Wore out my welcome pretty much everywhere, so I…' he clears his throat. 'I ended up homeless for a while.'

I can feel his pain, almost literally, and I can't bear to leave him out there with it alone. I put my free hand over his and squeeze it gently. Theo smiles sadly, but still doesn't look up. 'I used to sleep in this bus stop near a church sometimes. The Vicar there brought me food and coffee whenever she saw me. One night there was an early cold snap, it was so bitter out there, I didn't expect to make it through the night, and I was okay with that, you know? It would've been a relief.'

I abandon my coffee completely. Adjusting my position slightly, I lift his hand to wrap my other one over the back, enveloping it between both of mine, the closest I can get to wrapping my arms around him completely, which is what I actually want to do.

'But she… the Vicar… she brought me into the church to sleep. Let me use the shower in the rectory, gave me some clean clothes.'

Now I understand. 'She saved your life.'

Theo nods. 'Gave me another chance at one. I started helping out here and there – fixing things round the church, a bit of gardening, clearing up after services – and once she realised I wasn't dangerous or anything, she let me stay in her spare room. It didn't fix everything overnight, but it helped me start changing things. I couldn't have done that without her and her Church.'

'So that's why you became a Vicar? To pay her back?'

'Not exactly. When I got more involved with it, I just found it…' he searches for the words. 'It gave me *peace*. I'd been messed up for years – I told you I was a shitty teenager – and I never really figured out why. Nothing I ever tried – booze, drugs, sex—'

I try not to focus on that last one.

'It never really helped. But when I joined the Church, I felt… part of something. Something bigger than me. And somehow figuring out what had messed me up so much in the first place didn't matter so much anymore. I could just *be*.'

It's quiet for a little while as he deals with having said it out loud.

'So,' he murmurs eventually, his hand fidgeting between mine as he finally lifts his head. 'You still want to flirt with me?'

His face is so stunningly expressive, it's impossible for him to hide what he's feeling and in one look, I see it all. The hope, the fear, the shame, the longing. Not being able to bear the idea of his hurt for another second, emboldened by the way he looks at me with those achingly sad, big, puppy dog eyes, I deice to be either the bravest or stupidest I've ever been in my life. Gently, I let go of his hand as I stand up and move to his side of the table. Taking his beautiful face in my hands, I stroke the soft hairs on his cheek, looking for anything, any sign that this isn't what he wants. His eyes are wide on mine, his gaze unsure but full of expectation, and his breath catches in his throat as I lean down closer.

I kiss him.

18

Just once. That's all.

Soft, slow, gentle, just my lips against his, nothing more.

For a second, he doesn't respond – maybe it's the shock that I really, actually did it – but then he *does*, and it's warm and sweet and his mouth is just so soft, I feel like I'm melting into him, like we just *fit*. It's perfect, new and exciting but like we've done it a thousand times before. And then I feel his hands, one in my hair, one at my waist, pulling me closer to him until I find myself on his lap, and then his tongue's there, unsure, testing, probing, and I meet him with mine and then I'm just *gone*.

It's just a kiss, but it's the sort of kiss you spend your whole life wishing for. From someone I trust, someone I like, someone who cares about me. Someone I care about.

It's like coming *home*.

Oh crap. It's insane. I haven't even known him a week. How can I possibly feel any of this? How can it be real? I feel dizzy, like I'm seeing stars, and I pull my lips away from his, needing to catch a breath. When I look at him – scared, excited, wondering if I did the right thing – his eyes are glazed, and he smiles slowly back at me with something like amazement.

'You kissed me.'

How could it be anything but right when he sounds so damn *happy*?

'You kissed me back,' I point out.

'I did,' he admits breathily.

I can't help but smirk. It was a hell of a kiss, after all. 'You *really* did.'

One eyebrow pops up, intrigued. 'Really?'

'Oh yeah,' I'm half giggling. 'Definitely not always a priest.'

'Vicar.'

I lean back towards him, locking my eyes with his, searching for more. 'Whatever.'

This time he leans into me without hesitation, hand at the back of my neck, pulling me to him urgently, and when he kisses me this time, he's hungrier, more demanding, and I sink into him, never wanting it to end. I forget where we are, the horror of what's going on, everything. I'm just here, with Theo, enjoying him, and he's amazing, and it's just right. I even forget that I'm sat astride his lap until the development of a fairly insistent reminder.

I pull back again, breathless. 'Erm…'

'What's wrong?'

I nod down, shifting to give him some room. 'Friend of yours wants to join us.'

'Oh shit, sorry.'

'Don't apologise,' I reply quickly. 'I take it as a compliment.'

Theo smiles back at me. 'You should.'

'But I guess you… can't. Right?'

He knows exactly what I mean. 'I can, actually,' he corrects me cheerfully.

I raise my eyebrows, surprised. 'Really?'

'Yep. But only if I'm married.'

Disappointing. 'Shame.'

'Wanna marry me?' he asks playfully.

I love when he makes me laugh. 'Ah yes, lust. The foundation of all good Christian marriages.'

'I've known worse,' he replies wryly.

I wonder if he means his own broken engagement. 'How long have we known each other, a couple of days?'

'Three, technically. It's Wednesday now. Plus there was the party, so that makes four.'

'Hmm. Maybe we should give it till the end of the week,' I joke.

'Not sure I can wait that long.'

'I can see that,' I laugh again, one eye on the interloper between us. 'Maybe I should go back to my seat.'

'But I don't want you to go.' Theo gazes up at me, smile warm and inviting, one hand supporting the back of my waist, the other playing with my hair, eyes dark and wanting.

'And I don't want to leave you like this,' I reply honestly. 'But other than backing off so you can calm down, the only other ways I know to take care of it fall under the heading of stuff you can't do.'

He frowns sadly. 'Yeah. It's just…'

I stroke his face gently. 'What?'

His eyes flicker up, searching for mine. 'I'm scared if I let you go, you'll never come back.'

Awwwww. I think my heart just melted. 'I will. I promise.'

I'm making a lot of promises lately, and this one might be the hardest of all to keep. How would he and I even work?

For right now, though, I don't care. Screw the practicalities. We'll figure that out later.

He leans forward to give me one final sweet, gentle kiss, then lets me go. I slip off his lap and go back to my chair, but pull it close beside his before I sit back down and take his hand. We can at least have that much.

'It's been a hell of a day.'

'A lot going on,' I agree.

Theo nods quietly. His expression tells me he wants to say something, but isn't sure how.

'Go on, what is it?'

He swallows dryly. 'This afternoon, with that – thing. How could I see it?'

The question takes me by surprise. 'I'm honestly not sure. Hannah I could understand.'

'How come?'

'Kids,' I shrug. 'They often can. They're young, their minds are open, more attuned to pick up on things that adults don't.'

'That doesn't explain me.'

'It doesn't. I'm not sure I *have* an explanation.'

He doesn't look thrilled.

'It shocked me when I realised you could see it. It was written all over your face. I'd like to understand why too.'

I squeeze his hand tightly and he smiles.

'Although,' I go on, 'I'm more curious what Grace meant about taking you and leaving.'

'Maybe she didn't mean anything,' he shrugs. 'Maybe it was just a throwaway comment.'

I consider his suggestion. 'Remember how we thought it might be targeting you for some reason?'

'You still think so?'

I raise my eyebrows. 'I wonder if Grace does, and that's why she said what she did.'

'God,' he sighs uneasily, rubbing his forehead with his free hand. 'I hope you're wrong.'

'So do I.'

'But if you're not…'

'You know how to protect yourself,' I remind him firmly.

'Not from flying lamps,' he muses.

I put my other hand back on his cheek and meet his eyes steadily. 'Hey. Nothing bad's going to happen to you,' I tell him fiercely. 'I won't let it, you understand? Whatever the hell that thing is, if it wants to get to you, it'll have to come through me first, and I'd love to see the fucker try.'

The sudden strength of conviction in my voice surprises me. It better not even think about touching one hair on that gorgeous, wavy head of Theo's. I will personally take it apart piece by fucking piece, down in flames to the depths of hell myself if it tries to hurt him. I don't care *how* powerful Grace reckons it is.

'That might scare it off,' he teases. 'I wouldn't want to tangle with you when you're all worked up like that.'

'I bet you bloody would.' It's out of my mouth before I can stop it.

Theo cocks his eyebrow at me. 'I wish.'

'Sorry.'

He shakes his head with a wry smile, bringing my hand up to his lips to kiss it. It's a disarmingly sweet gesture, and I melt all over again.

'What happened today, Dot?'

'What went wrong, you mean?'

He nods.

'I don't think it was any one thing. She brought plenty of reinforcements, but it just seemed to catch all of them off guard.'

Theo frowns. 'So it's stronger than you thought?'

'Maybe. But I thought they were prepared for that,' I shrug. 'Grace knew from everything we told her it wasn't a normal run of the mill spirit. The possession thing alone proved it. Even the Guides can't take over like *that* when I let them in.'

His eyes widen. 'What? Your Guides possess you?'

'No,' I correct quickly. 'That's my point. These are spirits I've been connected to for decades. They can piggyback inside my head for whatever reason, but that's it. I'm still fully in control, it's just like I've got company in there. They can sort of… talk *through* me, I suppose. But they can't take over my whole body like some sort of puppet.'

'Isn't that weird?'

'Of course it is. But they only do it if there's no other option, usually if something they need to share that they can't get through to me otherwise. It doesn't happen often, plus I've been doing it so long, I'm used to it, and I trust them,' I explain. 'But for something to come out of nowhere and be able to get into Rebecca and Rob like that— especially with Rob, when it took him over— that's seriously powerful. That's why Grace brought so many people in the first place.'

'Strength in numbers, eh?'

'Exactly. Look, a normal clearance wouldn't be like that. I've done the odd one before by myself, no other help. All it usually takes is a bit of meditation, introduce yourself, figure out why they're there, and nudge them gently into the light. Piece of cake.'

'And instead, this thing—'

'Picked them off, one by one. Worked its way through, I'd guess, probably the weaker members of the circle, the least experienced, using their own energy against them.'

'I'm amazed it didn't go straight for us.' Theo frowns uncomfortably, and I immediately worry how all this talk of ghosts might affect how he feels about me.

'Thinking about burning the witch after all?' I joke tentatively.

'No,' he grasps my hand tighter. 'God, no.'

'You sure?'

My face must betray my fear, because he cups my chin with his other hand, holding it steadily, his eyes locked tightly onto mine. 'Dot. *No.*'

I'm grateful for the reassurance. I just hope it sticks. 'Okay.'

'I'm just still taking it all in. I haven't even got my head round what you did with Rob yet to get that thing out of his head, let alone what I saw you do in that circle.'

'Rob wasn't that big of a deal,' I try to play it down. 'It was mostly just a form of hypnosis, getting the part of him that was still *him* to block it out. He just needed to be shown how to do that, that's all.'

'Why does it even want to possess people? Just to scare them?'

'Partly that, maybe. Partly to show off, be intimidating. Also,' a thought occurs to me, 'I know you didn't see it before when it was with Rob, but it was bigger this afternoon. Like it'd grown.'

'Dot, it had *horns*.'

I grimace. 'You saw that? Yeah. This morning it was just a blob, but later it looked like it was taking some sort of shape. I wonder if the possession thing might be, somehow…'

'What?'

'How it builds its energy. Maybe.'

'Cheery thought.'

'Yeah.' I slide my fingers in and out of his, enjoying the easy, comfortable connection between us, despite the grim conversation. After a minute of quiet bliss, I sigh regretfully. 'It's my shift.'

'What?' Theo looks surprised.

'You need sleep. Well, also a cold shower,' I joke. 'But mostly sleep.'

'You want me to sleep after we've just sat here talking about possession and evil spirits with big horns?' He looks aghast. 'I'll have nightmares.'

'Well, what do you suggest to take your mind off it? You have to get some rest.'

He smirks back suggestively.

'Oh no,' I tell him quickly, 'no more of that tonight. You

definitely won't sleep.'

'Can we talk some more? Just for a bit. Not about horned apparitions.' He pauses briefly. 'Or horny vicars.'

God, he's sweet. 'Five more minutes,' I tell him sternly.

'Yes ma'am.'

'What do you want to talk about? More questions?'

'Just one. If that's okay.'

'Go on.'

'What does it feel like?'

'What does what feel like?'

'Seeing dead people.'

'Walking around like regular people?' I echo his line from before.

'Is it really like that?' he laughs.

'It can be,' I shrug, reassured by his ease. 'Sometimes.'

'Sometimes it's different?'

'It's different for everyone who has it.'

'How?'

'Most mediums get either visual, or audio, or they just… sense things.'

'One or another.'

'Yeah.'

'But not you?'

I shake my head. 'I get all of them. Not all together, not all the time. Sometimes just one, or two. But sometimes…'

'Sometimes all of it at once,' he finishes for me as I nod. 'Is that… usual?'

I open my mouth. At first nothing comes out, so I swallow. 'No,' I reply quietly.

'And this… this other Voice you mentioned. The one that isn't one of your Guides.'

'What about it?'

'Is *that* usual?'

I shrug. 'Not that I know of.'

'You don't think it could be…'

Psychosis? Schizophrenia? Early dementia?

'…God?'

'I'm not that delusional.'

Theo laughs lightly. 'So, all these different things that are so unusual. Is that why you're so…'

I frown back at him. 'Messed up?'

'I was going to say powerful.'

I could not be more surprised. 'What?'

'Well, yeah. What you did with Rob— and okay, I know you said you didn't do much, but I think you're bullshitting.' He looks at me like he can see straight into my head and wants to tell me off for downplaying my role. 'But what you did in that circle, after it all started going downhill… I've never seen anything like it.'

His voice is tinged with something that sounds remarkably like awe.

'Theo—'

'I mean it,' he says firmly. 'You stood there, between us and it, facing it down like it was *nothing*.'

'It wasn't nothing,' I remind him gently.

'Which is why it's all the more impressive.' Theo shakes his head, looking into my eyes with so much affection and warmth and pride that it makes me shiver. 'You're fearless.'

I'm proper blushing now. 'I don't think I've ever been called that before.'

He smiles broadly. 'And amazing.'

'Oh, stop it.' I'm not good with compliments, and he's clearly enjoying making me squirm in my seat as he leans in closer.

'And beautiful.'

I have to smile. He kisses it softly.

I shake my head as he pulls away. 'Such a smoothie.'

'I'm out of practice.'

Hardly. 'I think you're doing okay.'

'You reckon?'

'I do. But you really do need to go to bed.'

He moves close and I'm expecting another kiss, but instead he whispers gently in my ear. 'Come with me.'

It takes all my willpower not to drag him into the other room right there and then. Never mind keeping watch, never mind the sleeping family on the other side of the wall.

'Bad idea.'

He draws back, eyes wide. 'Just to sleep. That's all I meant.'

'Yeah, right.'

'I mean it. You think I'd do that with them all asleep on the other side of the wall?'

Damn, he has to stop reading my mind like that. I mean, I know he isn't, not really, but the way he picks up on whatever I'm thinking is just *uncanny*.

'Okay, okay, I believe you.' I fight the comforting vision of snoozing away cosily on that big sofa, wrapped up safe and warm in his arms. 'But it's still a bad idea. One of us has to keep watch, remember?'

He sighs from the depths of his soul. 'Yeah. I remember.'

I raise my coffee. 'Your five minutes are up.'

'Five more.'

'No more. Go to bed,' I plead.

'All right, all right,' he rises finally, yawning and stretching to pull out the knots in his shoulders, and I marvel happily at the glorious sight of him. 'Goodnight kiss?' he suggests cheekily.

Tempting, but I'm not falling for it. I point towards the other room. 'Go.'

'All right, I'm going. Sure you'll be okay?'

'Oh yeah,' I reply drily. 'Everything's perfectly under control.'

'Okay,' he smiles back sweetly, his handsome face framed by the soft glow from the lamp. 'Goodnight.'

I smile back. Just as he reaches the doorway, I can't resist one final flirt. 'Theo?'

He turns back expectantly. 'Yeah?'

I flash him a suggestive look. 'Sweet dreams.'

That gorgeous smile of his lights up every corner of my heart. 'I certainly hope so,' he winks back.

I giggle to myself like a teenager as he disappears. Dot, I tell myself resignedly, you have got it *bad*.

19

First priority next morning – after Theo and I got past the first few minutes of smirking and giggling – was to get the Hudson-Hicks clan out of the house, on the agreement we'd let them know once we were on our way back, so they wouldn't come in the house until we were all together again. There was some debate about palming off Hannah and Adam to friends or relatives further afield while we had the chance, but when Theo suggested it, both kids pitched a fit, clinging to each other and their parents with an impressive level of determination. They settled on a daytrip to Alton Towers – last chance before it closed for the season – and scuttled back and forth in a parallel version of their usual morning routine, departing in a whirlwind of noise and relief.

I would've preferred a change of clothes before going into the office, but being two sizes larger and several inches shorter than Rebecca made her offer to loan me an outfit redundant. The hijinks of yesterday's aborted attempt to clear the house had given my top something of a pasting in the freshness department, not to mention the effects of having gotten a little hot and heavy with Theo.

Not that it deterred him. He was in a visibly chipper mood as we saw Rebecca and her brood off at the front door. Before we had to get on our own way, he snuck in a quick, lingering kiss, laughing and joking and teasing as we headed to the car, as though we were about to embark on a romantic road trip. Every time I wasn't using the gearstick or handbrake he held my hand; played absent-mindedly with my hair almost the entire journey and managed to kiss me every time we stopped at a red light. I felt a bit like I was shepherding a giant golden retriever in human form, but I welcome the attention all the same. It felt like a respite, a sanctuary after the last few days. Well, after the last forty-odd years, truth be told.

After we park up in Snow Hill car park, I leave him to nurse a massive latte in the Costa next to the station and head up the road to the office.

I still don't have a plan yet.

Just an end goal: part Dickhead Scumbag from his phone, work out how to unlock it, find whatever vile stuff he has of Mags and delete it. Part of me wants to take it straight to the police as soon as I get my hands on it, but Mags made it clear she didn't want to go down that route. I'd already let her down once, and I wasn't about to repeat that. Before anything else though, I need to get upstairs, and without my staff pass which was back at home, I can't even get through the barriers in reception, and curse myself for not having the forethought to swipe Rebecca's before we left the house.

Thankfully though, Jackie's in, and waves me over to the front desk as soon as she spots me wander into the lobby.

'Dot! Hey mate, I was starting to think you weren't coming back.' She dashes round the edge of the desk as I reach it and embraces me in an unexpected hug.

'I wish.'

She frowns at me mischievously. 'Weren't you wearing that top yesterday?'

Busted. 'Erm...'

'Made the most of your afternoon off then,' she winks. 'Dirty stopout.'

I can't be arsed to set her straight.

'Has Mags been in touch? I heard she's not coming in for the week.'

I tense at the question. 'Yeah, she's not great,' I murmur half-heartedly, not wanting to lie to Jackie but needing to keep it vague.

'Aww, poor lamb.'

Jackie's the de facto Mom figure for practically the whole firm, and out-Work-Mom's me in all the ways that matter. Unlike me, her lack of kids isn't her choice, and bless her if she hasn't spent her life adopting every waif and stray that's fallen into her path to make up for it. I'd swap her for my egg donor in a heartbeat if I could.

'Listen, Jack, I'm sorry to ask, but I left my pass at home.'

'Not a problem,' she trots back to her seat. 'I'll set you one up.'

Popping a blank visitor pass into the machine on the desk, she clicks something on her screen, taps a few buttons and hey presto.

'Here you go,' she sings cheerily as she hands me the plastic card over the counter with a wink. 'Access all areas.'

'Thanks, mate.' I have a sudden thought. 'Actually, while I'm here, could I ask another cheeky favour?'

Reception's mostly empty. There's a couple of folks about, but only passing through on their way here and there, not slowing long enough to pay any attention. But I lower my voice anyway.

'Can you still see everyone's diaries?'

Our place give you access to online diaries of anyone you work directly for, along with other colleagues in the team with the same role as you. So, in my case, I have David's, Zoe's and Stephen's, as well as Mags' and all the other secretaries in the team. Jackie's supposed to just have diaries for Phil and the other post room folk, as they rotate holiday and lunch cover on the front desk. But the last time IT rolled out an upgrade of a certain major software product, a glitch suddenly gave her access to the diaries of the whole Birmingham office. She logged it with IT when it happened, and one of them even looked at her machine and was supposed to come back to her to get it fixed. But he never did, the IT call ticket got closed, and Jackie never got round to chasing them back.

She raises her eyebrows. 'Not if anyone asks.'

'Excellent. What's Dickhead Scumbag up to this week?'

Jackie turns to her screen, clicking on calendars until she brings up Nathan's diary. 'Want a print?'

She's the best.

'That'd be perfect. Thanks.'

'No probs.'

A couple of seconds later, she whips a sheet from the printer under the desk and hands it to me. 'Gonna let me in on what this is all about?'

I hesitate. Like I told Theo, it's not my issue to share. But in all honesty, I don't know how I can pull this off by myself. And Jackie, well – she's super trustworthy, she knows everyone, sees everything, and she loves Mags to bits, she'd be devastated if she knew what had happened to her – she genuinely might be able to help. But I can't tell her why. Not without betraying Mags' trust all over again.

'Let's just say he's outdone himself,' I tell her cryptically. 'I need to stop it escalating.'

Jackie frowns back, concerned. She was my main source of support when I went to HR about the work experience incident – even volunteering nuggets about his behaviour she'd witnessed, which I knew nothing, to back me up – so she has a good idea what I might be implying. 'Can I help?'

Music to my ears. 'Anything on the grapevine about it?'

'About him reaching new levels of depravity? Not that I've

heard. I'll keep an ear out though.'

'Thanks.' I study the print carefully.

'What are you looking for?'

'Meetings. Preferably tagged sensitive.'

'Why?'

'Because if he has any, he'll have to check his phone in with you.'

Most of our clients couldn't care less, but some of the more high-profile ones don't like the lawyers taking phones in their meetings. If Nathan has any of those scheduled this week, he'll have to check his phone in at reception before they start. Jackie locks them away for the duration, and he'd be parted from it for long enough that I could have her snatch it for me. But there's nothing. I sigh, frustrated. 'Damn.'

'No luck?'

I shake my head. 'I need to get my hands on that phone.'

'What are you planning to do with it?'

I meet her eyes carefully, trying to be subtle. 'Delete whatever I find on it.'

Jackie's eyes widen. 'Oh shit.'

'And whatever's in the cloud, and hope he hasn't saved it anywhere else.'

'*Shit*. Really?'

'Really.'

'Oh god, it's not...' she winces. 'You?'

'*Jesus*, no!'

'All right, all right.'

'Come on, Jackie.'

'But if it's not...' she looks at me curiously. 'Then why are you...'

A look of thunder crosses her face.

Uh-oh. Jackie's not stupid. She *knows*. She's right, there has to be a reason I'm involving myself in this. The second the penny drops, I can see it all over her face.

'Not Mags?' she whispers, pained.

Damn. 'Look, Jackie, I can't—'

'That *fucker*,' she hisses angrily.

'Jack—'

'I mean, I saw how cosy they were on Friday night, but…' she steams, more to herself than me. 'Shit. *Shit*.'

'How nice of you to join us, Dot.'

We both look startled towards the lobby as a familiarly hostile voice cuts through the air. It's Pat. I hope she didn't hear anything.

'So glad to see you back. With both you and your *little friend*—' her disdainful tone towards Mags immediately puts my back up '—out for the last couple of days, the work in your section's really piling up.'

Jackie glares at her. 'Good morning to you too, Patricia.'

Pat eyes Jackie with a look of utter contempt. 'Jacqueline.'

One of the best ways to spot your standard, garden variety office arsehole at fifty paces is to see how they treat the folks on reception and the post room and the canteen, anyone they mistakenly deem to be somehow beneath them. The same logic works for screening potential dates. Just watch how they treat the waiting staff, or anyone behind the bar.

'Well?' she looks back at me, tapping the face of her watch to remind me of the time like I'm a child, not a middle-aged woman who's been doing this job in their sleep for the past eight years. 'Chop, chop. Those dictations won't type themselves.'

She's supposed to split work out if people are off, to be covered between the team. Including herself, not that she'd ever lower herself to pitch in with the rest of us. Of course, I have no intention of staying long enough to clear down whatever work she's seen fit to abandon on my desk, but she doesn't need to know that.

'I'll be right along, Pat,' I smile sweetly. 'As soon as I've finished doing my statement for HR.'

Pat frowns. 'HR? What are you talking about?'

'My statement. You know, for my fall?'

'What?' she looks confused. 'What *statement*?'

'For. My. Fall.' I repeat the words slowly, exaggerating each one like she's the child now. 'For the health and safety investigation. With my solicitors.'

Pat's eyes turn into saucers. 'Solicit— you're *suing*?'

I shrug. 'Down to them, isn't it.'

'But you— I— you—' she blusters.

'Hmm?'

She looks between me and Jackie, increasing exasperation across her face, before rolling her eyes theatrically and stomping off towards the lifts. As soon as she's safely inside one, Jackie, who's kept an admirably straight face through the last few minutes, roars with laughter, shaking her head.

'You are so full of shit,' she cackles.

'Please. She deserves a wind-up just for how she talks to you.'

'I'll not argue with that,' she sighs gently. 'You fancy lunch later?'

I shake my head quickly. 'Sorry, Jack. I'm not staying. I only came in to try and figure out this phone business.'

'Hmm. Well, if you can get hold of it, I know who can unlock it for you.'

Hope surges through me. 'Really?'

'Oh yeah. Paul in IT. He's done it for some others when they've forgotten their passcodes.'

'Would he need to know why? It's not like it's my phone.'

Jackie shrugs casually. 'I promise he'll do it on the quiet if

I ask. He owes me a favour or three. And he especially will if he knows who it belongs to,' she adds. 'Nathan's always on their back in IT for nonsense. None of them can stand him.'

'Yeah,' I snort. 'Tell them to join the club. Look, I'm after it to delete whatever's on it,' I tell her plainly, 'not to go to HR again. I wouldn't waste my breath.'

Jackie rolls her eyes. 'After last time…'

'Exactly. It just needs to be gone. Even if that means taking it up to Gas Street to chuck it in the canal.'

Jackie takes a quick breath. 'You know, if you need to get it off him…'

'What? You have an idea?'

'I might have. But—'

'C'mon Jack, I'm clutching at straws here,' I tell her desperately. 'I'll take anything you've got.'

She pulls a face. 'I'd have to get someone else involved.'

I shake my head immediately. 'No, Jack, sorry. Thanks for the offer, but—'

'They're discreet, I promise.'

I mean, I do need all the help I can get. But I'm already worried Mags is going to hate me forever as it is, just for talking about it to Jackie.

'I can't, Jack. It's not my call to make, you know?'

She doesn't argue further. 'I get it. But keep it in mind, okay? And if there's anything else I can do…'

'Know any local kneecappers?'

She smirks darkly. 'I can ask around.'

I laugh ruefully. 'Thanks. Look, I'm just going to pop up to where he keeps it these days, then I'm off. Maybe I'll get lucky and he'll have left it on his desk.'

Jackie nods. 'You in the rest of the week?'

Hmm. Well, let's see: I have an unscheduled appointment to

interrogate my estranged narcissistic mother, a mind-controlling evil spirit to send packing to the Other Side, and the not-at-all unwelcome advances of an adorably besotted Vicar to contend with. What's left of the week is already shaping up to be pretty full-on. 'I doubt it.'

Jackie nods. 'Give Mags my love.'

'Don't know what you're talking about,' I shrug innocently on my way to the lifts.

'Course you don't,' she drops back into her seat to deal with the buzzing switchboard.

I head straight for my desk as soon as I reach our floor. Bonnie waves at me from the next pod over, grinning as she balances the handset of her desk phone against one ear. Casting one eye across my and Mags' adjacent desks – Pat wasn't lying, you could build a fort with the number of files strewn across them – I don't even bother dumping my coat and bag before I walk to the end of our section and peek round the corner.

Dickhead Scumbag is sat on the opposite side of the room, thick as thieves with Pat, regaling her with god knows what. Naturally, he's manspreading his arrogant self across the pod he shares with Zoe. Pat leans toward him, hanging on every word, batting her lashes and giggling like she thinks he's on the flirt. Just watching the interaction between them is enough to get my blood boiling.

Then Nathan pulls out his phone and my heart drops into my stomach.

He opens it up, shows something to Pat, and after a couple of seconds they both explode in conspiratorial laughter, loud enough to turn heads. I clock his slimy, sneering smirk of contempt and panic hits me right in the guts. It's not *that* surely? He wouldn't show it to Pat, would he?

Would he?

No, I tell myself, it could be anything. Probably just some shitty meme.

Right?

As I contemplate the possibilities with an increasing sense of desperation, he looks up, catching me watching. Grinning from ear to ear, he stares right back at me, dropping the skeeviest, most deliberate wink right in my direction.

Fucking scumbag. He couldn't. He wouldn't dare show it to Pat. He's just trying to bait me.

Right?

Maybe he can see the rage burning behind my eyes as I glare back at him, as he abruptly turns away, dismissing Pat now she's served her simpering purpose, and casually sticks his phone into the safety of his back trouser pocket. I'm definitely not getting my hands on it now then. But what *can* I do? I rack my brains, my thoughts spiralling at the idea that he might be sadistic enough to show his footage of Mags around the office, telling myself over and over that he *couldn't* be doing that, surely. But then I remember what sort of person he is to have taken it of her in the first place, to have used it to… *blackmail* her into doing stuff she didn't want.

He is *absolutely* capable of worse.

I go into myself briefly, to ask the Guides for help, inspiration, anything. But of course, when I need actual, practical help with a real, *earthly* problem, something that needs fixing with real-life ramifications, they're nowhere to be found. Fuming, I storm back to my desk and start piling the mess of files into three neat stacks, glancing at each set of instructions so I can put them vaguely in order of priority.

'Hey, Dot,' Bonnie frowns at me as she hangs up the phone. 'How you feeling? I didn't expect to see you back.'

'Yeah,' I smile weakly, forcing it past the urge to walk right over to Nathan and hit the smug, self-satisfied prick square in the face. I've never been in a physical fight in my life – I suspect I wouldn't know how to punch my way out of a wet paper bag – but the impulse remains. 'I don't think I'm staying. I still don't feel right.'

'Oh god, Dot,' she scampers quickly over to me, a concerned hand on my arm. 'For Christ's sake, get yourself back off home. Don't worry about this lot.'

'Yeah,' I nod quickly. I'd rather leave with more to show for my trip, but there's not a snowball's chance in hell I'm getting that phone out of his pocket. 'You mind telling Pat for me? I don't think I can deal with the lecture.'

'Oh, my pleasure,' her eyes light up at the prospect. 'We've all been volunteering to take the files, but she wouldn't let us, not even when Stephen started complaining. If only Rebecca was in—'

Hmm. Don't hold your breath.

'—I'd have gone straight to talk to her about it, but—'

'Thanks, Bonnie.'

She shrugs. 'You'd do the same for any of us, you always do. Look after yourself, okay? And please get some rest. You look absolutely knackered.'

Not a surprise.

Bonnie practically manhandles me to the landing, and I stew the whole way back down in the lift. As I step out, there's a lull at reception again and Jackie immediately clocks me. 'That was fast.'

I hesitate for a second.

Screw it.

I storm over to her, skipping any further pleasantries. 'This idea of yours. Can you do it without giving details?'

Jackie sees the look on my face and doesn't hesitate. 'Totally anonymous. He's on a shit list already and they're just *looking* for ammunition.'

I shake my head. 'I told you, Jack. No HR.'

She frowns back. 'I can't promise that. But I'll do what I can.'

I grimace, frustrated. I don't know what else to do; the damn thing lives in his pocket, for god's sake; how else can I get my hands on it? If I ran in dodgier circles maybe I could arrange a convenient mugging, or get some light-fingered friend to pinch it the next time he's propping up the bar at The Old Joint Stock, but I'm not that well connected.

If I go along with Jackie's idea, Mags may hate me. She might never forgive me for risking other people finding out what happened to her, when all she wants is for me to destroy the evidence so she can get on with her life and pretend it never happened at all. But if I don't, what chance do I have of actually helping her in the first place?

And if I don't get hold of that phone, what else might he do with that recording?

Or try to do to *her*.

'Do it.'

Jackie looks up, surprised. 'You sure?'

What choice do I have?

'As little detail as you can get away with. And no names but mine and his. Okay?'

She nods quickly. 'Okay.'

'I don't want to make things worse.'

'I'll do my best,' she leans forward sympathetically. 'You have my word.'

There are precious few people in my world whose word means anything at all. Jackie's word absolutely counts.

I only hesitate for one more second. 'Then do it.'

She breathes deeply. 'All right. I'll text you when I have news.'

I give her a brisk tip of my head in acknowledgement and head back out into the cold, all the while hoping I can find some way to get Mags to understand. She's going to be so hurt, and it's all my fault, and her words from our awful conversation last night echo through my brain: *You don't care about me, you wanted this to happen, you're jealous because nobody likes you.*

Nobody likes you.

My own name's always been at the top of that list.

20

I text Mags on my way back to Costa.

Couldn't get it yet, but there's a plan. See you in a couple of hours. Love you xx

Theo knew something was up as soon as I walked in.

'Did it go to plan?' he frowns doubtfully.

'Not exactly. You ready to go?'

'Still don't want to talk about it?'

I know he wants me to, and I understand why – he wants me to open up to him, to share my frustration, to help me – he wants to know that I trust him with it. But right now I just can't. I'm so angry, all he'll get is bluster and rage and none of it'll make any sense. Besides, I want to hold onto that feeling, use it to steel myself for dealing with Grace.

'Later, maybe. After…' I shake my head vaguely.

'After all this,' he suggests.

'Yeah.'

Although I haven't really thought that far.

'Just glad to hear there'll *be* an after,' he smiles. Its warmth is enough to drop my blood pressure from full raging meltdown to hacked off but strangely calm.

'One step at a time, Father,' I caution gently.

'Of course. Here, got you an Americano,' he holds a takeaway cup towards me shyly.

Of course he did, because he's lovely.

'Thanks.' I plant a quick, chaste peck on his fuzzy cheek as I take it to show my appreciation and he beams. 'I need this.'

'Ready for the next round?'

'Not really,' I groan, 'so let's go now before I lose my nerve.'

'Any idea what you're going to say to her?'

We hurry across the forecourt at Snow Hill, the chill in the autumn air turning it into a wind tunnel.

'I dunno,' I shrug, sipping as we trot briskly through the station before cutting across to the multi-storey car park. 'Ask her why she chickened out and did a runner? And what the hell's going on?'

'And why she told you to take me and leave,' he reminds me quietly.

'Yeah,' I look at him as we reach the car, all sad, dark eyes and gorgeousness, and my heart simultaneously aches for him and skips a beat with excitement. 'That too.'

Theo snickers happily.

'What?'

'We've done it again.' He lifts his hand and I see mine clasped in it.

I laugh in mild disbelief, amazed we've managed to walk all this without realising we were holding hands again. 'I don't even remember doing it.'

He twinkles back. 'You still are doing it.'

'So are you,' I point out.

'Yeah, but I think you started it,' he teases.

'Prove it,' I laugh, extricating my hand from his warmth as I fish around in my bag for the keys. 'It is weird though,' I admit, wondering which of us reached for the other first. 'Must be an instinctual thing.'

Theo's voice is suddenly low and needy as he leans towards me. 'I'll show you instinct.'

His kiss is unexpected, the closeness of him taking me by surprise, making my head spin. He tastes of coffee and sweet,

sweet bliss, the gentle caress of his fingertips against the bare skin of my neck sending shivers through me.

'*Get a room!*' a voice shouts from across the car park, breaking us up with a shared giggle as we turn to see a couple of teenagers laughing as they pass into the station.

'I wish,' Theo murmurs playfully against my ear.

'All right, down boy,' I admonish gently, choosing not to point out that if he wants to keep that dog collar of his, a room isn't a realistic option. More's the pity. 'We should get going.'

Theo shakes his head, sighing deeply. 'No time for love, Dr Jones.'

'Not right now, no,' the reference makes me laugh.

'After?' he raises a hopeful eyebrow.

'After,' I agree.

'Okay then.' He dashes to the passenger door, gesturing for me to open up. 'Well? Come on.'

I scoff my way to the drivers' side. 'Oh, now you want to go.'

'Hey, the sooner we go…'

I turn the key, both locks popping up as I reach to open my door.

'… the sooner it's after.' He winks over the top of the car before opening his side and scooting quickly into the seat.

'You're hopeless,' I feign despair as I climb in beside him.

'Hopeful,' he corrects me primly. 'Hope*ful.*'

I hand him my half-drunk cup. 'Here, make yourself useful and look after this.'

'What, they didn't have cupholders when you bought this car back in the 1800s?'

'Funny.'

It's a quick drive to the church from town; most of the morning traffic is heading into Brum rather than out of it. We joke around a little – he's noticeably less handsy than he was earlier though, and the closer we get, the more tension fills the atmosphere between us.

'You want me to come in with you again?'

I shake my head. 'Not this time. I don't want her to feel cornered. If she thinks we're ganging up on her—'

'—she won't cooperate,' he finishes.

I nod, taking a deep breath. 'Wish me luck.'

He reaches over and takes my hand back in his, squeezing it tightly. 'Go get her.'

His absolute faith that I can fills my heart, and I squeeze back as I get out. Here we go again, I think as I make my way towards the building. The front is still open as always, and as I step into the porch, I see the inside door has been propped wide with a heavy iron doorstop.

A voice echoes from inside as I cross the threshold. 'I wondered how long it'd take you to show up.'

Grace is sat in the front pew on the right, beside the aisle.

'You knew I had to come,' I reply simply.

'Of course. You want answers.'

She can't see me – she's facing the platform – but I nod anyway. 'Am I going to get them?'

Grace finally turns to look back at me with a weak smile. Today, she looks every bit of her sixty-eight years, every line suddenly etched deeply across her face, making her look fragile, almost defeated. It's the most human she's ever seemed in my whole entire life, and it takes me by surprise. 'Sit?' she asks tentatively, gesturing to the opposite pew.

She hasn't started a fight yet, and I'm not about to do it. Not today. I walk steadily down the aisle and take a seat at the end of the opposite pew, waiting to see what she has to say. Grace sighs, gazing wistfully up at the raised pulpit in front of us.

'Do you remember when you used to work the platform?' she finally asks.

The nostalgia in her voice catches me off guard. 'Not really,' I answer honestly. 'A vague impression here and there. I know I did it, but it's like…'

'Like what?'

'I dunno. Another life,' I suggest. 'Something that happened to somebody else.'

'Oh, Soteria.'

I fight back the instinct to react to the stupid name.

'You were a vision,' she says, voice full of wonder as she looks back to the platform, like she's picturing the memory. 'What you did for people, what you gave to them…'

The urge to roll my eyes at her rose-tinted recollection of my messed-up childhood is overpowering, so I force them tightly shut.

'…such *peace*. Such comfort. Oh, I mean, the rest of us who worked the platform – me, Shaun—'

I bristle visibly at the mention of his name.

'—the others who came and went over the years, we all passed our messages from the Guides to give people that solace, that belief in life after death. But you, you were *incomparable*. You were an inspiration, a whirlwind of hope and faith.'

'I was just a kid, Grace.'

My tone is measured, but with the best will in the world, I can't push all the simmering anger away, and some of it leaks out.

'A force of nature, a beacon of—'

'A fucking *kid*,' I snap. 'How old was I when you first stuck me up there?' I gesture up at the same platform she's going all misty-eyed over. 'What was I, eight, nine?'

I wait for her to bite back, but it doesn't happen.

'You were a prodigy,' she says quietly.

'For god's sake,' I shake my head angrily, not even trying to hide it now.

'You had a *gift*; I couldn't just let you waste it—'

'Some gift,' I rage, up on my feet. 'Do you remember how many friends I had at school? You remember how many times I came home crying to you because of bullies, kids torturing me because they thought I was some kind of fucking circus freak?'

Grace turns slowly in her seat to fully face me. 'Soteria, I—'

'Stop *calling* me that!' I explode completely. 'I am *not* your fucking Soteria, your little ghost-channelling puppet you can prance about on stage to boost your own inflated ego. I haven't been that girl since your precious fucking *boyfriend* pinned me face down in that room behind the platform and tried to rape me.'

'He didn't do it, did he?'

I'd like to say I'm shocked at the ice in her response, but it's basically the same one she gave me back when it happened, so. And okay, *technically* he didn't finish it. Doe she honestly think that makes it any better?

'Not for lack of fucking trying.'

'It was a difficult time, he was confused—'

'*Confused?!*' I yell, white heat through my veins as the long-suppressed memories of that time resurface back through years of careful burying. 'Where was he trying to put it, my schoolbag?'

'You know he wasn't—'

'I was twelve years old, for god's sake.'

'He'd been through so much, we all had, it was just—'

'You always made excuses for him.' I mutter dully. 'It was always him, always the Church, never *me*. I was just never a priority. Even after all that, you *still* kept making me work that damn platform.'

'The work you were doing was too valuable—'

'Not for one second did you even think about getting me *away* from it, away from *him*, or any other risks, any other harm it might all do.'

'What you could do was more important than—' she stops abruptly, realising she might have said too much.

'Go on,' I push her, 'say it. What I could *do* was always more important to you than *I* was. Bringing in punters to the Church with my special powers, your precious sacred cow. That always meant more to you than me being *safe*, or *whole*, or god *forbid*, just a normal bloody kid.'

Grace doesn't respond. She doesn't need to; it's not as though this has never come up before. My being 'difficult' as a teen was all because I wanted to give the whole thing up, I didn't want to do it anymore, and she wouldn't let me.

'Do you still remember what happened? With Shaun, I mean?'

'I've spent a lifetime trying to forget it.'

I never really have, not completely. Those fuzzy memories I mentioned before are still back there, lingering, and right now they're getting clearer again by the minute.

I came into church after school as usual, and he asked me to help him sort some study books in the back room ready for that night's circle. But when I got in there, he grabbed me, shoved me face down onto the cold tile floor, pulled up my school skirt, yanked down my knickers and got as far as having his fingers inside me before somebody pulled him off.

'Do you remember that Teddy was the one who… intervened?'

I remember *somebody* did. Was he one of the other mediums? My memories of the rest of the circle back then are as blurred as everything else. 'No. Who was he?'

'*Is*,' she corrects carefully. 'Who *is* Teddy.'

'Okay, whatever,' I bite, 'who *is* Teddy?'

Grace swallows awkwardly, unsure. 'Not long before that…

that business. There was a clearance. Do you remember that?'

I don't. 'Was I there?'

She nods. 'Teddy, too. You were only supposed to be there as a couple of extra hands. Both of you were too young to take part directly, we didn't even have you sit in the circle.'

I wait for her to go on.

'You had such… I'm sorry, I know you hate for me to talk about it, but you had *such* power as a medium, Dot. Nearly forty years I've been doing this, professionally, and I've never seen another with that sort of power. And I'm not just saying that because you're my daughter,' she adds quickly.

I wonder where all this is leading.

'So powerful,' she muses to herself. 'I honestly believed back then you were truly destined for a higher calling, that maybe you'd even end up leading the Church one day. And not just our little one here,' she gestures to the building around us. 'To watch you work, see what you could do, the link you had with the other side… you straddled the line between us and them as if the veil didn't even *exist* for you. It was… awe inspiring.'

I've never heard her talk like this before.

'But,' she goes on carefully, 'that was nothing compared to when you and Teddy worked together.'

Okay, now I'm not sure if I'm just super confused or if she's finally gone completely batshit insane. 'I don't remember anyone in the circle called Teddy.'

'There's a reason for that,' she nods quietly.

'Which is?'

'Let me tell it in my own way,' she urges. 'Please?'

I nod, indicating for her to go on.

'He joined the church with his parents a year or so before everything happened. The two of you were inseparable from the start. It wasn't until they'd been coming for a couple of months when we realised he was a gifted medium in his own right – nowhere near your level, of course, nobody in the circle was, but he had it in him, it was undeniable. And there you were, both of you so gifted in your different ways, and so lonely, no other kids your age to be friends with. You bonded so quickly, and the first time you worked the platform together, it was *electric*.'

I have zero memory of any of this.

'What happened to him?'

She eyes me carefully. 'After what happened… the clearance, Shaun. His parents left the church. They moved away.'

'What *did* happen?'

Grace takes a deep breath. 'The clearance went wrong.'

Uh-oh. This sounds familiar.

'It was more powerful than we realised. None of us were prepared for it. We tried to fight it, but it took control of everyone in the circle in turn, one after another. Like it was trying to feel us out, try each of us *on*. It was only later we realised what it wanted.'

I will myself to stay patient and let her get it out in her own time, but it's not a virtue I'm renowned for at the best of times and right now, it's wearing incredibly thin.

'The two of you kids had to step in. The power you shared is what sent it back into the light.'

She looks up at me now, hoping I understand.

I start to. 'Are you trying to tell me it's the *same thing*?'

Grace leans back, sighing with relief.

'Seriously? You're telling me the thing in that house that's been terrorising my friends, the thing that sent half a dozen of your mediums packing yesterday, is the *same thing* you couldn't get rid of all those years ago?'

She nods urgently. 'That's why I told you, you *can't* stay there.'

'But you said we sent it back before. Me and this Teddy guy.'

'It was so powerful,' she mutters, mostly to herself, '*so* powerful, I've seen nothing like it before or since, and if it gets what it wants—'

'Grace, what does it want?'

She witters on to herself.

'*Grace.*'

Her head snaps up.

'What does it want?'

She looks at me like I'm being wilfully stupid. 'Why, *you* of course.'

I frown back at her. What?

'*What?*'

'It wants *you*. To get into you, to have control over you, your power. Back then, when you and Teddy joined together and used your Voice you forced it back, but—'

How does she know about the Voice? 'What? The Voice? What do you mean?'

'Your *Voice*. It's your link with Teddy, the two of you created it together. Your bond, that faith in each other that could never break. The connection between the two of you was always so *fierce*, that's why I was so shocked when you turned up here yesterday and—'

Grace breaks off abruptly. Too abruptly.

I look at her suspiciously. 'What *about* when I turned up here yesterday?'

She reaches into the pocket of her cardigan, pulling out a tattered, folded piece of paper.

'Grace? What about yesterday?'

She opens the piece of paper, gazing at it sadly, and as I try not to completely lose my mind, not to mention my temper, I look at it and realise it's not a piece of paper at all. It's a photograph.

'After everything that happened,' she continues slowly, 'after the clearance, we had you both put under hypnosis. To block it out, you understand, to bury it, to make you both forget. You were both so young, you shouldn't have been dragged into it, either of you, you shouldn't have had to fight that thing when the rest of us couldn't.'

She leans across the aisle and reaches out to hand me the picture. I take the small square and unfold it carefully.

'When you showed up, I was so shocked. I thought you must—' she shakes her head sadly. 'When we came to the house, I realised you didn't know.'

It's faded, but not terribly. It's a group shot, taken in the very late eighties or early 90s, going by the clothes, and there she is, Grace at the peak of her glory days. There's Shaun, another couple I don't recognise, and in front, a kiddie version of my mousy haired self. But my eyes are drawn immediately to the last figure in the picture, a boy beside me, about my age, maybe a year or two older. The two of us are facing the camera, arms around each other, laughing as I playfully try to plant a big kiss on his cheek and he playfully tries to stop me.

I have no memory of this boy.

This boy who I was clearly incredibly close with, who according to Grace I was inseparable from, who I worked the platform with, who helped me fight this thing, who I forged some super-duper powerful psychic link with to connect us together when we ventured to the Other Side, so that we could look out for one another and protect each other and face the world – and the otherworld – safe in the sanctuary of our shared Voice.

No memory at all. Except...

... now that I look, there's something about the eyes. Something so familiar, a warmth, a sweetness. Something in the smile on his face as he teases me, in the unruly mop of dark brown hair, rudely distorted by the decades-old crease through the middle of the photo. When my brain finally catches up with my eyes, I nearly fall off the pew.

'No.'

Grace nods. 'Yes.'

'*No.*'

'Yes, Dot.'

The boy in the picture is Theo.

21

'It can't be.'

Grace is quiet.

'Grace, it can't be.'

'It is,' she replies simply.

My brain tries desperately to make sense of the truth I can see in front of my eyes but can't bring myself to accept.

'When I saw the two of you here together, I...' she starts hesitantly. 'I honestly thought you had to have found each other. Deliberately, I mean, sought each other out. It clicked when you told me his name, that's when I realised, but you didn't seem to.'

'His name?'

'Theo. Theodore? *Teddy?*'

I never made the connection. But then, I have no memory of *Teddy* ever existing.

'But I don't remember *any* of this,' I wave the picture vaguely in the air, hoping the movement might erase it like an old Etch-A-Sketch.

'I told you; we hypnotised both of you to forget what happened.'

'You said you hypnotised us to forget the clearance.'

'At first. But then, the business with Shaun, and Teddy—'

'Don't call him that,' I instinctively reply. 'His name's Theo.'

Grace nods calmly. 'With Theo being the one to stop Shaun...' She looks away briefly. 'After everything else that had already happened, his parents left the church a couple of months later and moved. When you two were separated, that's when you started… when things started going downhill. With both of you.'

Twelve. Twelve years old and that's what sent me off the rails. Losing him. Well, not *just* that, I realise – there was a whole bunch of other awful shit, clearly – but Theo was my final defence against everything tearing me apart, and without him…

'Without him, you were lost. Without you, *he* was lost,' Grace explains.

'But why don't I remember him? Why doesn't he remember me?'

'You were so hurt when they took him away.' Her voice is suddenly tiny. 'So desperately sad. You locked yourself away, wouldn't eat, couldn't function. When I spoke to his parents and found he was the same…'

My heart is thumping so loud in my chest that I'm amazed I can even hear her.

'We took both of you back. For more hypnosis.'

I can't speak.

'We agreed it was for the best.'

I look at her in horror. 'To *forget* each other?'

'To help you *cope* with him being gone,' she pleads. 'Him too. The bond you two shared was so strong. That Voice, we had to silence it so both of you could get on with your lives.'

Finally, I think understand. 'That's why you told me to *take him* and leave the house.'

'Yes. He fought it with you, that's what got rid of it all those years ago. If it's brought the two of you back together intentionally, he's just as much at risk as you are.'

'But that makes no sense,' I point out. 'If between us we can fight it, why the hell would it want to bring us back *together?*'

She shakes her head. 'Theo isn't what he was then. He's a priest now, for god's sake, he doesn't even know he has that power in him. And it attacked him before, targeted him deliberately, you thought.'

'Yeah? So?'

Grace shrugs unhappily. 'It's using him as bait.'

'*Bait?*'

'To get to you,' she goes on. 'As long as he's there, and can't use his power because he doesn't remember, it knows you'll do anything to keep him from harm. Which makes you vulnerable. It's just waiting for an opening— when your defences are down, when you're weak or you're tired from trying to protect him— for a chance to get in and take control of you. To get its hands on *your* power.'

'Why does it even *want* that?'

'Not for anything good.'

'What *is* it?'

'It's an old spirit, very old,' she replies wearily. 'An evil one. You saw its form start to take shape yesterday.'

I recall that vague but unnerving outline of horns and claws and shudder at the memory.

Now I understand how Theo saw it too. He's a medium.

Theo's a medium.

'Something ancient, about as close to an actual demonic presence as really exists,' Grace goes on. 'A spiritual demon, I suppose you could call it.'

I breathe deeply. This is an awful lot to take in.

'How do we stop it?' I ask her finally.

'You did it before, the two of you,' she reminds me. 'If anyone has a chance of doing it again…'

I shake my head, staring at my feet. 'He wasn't a Vicar then.'

Theo, a medium. How the hell is he going to take this?

Grace laughs, a little unkindly. 'What nonsense. Remember what I told you yesterday about his faith? How strong it is?

You had him use it in a chant, as the talisman to protect him, for him to help protect you, yes?'

I nod quietly.

Grace leans across the aisle. 'That faith of his has *nothing* to do with his church. It's faith in *you*.'

I raise my head to meet her gaze.

'I felt it,' she tells me fiercely, 'my Guides felt it, coursing through him. He has *such* faith in you.'

And I sort of already knew that, didn't I? I have this whole time. I felt it, I knew it, I just didn't really…*get* it.

'Such *love* for you,' she adds gently.

*And you for hi*m, she doesn't say, but I don't need to be psychic to read her thoughts.

'Somewhere in there, some part of him remembers what you were together.'

My mind is reeling. We were so drawn to each other at the party, we connected so easily and strongly from the start, like we'd know each other for years. Was it all just down to some deeply buried childhood memory? To the shared trauma which put both of us on the path to a lifetime of self-destruction, trying to outrun our teenage pain?

Was that all it really was between us? Is that all it *is*?

Is anything I feel for him even *real?* Is anything he feels for me?

'How do I even start to tell him.'

It's not a question for Grace, and she knows better than to answer. The silence hangs heavy around us for a minute. I need to leave – Theo needs to know all this, and soon – but my legs feel like lead, not to mention my poor aching heart. Oh, for a week ago when it was cold, coal-black and made mostly of stone. Mostly.

'You're still determined to go back there?'

I nod. 'I can't just leave them like this.'

'It doesn't want *them*,' Grace reminds me. 'It wants you.'

'That doesn't change their situation, Grace.'

Just because she refuses to put on her big girl pants and face up to deal with this once and for all, doesn't mean I won't. I am *not* my mother's daughter.

'I realise that.'

'Surely if anyone might have a chance of getting rid of it for good, it's me and him.'

Grace nods carefully. 'But he needs to remember who he is first. He's no use to you if he can't.'

She says it so callously, like he couldn't possibly have any other worth, and I hate her for it. For that, for burying my memory of him in the first place, for taking away my childhood with all this, for taking Shaun's side over mine, for constantly putting him and the church before me until I finally gave up on her. For all of it.

'He will.'

'And the love you two have for one another, if it's really—'

Uh-oh, old rolleyes is back. 'Yeah, yeah.' I stand abruptly, suddenly wanting to get as far away from her as I can as fast as possible.

'If it's as strong as I *know* you believe,' she stands to mirror me, 'and I know you do believe it, Dot, that's part of your power too. Just like that family you want to protect so much, the love that binds them together is what gave *them* strength yesterday.'

I turn to leave. 'Thanks for your help, Grace.' I even mean it, a little.

She grabs my arm as I turn down the aisle. 'Your love is your strength, remember. Yours and Teddy's.'

I wince at the name.

'*Remember* that, Dot,' she urges.

I nod miserably. 'I'll remember.'

'Good luck.'

I'm not sure what else to say. Goodbye doesn't seem like enough, and I don't know how likely it is that I'll see her again. Or if I'll even want to. Somehow, I doubt it. There's just been far too much water under this particular bridge.

'Look after yourself, Grace,' I tell her over my shoulder as I turn down the aisle and walk away from my childhood for the last time.

22

The moment I catch sight of him through the windscreen as I reach the car the floodgates just *open*. Proper, ugly, red-faced sobbing, tears pouring from everywhere on my face.

Then memories start to hit me. Little flashes, pictures of things long-since forgotten and now unlocked, trickling out of my buried consciousness like a second set of tears inside my head.

Me and Teddy playing tag around the church. Making patterns with sparklers together on bonfire night. Riding the waltzers they used to have at the old fireworks display at Perry Park, falling into one another as they spun us around in our shared little world. Getting the train into Birmingham, going to the pictures to see Indiana Jones and the Last Crusade at the Odeon on New Street, throwing popcorn at each other while he teased me about my crush on Harrison Ford.

Oh my *god*.

A memory which feels all too recently familiar comes crawling through from the archives into the front of my brain, as though I'm watching it unfold right before my eyes, and the force of it is overwhelming.

I think he was my first kiss.

Just then Theo looks up. Seeing the state I'm in, he jumps out of the passenger side and rushes towards me, fear and worry written across his face showing every facet of his good, sweet, open heart and I crumple helplessly into his arms.

'Jesus, Dot, what happened?'

I can't speak, I can only howl as memories of Teddy – no, *Theo* – flood through me like a tidal wave.

'Dot, shh, I'm here,' he tries to soothe me. 'Please, Dot, what's wrong? Talk to me, *please*.'

I force myself to catch my breath, gulping down my cries to stifle them as they burn through my chest.

'That's it. Deep breaths.'

I steady myself against him, breathing in the sensation of my head against his chest, of his arms wrapped around me, of his soft kisses on the top of my head, all the while wondering if this will be the last moment I get to have them.

'What did she say? Come on, Dot. Please tell me what's wrong.'

Looking up finally into those pleading eyes, his face desperately searching mine. I can't bear to tell him that all of it – everything we've felt over the last few days – might be nothing more than our shared ghost of the past. But he has to know.

Slowly, I reach up and hand him the picture, sniffing through my tears. 'She gave me this.'

'What is it?' he takes it from me, opens it, looks at it. 'A photo?'

Theo looks at it, bewildered.

'Wait a second. Is that *me?* And that's my parents.'

I wait for the penny to drop. Give his mind a second to figure it out. Maybe that'll ease the blow.

'But I don't recognise—'

Then he freezes, and his eyes fill with sudden confusion as he looks back at me, back at the picture, back at me. 'It can't be.'

I sigh dully. 'It is.'

'How is this possible? This is *you?* But— I don't— how can—'

'I know,' I look up at him, my heart breaking, tiny little ice chips already starting to settle back in there, piling up ready to protect me from his inevitable rejection once everything comes back to him and he realises the last few days have been a lie.

The seconds pass silently between us.

'I don't understand,' he finally says.

I nod toward the car. 'Can we sit?'

Once we're inside, I turn the engine on to run the heaters. We might as well be comfortable as everything we thought about ourselves and our pasts and our memories comes crashing down around us.

And then I tell him. Everything Grace told me, about him joining the church with his parents, about his being able to do what I can do, about us doing it together. I tell him about the clearance they did that went so wrong, that we were the ones who fixed it, about the first bout of hypnosis, what happened afterwards with Shaun and Theo's part in stopping it, his parents finally leaving and both of us coping so badly our parents decided to wipe us out of each other's minds for good. He just lets me talk, all of it tumbling out, probably not all even making sense, and after I'm done he sits there quietly, rubbing his head with his elbow propped up against the window, eyes closed. I'm not sure how long we stay that way. It feels like hours, although I know it's nowhere near. All I want is for him to react, to say something – anything – but at the same time, I'm so terrified he'll say he doesn't want to be near me ever again.

When he does eventually open his mouth, his voice is low and quiet, barely more than a whisper.

'We used to go to the pictures together. All the time.'

My heart flutters. He's remembering.

I nod. 'Yeah.'

He opens his eyes and turns to look at me, and I can see they're rimmed with tears. 'Did we go ice skating? At Silver—'

'—Blades!' I finish with a shocked squeal, his mention of it jolting a vivid picture suddenly into my head: holding hands as we dragged each other around the rink, him falling down onto the ice and pulling me with him, both of us laughing and terrified of losing our gloved fingers to the blade of somebody else's skates, getting burgers from the Wimpy down the road afterwards.

'They made me… *forget* you,' Theo murmurs, leaning forwards into the tiny passenger space, head in his hands. 'Jesus.'

'They made us *both* forget.'

'The thing with— what happened with that— *man*,' he glowers. 'I didn't ask you any more about it, I figured if you wanted to tell me, you'd do it in your own time. But I was *there*.'

I nod gratefully. 'You stopped it.'

And now I really do remember. What Shaun did – tried to do – it was never about me, not in the way you'd think. It was about my ability and his jealousy of it; what I could do that he couldn't. Attacking me like that was his twisted way of trying to take it, as though he could catch it from me like a disease.

'I always knew, I *knew* something was wrong.' There's an edge in Theo's voice I haven't heard before. 'Like there was a hole, something missing, and I could never figure it out, I could never fill it, but I always *knew*—'

I reach out, wanting to calm him. 'I know, Theo—'

'*No*, Dot, don't you see?' He turns angrily to face me, the words suddenly flowing so fast, tripping over one another to fight their way out of him. 'I was always looking for it, always trying to find it, to fill that hole, and that's how everything got so out of control and *nothing helped*, it just kept getting worse. Even since I sorted myself out, since I joined the Church, I still knew deep down there was something in me that wasn't really *right*, something I didn't understand, something that was missing.'

He finally breaks off, breathless, shaking his head as he takes my hand in his, cradling the side of my face with such tenderness that I can *feel* the wrench through my heart start to sob.

'I never imagined that the thing that was missing was *you*.'

Wait, so – he *doesn't* hate me?

He looks at me like I've gone crazy. 'What? Of course not, god no, how could I ever *hate* you, Dot?'

Oh. *Oh.*

Oh shit.

All those times he finished my sentences, said out loud something I'd just been thinking…

'You really *can* read my mind.'

'What?'

'What you just said,' I tell him, my heart beating at a rate that isn't healthy. 'About hating me. That's what I was just thinking. But I didn't say it out loud.'

Theo's forehead wrinkles in confusion. 'What? Are you saying…'

I look at him in shock. 'You've been doing it this whole time.'

'You mean— I—'

He knows I'm right.

'But *how?*'

I didn't get to this part yet. 'Remember what I told you about that Voice, that thing that isn't a Guide, the one I've never really understood?'

Theo blinks at me, oblivious.

'Grace said that's *you*. Or, it's this link we have between us, a psychic connection.'

He searches my eyes, trying to understand. 'But didn't you— I thought you said that at the party you went somewhere else in your head to talk to the Voice.'

'Yeah.' Finally, I see it. 'When you were right there next to me.'

'But how could I be— I don't— I didn't *do* anything.'

'It's not your conscious mind, Theo. It's another part of you, somewhere else, this part that's been locked away and forgotten about all this time. I used to hear it on and off through the years, like it was calling for me, like it *needed* me, but I didn't understand.'

'That was me?'

'I think so. Maybe. When you were…' my voice cracks at the thought of it, '…struggling. And I heard it whenever *I* was struggling too, like *it* was trying to help *me*.'

Theo looks shellshocked.

'Then there it was again on the doorstep of that house, telling me to stop, not to go in. And *you* were already in there. That part of you, the part in the back of your mind that you didn't even know was there, it knew something was wrong and felt me coming and tried to warn me.'

There are tears in my eyes again. This man, this beautiful, good, sweet man – without even knowing who or what he was – at his core, his subconscious instinct was to try and protect me, to stop me from walking into harm, even though consciously he didn't even know me. My heart swells, filled with emotion, with the pain of everything that he and I have both been through all these years separated from each other, with the sad thought of what might have been if only we could've shared them instead. And after a lifetime of thinking it wasn't possible, of believing it was something I'd never be capable of feeling, I suddenly know without a single doubt in my mind that I love this man.

When I look back at Theo, he's smiling, eyes shining. 'Really?' he asks happily.

Dammit. Mind reader. 'You have to stop doing that.'

He laughs warmly. 'I'm sorry, I swear I'm not doing it on purpose. I wouldn't even know how.' Then he stops, swallowing awkwardly. 'I love you too. And not just because of all this,' he stammers out quickly. 'I was already thinking it before, but I didn't dare say anything, I thought you'd think I was insane, because we barely know each other, but now, I mean, now it just…'

'Makes sense.'

That eyebrow of his pops up again. 'Now who's reading whose mind?'

'I'm not,' I protest, 'that was just—'

Theo leans in quickly to kiss me quiet, and the thought fades to nothing as he sweeps me back under the waves with him again. Then he pulls back, startled. 'Oh my god. That's why— last night, when you kissed me the first time, it felt so *familiar*. Like coming home.'

He searches my eyes for confirmation.

'Because it *wasn't* the first time. Right?'

I nod. 'Are you getting that one from me again? Or do you remember?'

'I remember there was popcorn,' he recalls slowly. 'So we must've been at the pictures. You were banging on about how gorgeous Indiana Jones was, and I think I might've been jealous, so…'

'You kissed me.'

'I kissed you.'

I shake my head with a smile. 'To shut me up.'

'Basically,' he laughs.

'I'd had *such* a huge crush on you, before that. For ages.'

'Not as much as you did on Indiana Jones,' he teases.

'Oh god, *so* much more,' I confess as the picture of my preteen hormonal self comes crashing into full view. 'I'd thought about kissing you hundreds of times, about what it'd be like, but I didn't have a clue what to do. When you actually did it, for a second I thought my head had exploded.'

'I was your first kiss, wasn't I?'

'You were. Hell of a first kiss, too,' I tell him wistfully. 'Ruined me for everyone else after.'

'I'm sorry.'

'I'm not.'

'You know… you weren't my first kiss, right?'

'I know,' I shrug. 'You had a couple of years on me, I didn't mind.'

Theo sighs suddenly, his arm around me. 'Can we just carry on like this?'

'What, talking about kissing and Indiana Jones?'

He looks at me seriously, reaching up and twiddling my hair in his fingers. 'You know what I mean.'

I know what he means. 'We can't just leave it like this.'

'But I can't… Grace told you we had a chance if we fight it together, right? But what if I… I mean, I *saw* you, Dot. I *saw* what you can do. I can't *do* that.'

'You can,' I correct him. 'You just don't remember.'

'What if I *can't* remember,' Theo counters, anguished. 'What if we go back there to fight it and I *still* can't remember, and you have to do it alone, and you—'

He breaks off abruptly, looking away.

'I don't want to lose you again,' he says quietly.

I reach out toward him, my hand stroking the scruff of his cheek as I turn his face gently back to mine. 'You won't,' I tell him firmly.

'If you got hurt because of me—'

'I won't.'

'If I let you down—'

'You *won't*.'

'I don't know if I could…' his voice breaks. 'I couldn't take that.'

I see where he's going, and I won't let him start down that road. 'Listen to me,' I tell him sternly. 'Your conscious mind doesn't remember, I know that. But *something* inside you does. The Voice, remember? You already warned me, you've already been in there with me, helping me.'

Theo doesn't look convinced.

'Sticking your nosy beak into my head,' I tease, gentler now, 'reading my thoughts.'

He smiles sadly. 'I told you. I don't know how I'm doing that.'

'But you're still doing it.'

'But I—' he sighs, knowing I'll just keep arguing. 'I don't want you to get hurt. I don't want it to hurt *you*.'

I shake my head. 'It's not going to. It can't, can it? If Grace is right, if what it really wants is to get inside my head, to take control of whatever it is it thinks I can do that's so bloody amazing, it can't *afford* to hurt me, surely? It *needs* me in one piece.'

'That explains why it only throws things at *my* head.'

'To bait me, she said,' I recall Grace's words. 'But I wonder if it's more than that. I wonder if it's scared of us. It wants to stop us from fighting it together.'

'Like we did before.'

I nod back, his face warm against my hand as I look into those endless eyes of his. 'To stop you from protecting me.'

'Hmm. Wants to stop me protecting you, eh?' The sound from his throat is low, almost feral, his jaw tightening along with his grip on me, which suddenly feels deeply, disarmingly possessive. As someone who's always been incredibly independent, I've never been keen on the idea of a partner thinking they own any part of me. I'm very much my own person, and the only one I've ever felt comfortable belonging to is myself. But I have to admit, coming from him, it's pretty hot. Even more so when he pulls me in for another frantically passionate kiss, growling in my ear. 'Let the fucker try.'

'That's the spirit, Father Gregory,' I smile teasingly as we come back up for air.

He groans. 'What the hell do I put in my pastoral care report. *Christ*.'

'Don't take his name in vain,' I tell him prudishly.

'You do it all the time.'

'I'm not a Vicar.'

'Not sure I will be after all this,' he mutters dully.

I eye him warily. 'What do you mean?'

'Come on, Dot. You know the Church's stance. You've beaten me round the head with it enough the last few days.'

'So?'

'So? Well, I can hardly be true to my faith and be a medium at the same time, can I?'

I frown up at him. 'Nobody's suggesting you start talking to dead people in the middle of Sunday service. This is a one-time thing, just to get rid of this thing for good. Then you never have to think about it again.'

Theo shakes his head firmly. 'I don't want to hide from what I am.'

'Don't know why not,' I shrug casually. 'It's worked for me for a lifetime.'

Has it, though? Really?

'And then there's that, as well.'

'What?'

'When all of this is over, there's you,' he sighs. 'Us.'

'You putting that in your pastoral care report?'

'I mean it, Dot. As long as I'm a Vicar, we can't— I mean, even if we're together, you know— we can't—'

'Unless we're married. I know. We had this conversation.'

'And even if we were married…'

My eyes are like saucers. What now? I know we joked about it before – when we were hot and heavy and horny – but he actually sounds *serious*.

'… even if I could bury that part of me again, nobody could ever know what you can do. You'd have to hide too.'

'I just told you, I've been doing that my whole life anyway.'

Theo looks surprised. 'You mean, *nobody* knows? I thought you were joking.'

'Well, paying clients do. But they don't know me outside of that. It's not like I advertise.'

'What about your friend? The one with the problem you've been trying so hard to solve? Does she know?'

'Mags?' I shake my head. 'God, no. Nobody from work. Rebecca didn't know until I got roped into this. Lisa, my roommate,' I go on, 'she knows I do readings. But she doesn't really get what it is, not properly. She thinks it's just tea leaves or tarot cards or some crap like that. I don't think she understands it's real.'

'Why? Why don't you tell anyone?'

I hold his gaze levelly. 'Would you?'

He hesitates for a second. 'I wouldn't be announcing it to people on the street. But the people around you, your friends, the people you care about... for them not to know about something that's such a fundamental part of who you are, it just seems...'

'What?'

Theo shrugs unhappily. 'It just seems like such a shame. For you, I mean. You must spend your whole life looking over your shoulder, worrying that somebody might find out.'

He's not wrong.

'That's true. I just...' I shake my head as he waits quietly. 'Look, I've always had a hard enough time making friends in the first place. The last thing I need is to scare off the few I *do* have by making them think I'm a nutter.'

Mags, Jackie, Lisa, Penny. Right now, Mags is tenuous at best, and depending on what happens with Jackie's master plan, that friendship might be damaged for good. If I were to leave my stupid job tomorrow, would Jackie bother keeping in touch? Will Lisa and Penny, once they inevitably end up getting a place of their own? Add my particular flavour of supernatural weirdness on top of all of that, and who knows if it'd even take *any* outside forces for all of them to just leave me in the dust.

'You don't trust them?'

His suggestion stops me in my tracks. 'Well, I mean— of course I do, but— I—'

I can't think of a way to finish that sentence.

Before Theo has chance to push it any further, a double beep rings out from my bag and I scramble to grab it. Saved by the bell, or in this case, a text from Jackie.

10am tomorrow. They want rid of him, so it's HR only IF you find what you're expecting. Is that a problem?

Dammit. I knew it wouldn't be straightforward. I have to talk to Mags about this.

I text back quickly.

I'll sort it.

Bubbles appear on my screen as I watch it intently, Theo watching me in turn.

Meet me at the back entrance, 9.45. I'll let you in and we can get the bastard x

See you then x

I sigh deeply, an uncomfortable feeling of foreboding creeping into the pit of my stomach. It feels eerily as though all sides of my life are on a crash course. Time to face Mags. And the music.

'Time to go. Belt up,' I tell Theo as I do the same.

'We're going back to the house already?' he frowns dubiously.

'Not that one. I need to stop off at mine, to see my friend.'

'The one with the problem?'

I nod, light raindrops starting to smatter across the windscreen as I pull out.

'Can you fix it?'

What a question. Can I convince Mags to be okay with

whatever Jackie's cooked up, if it means involving HR? Can whatever her plan is even work?

Even if it does, and any immediate threat to Mags is over… can anything *really* be fixed for her?

'I hope so,' is all I can reply.

23

Mags hasn't replied to my text as we arrive at my place. I park as close to the house as I can, noticing Penny's car in the spot I usually take. At least she's still here keeping Mags company, even though I'm the one who promised to do that, I think guiltily to myself. In the end I wasn't here for her at all.

When I turn to Theo, he's peeking curiously through the windscreen, still wet from the rain shower. 'Which one is it?'

I point it out.

'You rent it with your housemate?'

'Lisa. Not everyone's job comes with a free house, you know,' I tease gently.

Theo laughs. 'Is she home?'

'Nope, she's a paramedic, she'll be on shift until later. Her girlfriend Penny's here though, she stays over a lot.'

'Hmm. And your friend?'

'Margaret. But everyone calls her Mags.'

He does that thing again where I can tell he wants to say something but he's not sure how.

'What?'

'If you need privacy... I mean, I don't have to come in. I'd love to see it, but...'

'Leave you sat here on your lonesome in my cold, wet deathtrap of a car?'

'You did earlier.'

'Because it was *Grace*,' I remind him, wide-eyed. 'I would've stayed in the car if I could've got away with it.'

He considers for a moment. 'You sure you want me to?'

'Come on.' I interrupt him with a roll of my eyes as I climb out and wait for him to follow.

As we walk up to the house, I spy a sliver of light flashing through a gap in the closed living room curtains. Someone's got the telly on, and as I open up and step into the hall, Theo close behind, I hear noise, raised voices, not in English. I poke my head round the door and Penny's curled up on the sofa, lights off, a half-eaten Subway beside a glass of juice on the coffee table, entirely focused on some Korean thing with zombies.

'Pen?'

She jumps out of her seat, with a squeal sending cushions and the remote tumbling. 'Shit. Jesus, Dot, you scared the crap out of me.'

Theo hovers behind me as I open the door the rest of the way. His appearance shocks her all over again. 'Oh! Sorry, Father.'

He smiles awkwardly as she looks back to me.

'Is Mags having an exorcism?'

Theo chokes out a little laugh behind me.

'No, Pen. This is Theo, he's…'

I have no clue how to introduce him. In fact, I'm not sure if words which accurately describe who he is to me at this point even exist.

'Here for moral support,' he comes to my rescue.

'Not sure Mags is up for being saved by the power of prayer,' Pen muses dubiously.

'Moral support for me,' I explain. 'How is she?'

'Pissed you didn't come home last night,' she shrugs apologetically. 'Not eating. I guilted her into hanging out with me yesterday, but her heart wasn't in it. She's been holed up in your room all morning.'

None of this sounds good. 'Did she tell you what happened?

Either of you?'

'Not in detail. Little bits. Not hard to put two and two together.' Penny shakes her head angrily. 'Fucking *men*. Sorry, Father. Present company excepted, I'm sure.'

Theo makes a don't-worry-about-it gesture, then I feel his hand on my shoulder with a gentle squeeze. I wonder how much of Mags' situation he can see inside my mind right now. 'Why don't I go and make us all a drink?' he suggests warmly.

'Oh, sorry,' Penny steps forward with a start, 'where are my manners. I should've offered.'

'Don't be silly,' he waves her back amiably, turning to me. 'Just point me in the direction of the kitchen. You want tea? White, one sugar?'

I only have that when I'm stressed or sick, so he definitely plucked that information out of my head. He's only seen me drink coffee.

'Are you sure?'

'Of course,' he smiles back affectionately. 'Same for Mags, right? How about you Penny, you want a coffee?'

'I'd love one,' she drops back onto the sofa with a massive grin. 'Milky please, two sugars.'

Theo nods. 'Door at the other end of the hall?'

'Yeah, but—'

'I've got it.' He squeezes my shoulder again and turns down the hall. God, he's so good.

'He's *nice*,' Penny hisses in a stage whisper once he's gone. 'But since when have you been into men of the cloth? I thought you hated anything to do with the Church?'

'It's complicated,' I mutter. 'Look, I'm gonna go up and try and talk to Mags. Thank you, for looking after her I mean. I'm sorry I wasn't here.'

'Don't worry about it,' she shrugs matter-of-factly. 'Lisa and

I both know you wouldn't have stayed away last night unless it was for a good reason.'

The knot in my stomach settles a little. 'Thanks, Pen.'

'She knows that too, you know,' Penny tips her head up towards my room above us. 'She just… she was lashing out last night. You're the closest one to her, so you're the easiest target.'

'I hope you're right.'

'I'm always right,' she grins. 'I'll keep your nice Vicar company while you're up there.'

'How did you know he was a Vicar? Everyone usually assumes priest.'

Penny shrugs casually. 'He doesn't have that tightarse Catholic vibe. Met a lot of Vicars over the years. My dad's a Reverend, you know.'

Well, isn't this week just full of surprises.

Leaving Penny to the joys of South Korean horror, I head upstairs, hovering outside my closed bedroom door for a second while I gather myself together, then knock lightly.

No response.

'Mags?'

Nothing.

Letting out a deep breath, I open the door slowly and peek my head inside. 'Mags?'

It's dark in there with the curtains closed. The bag she packed when we left hers is slung up against the near wall, contents spilling out, toiletries and scraps of clothes littering the rug at the foot of the bed. On the floor in front of the bedside table, I can just about make out a plate of dry, untouched toast and a similarly neglected bowl of Cheerios, alongside half-drunk mugs of tea and a couple of small, empty bottles of orange Lucozade. Well, at least she's been hydrating.

'Mags?' She's curled up under the covers, cocooned in

darkness, facing away from me towards the window as I approach and perch down gently on the end of the bed. I'm not sure if she's genuinely sleeping, or just ignoring me.

Then she speaks, her voice hoarse from three days of crying. 'I saw your text. You didn't get it.'

'I'm sorry.'

'Why not?'

'He had it in his pocket.'

I don't tell her that before he put it there, he was cackling with Pat about something. A part of me still holds out hope that whatever they were looking at was nothing to do with her.

A long, defeated sigh comes from the pile of bedclothes as she pulls them closer around her.

'I thought he might have to turn it in for a meeting and maybe I could get it then. But there's nothing booked in.'

'That's not your plan? Your text said there was a plan.'

Not my plan. Jackie's plan. I hesitate. I need to tell her – she needs to understand the implications if Jackie's solution works, whatever that solution is – but I don't know how well she's going to take it, especially now I'm seeing up close for myself just how hard she's given up already.

'There is.'

Mags finally lifts her head from the pillow, pulling the duvet away from her face. Even in this dim light, I can see the puffiness, eyes blown up and crusted with sleep, hair in disarray. 'What is it?'

Okay. Deep breaths.

'I can get it. Tomorrow morning, ten AM. But you might not be happy about how. And I don't know if it's worse to do that or leave things as they are.'

'How?'

Here we go. 'I've had to get help.'

'You *told* someone?!' she explodes.

'I didn't know what else to do, okay? And I didn't tell her anything, not anything specific, but…'

'Who?' she demands. 'Who did you tell?'

'I didn't really tell anyone,' I backpedal, panicking. 'I asked Jackie if she could see his diary, but I didn't tell her why. Not exactly. But you know her, she's not daft. She sort of…'

'*What?*' The harshness in her voice punches me in the gut.

'She put two and two together.'

Mags groans deeply, head in her hands.

'Look,' I go on, 'she doesn't know exactly what happened. Just that he did something wrong. And I didn't tell her it was you, but with you being off, she assumed.'

'No, no, *no*,' she moans to herself, over and over.

'I don't know exactly what the plan is, it's something she's cooked up. I'm supposed to meet her round the back of the office, and then do what she tells me and I'll have it.'

Mags looks back up expectantly.

'There's a catch, though,' I tell her carefully.

'What catch?'

I swallow, my throat bone dry. 'If the… if I find… *that*… on his phone. It has to go to HR.'

'What? *No.*'

'If it turns out he's deleted it already, nothing else happens.'

'One thing,' she murmurs irritably, her anger building. 'I asked you for one fucking thing, Dot. Don't tell anyone! Don't let anyone else find out. I asked you to do that *one* thing for me.'

'No, Mags, you didn't,' I correct her quickly.

She stops mid-rant. 'What?'

'You didn't ask me for *just* one thing,' I remind her. 'Yes, you asked me not to tell anyone, and I've done the best I can to honour that. Jackie loves you to bits. She also knows that piece of shit bastard and what he's capable of, and as soon as I started nosing around, she was bound to figure some part of it out, even if she didn't have the full story. But you *also* asked me to get that phone from him, and to get *rid* of the video somehow. How did you imagine I was gonna manage that exactly? I don't have fucking superpowers, you know.'

Mags looks back at me, fighting back tears.

'I'm sorry I talked to her,' I shrug, 'because I know you didn't want me to, and you'll probably hate me for it. But then again, I'm not sorry, because I can't get to his phone without help, and even if I could, I wouldn't even know how to unlock the thing to get into it. Telling her means there's a chance I might actually be able to *do* all that.'

She sniffs. 'I don't— I just—'

'Jackie would *never* do anything to put you in a bad position. You know that. She says there's someone behind the scenes who wants rid of that bastard as much as I do. They're willing to set up whatever this plan of hers is, but only if they can use what I find as proof to end him there for good.'

Mags nods slowly. 'Which means HR. And telling people.'

'I'm sorry. I know you don't want that. But I don't know what else to do to fix it,' I tell her hopelessly.

'But you don't know exactly what her plan is.'

I don't. I shake my head.

'And who's she told? Who's behind this masterplan of hers?'

'I don't know that either.'

'Don't know much, do you,' she mutters sullenly.

Mags reaches for a tissue from a pile of half-used ones discarded on the other bedside table.

'People will find out,' she starts slowly. 'They always do when HR get involved. They'll know what happened. What he did.

What I…' her voice cracks into a trembling whisper. 'What I *let* him do.'

I move along the bed closer to where she's sitting, wanting so much to reassure her. 'If the worst happens, if people *do* find out, none of this says anything about you. *He's* the one at fault, he's the fucking dickhead scumbag bastard piece of shit who took advantage of the situation.'

'You know they'll say I asked for it.'

'Some people probably will,' I agree sadly. What a world we live in. 'But only the arsewipes.'

She laughs a little at that.

'Nobody whose opinion is actually worth giving a crap about is gonna think this whole thing reflects badly on anyone but *him*.'

We both turn at a gentle knock on the slightly ajar door. Theo's hesitant voice drifts through the gap. 'Er, Dot? I've got the tea.'

Mags frowns. 'Who's that?'

I stand abruptly, hoping to beat him to the door, but just then a tray appears in the room carried in by a familiar pair of hands, loaded with two mugs and a big plate of biscuits.

'Hi. Sorry,' he smiles over at Mags. 'Tea?'

The disbelief on her face tells me that she definitely recognises him from the party.

'I'll take it,' I smile at him and close the distance between us, hands brushing as I nudge the tray from his grasp. 'Thanks, Theo.'

Mags coughs from the bed, flashing me a what-the-hell look, eyes darting back and forth between us.

'Sorry, Mags. This is Theo. Theo, Mags.'

'Hi,' Theo waves brightly.

'*Hi*,' Mags replies emphatically, a smirk spreading across her face as she looks back at me.

'You were there on Friday night, right?' he asks her.

'Yeah. You were the one dressed as a...' Mags trails off as she spots the dog collar at his neck. I didn't think it'd be physically possible for her eyes to get any wider, but evidently I'm wrong.

'Wait— so you actually *are* a...' she points towards the collar.

He shrugs back good-naturedly. 'Guilty.'

I close my eyes with a sigh, suspecting the Spanish inquisition is about to be incoming.

'Well,' Theo clocks my expression and sensibly decides to make himself scarce, 'I'll leave you two alone.'

The second he closes the door Mags folds her arms, giving me a look of utter self-satisfaction. 'So that's why you haven't been home for two days.'

'Mags, I—'

'I knew he was your type,' she cackles with glee.

'That's not— I mean, he's just—'

'An *actual* priest,' she shakes her head, enjoying the situation far too much. 'I never thought that'd would've been your thing.'

I groan. 'It's really not like that.'

'*Really?*'

'Well... okay,' I relent. 'It's not *completely* like that.'

Mags gives me another stern look.

'It's a long story.'

She pats the bedclothes beside her. 'Spill.'

I carry the tray over and place it on the bed between us as I sit down carefully, trying not to disturb the drinks. 'He's *not* the reason I didn't come home,' I insist. 'I would never have stayed away, not just for some bloke. Not when I promised you I'd be back. But something else came up.'

'Where have you been then?' she lifts her tea from the tray. I'm happy to see her take a bourbon from the plate along with it.

How much do I tell her? How much *can* I tell her, without

having to tell her all everything? Theo's words from earlier ring in my ears, and I decide to take a risk.

'I've been at Rebecca's.'

I hope I don't regret it.

Mags looks back at me in bewilderment mid-dunk. 'Rebecca's? As in, Big Boss? Why?'

I'm still hesitating. 'It's hard to explain.'

'What,' she scoffs back, 'harder than what I had to tell you this week? I doubt it.'

She's got a hell of a point. 'Okay. Just... please just try and keep an open mind, yeah?'

Mags eats her biscuit, gesturing for me to get on with it.

'Okay. Well...' I clear my throat, wondering where to start. 'So... since I was little, I've been able to see things. And hear things. That other people— *normal* people— can't see and hear.'

'Oh yeah,' Mags interrupts through a mouthful of biscuit, 'your witchy thing. What about it?'

Now it's my turn to be confused. 'My— *witchy* thing?'

'Yeah,' she shrugs dismissively. 'You know, how you always know people are pregnant before they tell anyone, and if someone's sick you always know what's wrong with them. Hey,' she goes on quickly, 'remember when Joe's nan died and Zoe's mom as well, you knew just what to say to both of them to make them feel better while the rest of us looked like idiots not knowing how to talk to them? Jackie and I joked that you must have a direct hookup to the afterlife and they were feeding you the words.'

It's not often I'm completely gobsmacked. This is one of those rare occasions.

'Cos you're a witch,' she shrugs again.

I don't know what to say.

'What's you being a witch got to do with Big Boss?'

I struggle to get any words out for a good half a minute. 'Could you… maybe not call me a witch?' I finally croak out.

'Okay. What do you call it?'

So many things, over the years.

'A medium,' I sigh eventually. 'I'm a medium.'

It feels weird saying it out loud. It might be the first time that I have. Without apologising for it, at least, or trying to justify it.

'Fine, medium then. What about Rebecca? Is her big fancy new house haunted or something?'

'Erm…' I can't decide if Mags is taking all of this really well, or absolutely ripping the piss out of me. 'Yeah. It is.'

'Really?' She stops mid-sip, eyes wide. 'Oh, wait— is this because of all that weird stuff that happened on Friday night? With the Ouija board? I knew that was dodgy.' She shakes her head knowingly.

'Kind of. Sort of.'

'So? What then? And what's your hot man got to do with it?'

I can't help but laugh. 'He's not *my* hot man.'

LIAR.

I look up, shocked. I heard the word clear as day, but it sure as hell wasn't Mags. It's the Voice. Mags is, of course, oblivious. 'So you do think he's hot then.'

TELL THE TRUTH.

I can't decide if it's cute or intrusive. I don't even know if Theo's doing it on purpose, but I need to tell him to back off and give me some privacy.

'Sorry, Mags, can you just give me a sec?'

She frowns. 'Oh-*kay*…'

I turn away from her briefly, closing my eyes, dropping quickly into my deep-dive meditative state, searching for him in the mist, looking for the part of his mind that links to the Voice. I'm in the fog like before, my subconscious somewhere in the ether, but it's different now. The fog isn't so thick, the space not so dim.

Nor so empty.

Theo's here.

At least, my subconscious' impression of him. Not entirely solid, not exactly real, but a moving representation of the picture of him I have in my mind, sort of like an animated avatar. He's smiling. 'Go on,' he says. 'Tell her.'

And the Voice. It's no longer an unrecognisable, disembodied sound. It's his voice. Theo's *actual* voice.

I've never been so happy for Grace to be proven right.

'Can you leave?'

'If you tell her the truth.'

'You can't just pop in here whenever you feel like it.'

'Why not?'

'Because it's *weird*.'

'I like it here.'

'Emergencies only, Theo.'

'Fine, I'll go. But tell her the truth.'

'*Out*.'

The exchange lasts only a few seconds – again, time moves funny in the ether – and as I open my eyes, Mags is watching me cautiously. 'Did you just do a witchy thing?'

I ignore the question, revisiting her previous one instead. 'Yes, I think he's hot,' I admit with a sigh. 'And yes, I suppose he *is* mine. Sort of.'

CLOSE ENOUGH.

A second's pause, and I don't feel him in there anymore.

'So what is he then, an exorcist or something?'

I shake my head. 'He's not Catholic. He's Rebecca's local vicar, he was at the house when I went back on Monday to warn them something was wrong.'

'That's where you were all afternoon? That's why you missed my calls?'

'Yeah. There was a lot going on,' I shrug apologetically.

Mags nods. 'That's where you went yesterday, after you dropped me here. And where you were last night.'

'Yeah. Stuff there kind of…' I debate the most succinct explanation. 'Kicked off. I couldn't leave, I wasn't sure they'd be safe.'

'Are they safe now?'

'Short of a dodgy burger or a couple of loose screws, they should be for the minute. They're at Alton Towers for the day.'

'And when they get back?'

'Not so much,' I grimace.

Mags nods, taking a massive gulp of her slightly cooled tea. 'So you're going back there again tonight.'

'I have to, Mags. I'm sorry—'

'No,' she shakes her head quickly. 'Don't apologise. They need you there. I get it.'

I can't get over how well she's taking all this. How she's *accepting* it, like it's a perfectly normal, rational, pedestrian sort of conversation.

'So you don't think I'm batshit insane?'

Mags laughs. 'Oh, I've always thought that,' she teases. 'But not for this.'

We sit that way for a minute, me in stunned silence, her sipping from the mug in her hand, dunking more biscuits an inch at a time.

'I'm going with you tomorrow,' she says eventually.

'What?'

I meet her eyes. There's steel in them.

'Mags, no. You don't have to do that.'

'I want to. I want to be there to know when it's over.'

I can hardly blame her. But of course, there's a chance it might not be.

'What if I get hold of it and there's nothing on there?'

She shrugs. 'I'll hand in my notice and get signed off sick till it's up.'

I don't think she's joking.

'I don't know, Dot,' she goes on wearily. 'I suppose I'll have to figure that out when it happens. If it happens.'

I nod quietly.

'But if we do find it, if it is on there…'

I wait for her to go on.

'If they really *can* use it to get rid of him, to do— anything— I want to be there to see it happen.'

'There'll be HR, meetings,' I remind her. 'You'll have to talk about it.'

'I know. I don't love that. But you'll be there to hold my hand, right?'

I reach out and grasp hers tightly. 'Of course, Mags. *Always*.'

Mags nods. 'Pick me up in the morning then?'

'Yep. About ten to nine? Jackie said to meet her at quarter to ten.'

'I'll be ready.'

'Do you need me to pick up any clothes from your place first?'

She shakes her head, indicating the bag I saw when I came in. 'Still got plenty. I've been living in these pyjamas since yesterday.'

'Okay.'

Mags smiles. 'He makes good tea.'

'Better than mine,' I nod in agreement.

'You always use too much milk.'

'I always forget I'm not making coffee.'

'Hmm,' she snorts. 'You know, I saw a ghost once.'

That came out of nowhere. 'Really?'

'Uh-huh. I was… fourteen? Fifteen? My nan. Couple of months after she died.'

Woah.

'I was off sick from school, a stomach bug I think. I was lying on the sofa watching Octonauts. She sat down next to me, asked me how I was getting on, how were Mom and Dad, how was school. Talked to me like she'd never been away.'

I can picture it almost exactly.

'Mom didn't believe me. Told me it was just my temperature,' she scoffs, irritated as she looks down, fiddling with the edge of the duvet. 'It wasn't my temperature.'

Instinctively, I know she's right. If it had been just her temperature, I wouldn't be able to see the picture of it so clearly now, someone showing it to me from somewhere. 'It wasn't.'

Mags looks back up with a smile. 'So you don't think *I'm* batshit insane?'

'No more than I already did.'

We both laugh.

'You'd better rescue your hot man before Pen bores him to death,' she eventually suggests. 'I love her to bits, but there's only so many zombies I can take in one day.'

'Yeah. I'll see you in the morning.'

She nods as I turn to leave.

'Dot?'

'Mmm?'

'Whatever it is you're doing tonight for Rebecca. I hope it works out.'

I look back at her from the doorway. 'Thanks, Mags.'

Me too.

24

Changing my clothes while I have the chance, I chuck some extra in a bag before I extricate Theo from Penny's effusive clutches. Once we're safely back in the car, I bring up his little mind-poking escapade.

'Were you…' I muse casually as we get settled. '*Doing* something back there?'

His bewildered confirms it wasn't on purpose. 'What do you mean? Making the tea?'

'No, not the tea. Which was lovely, by the way.'

'Oh, wait. You thought I did something… mediumy?'

It's an improvement on witchy, I suppose.

'You did. I just wasn't sure if you *knew* you did.'

Theo rubs his jaw awkwardly, not quite sure what's happened or exactly how he's involved. 'What did I… do?'

'You talked to me. In my head, I mean,' I clarify.

'What did I say?'

'Mags and I were talking about you,' I shrug. 'And you told me off, said I was lying to her and to tell her the truth.'

His bemused smile develops into an amused smirk. 'Why, what did you say to her?'

'Never mind that,' I tell him, trying to be at least a little bit cross but finding it difficult against the power of those big puppy-dog eyes. 'I went… *inside*, to tell you to stop it and get out of my head, and you said you liked it there and didn't want to leave.'

Theo laughs heartily, slapping his leg. 'Oh, wow. That's just—*wow*.'

'What?'

'I didn't do it on purpose,' he raises his hands placatingly. 'I swear.'

I wait curiously for his explanation.

'Promise me you won't be cross.'

'Theo…'

'All right. I was sat on the sofa with Penny and she's lovely, but she was going on and on about whatever it was she was watching, and I tried to be polite and pay attention, but it just wasn't my thing. So, my mind started wandering. I was thinking about you, and this Voice business, and I thought to myself that if I really could, you know… visit you, inside your head, well…'

I push him to finish. 'Well?'

'I thought that wouldn't it be a lovely place to visit, and I bet I'd like it there and I'd never want to leave.'

I have to smile. 'Okay. We *have* to teach you to control it.'

'I'm sorry, Dot,' he frowns now, concerned.

'I'm not cross with you,' I reassure him quickly, a hand on his. 'Really. Look, this is a good thing. This means it's coming back to you. You thought it in some part of your mind, and you did it. You just didn't *realise* you were doing it.'

'How does that help though? I still can't do anything like way you can.'

'Yes, you can,' I squeeze his hand. 'Look, if you can go to that place where the two of us have this connection, wherever that is, then you can go to where your Guides are.'

'I have Guides?'

'We all do, remember? And now that you're—' I reach for the best way to phrase it. 'Now you're getting back on the horse, so to speak, they're probably champing at the bit to reconnect to you, to show you the way.'

Theo looks at nothing in particular as he lets it all sink in.

'Hey,' I move my hand to the side of his face and bring his attention back to me, the soft hairs tickling my palm. 'Most importantly? You can come with me to wherever that thing is, and help me send it packing back to where it came from. You just need a bit of practice.'

He takes a deep breath, letting it out slowly. 'Okay,' he nods back, trying to convince himself. 'Practice. Okay.'

'You want to text Rebecca, let them know we're heading back?'

'Yeah. How long?'

'Well, we missed lunch,' I point out, 'and I don't know about you, but I'm starving, so we should grab food on the way. There's a drive-thru Maccy's round the corner, so if we stop off there, then back to Lichfield… say an hour and a half, just in case?'

Theo nods, putting his seatbelt on and grabbing his phone as I start the car.

It's late enough in the afternoon for Maccy's to be quiet, so we're the only car in the queue. We're a good twenty minutes ahead of schedule when we park back on Rebecca's drive.

'It looks like a haunted house, doesn't it,' Theo muses as I eat. He already scoffed his while I was driving us back, he couldn't wait.

'What do you mean?' I ask through a mouthful of fries.

'You know. Old house, out here in the middle of nowhere, all shadows and creepy. You'd expect it to come with a ghost.'

I slurp my chocolate milkshake noisily, releasing the straw with a pop. 'It's not just old houses that have ghosts. Besides, that thing isn't one, according to Grace,' I remind him, 'not in the usual sense. And technically it's not even haunting the house either.'

'How is it not haunting the house?'

'It's stuck in the house for whatever reason. But it's haunting the people. It doesn't really even care about Rebecca and her family, either. So I suppose if anything, it's haunting *us*.'

Theo frowns at me. 'Cheery. Thanks for that.'

'This is assuming Grace is right about it, of course.'

'You think there's any chance she's not?'

'I wish I did. At least we have a better idea of what we're up against. And if we did fight it off before, the two of us, something inside us will remember how to do it again. I'm sure of it.'

'Hmm.' Theo murmurs noncommittally as his phone vibrates on his lap and he looks down. 'They're nearly back.'

I chase the last of my fries with the dregs of the shake before I stuff the packaging in the brown paper bag and chuck it on the back seat. 'Okay. Let's go.'

'Wait,' he reaches to stop me as I turn for the door.

'What?'

'We've still got a couple of minutes,' he smirks shamelessly, hand sneaking gently along my arm, making my skin tingle.

'*Now?!*' I feign outrage, trying pathetically to suppress a smile.

Theo leans towards me, his face stopping just short of mine. 'Just for a minute. Before we go in there and have to hide it again.'

This close, I can see every crease, every freckle, every moment of the last thirty years I've spent without him etched across his face. I look back up into those big eyes, dark and warm and gentle, and I have no idea how the hell we're going to make this work. But if the alternative is another thirty years without him, well, that's just not an option.

He takes my silence as hesitance, second guessing himself. 'If you don't want to, it's fine,' he spills out quickly. 'I just—'

I hold a finger to his lips to shush him. 'Thought you could read my mind,' I tease gently.

He relaxes. 'Thought you didn't want me to.'

'Can you read it now?'

Theo cocks his head to one side in thought, eyebrows raised. 'We can't do that.'

I actually wasn't thinking that at all and roll my eyes at the joke, but kiss him anyway. It's slow, and warm, and easy, and so familiar now that as we take our time, I just want to keep coming back to it over and over again. Back to him.

He smiles as we pull apart to take a breath. 'You taste like chocolate milkshake.'

'Sorry. I know you prefer strawberry.'

'I can live with it,' he shrugs sweetly, tipping his head forward, touching his forehead to mine, eyes closed.

The distant sound of an engine from beyond the trees warns us the others are close.

'They're here.'

'Mmm.'

'Theo?'

He doesn't move.

'Time to go.'

He frowns, eyes still closed against me. 'Just another minute.'

'I don't think we have that long.'

He sighs. 'Can't we mind control them to stay where they are?'

I laugh gently. Nice thought, but sadly outside either of our ability.

'Just to keep them away a bit longer.'

It takes all of my willpower to pull myself away. 'It doesn't work like that. Sorry.'

Theo finally opens his eyes, smiling sadly at me. 'Not much use this medium thing, is it?'

'Told you so,' I sigh with a shrug.

He looks at me hopefully. 'After?'

'After,' I nod in firm agreement.

He leans back in to give me one final, quick kiss before turning to open the passenger door. I follow suit, easing myself out just as Rebecca's car pulls round from behind the trees. They all wave and she parks beside Rob's car: the kids look pretty smiley and I can see a pick and mix bag in Hannah's upturned hand, so whether they've had a great time or are just hopped up on sugar, I'm not sure.

'Good day?' I ask as the four of them pile out.

'Great day,' Rebecca replies. She looks relaxed, like she's finally been able to take a breath, and it's nice to see a proper smile back on her face. 'Got rained off a couple of rides, but I think we did all the ones you were bothered about, didn't we kids?'

'Adam was jealous cos I got to ride Thirteen and he was too short,' Hannah announces smugly.

'Was not,' Adam sulks back.

I frown at him sympathetically. 'Those big rides are horrible. I'm too scared to go on them.'

He smiles a bit.

'And of course the rapids were closed,' the older girl sighs dramatically.

'The weather,' Rob shrugs by way of explanation.

'How about you?' Rebecca's smile falters as she turns the conversation back to the present. 'Everything go okay?'

Theo looks at me to take the lead.

'Well,' I start brightly, 'there's some— sort of— good news.'

The couple exchange glances as the kids hover between them, Adam making the occasional play for the remains of Hannah's sweetie bag, her snatching away.

'Sort of good news?' Rob frowns, looking between Theo and I.

'It is good news,' I almost convince myself. 'So, Grace did know what it is. She's seen it before, a long time ago. And it was got rid of, back then.'

'Wait, I thought…' Rebecca looks confused as she glances to her husband. 'Didn't she say that they couldn't fight it, that the house couldn't be cleared? So how did they get rid of it back then?'

I swallow as I look at Theo, silently asking his permission to share the story. It's his too, after all. He nods back.

'They didn't. *We* did.'

'We. Who's—'

Rebecca's far from stupid, and she immediately sees the glance that passes between Theo and I.

'You. You *two?* Wait, so you— you *know* each other? From before all this, I mean?'

She looks back and forth at each of us incredulously.

'Apparently. But we didn't know that until today.'

Hannah looks up from her sweets. 'Were you two boyfriend and girlfriend?'

Theo laughs at the blunt question. 'Sort of.'

'Are you now?'

'Of course they're not, Hannah. Father Theo's a Vicar, sweetie, remember?' Rebecca explains. 'Vicars don't have girlfriends.'

I can see from her expression that she doesn't believe a single word she just said. Not one bit.

'Okay,' I try to improve my explanation. 'So, it turns out that we knew each other when we were kids, and we did this sort of stuff together.'

'What?'

I ignore Rob's shocked reaction. 'There was this big kerfuffle with this same thing that's been bothering you guys—'

'*What?!*'

'And we fought it, between us, did something that got rid of it. But we were really young, well, I was only a couple of years older than Hannah, and it was this big traumatic thing.'

I realise I'm babbling.

'So, our parents— Grace who you met, and his, who were in the church too— they had us hypnotised to forget about it. But then some other stuff happened so they also hypnotised us to forget each *other*, so when we met, I didn't recognise him.'

I finally take a breath.

'And I didn't recognise her,' Theo adds.

'We had no idea about any of it. But Grace gave me this.'

Theo still has the photo from earlier and I nod at him. He pulls it out of his trouser pocket and hands it to Rebecca, who looks at it and promptly does the most comical double take I think I've ever seen in my life.

'Bloody hell.'

It's like Theo's reaction all over again but multiplied, as both she and Rob look from the picture to each of us and back again, the kids straining to see, wanting to understand what all the fuss is about.

'That's— *woah*.'

'It's really you. Both of you, I mean,' Rebecca looks stunned as she hands it back.

'Yeah.'

'You don't remember each other?' Hannah pipes up.

'We didn't,' Theo replies patiently. 'But we're starting to.'

'Wait.' Rob considers the story for a second, his face filled with hope. 'This is better than good news, right? You've already fought it, you've done it before, the pair of you.'

'Well…'

'You can do it again, right?'

Theo steps in. 'It's not quite as simple as that.'

Rebecca smiles, shaking her head resignedly. 'Of course it's not.'

'First of all, I'm long out of practice with any of this,' Theo explains. 'Bits of it are coming back to me, but it's barely even been a few hours since I found out, so I'm not exactly match fit.'

'And second?'

I look at Theo curiously, wondering myself what the second thing is.

'Second,' he begins carefully, 'this thing. It doesn't care about any of you. Its goal isn't to hurt you guys.'

Oh yeah. I'd almost managed to forget about this part.

'That's a good thing,' I cut in quickly. 'It's messed with you but only as a means to an end. It's not about to zap one of the kids into the telly or anything. That's not what it's after.'

The couple exchange looks, holding both of the kids close now.

Rob frowns. 'So? What *is* it after?'

I shift uncomfortably. Theo puts a reassuring arm around me, a slight tip of his head in my direction.

'Her.'

A sudden silence hangs between us all.

'You?' Rebecca finally looks at me, pained.

I shrug back, trying to sound nonchalant. Like being the target of a demonic spirit is all in a day's weird work. 'It's a possession thing. I have... these gifts. It wants to use them.'

She frowns. 'For what?'

'Nothing good,' Theo replies quietly, echoing Grace. His hand gently rubs the bit between my shoulder blades in an effort to remind me that he's with me.

Rebecca looks down, concerned, then back to me. 'So, what it did to me and Rob. That's what it wants to do to you?'

'Not quite.'

'What then?'

'Well, no offense, but you two were just...' I falter. 'A warm up. A distraction. With you two, it had no intention of staying.'

'*Staying?* So, you mean, if it does it to you—'

'It won't,' I meet her eyes quickly.

'It's what, going to just set up home permanently in your head?'

'Trust me, Rebecca,' I interrupt. 'I have no intention of giving it that chance. Look, you saw what happened when it appeared before. We pushed it back, all of us, together—'

'With a little help from your mother and her friends.'

'Not much,' I scoff. 'And that was before we knew what Theo could really do. Look, according to Grace, him and me together—'

My face flushes slightly, and I see Theo fighting back a smile at the implication in my poor choice of words.

'Our combined power,' I elaborate quickly, 'gifts, psychic energy, whatever you want to call it, according to her was a big deal. And this was back when we were kids. These things can develop more over time.'

'But he doesn't remember how to do it,' she points at Theo.

'Yet,' I correct her, 'he doesn't remember *yet*. But what he *is* remembering is already coming fast. It's not going to take long for the rest to catch up.'

Theo frowns at me dubiously.

'It's not,' I insist to him. 'You've already been poking around in my head without knowing it. We just need a day or two. Maybe not even that, if the house is quiet like last night and the two of us can sit down and practice.'

'So what do we do? Just carry on as we are?'

I shrug. 'Not for long. Just enough for the good Father here to get his mojo back. Like I said, if we can just practice.' I turn back to Theo again, 'If you can hook back up with your Guides, I honestly don't think it'll take any time at all.'

The family exchange glances.

'We just have to hang on a bit longer,' I tell them, quietly confident I'm right. 'We can do the same again tomorrow— go out again, I mean. I have to go into work—'

'*Again?*' Rebecca groans. 'Why, for Christ's sake? Sorry, Father.'

Theo shrugs.

'I'm not getting into it now. But it's non-negotiable.'

'But—'

'No.'

'If this is because—'

'*No*, Rebecca,' I tell her firmly. 'Leave it, please. Look, let's get through tonight, which with any luck will be a nice quiet repeat of last night.'

I try not to picture Theo and I back in the Orangery.

'Theo and I can get some practice time in this evening while you guys are still up, then we'll keep watch again.' I set out my cunning plan. 'Tomorrow morning I'll deal with the work thing, a bit more practice, and by tomorrow night, or Friday at the very latest, he and I take it on, and we get rid of it. For good, this time.'

They look uncertain.

Theo clasps my shoulder reassuringly.

'There's light at the end of this tunnel, okay? I promise,' I tell them, and I really, honestly believe it.

Right up until the moment Rebecca opens the front door.

25

Inside lie the remnants of chaos.

The hall – that grand space where I stood with Mags only a few nights ago, giving her a crash course in the history of the Hudson-Hicks' legendary shindigs – is littered with debris, like an extremely localised tornado passed through during the hours we'd been away. The stylish sideboards have been upended, drawers and doors opened and contents spilled across the marble, the carefully curated ornaments displayed atop them scattered into a million tiny pieces on the floor.

'Dot…' Rebecca squeaks out my name as she stands frozen at the precipice, not daring to step forward from the porch to breach the threshold.

I put what I hope is a reassuring hand on her shoulder as I slip between her and Rob, whose expression is just as fearful. His hands firmly grip each of the kids' shoulders in front of him, holding both against his body as they stare wide-eyed into the confusion before them. I take a couple of tentative steps into the hall, careful to avoid the wreckage, and stop a few feet inside to listen for any sign that whatever caused the violent disruption might still be hanging around.

The house is quiet. Too bloody quiet.

It certainly sounds empty, but it doesn't *feel* like it. I remember playing sardines as a kid, going into a room to look for someone hidden, not wanting to be caught. Somewhere in the room they're holding their breath so you don't find them. A room like that might sound quiet, but it doesn't *feel* quiet. Part of you knows that someone's in there somewhere, behind a curtain, or in a wardrobe, or under a bed.

That's how the house feels.

The last shards of late afternoon light are still coming through the windows, and from where I'm standing, I can see past the open living room door to make out a mess of sleeping bags, blankets, Lego bricks and schoolbooks strewn across the floor. It didn't look like that when we left this morning. I mouth a silent but clear instruction for the group to stay put, Theo included, and inch gingerly towards the doorway for a better look. There's no obvious sign of the creepy, misty form, and it seems still enough. Maybe it just threw a tantrum because we all did a bunk and it had nobody about to mess with.

As I pass the bottom of the stairs, Hannah *shrieks*.

'Up there!'

I follow her outstretched arm towards the landing, where a shadowy mass is beginning to billow above the banister.

'What do we do?' Theo tries to bury the panic in his voice for the benefit of the others, but he can't hide it from me. He's not ready for this, not yet, and we both know it.

And I can't do it alone.

'Get out,' I hiss over my shoulder, backing up slowly.

'It's gone!'

I look up quickly.

Hannah's right. It's gone.

But *where*.

I don't like this.

Now Adam screams, tumbling forwards into the hall, crying for his parents as they trip inside after him. 'I felt it,' I hear him howl, 'I *felt* it—'

There's a shadow filling the open front doorway, misty tendrils reaching out, searching.

'Theo!' I warn quickly.

He scoops Hannah up from where she's frozen in place beside him, skipping deftly into the hall out of reach of its probing… fingers? Antennae? Tentacles? I don't know anymore.

'Dot…' Theo's gaze is locked on the mass beside the front door as Hannah clings to him, eyes tightly closed.

'I know.'

Actually, I don't, and that's a problem. A minute ago, I had it all figured out – at least, I thought I did. Get Theo back up to speed and then between us, kick its arse into the light, or dark, or wherever. But now? They could group up again like they did before, protect themselves while I try taking it on one-on-one with the help of the Guides. That might knock it out of commission again, buy us more time. But when I did that yesterday, the Voice was there to help me, but now the Voice is Theo, and Theo is *not ready*. These thoughts race through my brain in a split second and while they whirl in the back of, out here up front, the sight of the hovering, undulating cloud of fog near the door throws up a separate train of unwelcome thoughts. Why is it at the door? Is it leaving? Of course it isn't, don't be daft. It can't do that, not without being attached to someone.

Then I realise. It's put itself between us and the door.

It's a *trap*.

The thought dawns on me at the exact moment the front door swings away from the wall and slams firmly and loudly shut.

'Oh shit. It doesn't want us to leave.'

Theo and I exchange a pained glance. We might not have a choice. We might have to do this now, ready or not.

Just to labour the point, one of the collapsed sideboards slides abruptly across the floor towards us and we stumble out of its path as it lands squarely across the closed front door, blocking any chance of a path back the way we came.

'Back door. *Now!*'

As I jostle the others on ahead, mindful to keep myself between them and it, part of me already knows we won't be able to get out that way either, we'll be stopped somehow. Surprise, surprise, when we reach the equally chaotic kitchen, the giant American-style fridge-freezer is wedged diagonally across the back door, surrounded by a pool of melting frozen food packets and smashed condiments.

'There's the balcony upstairs,' Rob suggests. 'We could jump.'

'Are you insane?' Rebecca argues. 'It's at least twenty feet, we'd break every bone.'

'Would you rather have that thing get back in our heads again?'

'Guys,' I shush them as I hear something. 'Wait.'

In the silence, it's audible. There's a low, deep vibration coming from somewhere inside the house, within the walls, the foundations.

Déjà vu. My vision, brought to life.

I turn back to them. 'Stay here, stay together. Protect yourselves. Like before, remember?'

Theo steps toward me, passing Hannah to her mom. 'Dot, *no.*'

'It's fine, it'll be fine,' I shrug back, pretending I'm calm. 'I'll push it back again, just like yesterday—'

'Yesterday was different,' his hands are on my shoulders, desperate, pleading. 'Yesterday we didn't know what it wanted.'

'Theo—'

'You can't fight it alone.'

'But you're not ready.'.

'What if it *wins?*'

'I don't know what else to do!' I explode back, harsher than

I mean. Theo looks down, stung, and I reach a hand gently to the side of his face. Once his eyes are on mine, I shrug a gentle apology. 'We're trapped in here with it now. *They're* trapped in here with it,' I nod towards the others. 'I don't know what else to do.'

He looks back at me steadily. 'I can't lose you,' he says simply. 'Not again.'

'You won't,' I try to reassure him, but it's hard to sound convincing.

'Let me help.'

I appreciate his earnestness, I really do. But from a practical perspective, he doesn't remember what to do. I can't hold his hand through the process and deal with this thing at the same time.

Rebecca's voice interrupts my train of thought. 'Let us *all* help.'

That gets my attention. 'What?'

'You said before that what we were doing helped protect you as well as us, right?'

She is right. 'Mmm.'

'So, let us come with you and we'll do it again.'

'Rebecca,' I start carefully, 'I appreciate the offer. I really do. But look at your kids, for god's sake. They're terrified.'

'We're *not*,' Hannah shoots back indignantly.

'Yeah,' Adam chimes in, 'it's a big meanie. I want to fight it.'

'And we can *see* it,' she points out with the perfect derisive nine-year-old eyeroll in the general direction of her less supernaturally-blessed parents. 'They can't.'

Around us, the rumble starts to build.

'Anyway, *I'm* not scared of it,' Hannah goes on casually, ignoring the steadily increasing din. 'It wants you, not me.'

My stomach drops into my feet. 'Thanks, Hannah.'

Theo turns me back gently to face him. 'Look, I know I can't fight it. I don't have a clue what I'm doing. But if we really are that much stronger together, let's *be* together.'

'What do you mean?'

'Let me stand with you,' he takes my hands in his. 'I might not know how to go with you wherever it is you need to be to fight it. But I bet you can get into *my* head and find whatever hidden talent is back there. *You* use it.'

I hadn't even thought of that. Maybe that could work? Maybe I don't need him to use his abilities, maybe I don't need him to actively do anything at all. Maybe I just need him to be there with me so *I* can tap into *him*. The alternative is to leave them all down here together, hidden as best as possible to protect themselves as best they can while I keep it busy. Part of me wonders if that's the right thing to do – if it's only after me, isn't keeping them away and facing it alone the sensible option?

But Theo's words echo in my head.

What if it wins?

What if I come back to them and I'm *not me?* Then what happens to them?

To Theo?

I'll admit, when I stepped in yesterday after Grace and Co. lost the plot, when it backed off, I felt like quite the badass. Like a switch flipped somewhere in my brain and said: *Yes*, this is *it*, *this* is why you have this thing in you, *this* is what you were *born* to do. For a minute, I felt invincible, for the first time ever. Then Grace told me what happened all those years ago, about Theo and what he and I did together. As messed up as both of our lives ended up for so many years afterwards, realising there was a *reason* I was so immediately drawn to him, there was a *reason* we'd been pushed together now, it felt perfect, like all the stars were aligning. He was the missing piece of my puzzle, and together we were a *force*, and now that we knew, once Theo got his groove back, that thing wouldn't stand a chance against us. It was all meant to be.

But the thing we were fighting – a spiritual demon, Grace had called it – clearly had a different idea. It wasn't giving us the chance to get that far. So I had a choice: face it completely alone and take the risk that if I wasn't up to the challenge, even with the help of my Guides, it might end up getting what it wants. Or have the others with me, and hope their extra strength could be enough to boost my own and hurt it, enough at least so we could get out of the house and regroup elsewhere, enough to give me and Theo the time we need. Then we could come back again to finish off the plan. But then they'll all be at risk. I'm damned if I do and damned if I don't. And I suspect I'm also rapidly running out of time, as above us the rumble builds enough to make the pendant lights clatter with a nerve shredding tinkle as they sway precariously above the kitchen island.

'You sure you want to do this?'

I'm looking at Rebecca and her brood. There's no need for further confirmation from Theo: his answer's right there against my fingers as he laces them with his own and clasps them tight. Rebecca shares a look with Rob and the kids, then turns back to me with a short, determined nod.

I sigh deeply, pushing away my doubts, trying to replace the instinctive fear with a modicum of positive faith. Faith in what I know I'm capable of, in these people standing beside me and their conviction, in the warmth of Theo's hand wrapped around mine and the power I know he has tucked away somewhere in his subconscious, if only I can find it.

'Okay,' I breathe it all out. 'New plan then. You guys stay together, behind us. Use the wall, use your mantra.'

'You,' I round on Theo.

'What do you need?'

'Do the same. Use the wall, protect yourself, use *your* mantra. But stay upfront with me, do *not* let go of my hand, okay?'

He nods firmly, clasping my fingers again tightly to underline his understanding.

'Now, this is important,' I go on carefully. This is the bit I'm less comfortable about. 'I need you to use the wall to protect yourself, but you also have to let me get *in* there. So you're going to have to put a crack in it somewhere for me to find.'

Theo considers it. 'I can do that.'

'You let in me and only me,' I insist. 'You feel anything else trying to poke its nosy fingers around in there, you shut it back up tight straightaway, you don't hesitate. Understand?'

He nods.

'*Only* me,' I stress again.

'Only you.'

'Okay then.' I glance back at the windows. Most of the light has faded now. 'We'll put the lights on as we go.'

'Where are we going?' Rob asks tentatively.

'The landing. Hands out,' I nod. 'I know you can't make a circle while you're moving, but hold hands in the meantime, kids in the middle. Then close the circle as soon as we get upstairs.'

Rob nods back as they make a chain.

'Your love is your strength, remember? Start it now.'

Rebecca leads them in their mantra as I take one final deep breath and turn back to Theo. 'Ready?'

He smiles back with pure, absolute love. I can see it all over his face – I can *feel* it coming off him in waves, washing over me, basking me in the light of it – and it's the most overwhelmingly beautiful thing I've ever experienced. 'My faith is my strength,' he squeezes my hand again.

And I know in that moment that Grace was right about that

too. He's not talking about his faith in God, in the Church. His talisman is his faith in *me*.

'Then let's go.'

With my free left hand, I flick on the kitchen light as we move back into the corridor and turn down the hall where we came from. Every time Theo and I pass a switch on either side of the wall, one of us reaches to turn it on, never letting go of each other's hands, gradually lighting up each area downstairs as we go. Around us the rumble continues, getting noticeably louder as my right foot touches the bottom step of the staircase. At the same time, I flick the bank of light switches on the wall for the stairs and the landing.

Nothing happens.

Theo's hand tenses in mine.

'Don't worry,' I say loudly for the benefit of the unwelcome guest, my voice laced with contempt. 'It's just a cheap parlour trick. That's what all of this is, the noise, and the mess, and the furniture. It wants to scare us, because it's scared *of* us.'

The noise *does* dial down in response to my words – only a fraction, but enough that I can tell – and when I strike the switches a couple more times, the lights come on. Not all the way – it's like they're on a dimmer, but they're there, and that'll do.

It doesn't want to look weak, I think to myself. It has an *ego*. That's interesting. Can I use that?

I tug gently at Theo's hand as I start up the stairs and he matches me step for step, his own mantra quiet on his lips as he mouths it gently, over and over. Each time we pass one of the lights, positioned every couple of metres along the curve of the wall, the bulbs in them flicker briefly, as though reacting to our presence, and the closer we get to the top, the colder the air feels. Taken all together, it's an intimidating scene, but after its reaction to my insult of its ego a second ago, I can't help but wonder if it's doing all this to compensate for something.

I hesitate on the threshold of the landing, surveying the scene quickly. The space here is just as we left, neat and mostly empty but for a couple of decorative chairs and the small, neat sideboards and tables. Maybe the tantrum was just confined to downstairs. The master bedroom door is still closed, but the door to Hannah's room is ajar and through the gap I can tell it's not been affected. Why is nothing disturbed up here? Did it just want to give us a scare as we came in, to put us on edge, make us vulnerable, so it could use that opening to trap us inside before we realised what was going on?

More importantly, although I don't see chaos, and I don't see mess, I also don't see *it*.

Where is it hiding?

What is it up to?

Hand in hand with Theo, I walk slowly to the centre of the landing, right beside the spot near the banister where Hannah saw it only a few minutes before.

'Guys, make your circle. Stay over there, near the stairs.'

They follow my instructions. Theo leans in, picking up on my confusion as I try to figure out where it is and why it hasn't appeared yet. 'What is it?'

'I'm not sure,' I whisper back.

'Can't you start?'

I shake my head, glancing around quickly, eyes darting across the landing for any sign. 'I don't know what it's playing at. Dammit, where *is* it?'

'Does it matter?'

'I guess not, but…' I hesitate. All of a sudden this whole thing just doesn't feel quite *right*.

A jarring clank comes from across the landing as the closed door to the attic staircase starts to rattling violently against its frame.

'Maybe it's up there,' Theo suggests.

Maybe—

Hannah's door slams shut with a sudden *bang* and we both jump.

The master bedroom door begins to shudder.

Adam's door opens, closes, opens again.

Each of the doors leading off the landing repeat their movements in turn, faster and faster, speeding up until they all end up going at once, the cacophony drowning out the family's talisman. They try collectively to shout above it, the clamour almost unbearable.

Then as quickly as it started, it all very suddenly, very abruptly, just *stops*.

I wait, heart in my mouth.

Then the lights go out, Hannah screams, and Theo lets go of my hand.

26

The lights blind me, blazing back up suddenly as I'm reaching around frantically for Theo. When the scene comes into focus, I see Rebecca and Rob huddled against the wall with the kids, Hannah sobbing frantically. There's no more rumbling, no more cold, no more flickering lights.

And there's Theo.

He's lying on the floor, inches from where I'm crouched, his eyes closed, out cold. The second I see him, I fly down on my knees beside his prone form, checking desperately for any injury, any sign of what's wrong, *anything*.

'Come on, Theo,' I shake his shoulders gently, desperately. 'Wake up.'

'Is he okay?' Rob's voice behind me.

'I don't know,' I reply tightly, hearing my own fear.

'Maybe he fainted,' Rob suggests hesitantly as Rebecca and the others close in beside him, Hannah's hysterics dampened to a sullen sniffle. I ignore them all.

'Please, Theo. *Please*.'

I feel the tears rising. I don't know what to do.

With one hand on his face as I gently stroke his fluff, I put the other over his where it rests across his chest, leaning down to listen for a heartbeat, and—

—his fingers close slowly over mine.

I sit up quickly then, remembering how to breathe. His eyes flutter open, unsteady, unfocused, but *there*.

'Thank god,' Rebecca mutters.

I lean forward, moving to brace his head, beside myself with relief and joy after my brain having been obliterated by sheer, raw *panic* at the thought he might be injured. 'Are you okay? Are you hurt? Can you sit up?'

Theo starts to pull himself upright, sitting beside me on the floor, and I don't even care that Rebecca and the others are right there, I throw my arms around him, eyes stinging as I bury my face in the side of his neck. 'Oh god, I thought I'd lost you. I thought I wouldn't— I thought you— I—'

I pull back to see his handsome face through my tears, so grateful he's okay, leaning back in to gently press my lips against his, realising how *terrified* I was that I might never be able to do it again, ignoring the gasps from Rebecca and Rob and the giggles from the kids.

Something's wrong. I can feel it.

When I pull back, he's smiling at me, but…

I cover my mouth with my hand as the realisation dawns on me and my heart crumples like cold ash into my stomach. Oh, god no.

It's not him.

He – *it* – reaches a hand out toward me and I scoot back on the floor away from him, jumping like I've been electrocuted, climbing quickly back to my feet in horror. The others haven't cottoned on yet, and after my blatant show of affection towards him, now they're confused.

'Dot?' Rebecca frowns at me. 'What's wrong?'

'Yes, *Dot*,' it watches me steadily as I back away, its grin distorted behind Theo's smile. 'No more of your lovely kisses for me, *dear girl?*'

'Get away from it.'

'What? Why—'

'It's *not him*,' I hiss harshly.

It takes a second for them to catch up, but as it climbs smoothly up to its feet, Rob suddenly clocks what I mean and grabs the others, yanking them back, away from it. 'Oh *shit*.'

He – it – watches me steadily, at full height now, looking me slowly up and down as though it's seeing me for the very first time. When it speaks, the voice is Theo's, but at the same time it's not – it's hard, and brittle, and there's no warmth, no affection – it's just *wrong*.

'So nice to finally meet you *properly*, dear girl. In person, so to speak.'

It's so, *so* wrong.

'What do you want?'

'Oh, I think you know.' It raises Theo's eyebrows, directing a curt nod in my direction. 'I want in there. In *you*.'

My heart is threatening to beat out of my chest. The rage and pain at what it's done to Theo – what it's *doing* to him – is so palpable, so overwhelming. But I do the best I can to sound like I'm still calm and in control. 'Come on then,' I beckon it toward me. 'What's stopping you?'

It laughs, and everything in my soul breaks as I see his face, Theo's beautiful warm eyes and smile and his little creases turned into this mockery in front of me, a shell of a puppet filled with something unspeakable, tainting everything in him. 'Nice try,' it winks at me, sauntering casually across to the banister where it leans back, arms folded. 'I expect you will roll the red carpet out for me.'

I shrug casually. 'It's not doing you any good where you are now.'

'But dear *girl*, this is a perfect fit for me, for the moment. As long as I have him, I have *you*.'

Grace's warning that it was using Theo as bait rings in my ears.

'Why me?' I face it down across the landing, equal parts incensed and horrified. 'Why do you want into my head so badly? What's so useful in there?'

It takes a deep breath, sucking air through its teeth, eyes closed as its head drops back. For a second, I wonder if it's sleeping, or fallen out of him, or its batteries have gone. Then its head snaps back up, eyes burning viciously through me.

'Imagine a grid of electricity. Hundreds of thousands of buildings, linked by the same conductor, interconnected, pretty lights dancing across a screen somewhere.'

Pretty modern analogy for a centuries-old demon spirit.

'Whoever controls that conductor, controls all of that power. They let all the people have their pretty lights, or they turn them off again.'

I shrug. 'Okay.'

'Now, it also works the *other* way. By flicking a different switch, instead of sending electricity *out* to all those hundreds of thousands of buildings, you can harness it, pull it back from them to use for yourself. And because all of them are connected to one another, not only do you get to *use* that power, but you get to *control* all of the buildings.'

I'm beginning to see the picture it's trying to paint. A massive network of lights, criss-crossing like a spider web, at each junction a building sharing its power supply, being controlled to do… what?

'That is what the other side is made of, but they are souls, I suppose you would call them, rather than buildings. Untapped energy, galaxies of it, an infinite capacity of power, connected for eons,' it explains, awestruck with its own story. 'It never runs out, and more join it every day, thousands upon thousands of them. But to harness that power, to *use* it, you need a conductor.'

Why do I feel like it means me.

'*Ahhhhh,*' it sighs wistfully. 'What a *dream* that would be. To have all that power within oneself, to use at your command.'

'Use it for what?'

'For what? For *this*.'

It clicks its fingers, and a narrow corner table against the wall jumps up, spilling its contents before whizzing past my head by barely an inch, shooting over the banister behind not-Theo and clattering into pieces on the marble floor downstairs.

'Shit.' Rob mutters nervously from across the landing.

In an instant, its attention snaps towards them and its eyes glint with evil intent. As it flashes me a twisted imitation of Theo's usually warm smile, a tall vase from another corner hurtles in their direction without missing a beat.

'Move!' I beckon quickly for them to get behind me. The bauble smashes into dust against the wall a second after they do.

It can't hurt me, though. Not if it wants me.

Time to test that theory.

'*This* is what you want?' I shake my head defiantly, fighting not to see Theo's face as I focus all of my rage, all my *hate* towards it. 'You want to throw shit around like a toddler?'

It cackles again, resting its hands casually on the banister behind it now, spreading its arms and leaning back lazily. 'Dear *girl*, of course not.'

It tips its head, watching as the others situate themselves behind me, eyes flashing maniacally as it raises a hand to wave teasingly at the kids.

'*Chaos*, dear girl. You said it yourself, furniture and lights… parlour tricks. But with *real* power, with all of that wonderful energy that exists there in the light, beyond the veil… *chaos*. That. Is. What. I. *Want*.'

Talking to this – *thing* – that looks so much like my beautiful Theo and yet isn't, is pulling me apart. 'What does any of this have to do with me?'

It shrugs, straightening its long form back up idly, bored of our conversation. 'To use that energy on this plane, you need the conductor. To connect all of that immeasurable power from the light, to bring it all through to this side and focus it. Suitable conductors, powerful enough themselves to link to the other side and harness it, and more importantly, powerful enough to control it, do not come along like *buses*, dear girl.'

It smirks playfully., 'I've been waiting for *you* for a long, long time.' It looks me up and down slowly, leering.

It's not him, I tell myself, trying not to break down. It's not Theo.

'You *are* that conductor. With not only the power to summon all of those souls out from the light, to draw on their power, but the strength to channel it, to control it. At least,' it adds teasingly, 'you will once *I'm* inside that pretty little head.'

I wonder why it isn't already, and decide to chance the question.

'If I'm the one you wanted all along, if nobody else was ever any use to you, why all this fucking about? Why even mess with Rebecca and Rob in the first place, why *any* of this?'

I stop short of mentioning what it's doing right now to Theo.

'Ah yes,' it grins coldly, eyes flashing, knowing exactly what I didn't say. 'The poor, lovesick *priest*. You realise, that misguided fool is in here trying to *fight* me?'

I feel sick. Oh god, Theo.

'Since the second I slipped in, when his proverbial back was turned. Too busy, too distracted by being so, *so* in love with *you*. What a liability. Would you like to see?'

It's hard to describe exactly how his face changes, but somehow it does, enough for me to see *him*. He's Theo again, and his face is all anguish and pain and fear, his big brown eyes are wide with it, and when he says my name and it's really Theo's voice, I know that he *is* still in there, he *is* fighting. I don't know how much of what else it's said is true or not, but it wasn't lying about that.

'Dot, don't listen to it,' he urges desperately, 'don't you *dare* do what it wants—'

And then just like that he's *gone*, and back in his place is *it*, cackling horrifically under a twisted mask of Theo's face. 'Enough out of *him*.'

'Why don't you just get in here if that's what you want,' I rail at it, the anger in me rising like bile, threatening to choke me. 'Leave him alone.'

'But my dear girl, it's so nice and cosy in here,' it taunts. 'I might make myself comfortable for a while.'

'You don't want him.'

'Oh *yes*,' it ignores me, pacing slowly up and down the edge of the landing. 'I could really enjoy taking *this* one out for a test drive. He has such... *thoughts* of you, dear girl.'

I try not to rise to its bait, but the idea it can see inside Theo's mind, that it might know everything that's passed between us – that *violation*, that defilement of something so good and right and beautiful – it makes me feel sick to my stomach. It saunters forward in my direction, blinking mischievously.

'Maybe I should show you exactly what the good *Father* would like to do with you.'

My hackles rise. 'Shut up.'

'I do think you would *enjoy* it, dear girl. I most certainly would.'

'Shut *up*.'

It reaches out towards me. 'I think I might just be able to have you *beg* me—'

'*Shut up!*'

I smack its outstretched hand away, reminding myself again and again that it's not Theo, it's *not him* saying these things, it's *not*. It recoils sharply, stepping back from me as if I've burned it. My frustration and anger spills over and for a moment, I see the absurdity of the situation from the outside. Apparently, this is my life now: being sexually harassed by a power-hungry demonic spirit wearing a human suit that looks like my new old boyfriend. I have no patience left for this nonsense anymore, and I want my Theo back.

'You know what I think?' I challenge it, steam practically coming out of my ears. 'I think for all your bluster and bullshit, you're not anywhere near as badass as you make out.'

It sneers back at me, amused. 'Is that so?'

'The lights, the throwing things around, even your sad little attempts at possession.'

That last one might have me skating on thin ice. Any level of possession requires a good bit of power, just like Grace said, and it's a damn sight more than just misdirection and showmanship.

'If you were really what you claim, you'd be *in* me already,' I spit at it. 'Smoke and mirrors. That's all you are.'

It tips its head slyly, its lizard gaze not leaving my eyes.

And suddenly Theo's there in front of me again, completely normal as if nothing ever happened. 'Dot? What the—'

Then he falls to his knees, face contorted in pain, screaming, head in his hands. '*Nooo*, make it stop, make it *stop, Christ, Dot, help me*—'

But it's over as quickly as it began. My heart seizes in my chest as it lifts its head quietly to look back up at me, its eyes narrowed in warning.

'Careful, dear girl,' it hisses, rising slowly back to its feet. 'Using him to hurt *you* would be a good deal more fun for me, but I can just hurt *him*.'

It's clearly not planning to leave Theo willingly. But why isn't it even trying to get into me?

'You can't,' I suddenly realise aloud. 'You can't get into me, can you.'

It shrugs dismissively.

Oh, please. I know fake casual when I see it. I practically invented it. 'Why not?'

It heaves a light sigh. 'For what I have in mind... as a host, I require you to be... *compliant*, dear girl.'

'As a *host?*' Eek, that sounds creepy.

'Well, of course. You already understand that this would not be a temporary arrangement.'

I'd already figured – I said as much to Rebecca half an hour ago – but it sounds so much worse coming out of *it*.

'In order for it to be effective, the host must be completely acquiescent. Give their mind, their power over to my control *willingly*. Invite me in, if you will.'

Like a vampire. Figures. So I was right. It *can't* come into me, not completely, not the way it needs to. Not without an invitation. 'Can that even work?'

'It can. It has.'

It *has?* 'You've done it before?'

'Rarely. As I explained, conductors of your... *talents*... are maddeningly uncommon. Maybe one or two in one of your centuries, and again, they must also be *willing*. Even then, the connection can still end too abruptly to be... worth the effort.'

'How?'

Another tip of the head, as it raises its eyebrows. 'Other humans often do not care for chaos. The last time, a century ago in your understanding, the host was more than willing. I had no need at all to create such an encouraging set of circumstances as I have with you. But he had his own agenda. His own lust for power, which affected others. As a host, his body became... *unviable.*'

'Unviable.' I blink in understanding. 'You mean *dead?* Somebody killed him?'

It shrugs blithely again. 'Repeatedly, if the rumours are correct. And just as our delicious chaos was beginning to take shape. Such a waste.'

I'm starting to realise the enormity of what it wants, and it's not a pretty thought.

'So let me get this straight,' I slowly set out what I think I understand from the last few minutes. 'You want me to invite you into my head, let you take over, and then what – you use me to channel energy from the other side and create chaos on this one until I eventually die?'

It smiles broadly, and for a second it almost looks like Theo. But it's only an unnatural, uncanny-valley perversion. 'Dear girl. I am so *pleased* you understand.'

Theo *is* in there, though. Somewhere.

I *have* to get him out. Or get *it* out of *him*. I can't leave him like this, to be puppeteered or tortured or god knows what else even worse it might come up with.

'What I offer is a simple trade,' it shrugs. 'You give me what I want: freely, willingly, without resistance, and he shall be returned to you.'

Except for the catch. 'But I won't *be* me.'

'A minor detail. And of no concern to me.'

'If I do this,' I begin carefully, 'if I go along with it... How can I possibly trust that you'll do what you say?'

It rolls its eyes. 'Dear *girl*, I cannot possess more than one of you at a time. If I come into you, I am *obliged* to leave your precious priest behind.'

Either I give up myself, or I give up Theo. If I give up myself, and this thing really goes ahead and does what it claims it wants to, what the hell might I unleash?

But if I give up Theo…

I can't. I just *can't*. I'll never forgive myself if I leave him trapped in there, with that *thing*. And I'll never, *ever* recover from it. What might it do to him? What might it make *him* do, in an effort to try and make me comply?

'Your hesitation is understandable. This is no small undertaking. If it were, there would be no need for all of this…' it gestures to the space around us, to the others, to Theo's body cocooned around itself. 'All of this *motivation*.'

It's painted me into a corner. I won't – *can't* – abandon Theo, and it knows it.

'But perhaps… a sweetener? If it will make you more… *accommodating*.'

I frown back dubiously. I don't trust a bloody word this thing says.

'What do you mean?'

'Time,' it suggests simply. 'For me it makes little difference; in the light such a concept does not exist, as well you are aware, dear girl. But maybe for you… to feel you can reach some peace. Some closure. I might even… let you say goodbye to him. *Briefly.*'

Tears sting my eyes at the thought. This is real. This is actually real: this is going to happen. What else can I possibly do?

'As a show of good faith,' it goes on, 'I will not harm him. I will not use him at all. He will simply sleep, like the boy.' It nods at Adam, huddled back behind me with the rest of his family. 'Until it is time.'

My mind reels, desperately clawing for something, *anything*, inspiration, idea, a plan.

But there's nothing.

I have no choice.

I nod once, eyes closed in defeat.

It returns the gesture. 'A day. I will give you a day. Until this time tomorrow.'

And with that, Theo collapses.

27

A day.

How did it all go so wrong so fast?

Doesn't matter now. This is where we are. This is how it ends.

I'm barely conscious of the hubbub of noise and panic as the others rush to Theo's body as it hits the deck in front of me.

'Is he conscious?'

'Father? Father Gregory?'

'Dad, is he okay?'

'Dot?'

Somewhere in my numb paralysis, I hear Rebecca's voice as she lays a gentle hand on my shoulder. '*Dot?*'

It's only as I look up and notice how blurry she is that I realise I'm crying.

'What do you want us to do?'

I look dully over at Theo, prone on the floor as they hover, pointlessly trying to wake him. 'Look after him.'

'Well of course,' she shrugs quickly. 'But I mean, what do you want us to *do?* To fight it?'

I shake my head slowly. 'You can't fight it.'

'But—'

'*I* can't fight it.'

She does a double take. 'What?'

I've run out of words to explain. Words, energy, balls.

'You're not seriously going to do what it wants?'

I shrug back, empty, utterly beaten.

She raises her voice. 'No. Dot, you can't.'

'I don't have a choice,' I murmur quietly, on autopilot.

'You *can't*.'

'I don't have a *choice*,' I repeat angrily. 'What else can I do?'

'You can *fight*.'

'It *has* Theo,' I round on her sharply. 'He's trapped in there, with that— with that *thing*.'

'I know. I saw.'

'Even if I *could* fight it without him, if I try— if I try and do *anything* while it has him, it'll *hurt* him, Rebecca. It'll torture him in there. Or make him do god only knows what awful shit out here.'

'And what do you think's going to happen if you give it what it wants?' she argues back. 'What do you think it'll do once it has *you?* Just leave all of us to live long, happy lives, Father Gregory included?'

'I don't *know!*' my voice breaks as I drop to my knees, the tears flowing hard now along with the despair. 'Maybe? Probably not, but…' I look back up at her. I've never felt so desperate and lost in my life.

Well, maybe once before. The first time I lost *him*.

'I can't just leave him in there, Rebecca. I *can't*.'

'I know, I know,' she crouches down beside me, sympathy in her voice. 'But there has to be something else. There has to be another way.'

I shake my head sadly. 'It'll only leave Theo once I let it in. *All* the way in. And once that happens, it has control.'

Rebecca frowns. 'Maybe not.'

I look back at her blankly, unable to think, let alone follow what she's getting at.

'It said the last time it did this, the person had their own agenda,' she reminds me. 'They had a lust for power, and that got them killed, so it couldn't use them anymore.'

'So?'

She continues along her own train of thought. 'Well, if their lust for power got them killed, doesn't that imply they had some agency? That they acted for themselves, not completely under its control?'

I don't know about that. But her words spark another idea in my mind, a very different one. A grim one, too, but potentially effective. 'It also said it only gets one or two chances in one of our centuries,' I recall.

'Right. So, what are you thinking?'

I climb resignedly back to my feet. 'I'm the only one that's any actual use to it. All of you, Theo, you were all just – what did it call it – *motivation*, to beat me down enough that I'd go along with it. If I'm not available, it'll leave until another useful host pops up. But that won't be your problem. That won't be anyone's problem for another century,' I go on. 'And let's face it, with the state of the world, there'll probably be nobody left alive by then anyway.'

Rebecca frowns. 'What do you mean, if you're not available?'

I told you it was a grim idea.

'Just what I said.' I meet her eyes wanting her to understand that I mean what I'm about to suggest. 'It told us itself how to get rid of it. When the last host was killed, it was forced to go back to where it came from, until I came along.'

She shakes her head as she catches my drift. 'You're not seriously suggesting…'

'That's exactly what I'm suggesting,' I nod firmly. 'I invite it in. It leaves Theo, it comes into me. Once you're sure he's okay, that he's him, and I'm not me anymore, you… *take care* of me.'

'I can't believe I'm hearing this,' she storms as Rob heads over.

'I'd do it myself, but I suspect once it's in there, it won't let me.'

'He's out cold,' Rob interrupts, 'but he's definitely alive. Just like Adam.' He hesitates for a second as he notices Rebecca's stony expression. 'What's going on?'

'Oh, nothing much,' she shrugs dramatically. 'Dot just wants us to kill her, that's all.'

'*What?!*'

'Not me,' I correct her. '*It*. I won't *be* me anymore, not once it's in here. That's the whole point.'

'That's insane.' Rob shakes his head, eyes wide in disbelief.

'Absolutely not.' Rebecca fumes. 'No. Not going to happen, sorry. There has to be another way.'

I scoff lightly. 'If you've got a better idea, Rebecca, I'm all ears.'

'What about what I just said?'

'What, *agency?*' I shake my head. 'We don't know how true that is. Even if it was for the last host, it might not be for me. We just don't know.'

'But if—'

'*If,*' I parrot back angrily. 'If. You want to risk your lives on *if?* You want to risk *theirs?*' I nod towards the kids, sitting either side of Theo's body, each cradling one of his huge hands in their tiny ones. 'We can't be *sure* how much agency I might have until it's in there. And if it turns out I don't have *any*, well then, it's already too late and we're all screwed.'

'But we can't—'

'You have to.'

Rob turns away, muttering as he wanders dully back over to the kids. 'This isn't happening.'

I turn back to Rebecca. 'Look, I know it's not ideal.'

'*Ideal?!*'

'Trust me, it's not exactly my first choice either,' I snap. 'A couple of hours ago, I thought Theo and I were going to fight it together, get rid of it, *together*, and then once it was all over the two of us might actually have a chance at a *life*.'

I stop myself. I can't think about that, any of that. Not now. Not anymore.

I lay it out for her plainly. 'We can't leave it in Theo. We can't get it out of him without letting it into me. And we can't let in *me* without it bringing down god knows what chaos and destruction. Not just for all of you, but for *everyone*.'

Rebecca stares back at me, shaking her head.

'Now,' I go on, 'if I let it in and straightaway I realise there's something I can do, great. But considering I couldn't get rid of it completely when I fought it from out *here*, I'd say the chances of my being able to do that after I've given it an open invitation to take over my body are likely to be slim to none.'

'I— I don't...' she hesitates, then sighs. 'How would we even...'

'I don't know,' I reply flatly, 'and I don't want to. The less I know about the details, the better. I don't want it peeking into my head the second it gets in and immediately figuring out the plan before you have chance to execute it.'

She pulls a horrified face.

'Sorry. Bad choice of words.'

Rebecca looks around blankly at nothing in particular, lost.

'Just make sure it's something you can make look as though I did it myself. It'll be easier for all of you, after I mean. With the police and stuff.'

'This is— what— *how*—'

I shrug back at her. 'You've got a day to figure it out.'

She sighs back at me sadly. 'This can't be how it ends. It *can't*.'

'Don't feel too bad about it. The one thing it hasn't banked on is that I'd actually rather be dead than let anything control me but *me*.'

As it is, I'm starting to feel oddly calm about the whole thing.

It's not as though my life was all that great anyway. Other than Theo – and right now I can't allow myself to think about what this might do to him, I can't, or I might chicken out – I'll barely even be missed. I mean, Lisa'll have to get someone else to split the rent, but she'll probably just move Pen in full time. Grace might notice a disturbance in the Force, but that's about it; we've already established she never really gave a crap in the first place. No doubt Jackie'll raise a glass for me on the next work do, and Mags…

Damn. *Mags*. I still have one more thing left to do. But I do have the day it so graciously allowed me, so I can fit it in. If nothing else, at least I can shuffle off this mortal coil knowing I've done *one* decent in my crappy stupid life. 'I need to ask you a favour.'

Rebecca laughs bitterly. 'This doesn't count?'

I ignore that. I do appreciate what I'm asking them to do tomorrow will probably scar them both for life, but at least they'll still have one. Unlike me.

'It's a work favour.'

'A *work* favour?' she squeaks, wide-eyed. 'Are you serious? In the middle of all this?'

I nod quickly. 'This thing I've been trying to sort out all week.'

Screw it. Mags can't be pissed at me if I'm dead.

'I'm going in tomorrow, hopefully to get it done and dusted for good.'

'You're still going in tomorrow?! Have you completely lost your mind?'

'Non-negotiable, I already told you,' I remind her. 'None of this changes that. I'll be done by lunch, that's plenty of time before the deadline runs out.'

'But what if it—'

'It's not going to do anything now, is it,' I sigh. 'It's showing me its good faith, remember? So I don't go and rope in my Guides, or Grace, or any other medium who could help trip it up. It's got Theo already, it knows damn well he's all it needs to keep me in line.'

'Okay. So what's the work favour? You want a memorial plaque in reception?'

'Funny. No, I want you to promise me that when I come back tomorrow, if I haven't sorted things out, when you go back you'll speak to Jackie and Mags about Nathan and find some way to finally *sack* that fucker.'

Rebecca groans. 'Oh god. What did he do this time?'

'If tomorrow goes to plan, you'll probably find out. But if not, talk to the others and fix it. I don't care how you get rid of him, I don't care what for, even if it's not for what he's done. But you *get rid of him*.'

'That's your work favour?'

I shrug. 'Unless you happen to know anyone who does kneecaps, which would be my preferred solution.'

She shrugs. 'Okay.'

Something else occurs to me. 'Actually, while I'm asking...'

'I'm not a genie, Dot. I don't have infinite wishes.'

'Give Mags a proper job. She's smart, she's capable, she's working her arse off trying to get qualified. Stop letting her rot doing the same boring shit as me.'

'Such as?'

'Figure something out.'

'Anything else on your shopping list?'

'That's it.'

Rebecca takes a second to think then nods, all business, one hand out so that we can shake on it. 'Done.'

I realise how much I've missed Big Boss – how she is when she's in her element, where nothing touches her. I'll likely never see that again.

'One last thing,' she frowns back at me sadly, then looks over at the group across the floor. 'When he comes out of it, when you're… you know. *Gone*. What do you want me to tell him?'

God. That thought *hurts*.

'Tell him…' I choke back sudden tears. 'Tell him I'm sorry.'

She nods dully.

'But I'll visit him and explain. *After*.'

28

Rebecca ordered a takeaway for dinner, my choice. I opted for Chinese. One final pancake roll before the end became nigh. The family huddled up together on one of the sofas in the cleaned-up front room to watch a film, something Disney-ish I didn't recognise. You could be forgiven for spotting the scene through the window and assuming it was just a normal, cosy family evening in.

I didn't join them. Instead, I spent all night in the back room, well into the early hours. Between us three adults, we'd just about managed to get Theo's comatose form down the stairs while the kids offered helpful directions on how not to drop him. Settling him gently on the sitting room sofa – the same one he and I had taken it in turns to sleep on the night before – I pulled up a chair beside him, tucked him under a blanket, and talked.

Not out loud.

I started by telling him everything I'd begun to remember about us, the us from before. How lonely and different and apart from the world I'd always felt as a kid, and how that all changed overnight when he first appeared in my life. How much I'd adored him from the start, all sighing and does eyes every time he smiled, trying to hide my childish blushes every time he directed its beam of sunshine at me. How I'd never really noticed boys before, and then all these new, confusing feelings surfaced that I couldn't name and didn't know what to do with. How the thought of telling him how I felt was so utterly terrifying to twelve-year-old me – what if he doesn't like me the same way?

What if I'm not pretty enough? What if he thinks I'm just weird? What if, what if, what if? There was a notion that it could all go wrong so easily, that telling him might mean losing him, and that was unthinkable.

I told him about how, after I eventually *did* lose him, everything in my life spun out of control.

I told him how amazing he is, how strong, how brave for going through all he had and becoming the man he was now. How much I wished I could've been there beside him back then, how things might have ended up differently for both of us, and how I'd do anything to be able to go back and take away all of his hurt, all of his pain, to protect him and care for him and love him the way he deserved.

I told him I love him. As many times as I could.

I apologised for letting him down so completely, letting him get in this position in the first place, letting him get hurt. I begged him to forgive me for what was coming next, although I didn't specify exactly what that was, in case the stowaway might also be lurking, listening in the shadows, within him or without. I told him if there were any other option, any way in the world we could both get out of this messed up situation whole, *together*, that I'd do it in a second. But I didn't know what else to do. Without him, by myself, I'm not strong enough to fix it. I'm not whole enough. I'm not enough.

I told him how much I'd miss him.

It was a good job I wasn't trying to tell him any of it aloud. I wouldn't have been able to get the words out, what with all the full-on ugly crying. And I got nothing back from him, of course, not that I expected to. Wherever he was, I couldn't see him, I couldn't hear him. I could barely even feel the sense of him, although it was definitely there, *somewhere*, and I was grateful at least for that. All I could really do was hope that as I sat tearily beside his sleeping form – stroking his face, his hair, his scruff, holding his unmoving hands in mine, desperate to never let go – that somehow, some part of him might hear me. And understand.

There was just about enough room for me to curl up beside him, after I'd finally finished silently sharing everything I needed to say. I wrapped myself around him and took out the photo of us as kids for one last look. Then I carefully tore away the top half, erasing Grace and Shaun and his parents from the memory and leaving just the part with the two of us together, slipped it carefully back into his trouser pocket and tried to sleep.

Not that I got much rest. I woke repeatedly through the night, panicking he might be gone, checking his heartbeat under the blanket pulled over us, feeling the slow rise and fall of his chest beneath my fingers. It didn't matter, though. All I really wanted was to spend those few hours alongside him, giving him my warmth, my comfort, in the only way I knew how, for as long as I could get away with it. Had it not been for the other big obligation left on my To Do list for this week, I would never have moved at all.

When Rebecca saw me off in the morning, it was an awkward parting. It's not every day you wave goodbye to a departing guest, knowing that once they're gone you'll be Googling ways to kill them later. She promised me they'd take turns to babysit Theo until I got back, that he wouldn't be left alone for a minute, and if anything – *anything* – happened which suggested our mutual enemy wasn't sticking to its part of our 24-hour bargain, she'd summon me straight back.

Mags was already waiting for me outside mine, perched on the front wall, immaculately dressed and projecting a zen-like appearance of calm. Eager to get the whole thing over with now, I didn't even bother turning off the engine, just bibbed the horn a couple of times and leaned over to pop the passenger door open. She was silent as she slipped inside.

'Ready to go?'

'Ready,' Mags nods, her expression resolute. When she turns and finally catches sight of mine – puffy, blotchy, eyes red – her expression softens dramatically. 'What's wrong?'

'Nothing. Seatbelt,' I nod back.

She clips it dutifully into place. 'Did something happen at Rebecca's? Did you get it all sorted?'

My teeth set tightly. 'Not yet.'

'Come on, Dot, it's obvious something's wrong—'

'Look,' I turn to her quickly. 'I'll explain later, all right? For now, let's just deal with this.'

The last thing I want to do is burden her with my own ridiculous life when she's about to face her own demons. Mags starts as though she wants to argue, but I give her a pleading look and she retreats.

'Let's get it done.'

Relief floods me as I check my blind spot and pull back out. I can't talk about it now – about what happened, about Theo – I *daren't*. I won't be able to keep it together, and I have to. I have to get through this for Mags, this one good thing left that I might actually be able to pull off. Not like everything else I've stuffed up so colossally this week.

The tape deck is all that fills the silence as we head into Brum, leaving the car in the quietest corner of Snow Hill car park and heading the back route to the office. When we reach the delivery entrance to the building at twenty to ten, Jackie's already hovering beside the security hut, smoking nervously.

'Haven't seen you with one of those in a while,' I chide gently she gets the guard on duty to swipe us through the gate.

She ignores my observation. 'You're early.'

'By all of five minutes.'

'And you,' she turns to Mags, stomping out the remains of her cigarette on the ground, enveloping her in a giant bear hug. 'You my lovey have balls of absolute granite. I didn't expect you to be here.'

Mags forces a half-smile as Jackie lets her go. 'Thanks, Jack.'

'Are you going to let us in on your cunning plan?'

'Of course,' she looks back at me, taking hold of Mags' hand. 'I'm sorry I couldn't give you details yesterday, but it was all a bit frantic setting it up. I had to email invites, sort catering with the canteen and you just *know* how much they hate those last-minute requests, especially for so many people.'

'Jack,' I interrupt, 'you're talking like we know what's going on. What do you need *catering* for?'

'Izzy wanted it to look legit.'

'Izzy?'

'Yeah.'

'Izzy Ramsay?'

'Yeah,' she repeats. 'This whole thing is their show, mate.'

Beetlejuice again. From the party. The one who sent me home on a bonus half day and told me not to worry about Pat.

Mags looks at Jackie wide-eyed. 'Aren't they the one who sacked half the Technology guys?'

'Just the bad half.'

'By all accounts,' I add for Mags' benefit, 'they're quite the badass. *They're* your secret weapon?'

Jackie grins broadly. 'They already know his history, things he's done, what he's got away with. Everything the firm's brushed under the carpet in the name of client fees.'

'He's been getting away with all that for years, though,' remind her dubiously. 'The Senior Partners on the Board have never cared before. What's different?'

'Izzy is. They have clout.'

'Clout?'

'They're *part* of the Board, remember? They threatened to report the firm to the Law Society themselves,' she explains, eager to share, 'whistle blow on the lot, all the other dirt they've been collecting since they started. Also to blast them on socials, which of course scared the hell out of the other Senior Partners. Most of the old guard don't understand how it works, so any mention of it scares the bejesus out of them.'

I'm genuinely quite shocked. In a good way. 'So, what's happening?'

Jackie straightens up proudly. 'Office-wide seminar in the conference room. Compulsory attendance for all fee earning staff.' She pauses for a second to enjoy the drama of her big reveal. 'And they all have to hand over the phones as they go in.'

Wow. That'll do it, all right.

'For internal security purposes,' she adds solemnly.

'I'm impressed,' I tip my head in congratulations. 'And the catering?'

'Well, they do actually have to sit through a *real* three-hour seminar.'

'What about?'

Jackie smiles awkwardly. 'Sexual harassment and coercion in the workplace.'

Mags laughs lightly as she and I exchange glances. 'That your bright idea, or Izzy's?'

'Joint effort. There's only so many external presenters available at such short notice, and when the one we could book happened to have that on their list.'

'Couldn't resist the irony, eh.'

'Something like that.'

I nod. I've got to hand it to her, her and Izzy both. It's certainly a cast iron way to part him from his phone, and get it into our hands. 'So, what now?'

'It's a ten AM start, so they'll be heading in soon. Phil and I are on phone collection duty. Nobody gets through the door without handing theirs over, so woe betide anyone who's been daft enough to leave theirs on their desk.'

'Wouldn't that have been easier? Tell them all to leave them behind, then I could've gone up and swiped it.'

'Couldn't guarantee he wouldn't lock away,' she counters. 'Or that his little minion wouldn't hold onto it for him for safe keeping.'

'Minion?' Mags frowns.

'She means Pat,' I explain.

'Once they're all inside and the presentation starts, my IT guy will come and do his magic to unlock the phone.' Jackie nods at me. 'Then it's up to you.'

'And if I don't find anything?'

She shrugs. 'Then he'll never know. Even if he thought someone had been nosing in it, it wouldn't matter. It's a company-issued phone, remember? They can take possession and check the contents any time they want. And there's no *specific* instruction about who checks it for them.'

'You've thought of everything.'

Jackie checks her watch. 'I'd better go. Give it a few minutes, just in case there's any stragglers, then come up through the fire exit stairs and wait for me behind the door to reception. I'll bring it to you there.'

One final hug, for both of us this time, then she disappears through the fire exit door – propped open with an extinguisher, naturally – and into the stairwell beyond with a wink and a gleam in her eye, leaving Mags and I outside.

'You okay about all this?'

She shrugs. 'Much as I can be.'
I nod. 'At least it'll be over soon.'
'Yeah. This part, anyway.' Mags hesitates. 'Dot?'
'Mmm?'
'What if you don't find it? If he's deleted it or something, I mean?'
I frown. 'Wouldn't that be good?'
'In one way, yeah. But then…' she trails off unhappily. 'I'll never know for sure, will I?'
She's not wrong. I had wondered about that possibility myself.
'And if it's not there, if you don't find anything, they'll have nothing to use to get rid of him.'
I remember my talk with Rebecca. No point telling Mags about it now and upsetting her all over again. If it comes to that, she'll find out soon enough.
'Let's just see happens, okay? We'll deal with that if we have to.'
Mags is quiet again. We stay like that for a while, until I get fed up of waiting.
'Come on,' I nudge her. 'We've given it long enough. It's cold out here.'
She looks up, taking a deep breath.
'Ready?'
Mags nods slowly, eyes locked on mine. 'Ready.'
'Then let's go.'

23

We're both tense as we trudge our way up from the basement exit to the ground floor stairwell where Jackie's meeting us. Through the glazed strip in the door, I can see her sitting at the reception desk, leaning forward over the desk with her back to us. Across from her in the other is Paul, her IT guy, one of the Tetriminos from the party. He's messing with something which looks very much like a standard work-issue phone.

Nathan's phone.

Seconds after I see the both of them, they shoot up from their seats and cross the floor briskly in our direction. That didn't take long. The heavy, one-way fire door opens with a creak as Jackie pushes the metal bar down on the other side to unlock it and leans into the gap.

'Here you go,' she hands it to me.

We've got it. We've actually, *really* got it.

'Paul'll hover out here for a few minutes. You have any problem with it, just give him a nod and he'll sort you out.'

Paul gives us a friendly wave from the reception side of the doorway.

'Thanks, Jackie.'

She nods purposefully, smiling reassuringly at Mags before pulling the door back shut with a thud.

I turn to Mags. 'You sure you want me to look?'

Mags closes her eyes. 'Rather you than anyone else.'

So, I look.

I scroll through photos and videos, anything dated from the

last week. Then further back, in case there's any way he could've moved them into the older part of the camera roll. Then I check through all the albums – there's no obvious labelling to indicate what they are, but I guess even he wouldn't be stupid enough to name it 'Illegal Rapey Blackmail Videos.' I go into each folder in turn, tap on every banal cover icon to check the contents.

There are loads of pictures: rugby games, selfies at the bar with what I assume are probably his equally slimy friends, pictures of his fancy car. There are quite a few of him with different girls, arms slung around each of them, all smiles, all much younger than are age appropriate for his middle-aged arse. Icky, but not illegal. Mags watches me the whole time, sitting on the stairs, trying to hide her distress, but the longer I stand there scrolling, the more upset she's getting.

'Anything?'

'Not yet,' I try to keep my voice even.

There's nothing there.

I check his other files just in case. I never realised my phone had different areas to store stuff until last year. when I downloaded a free ticket for the Glee Club and couldn't find it. Lisa showed me where to look. But there's nothing. Nothing in the Cloud, nothing in deleted items. Could he have transferred the footage somewhere and then permanently deleted it, right after she left his place?

Mags catches the look of despair I'm failing to hide and struggles to hold back tears. 'Dot?' she croaks desperately.

Shit. *Shit*. There's nothing here.

After all this, how can there be *nothing here?*

'Just a second, love.' I try to think. What else? What else might I have missed?

I tap on the door to get Paul's attention and he opens it straightaway, popping his head through. 'Any joy?'

'Not yet. Is there any way to tell if he's – I dunno, uploaded something from the phone, then deleted it?'

Paul shakes his head. 'No. Not that I know of.'

'Any way he could have something on it but have…' I shake my head, grasping frantically at straws. 'Hidden it somehow?'

'Depends what. Jackie didn't tell me exactly what you were looking for, but some file types you can hide. Like—'

'Pictures?' Hope surges in my chest.

Paul nods. 'Photos, videos, downloads, you can—'

'How can we see if there's something like that? Something hidden?'

He reaches out. 'Pass it here.'

I hand it back to him, so fast I almost drop it.

'It's just in Settings,' Paul explains matter-of-factly, tapping away. 'Photos…ah. There we are. You see?'

He shows me the screen. There's an option called 'Show Hidden Album,' with a little green toggle button, currently greyed out.

My heart thunks loudly in my chest as Paul taps it and hands the phone back to me.

'There you go. If there *are* any hidden files on there, they should show up now.'

I scroll quickly back to the camera roll.

'I'd be surprised though,' he goes on. 'Most people in this place don't even realise that's a feature. The default is set for nothing to be hidden, so if it *was* enabled…'

I keep scrolling. *Albums.*

'It would definitely be deliberate,' he finishes.

My eyes widen. Holy shit.

There are *loads* of them.

And judging by the cover icons, way, *way* more than of just Mags.

'Jesus.'

Paul clocks my horrified expression – coupled with Mags on the stairs, head now buried in her hands – and steps quickly back out of the doorway uncomfortably. 'I'll leave you to it. Knock if you need anything else, okay?'

'*Jesus.*'

I don't know what else to say as I swipe up and down on the screen. I count ten – no, more like twelve – but wait, there's another, and *another*, further down as I keep scrolling. Each icon is a woman's feature: a head of hair, a tattoo, a set of freckles. I don't know how to work out if Mags is in here amongst all of these, not without going into individual folders to look. But god, I really, *really* don't want to do that if I don't have to.

What the hell *is* all this?

'Mags? Love?'

A muffled acknowledgement reaches me from beneath her hair.

'You don't have any tattoos, do you?'

She sniffs, looking up suddenly, confused. 'What? No. Why?'

'Then this one definitely isn't you.' I frown at a folder showing a snippet of a tattoo, a fierce-looking Chinese dragon.

'*This* one?' she blinks back, standing slowly from where she's been sat hunched on the stairs and stepping close enough to peek tentatively over my shoulder. 'What do you mean, this one?'

Mags stops short at the sight. 'What the—'

She snatches the phone from my hands, scrolling furiously.

'There's about fifteen of them, I think—'

'There's more than that,' she shakes her head, eyes wide, fixed on the screen. 'Did you see all the ones at the bottom?'

Now I look along with her. 'Shit, no.'

'These go back for, what—' she scans the dates as they change on the index screen. 'Right back to when he first started.'

I can't get my head around it.

'And I'm in here somewhere…' Mags muses quietly. 'At least I'm not alone.'

I register the dispassion on her face and raise my eyebrows. 'You're very chill about this all of a sudden.'

As she meets my eyes I see a faint spark, a flash of the joyful girl I know, the one from before last weekend. 'It's not just me. Don't you see? I didn't… I wasn't… if he's done this to all these other—' she breaks off, struggling to get the words out.

'If he's done it to all these other women, that means it wasn't my fault.'

'Oh, Mags.' I put my arms around her quickly. 'Love, it was never your fault. None of it was your fault.'

She sniffs quietly against my shoulder for a minute before pulling back. 'We need to be sure. *I* need to be sure. That I'm there, I mean.'

'Yeah. Well, we can eliminate tattoos, redheads, anyone of colour.' I frown at the screen in her hand. 'That still leaves a lot of folders, though.'

'I could probably…' Mags hesitates. 'Tell. From the icons. If it's me. I'd still need you to check what's in the folder, though.' She swallows. 'Just to make sure.'

I nod. 'I can do that.'

I don't want to. The thought of looking at *any* of it – not just her, any of it – makes me sick to my stomach. But if she can bear to see even the smallest reminder of what she's been through, I can pull up my big girl panties and get through this for her.

Mags scrolls back towards the top, to the newest data.

'That one,' she points eventually. 'That could be me.'

The icon is a patch of skin, pale, with a couple of large moles and the ends of some wavy fair hair just visible. 'Okay. Do you want to…' I nod toward the other side of the stairwell, thinking she might be more comfortable being out of sight while I look. She can't get over there fast enough and even takes a few steps back downstairs, finally stopping about halfway. Once she's settled, I take a deep breath and click on the folder.

There's just one video inside, framed with the same icon. Which tells me nothing. Am I really going to have to watch this? There's nothing else to identify the album, not even a date, so he must've deleted the timestamp.

I don't think I have much choice.

As I press play, I only half look at the screen, the same way I watch most of those horror films I love so much.

It only takes a few seconds of anxious squinting to question if the woman in the video is actually Mags. All I can see is her back, moving with him – as well as a brief shot of him turning the camera round to focus on himself, smirking like the Dickhead Scumbag he really, truly is – but her body looks shorter than Mags, her shoulders wider.

I don't think it's her.

'I don't think this is you,' I call down the stairs as it plays, the audio faint in the background.

'Are you sure?'

'Pretty sure.'

I turn back to the image and almost drop the phone again in my haste to unsee it. 'Fucking *hell*.'

'What?'

I close my eyes and breathe, turning the screen down against my leg, momentarily forgetting in my panic how to make it stop. I see him grab her hair, yanking her head back; I see her face, wet with tears and mascara as she sobs, *begs*—

Thank god it wasn't Mags.

'It's definitely not you,' I tell her croakily.

But some poor other woman went through this. How many?

How long has he been doing this? Had he done the same to them that he did to Mags, threaten them, demand more, hold it over them? My brain short circuits abruptly back to those few months I worked for him when he first started. All those phone calls I used to field, those women, a parade of them, distressed and on the verge of tears…

Oh god. Oh god, *no*. Were they… are those women *here?* Was that what was going on back then? Has he really been doing it *all this time?*

Tears sting my eyes as the memories of those months come flooding back. Telling the old Division Head – pre-Rebecca taking over – that I thought something was wrong, talking to one of the girls in HR and trying to explain how the desperation in these women's voices didn't feel right, like there was more to it, beyond his explanation of bitter, jilted exes. All those women – have they been living like Mags all this time, looking over their shoulders, constantly waiting for the other shoe to drop?

Then the guilt hits me.

Could I have done more?

Could I have *stopped* this?

In my daze, I haven't noticed Mags make her way back over. 'Was it bad?'

I can't think of an adequate response, so I just nod.

Mags takes the phone, flicking back and forth again. 'Okay, let me have another look. How about… *oh*.'

I look up at her. She looks like she's seen a ghost. The irony. 'What?'

She swallows dryly and points. 'I missed that one before. I think that's me. Birthmark,' she explains dully, tapping her right hip. 'Here.'

I see the icon and nod back toward the stairs. 'Go on. I'll call you back when I'm done.'

She doesn't need telling twice. Once she's out of sight, I still don't open it. Not at first.

You can do this, I berate myself over and over. Your last good thing. Do it for *her*.

With tears in my eyes, I open the folder.

There's more than one video in it. I count three… four. All short. But there are pictures, too. A lot of them. And I don't need to tap on any of them to be certain. About halfway through the album, I see part of a face, big blue eyes behind strands of hair, a bit of an ear, the flash of a gold necklace I recognise.

It's unmistakeably her. This time, the bile rises in my throat so fast I don't have time to stop it and I lean over quickly into the corner, retching. Nothing comes out, but I can taste it in my mouth all the same.

Mags' voice echoes from the staircase. 'Dot? Are you okay?'

'I'm so sorry, love,' I sniffle in reply, unable to fight the tears. 'Oh, I'm so, so sorry.'

She dashes back up. 'You found it?'

I nod, wiping my face with my hand.

'You're *sure?*'

I meet her eyes sadly. 'Positive.'

She looks down briefly. When she meets my eyes, she's pure steel again. I don't know how she's managing it. 'So we've got him?'

'I think so. God, I *hope* so.'

With a thin smile of triumph, Mags strides purposefully across to the door and taps on it gently.

Paul opens up. 'Everything okay?'

'Could you get Jackie, please?' she asks politely.

He turns and waves and Jackie's footsteps echo as she trots swiftly over to join us.

'Well?' she looks through the doorway, back and forth between us, impatient for news. 'Are you done?'

I nod. 'We're done.'

'So…' she glances hesitantly at Mags. 'Should I call HR?'

Mags turns back to me, a quick glance at the phone in my hand, fire in her eyes.

'No.'

She shakes her head briefly, turning back to Jackie.

'Call the police.'

30

Jackie called the police first, HR second. Mags and I hung about in the stairwell, waiting for one of the HR bods who came down for an informal chat. Right when the seminar was stopping for a comfort break, a couple of coppers showed up. Impeccable timing. Jackie herded us into a smaller meeting room, away from prying eyes, although not fast enough to avoid being spotted by Zoe, Paula and three other fee earners from our floor.

The police weren't keen on either me or HR being there, but Mags refused to let go of my hand, which she'd been holding since the moment Jackie went to call them. So, they took statements from each of us, along with Dickhead Scumbag's phone and a bundle of copy documents which the HR rep handed over – his personnel file. By the time it was done – that first step, the push to get the ball rolling – it was nearly lunchtime, and we were both drained, feeling we'd been through a couple of weeks in the space of as many hours.

Izzy Ramsay is waiting as we leave the meeting room and smiles kindly at Mags. They waste no time on pleasantries.

'Security will escort him to clear his desk once you're out of the building. He's on immediate suspension.'

My heart sinks. 'Only suspension?'

'For now. Just until he's formally charged. Then he's gone.'

'For good?'

'A charge is enough, even if it goes nowhere. He'll be reported to the Law Society,' they explain. 'They might not strike him off without a conviction, but… he won't be our problem anymore.'

'Hope springs eternal,' I mutter.

A curt nod. 'It certainly does.'

Mags smiles at them. 'Thank you.'

'Thank *you*. What you did took a lot of courage. And it's not over yet. You do realise that?'

She nods. 'I do.'

'When you're next in the office, come talk to me. I might have a more engaging role coming up in my team, if you're interested.'

Mags beams, thrilled.

'Erm, you might want to have a chat with Rebecca,' I suggest sheepishly. 'She might have her eye on Mags for something else as well.'

'What?' Mags turns to me quickly.

'She owes me a favour,' I shrug.

A big one.

Izzy raises their eyebrows. 'You're quite in demand. I'm sure Rebecca and I can figure something out between us when she's back.'

I elbow Mags in gentle encouragement. Things are looking up.

'In the meantime, you two are both signed off sick, I understand. So I don't want to see either of you back here for what little time remains of this week,' they order with stern sarcasm.

'No chance of that,' I nod, trying not to think about how little time remains for me at all. I can almost hear the Countdown music in the back of my head.

'I believe Jackie has the benefit of a corporate credit card. Why don't you let her use it to take you both for lunch?'

Jackie's already waving from the front desk, twiddling the plastic merrily in her hand. I feel myself hesitate, needing to get back to Rebecca's. More importantly, to Theo. But with no appetite first thing this morning, I skipped breakfast completely, and now I'm actually hungry. There's only one thing left I can do for Theo now, and once I've done that, it's *all* over. If I'm never going to see Mags or Jackie again after today, I can at least spare an hour to say goodbye. 'Why not.'

'Very good.' Izzy nods briskly in acknowledgement and heads towards the lifts.

Jackie dashes over to us with a squeal, grabbing Mags and clutching her tightly, practically giddy as she dances her across reception, 'I'm so proud of you, Mags. You did so well.'

'Thanks, Jack.'

'I wish they'd arrest him now, though,' she shakes her head mournfully. 'I'd have paid good money to see him marched out of here in handcuffs.'

'You're not the only one,' I nod.

'And we get a free lunch!' she babbles excitedly. '*And* Izzy's given me the afternoon off!'

'Really?'

'Told you, they're a good one. So, what will it be, ladies? Oysters at Adams? The tasting menu at Opheem?'

'I don't think Izzy wants you to completely take the piss with that card,' I frown dubiously, turning to Mags. 'What do you fancy?'

'Me?'

'It's your day,' I shrug.

And my last, I don't say to anyone.

Mags looks between us, uncertain. 'Actually, I could murder a Starbucks.'

I laugh as Jackie groans in disapproval. 'Of course you could. New Street, or the one down on the corner?'

'How about the Bullring?' she suggests. 'Less chance of bumping into other work people.'

So off we head across town, not too far but far enough to put some distance between us and recent events. I walk a little way behind them – Jackie yammering on at Mags in that unflappably cheery, personable way of hers, Mags relaxing under her arm, enjoying the slow beginnings of normality creeping back. Selfishly, hearing her laugh properly for the first time in a week brings me some comfort of my own.

I did it.

I did a *good* thing.

Even though most of it was down to Jackie, and Izzy, I still get to feel like I helped.

Soon, I have to do something much, *much* harder.

Oh god, Theo. Thinking about him sends a bolt straight through my heart. I miss him, and it *hurts*.

After Jackie thoroughly enjoys herself at the till abusing the corporate card, we get settled at a window table, decanting trays of drinks, sandwiches, a salad for Mags and cakes for us all.

Then, out of nowhere, Mags blindsides me.

'Right then. Now you can fill us in.'

I look back at them, barely halfway out of my coat. 'What do you mean?'

'This business with Rebecca,' Jackie lilts.

I flash Mags a look. 'You told her?'

She shrugs. 'You told her my thing. Figured it was fair dos.'

'That was different—'

'Bollocks,' Jackie growls. 'What's going on? And why were you all upset when you picked this one up this morning?'

I should've paid more attention on the walk over. They looked conspiratorial, the two of them, scheming little pair of—

'More importantly, what's up with the sexy Vicar?' Mags adds cheekily.

'Ooh yeah,' Jackie leans in, eager for juicy gossip. 'Is this the one from the party?'

'You should've seen her with him yesterday,' Mags giggles.

'He walked into her bedroom with a tray of tea and biscuits—'

That's it. That's what finishes me off. That perfect memory of him, so sweet and thoughtful, like he'd done it a million times before, like it was just so normal.

A snapshot of what our life together might've been, if only we'd had a real chance at one.

I collapse into my chair in a bawling heap of sobs.

'Oh shit.'

'Dot, oh no,' Mags moves quickly over to crouch beside me, a reassuring hand on my leg as Jackie looks on. 'I knew something was up.'

'Come on, lovey,' Jackie encourages gently. 'Talk to us.'

'Please, Dot.'

I can barely breathe, let alone form words.

'*Please*,' Mags urges. 'You never…' she trails away, looking to Jackie for backup.

'You never talk to us,' Jackie steps in. 'You never let us look after you.'

Mags nods, pulling a pocket tissue out of her bag with her other hand and pressing it into mine. 'You always look after me,' she says quietly. 'You always look out for me—'

'For both of us,' Jackie interrupts. 'And not just *us*, either.'

'You're always helping *someone*. Me, Jack, the other secs at work, Lisa, her girlfriend.'

My chest starts to ease.

'But you never let us help *you*.'

The tears slow, and finally still. I sniffle into the tissue, glancing tentatively at Mags. 'How much have you told her?'

'As much as I know. What you told me yesterday.'

Jackie raises her eyebrows teasingly. 'Always knew you were a bit of a dark horse.'

Mags inches gradually back into her seat. 'Well?'

When I told her what little I did yesterday, about me, she didn't point and laugh. She didn't turn me away, she didn't look at me with disgust, with disbelief, with horror.

The world didn't end.

Mine might be about to, but maybe before that happens, I should tell them both the truth.

So I do. I tell them the truth. *All* of it.

It's a jumbled old mess, pretty garbled in places, as I fight to maintain my bearings and calm myself down. But eventually, it all comes out, as coherent as it is unbelievable. Me, my bizarre childhood, my spooky side hustle. The appearance of the Voice on Friday night, before we set foot in that house, before I learned what it actually *is*. The real reason I passed out in reception on Monday. Everything that's happened at Rebecca's since, including dragging old Grace out of the woodwork to stick her oar in how well that all worked out. Yesterday's revelations, desperately trying to claw back those memories before I introduced Theo to Mags. Everything that kicked off after that back at the house.

And, of course, all about Theo himself.

Lovely, sweet, funny, gorgeous Theo. How he was so cheeky, but so shy. How one look at his smile lit up every corner of my otherwise dusty, neglected heart. How we promised each other we'd figure it all out between us… after all of this. But now, I had to break that promise. Now, there was no after.

'So this gorgeous man of yours is stuck somewhere?' Jackie's been watching me carefully as I've been sharing my outrageous story.

'Yeah.'

'And the only way to get him back is to get the thing that's stuck him there to shift out from him and into you?'

I frown, feeling I know where this is going. 'I know how it sounds, Jack, really, but— I swear—'

'No, no,' she waves away my defensive auto-response. 'I believe you. I just— can't you just move it into someone else instead?'

'Or some*thing* else,' Mags suggests. 'Like, I dunno, a vase, or a pot, or their cat or something.'

I appreciate the sentiment. There's no trace of sarcasm from either one of them. They're both utterly earnest. 'They don't have a cat, and it's not a genie. I can't just seal it up in a magic lamp.'

'Can't you *force* it out of him, though? Back to how it was before?' Mags blinks at me like it's the most obvious solution in the world. 'You said he— Theo— can get into your head because of your connection, this shared Voice. So if he can get into your head, why can't you go into *his* and kick it out from the inside?'

I catch myself. It's so simple. I can't believe it never occurred to me.

I shake my head slowly. 'I never even…'

Mags frowns as I trail off. 'You never thought of that? Seriously?'

'You see,' Jackie rolls her eyes at me, teasing gently, 'this is why you should tell us stuff more often. Bloody hell, Dot, what sort of half-arsed medium *are* you, anyway?'

'A stupid one, apparently,' I murmur, thinking it over.

Could it work?

Could I really just leave myself, go into Theo, and push it out of him? Once I leave myself, if it realises, it'll head straight into me.

'Come on, Dot. What are you thinking?'

I don't know how long it takes for it to go between hosts. Is it instantaneous, in the way we understand time, or is there a gap? If it catches me in Theo's subconscious, would I have time to get back into myself, before it could slip out while I'm vulnerable and take me over?

'There's so much I don't know,' I sigh, troubled. 'The only way I can *guarantee* it letting Theo go is by giving it what it wants.'

Mags leans across the table. 'What happens to you, though? After that?'

Ah. Yeah. I haven't told them this part yet. 'Well, erm...'

They both stare at me intently.

'I, er... we can't let it stay in me,' I explain vaguely. 'It's too dangerous for it to have control of that power. It can't get what it wants.'

'But aren't you doing just that?'

I shift uncomfortably in my seat. 'Um... well, not exactly.'

'Meaning?'

'We're just— I sigh wearily. Here we go then. 'We're letting it *think* it's getting what it wants, letting it inside me, so it gives Theo up.'

Mags frowns suspiciously. 'How?'

I clear my throat awkwardly, 'Well, once it's in me, if it can't stay there, it'll have to go back where it came from, you see. It can't use anyone else the same way.'

'But why couldn't it stay in you, Dot?' Mags is leaning so far across the table now, her face is barely inches from me, her eyes boring into mine, her sleeve threatening to drag into the dregs of my coffee.

I grimace hesitantly. 'Because I won't be here.'

Jackie looks at Mags. 'What does she mean?'

Mags ignores her, laser focused on me. That fire is back in her eyes as she glares, her mouth set harshly. I think she might have figured it out. '*No*,' she says firmly.

'What does— why won't she be here?' Jackie still hasn't caught up, nudging Mags for an explanation before she turns back to me. 'Dot, why won't you be here?'

Mags refuses to look away, so I do it for her, looking down at the table and fiddling with my scrunched-up napkin.

'She's going to kill herself.'

'What?' Jackie exclaims.

'That's your foolproof plan, right?' Mags simmers. 'You're going to let it get inside you, then kill yourself so it can't finish its evil plan?'

'Dot,' Jackie shakes her head, 'you're *not*—'

'Of course I'm not.' When I swallow, my throat feels thick. 'Rebecca's doing it for me.'

'What?!'

'*What?!*'

Heads turn as they exclaim in unison, wandering what drama's unfolding at our table. I shrug, refusing to look at either one of them. 'Or Rob. I don't know. One of them has to, in case it stops me before I have chance.'

'What if as soon as you let it in,' Mags drops her volume to a harsh whisper, 'it turns around and uses you to kill Rebecca and her whole family before they have chance to finish you off?'

'Not to mention this lovely Vicar of yours,' Jackie frowns.

Now I look up, my eyes darting uncertainly between them. That's a hell of a flaw in my plan I hadn't thought of.

'I…' I shake my head despairingly. 'It's the best chance we've got.'

'What about what I just suggested?'

'Go into Theo and push it out? I don't even know if I can *do* that,' I sigh. 'And if I try, I'll be leaving my body vulnerable, open to it. It could still get in there.'

'And your Guides can't protect you while you're gone,' Mags muses, 'because if it realises they're helping, it'll hurt Theo.'

I nod. 'Yeah. Same with Grace, or any other mediums. I daren't. I won't risk Theo.'

She tips her head in thought. 'Didn't you say Rebecca and

the others helped protect you before? They're not mediums. Can't they do that again?'

'They've got to protect themselves at the same time,' I explain. 'And protecting me when the thing is randomly pratting about is different to stopping it from…' I search for an appropriate word.

'Invading,' Mags suggests.

That covers it unpleasantly enough.

For a minute we're quiet in our own trains of thought, and I pick unenthusiastically at my lemon loaf. I would've preferred a brownie for my last meal, but they were all taken.

'What if you had more protection than Rebecca and her family?'

'I already told you. I can't call Grace or my Guides—'

'I don't mean them. I mean us.'

Mags points to Jackie then back to herself.

'Hell yeah,' Jackie chimes in, reaching over to Mags for a fist bump. 'Let's kick some demon spirit *ass*. I'm up for that.'

'Don't be ridiculous.'

'Why is it ridiculous?' Mags glares at me.

'Because there's no way in a million years I'm dragging you two into this,' I hiss back, trying to keep my voice down. 'You're not going within a mile of that bloody house.'

'Will you just listen? For *once?*'

More heads turn, and the Baristas exchange uncomfortable glances. I wonder if they might ask us to leave.

'It's not ridiculous,' Mags lowers her voice as I sit back, arms folded stroppily across my chest. 'You said the others were able to protect you before because they love each other. That gave them strength and power to help you. And they're not mediums.'

I shrug, irritated that I'm even entertaining any part of this conversation.

'So why can't we do the same? We love you.'

'Love ya babe,' Jackie winks in confirmation, grinning cheesily as she grabs my hand across the table.

I can't help but laugh.

'Lisa too, and Pen.'

I shake my head. 'No.'

'But Dot—'

'It's too *risky*.'

'Too risky?' she splutters in disbelief.

'There's no guarantee it would work. And if it didn't—'

'*Guarantee?*' Mags is outraged. 'There's no guarantee your stupid kamikaze plan'll work either, but you're willing to risk making Rebecca and her husband murderers in the process.'

I flinch. 'That's not fair, Mags.'

I glare back down at the table, sullen and annoyed. Mostly because she has a point. Several of them, in fact.

She reaches back across the table, gently taking my hands in hers. 'Dot, just tell me one thing.'

I blink back up at her. 'What?'

'What would *Theo* want you to do?'

Her words slap me cold right across the face. Ah, *bugger*. Well, I know the answer to that, don't I? And it wouldn't involve me dying, no matter how noble the cause.

'That's low.'

She shrugs. 'Did it work?'

I push my barely-touched, dry slice of cake away.

I miss Theo. I don't want to leave him.

I want this whole miserable business to be over with. For better or worse.

'Dot, come on,' Mags urges gently. '*Please*. Just let us help.'

Finally, I nod back at them resignedly.

'Okay.'

If Mags and Jackie could replicate what Rebecca and the

others did before, if their presence could amplify the effect, to stop it getting into me while I snuck away into Theo's head, maybe Mags' idea could work.

It's *possible*.

It relies heavily on me being able to get into Theo effectively enough to tap into his buried abilities, the parts of himself he hadn't remembered yet, and use that to push the thing out.

I'm not completely convinced. But Mags' suggestion that the second Mr Demon Spirit got cosy in me, it might immediately turn around and dispose of every remaining live body in that house stuck a horrific mental picture in my mind that nothing could shake loose. It is a deceiver, after all, A liar. It was from the very beginning.

If I can force it out of Theo, and the others can stop it getting into me...

I can fight it.

I'd be doing that alone. Even if Theo snapped straight back out of it once he was freed, having been occupied for so long and to such an overwhelming degree, he'd be exhausted, at his lowest ebb. The others would do what they could to protect him as well as me, but when I'm inside him, I'd need to put his wall back together as best I could, make it strong enough to stay standing after I left. I couldn't risk the sneaky fucker turning around and jumping straight back into him once it realised it had nowhere else to go.

The question was, was I up to it?

I went through with them in painstaking detail what they'd need to do: how to use the wall, how to chant, what sort of nonsense to expect from the demon. Then we parted ways, aiming to meet back at Rebecca's in a couple of hours.

In the meantime, I went back to the house and pulled Rebecca out into the garden, the safest place away from prying ears. Her relief at the change of plan was palpable, but there was no guarantee it would work, and I needed her to understand that if it all went wrong – if they couldn't collectively stop it from taking over me after all – we'd be back where we'd started, and she or Rob would still have to do the necessary to get rid of me, in order to get rid of *it*.

Assuming it gave them the chance, of course.

What little time was left I spent with Theo, quietly holding his paralysed hand in mine, until the doorbell rang. Rob beat the rest of us to the front door, just.

'Surprise!' Mags sings as he opens it, Jackie in tow.

Plus Lisa and Penny.

Mags grins broadly up at me from the steps. 'I brought reinforcements.'

They wave cheerily behind her.

'What? But—'

'No arguments,' Mags shakes her head sternly. 'We told them what was going on and they wouldn't take no for an answer.'

'Yeah, mate,' Lisa folds her arms with a frown. 'I always thought your weird side hustle was just that, a hustle. Never occurred to me it might be real.'

'We prepped them,' Jackie adds before I can ask, 'with everything you told us to do.'

'So we're good to go,' Pen pipes up behind her.

I sigh, rubbing my forehead, feeling ganged up on. Is this really a good idea? Or a bloody awful one? I don't even know anymore.

'Strength in numbers,' Mags suggests hopefully.

Rob leans toward me. 'We can use all the help we can get.'

I look from him, back to the huddled group. I mean, Mags and Jackie are already taking such a huge risk. What's two more people in the firing line because of me, eh?

'Do I have any chance of actually winning this argument?'

The four of them exchange glances.

'No,' their collective voices reply in comical unison.

Well, that's me told.

I step back from the doorway to let them through, Rob leading them politely to the front room, and hear voices as a round of awkward introductions are made.

Mags hangs back with me as I close the door. 'Dot, before all this starts,' she grasps my shoulder gently. 'I just wanted to say... I didn't— I mean—'

'Come on mate,' I nudge gently, 'spit it out.'

She matches my warm expression. 'I never apologised to you.'

I'm mystified. 'For what?'

'For what I said on the phone,' she explains. 'About you. Saying nobody likes you, and...'

The unpleasant memory of our conversation settles uncomfortably back on my shoulders. 'Oh. That. No need.'

'It's not true,' she exclaims. 'None of it. I didn't mean any of it. I was just hurt, and angry, and it wasn't your fault.'

'Hey, I know that,' I reassure her, quietly relieved to hear her say so out loud. 'You had so much to deal with.'

'I lashed out at the wrong person,' she goes on firmly, determined to get out what she wants to say. 'I said it because I knew it'd hurt you, and I wanted someone else to feel as crappy as I did. But it wasn't true, not a word. I need you to understand that.'

'I do,' I nod back. 'I *do*. I promise.'

Mags leans forward, embracing me tightly. 'I'm so, *so* sorry Dot. To say something like that, so deliberately, knowing what it'd do to you, that was awful of me. I'm a terrible person.'

'Don't be silly,' I laugh lightly as I hug her. 'You're no such thing. You're just human.'

Pulling back, I meet her eyes and I understand – I really get it – for the first time. Mags is my good friend who actually cares about me. She wants to be there for me, to help, to accept me as I am, good and bad, warts and all, if only I'll let her. Jackie too, and Lisa and Penny.

'We both are,' I shrug.

I love all of them.

Mags smiles, dropping her arms as she takes my hands in hers. 'Let's go get your boyfriend back.'

I roll my eyes as we wander towards the front room. 'Don't call him that.'

'Why not? That's what he is, isn't he?'

I cringe slightly. 'I suppose, but...'

'Then what?'

I pull a face. 'I'm a middle-aged menopausal woman, mate. *Boyfriend* sounds so...teen.'

'What would you rather I call him, your luuurrrver? she teases.

'Hardly,' I laugh. 'He's still a Vicar, remember?'

Well, if I can get him back, he will be.

'Introductions all made,' Rob nods over as we walk in, the kids giggling on the sofa in cahoots with Jackie while Lisa and Pen watch, bemused. 'Becs has just popped next door to check on him.'

'Okay. I'll start in there to wake it up and then... see what happens, I suppose.'

There's a sudden tension in the room as everyone hushes, quiet, serious, all eyes on me, waiting for what comes next. 'You all clear on what you need to do?'

Nods and murmurs ripple through the group.

'Don't take any chances. You guys stay in here, stay together in your groups at all times,' I stress firmly, 'no exceptions.'

Another wave of assent. I nod slowly, giving them all another couple of seconds.

'Anyone want to change their mind? Nobody'll fault you for not wanting to go through with this, but now's the time to speak.'

Some laughs and sighing, but no takers.

'It's a bit late for that,' Rebecca's voice chimes smoothly as she reappears from the other room. 'For us, anyway.'

I breathe finally. 'Okay then. Let's get started.'

I cross the floor, heading into the back room where Theo sleeps. My plan is for the others to hang back here, keep some physical distance between them and it, give them extra time to build up their protection, and the strength they'll need to give me mine. When I first wake it – still working through Theo – I'm concerned it might look one of them in the eyes, see straight through them and know *immediately* what we're up to. I'm less concerned about it doing that with me – I can still block it from probing – but there is one thing that risks me giving it all away.

Seeing Theo himself.

If it were really him, I'm not sure there's anything I can keep from him. I don't trust myself to look Theo in the eye and not become an open book.

And anything Theo sees, whilst it has him, that thing sees it too. So I have to tread carefully.

There's a chair still next to the sofa where his body lies. I pull it a few feet away and sit facing him, then close my eyes. A couple of deep breaths to centre myself tap into the frequency I need, and it's time.

'I'm here,' I murmur aloud. 'Come out.'

A pause.

Then a voice. *Its* voice. 'You are here early, dear girl. You must be keen.'

I open my eyes. Theo's form is alert, upright in the middle of the sofa, still and straight, feet planted evenly on the rug.

'There remains at least an hour until our deadline.'

I shrug. 'I've made my peace. Rather get it over with, if it's all the same to you.'

It raises its eyebrows with a curious tip of the head, then shrugs dismissively. 'Do you wish to say your goodbyes to him now?' Its voice drips with disdain.

'No.'

It starts at that, surprise briefly crossing its features. '*No?*'

'No,' I repeat calmly. 'I've told him everything there is to say.'

It frowns suspiciously. 'You do not wish to hear his voice? One last time?'

'What would be the point?'

It glances briefly around, as though looking for an answer. 'Dear girl, I really have no idea. You humans are usually so… *sentimental* about such things.'

'I've never been much for sentiment,' I reply truthfully. I never have been.

Not until extremely recently. Like in the last three days.

It nods, turning pointedly in the direction of the living room. None of the others are visible to it, but the low murmur of their voices, already joined in chant, is just audible. 'I see you brought friends.'

'Moral support. For Rebecca, and the others.'

Its head snaps abruptly enough I hear a crack in Theo's neck, and I bury my flinch hard, not wanting to show it any concern, any weakness it might exploit. But deep down, I worry what it might do to his neck for real if it realises what they're really up to next door.

Its eyes narrow sceptically. 'Is that so.'

'Some extra protection to back them up,' I reply, not entirely untruthfully.

It considers my answer with an offended frown. 'I begin to wonder if you trust me, dear girl.'

'Of course I don't.'

It bellows with throaty, coarse laughter.

'You said no mediums,' I shrug. 'None of them are mediums.'

'That is *patently* clear,' it spits contemptuously, rolling its eyes.

'What do you care then?'

It considers for a second, then decides to dismiss it, comfortable in its arrogance, its certainty in its superiority. When it speaks again, its voice is eager, tinged with malevolent glee. 'Shall we begin?'

I nod slowly, close my eyes, relax my shoulders, and prepare.

31

Breathing steadily, I slow the pace gradually in my mind, until everything inside me is still.

Silent.

Open.

I hope I can do this. No Guides, no Grace, just me.

I drop into the deepest state of meditation I can reach, and as I slip into the mist, I leave a metaphysical door tantalisingly open behind me. Only a tiny door – Alice would need half a dozen Drink Me potions to get through – but enough to show willing, encourage it to tiptoe out, make it believe if it releases its tentacled grip on Theo, it'll get what it wants from me.

When Mags presented her suggestion earlier, filling my head with images of potential bloody, horror for the Hudson-Hicks' once I let it inside me, the strongest and most disturbing sight was of Theo. Left alive, but a broken shell in every way possible, his psyche permanently damaged from the overwhelming malevolence left by its lingering presence, and by some final, twisted parting gift it planned to leave behind as it departed from him: a single seed of doubt. The torturous idea that some part of it might still be there, would always be there, looking over his shoulder from deep within his mind. On top of that, the guilt and loss and desperation he'd return to – me lost, us lost, the family murdered in the sickest ways imaginable, utter carnage – and there it would leave him, abandoned, swallowed utterly by despair, refusing to give him a way out, forcing him to relive the nightmare over and over until he finally took sweet release for himself.

It wasn't *just* a mental picture Mags painted. It sparked a vision in my mind, clear as day, of what would happen if we went ahead with my plan. This is what I *know* now: this evil thing, this demon spirit which thrives on chaos and malice and darkness, will *not* merrily skip its way on out of Theo's consciousness, dance into mine and leave him behind whole. Not a chance.

Which is why I'm determined to escort the fucker out myself.

As I head into the mist to look for Theo, and find my way into his head, I can only hope the others lock and bar my little Alice door enough behind me. Because for now, I'm back in the fog, passing places which feel oddly familiar, despite appearing to simply be variations of the same otherworldly nothingness. There's a spot here which evokes the feeling I had in that first moment Theo spoke to me at the party, in the food queue, thinking he looked tastier than anything on the menu. I can almost smell the smoky pork being dished out, the warm bread rolls and gravy and apple sauce. Another, now: the moment he crossed the library to check on me, narrowly missing being hit by low flying occult devices. The concern and care in his voice as he asked if I was okay, before I knew the *other* Voice I'd been talking to was *also* him, some other part of him, long locked away. And one more: Grace's reaction to seeing him and I together for the first time in god knows how many years. And the circle, fighting it, pushing it away, realising he saw it, wondering what that meant.

Then, suddenly I find myself *flooded* with emotions. I'm back in the Orangery with him: he's reading his book, we're talking, I'm sitting in his lap, and everything that happened that night envelops me in joy, those precious minutes we shared in the stillness of the early hours.

I begin to understand.

Every moment I'm reliving is one we shared. One we felt *together*. It's like a map, or road signs, each one marking a spot along the path the two of us have been walking side by side over the last few days.

No. Not road signs.

Breadcrumbs.

The book he was reading that night. The fairy tales. He's Hansel, and he's left a trail of breadcrumbs for me to follow.

So that's what I do.

I move on towards the next impression, and it's the strongest feeling yet, the pull of it enough to overwhelm even that heady memory of us together in the Orangery.

It's the moment I showed him the photo.

Now I realise. The feelings I'm having aren't my own.

They're his.

They're what *he* felt in those moments we shared. What he felt when we talked, when we kissed. What he felt the first time he saw the picture, the split second when he realised what it had to mean.

I feel it all: his confusion, not understanding how it was possible, then a little fissure opening in his fogged mind as the light of his memory started to poke through. His anger – towards his parents, towards Grace, for taking us away from each other – how powerless he'd felt back then, how hopeless, how lost. But he was just a kid too. As he got older and his life unravelled, his instinct that something was missing, some part of him that once existed but somehow just disappeared, that he could never put his finger on.

How every so often he'd have a random, consuming feeling out of nowhere, tickling in his brain, crying out in loneliness like it was searching for him, and all he could do was tell it not to worry, that it'd be okay, he was there, whatever was wrong would pass. But he never understood what the feeling was, or where it came from. Until that moment when he looked at the picture and it started to come rushing back, and that part of him which had never been able to find the answer forever on the tip of his tongue suddenly knew that feeling had been *me*.

In my worst moments, the depths of my loneliness, when I hadn't been able to breathe or think or see any way out – in my mind, I had called to the Voice, begged it to help, to hold me up, to stand me on my feet again, and the Voice came. *Theo* came. When he didn't even know that he could, when he didn't even understand what was being asked of him or why. On some level, he always knew. He knew he was needed, he knew *I* needed him, so the Voice spoke for him, sending me the comfort he couldn't.

I'm surrounded in nothingness, swallowed whole by this moment, by the fullness of it, its purity and its joy.

It's the moment he knew he loved me.

None of these memories, these thoughts, these feelings, are mine. This is no part of my mind. This is all *his*. I've a feeling we're not in Kansas anymore.

And then there's nothing, just fog, but filled with light, and then—

There he is.

I see him in the distance, just like I had when we talked in the 'other' place yesterday, when he accidentally on purpose took a daytrip into my head. But this time, he's on the floor, curled up on his side in the foetal position, head tucked down tightly, shielded by his arms. My first instinct is to go to him, but as I start to close the gap between us, there's an audible *thunk* as I walk straight into something hard and unyielding.

It's his wall.

I hadn't noticed it before, because it's transparent. Looking closer, I can see the opaque bricks, shimmering as they line up tightly, and I immediately wonder why on earth he'd make a see-through wall, of all things. But then I hear a growl from somewhere nearby, and when I look up, I understand.

The noise comes from the depths of a different mist, floating some distance from me. Tinged with purple-red edges, at its core it looks like a black hole, heaving and pulsating as it searches the edges of Theo's barely visible structure, the creeping vacuum at its centre sucking and probing as it tries to find purchase. Theo's form shifts slightly, and the wall trembles beneath my fingers as the section where the amorphous creature searches for a way in changes into solid, hard red brick. The mist recoils, tottering away quickly, its oily purple-red tendrils wrapping briefly around the rest of its form, as if soothing itself from an attack. Abruptly, it advances to a different section, only for another shudder to run through the structure at that exact spot, firming it up just as quickly. The creature reels, shrinking away, far back into the distant fog until finally, it's nowhere to be seen.

For now.

Where I'm standing, Theo's structure is less hardy. There are bricks crumbling at their edges and some blown altogether, and I realise he must only invoke its solidity when the creature attacks, when it tries to reach him. That's why the wall is clear, so he can watch for it and react when it approaches. In his defensive ball on the floor in the centre, I know instinctively it's all he has the strength left to do.

In some other part of my own mind, I hear the distant chants of the others: 'Our love is our strength, our love is our strength.' Beyond that, the faintest of something sliding towards my tiny open doorway, an oily, evil, probing *thing*. It's trying to get into me already, despite not having let go of Theo yet. I knew that fucker was lying.

There's a sudden, ear-splitting *clang* as the others put the plan into action by slamming a steel trapdoor closed against it, shutting it out and forcing it to hover helplessly outside me.

I feel the thing bustle in confusion for a second, then a sudden high-pitched, guttural scream pierces through everything as it realises what just happened.

Back where I am with Theo, the form which just retreated screeches back into view with a hideous howl, barrelling back in our direction.

Time to focus.

Before Theo has time to force what's left of his battered subconscious to fight once more, I take over, filling his wall solid. Every blown, damaged brick is replaced, every inch bricked up hard and full all the way around, so I can't see Theo anymore, and neither can it. The form halts abruptly as it sees the solid obstacle – no longer a hazy, weakening barrier ripe for breach, but a complete, fully formed wall. Not even a wall anymore, in fact, but a bunker. For good measure, I add a layer of steel plate, rings of barbed wire, giant vines of thorns, twisting around one another, anything I can think of to make it even more impenetrable. With every addition the thing pulls back, unsure, a little farther each time, knowing Theo was almost beaten and not understanding how he can be fighting so hard again when he had next to nothing left, not being able to grasp what could have changed since the last time it approached—

Until it spots me.

And then it comes for me. *Straight* for me.

Good. Let it.

It hurtles in my direction, shrieking, oily tendrils stumbling over each other, the abyss at its centre pulsating furiously.

You want what I've got?

Come and get it, you fucker.

I stare it down, unflinching where I stand in this other place, somewhere not entirely of its reality or of ours. At the moment it lands close enough that I almost feel its touch, I breathe deeply and concentrate.

Light surrounds me. I conjure a simple sphere which encloses me completely, putting a glossy, smooth barrier between me and it. It grapples desperately, looking for a hold, feeling for any weakness, anything at all it can exploit.

Good luck with that, mate. This is not that kind of a wall.

Its tendrils meet each other around me as it tries to envelop my sphere in its grasp, and me inside with it. I hold its dark gaze, waiting patiently as its remaining form surrounds me and my ball of light completely, the only thing it can do.

Focus.

I sheathe my sphere of light in a thin film of white-hot lava.

The thing *screams* in sudden agony – *good* – and tries to pull away, understanding too late that this sphere of light surrounding me isn't the protective bubble it appears to be. Understanding that it's not a shield at all.

It's a *weapon*.

The sticky lava doesn't allow it to release its grip. As it tries to pull back a single tendril, it yowls in distress as the limb rips violently away from the rest of its form, the connective mist in between disintegrating into nothing.

Gotcha, asshole.

The diabolical thing surrounding me whines and claws desperately, looking for any way out of my fiery trap, and I concentrate my energy once more.

My sphere inflates.

As it expands, the wide-eyed form stretches with it, shrieking around me in tortured anguish, fused to the bright orb by the phenomenal heat, unable to free itself, to fight back, to do anything but stare in terror at its own distending form, facing its inevitable and unpleasant end. I'm not I've ever had a sadistic streak, but as I enjoy every moment of its suffering, every one of its agonised screams, it occurs to me that maybe this is what happens when someone – or some*thing* – comes for someone you love. You want to cause them pain, you want them to *hurt*.

The light around me continues to grow, morphing effortlessly around the confines of Theo's bunker, until it finally fills all the space this other place of infinite nothing can hold, the creature's form splitting and pulling around it into smaller and smaller fragments, until it's finally stretched beyond any means of comprehension and the malevolent mist explodes with a *bang*.

But I can't celebrate just yet.

The dregs of it are out of Theo – no coming back from going *splat* like that – and I've left him with more than enough protection back there if it tries to send another part of itself back in. But now it's loose, and I still have one last job to do, back on our side.

Time to finish this.

In a split second, I'm back in my own head again and aware of the room around me. The chanting continues in the other room, but something's disrupting them in there now, interrupting the mantra: I hear a scream, a slam, panicked gasps, fear and chaos. It knows it's been played, and it's back to its old tricks, throwing a toddler tantrum. And not just in the next room with the others – around me, bookshelves clear themselves, knickknacks dive from display spots, light fittings clatter on the walls and in the ceiling.

Theo still lies prone on the sofa, stirring very slightly, but not enough to get him up. I can't leave him alone in here with this chaos, so I dash to the doorway and yell for the others, struggling to be heard above the din.

'Guys, in here!'

We have to be together for the final showdown. I need as much good energy around me as I can possibly have at my disposal.

Rebecca looks up, Jackie too, but they're too panicked to react.

'Quick!' I take two steps in. Jackie's group of four is closer to me so I grab her arm, pulling her towards the sitting room. '*Now!*'

Jackie snaps to attention and grabs Mags' arm, then yanks at Penny's hand to force both of them and Lisa forward. As they scramble towards me, Rebecca understands and follows suit, Rob and the kids tumbling in front of her as she pushes them all through the doorway past me. The noise around us is building, that all-too familiar roar reaching almost unbearable levels as it echoes around the house, surrounding us in every direction.

I turn to the others.

'One group now. Make a circle, all of you, around him.' I nod toward Theo. 'Me in the middle.'

They assemble themselves quickly.

'Chant again.' I almost scream to be heard over the whirlwind carving through the room. 'But follow me.'

Eight sets of wide eyes surround me now, their expressions terrified.

'I will to will Thy will,' I cry, looking at each of them in turn to follow my lead. 'I will to will Thy will.'

Jackie. Lisa. Penny.

They start to pick it up.

'I will to will Thy will.'

Mags. Hannah. Adam.

'I will to will Thy will.'

Rob. Rebecca.

A deep, ominous cackle booms from the walls around us. 'You think you can stop *me*, dear girl?'

'Ignore it. Focus on me. I will to will Thy will.'

'*I will to will Thy will.*'

'I am *eternal*. I am—'

'Look at me, *only* me. Don't stop chanting. Picture a light, the brightest light you've ever seen, but you can look at it—'

'*I will to will Thy will.*'

'You are nothing but *dust, puppets*—'

'You can look directly at it, and everything beautiful you can possibly imagine is in that light—'

Back near the door to the living room, our old friend the mist appears, hovering and vibrating and dark.

And *growing*.

'There's nothing but you and the circle and the light—'

'*I will to will Thy will.*'

The mist expands, reaching, curving, curling around the group, closing its own circle around ours.

'You *dare* try to trick *me?!*' it bellows, enraged. 'You *dare* try to challenge *me?!*'

'Just you, the circle, the light and the chant—'

The darkness thickens around us and as the shadow swallows us all whole, clear in my mind's eye, *I see it*.

Grace was wrong. It's not a demonic spirit, not at all.

'*I will to will Thy will.*'

It's a *demon*. An actual, honest to god *demon*. Trickster, liar, deceiver, impostor, those were the things the Voice called it that first night it intervened. The claws, the horns, everything I'd started to see before, right there in front of me as it stands outside of our circle, growing in size along with the mist, features half humanoid, half animal, dark and imposing and terrifyingly, utterly *evil*. With a twisted smirk, it vanishes suddenly from my sight and I know it's not gone, I *know* it's not finished yet, but where is it? Where did it go?

Oh *god*.

'I will to will Thy will.'

Rebecca's voice, but *not*. The tone is mocking and spiteful and as I turn, I see her face in a snarl, features contorted and marred by shadow as she stops chanting and instead throws back her head, *braying* with inhuman laughter. Before I even have chance to register my own horror at the sight, it's gone, her face back to normal.

'I will to will Thy will.'

The same nightmarish sound peals out behind me, its cold, cackling imitation of laughter. I whip round and see its shadow pass through the features of Lisa's face. Then it's gone again.

Now it's Rob.

Then it's Mags.

Then Penny, Adam, Hannah, Jackie.

I join the chant. Picture my own Light, invoke my Guides, beg all the Powers That Be which might occupy universe to send me anything, *everything* to help me fight it. The tornado swirls around us, a cacophony of thunder blaring from the walls, the darkness of the enormous shadow threatening to consume the room completely, and all of us with it. The thing speaks through Jackie now, raging.

'*I will show you what real power can do.*'

Jackie's body starts to rise slowly, dragging her up from her place in the circle, threatening to break it. Penny and Rob, either side of her, reach up, trying to hold onto her, to pull her back down and away from it.

I close my eyes and give myself up to the universe utterly and completely, feeling the light from the others pour into me, engulfing me as I become a part of it and the void. I feel rather than see as Jackie is pulled higher, the others' hands finally wrenched away, fracturing the circle.

They all rear back, scrambling, terrified, the chant forgotten.

Everything in the room that isn't nailed down is flying now, debris surging around me, bookcases and chairs and side tables shooting in all directions, the others dodging and pulling each other desperately out of harm's way as best they can. Somewhere in the middle of it I hear Rob's voice, a plea to make for the door, cut off as something whips across towards wherever he is and stops him, stops all of them from doing anything more than freezing in terror. No more circle, no more chant.

The only thing still in the room is the sofa beside me, Theo still lying on it, slowly regaining consciousness.

And none of it touches me.

I'm in the epicentre, the eye of the storm, but at the same time I'm also somewhere else, somewhere *other*, between here and the Other Side and whatever plane it is where the demon exists. I'm nothing but a channel, and there's nothing here but me and the demon and the light.

Then—

Something else.

Something familiar. Someone I know. Someone I *love*.

A beautiful, steady, low voice, all calm and faith, filling every remaining corner of my heart.

'I will…'

Somewhere outside of the ether, in the middle of the whirlwind of shadow, a large, warm hand closes tightly around my own.

'… to will Thy will.' I join my voice with his.

And with that, the light *spills* from me, enveloping the room and everything in it with its brilliance. In one final thunderous roar, the shadow shatters into a million fragments, obliterated into the nothingness, as it's swallowed back up by the eternity of the light.

32

The world comes back into focus.

There are moans across the room, one of the kids crying, Lisa asking someone if they're okay. I'm on the floor beside the sofa, sat with my back propped awkwardly against the front of it, Theo's hand still somehow in mine.

Theo.

I turn quickly to check on him, praying he's back, that he's *him—*

He blinks at me, grinning. 'Hey.'

My voice can barely escape past the lump in my throat. 'Hey.'

'We have to stop meeting like this.'

I roll my eyes. After all this, all he's been through, and he's still making stupid jokes. Ridiculous man.

Ridiculous, gorgeous, wonderful man.

Correction. *My* ridiculous, gorgeous, wonderful man.

'Shut up,' I scold gently as I climb up from the floor and into his arms, wrapping myself around him like I never want to let go.

I *don't* ever want to let go.

'Hey,' he reassures me gently, startled by the force of my siege. 'It's okay. I'm okay. It's gone, right?'

I nod into his neck, tears drizzling into his clerical collar.

'Know what that means?'

I pull back to look at him, sniffling as I shake my head. 'What?'

'It's *after*.'

Theo smiles at me, all warmth and love and everything I never realised was missing from my life.

'We made it to *after*.'

He flashes a cheeky eyebrow, and he's so silly, and I love him so much, and I lean in and kiss him and the world disappears.

But not for long enough.

'Dot?'

It's Mags. I break off from Theo and turn to face her, still high on the closeness of him, on him really being back here in my arms again—

My happiness sinks as I see the tears in her eyes.

'Jackie. It's—' her voice breaks.

Jackie.

I'm up in a flash, Theo close behind as we rush over to the others. They're grouped together near the window, the kids hanging back, holding each other and crying. As we reach them, I see Rob with his arm around Rebecca, a nasty cut spilling blood over his right eye as the two of them block the kids' view. On the floor, Penny crouches, talking into her phone opposite Lisa as she leans over—

Jackie.

Lisa's doing CPR on her, methodically switching between breathing and chest compressions. I don't know how long she's been going, but it doesn't look like she's getting any response.

I fall to my knees beside Jackie's prone body. 'Oh no. Oh god no.'

'Ambulance is on the way.' Penny puts her phone away as Lisa nods in acknowledgement.

'What happened?'

Rebecca replies through gentle sobs. 'It had her up in the air still. When it all—'

She breaks off, unable to finish.

'Penny and I tried to pull her down,' Rob goes on sadly. 'But it kept pushing us back. When it all stopped, with that light, she just – she just—'

Penny puts a gentle hand on my shoulder. 'She fell.'

The realisation dawns on me. It had attached to her, was lifting her, was going to use her, hurt her... but the light broke the connection.

So it had to let her go. It had to drop her.

The light made it drop her.

I was the light.

I did this.

This is my fault.

'Jackie, no.' The tears spike my eyes as I grab her motionless hand, flinching at the coolness of her skin under my fingers. I look desperately over at Lisa, focused, working so hard trying to force life where there is none. Theo comforts Mags as they stand hesitantly behind me, and as I look around at the others, dishevelled, dazed, hurt, all I can think is that this is my *fault*.

I did this.

Jackie shouldn't have been in harm's way; she shouldn't have even been here. None of them should've been; it came here because of me, because it wanted me. Jackie shouldn't have got hurt.

It should've been me.

'*No.*'

Theo's down beside me in an instant.

'Don't think that. Don't *ever* think that.'

But I do think that. I can barely look at him as I nod dully through my tears, my guilt, my shame. My fault.

'It's *not* your fault.' He grabs my arms tightly.

Then whose fault is it?

'That thing,' Theo responds to my silent question. 'Not yours.'

I finally croak out actual words, forcing them past the bile threatening to rise in my throat. 'That thing was only here because of me in the first place.'

Theo shakes his head. 'You didn't invite it. It came because of what you have in you, not who you are, and that's nothing you could control.'

Lisa's steady voice stops him going on. 'Guys, you might want to figure out how you're going to explain this.' She nods to the room around us, littered with debris and upended furniture.

'Yeah,' Penny nods. 'Police probably won't be far behind that ambulance. And this place looks…'

'Like something kicked off,' Lisa finishes for her.

'What should we do?' Rob looks from them to Rebecca. 'Should we try and clean it up?'

'No,' Lisa interrupts sharply in between the breaths she's sharing with Jackie. 'You mess with the scene, they'll be able to tell, and that'll be worse.'

'Then what do we tell them?'

'How can we possibly explain—'

I hear their voices around me, but I can't register the conversation. All I can think about is Jackie and how still she is and how cold she feels and how if I'd just told her and Mags *no*, if I'd kept the whole story to myself, if I just hadn't told them the truth—

Theo's voice, low and commanding, rings out above the chatter amongst the others as he puts a reassuring hand over mine.

'We tell them the truth.'

The others hush suddenly, looking at him in surprise as he squeezes my hand then lets it go, standing slowly beside me where I kneel on the messy floor.

'Are you insane?'

'That's crazy—'

'They'll never believe—'

'We tell them the truth,' Theo repeats steadily. 'But the short version. We held a séance to get rid of something in your house, and Jackie got hurt.'

Rebecca and Rob look back at him, speechless.

Theo shrugs. 'They might think we're crazy. But better that than they think we're trying to cover something up.'

Oh god. The police. Again.

'They'll have a lawyer, a doctor, a paramedic and a priest, all telling the same story. And it's not like there's any evidence here to contradict it, because that's what actually happened.'

I'm not a lawyer, or a doctor, or any of those things. I'm just me. The medium in the middle of it all.

Who caused it all.

'Besides, it's a hell of a lot easier to remember the truth.'

They all exchange uncertain glances. I can only look at Jackie.

'We just have to leave one thing out.' He turns to Mags, somewhere behind me. 'Mags, you've had enough dealings with the police for one day.'

My heart calms a little at that. Yeah, that's good. Protect Mags. Keep her out of it. She's been through enough already.

'You take Dot and leave.'

'What?'

'*What?!*' I'm on my feet now, my brain suddenly back in the room.

'Now, before the ambulance gets here,' Theo urges. His instruction to Mags is calm, but there's a note of desperation in his voice. 'We'll tell them what happened, but miss out all the stuff about that demon wanting to take over Dot, and then we can leave you two out of it. I'll tell them the séance was my idea.'

I shake my head. 'Theo, no—'

'Please.'

He turns to me now, taking both of my hands in his, eyes fixed firmly on mine. 'I can read your mind, remember? You're spiralling, you think it's all your fault, and if you're here when the police turn up, you'll self-destruct completely and try to take all the blame.'

I can hardly argue with him. It's not like he's wrong.

'You've been through enough. You've done enough. Let me do this.'

'But—'

The Church. His job. His *life*. If he tells the police the séance was his idea, if they look into any of it, even a little, and the Church find out…

He'll risk losing everything.

Theo smiles at me lovingly as he hears my thought. 'Not everything.'

I feel like my brain's been broken; I can't take all of this in and I don't know what to do.

'But Jackie—'

'Is not your fault. Is nobody's fault.'

I look back down at her prone figure, Lisa still working away diligently, despite it being obvious to all of us by now that it's probably hopeless.

Then I hear sirens. Distant – not at the house yet, not even close enough to have reached the drive, but they're somewhere nearby.

Mags puts a hand on my shoulder. 'We should go.'

I turn to look at Rebecca, standing with Rob, the kids standing sadly between them now. She nods back at me, gesturing to the doorway. 'Go on. We'll take care of this.'

So much is running so fast through my head all at once, I can't get a grip enough to make sense of any of it. As I look back up into Theo's face, tears in my eyes, he squeezes my hands tighter before pulling me in close, holding me like it could be for the last time, fighting back tears of his own as he pleads in my ear.

'Go now. Please.'

'Come on, Dot.' Mags pulls at my arm as the sound of the sirens inches closer. 'We have to go.'

Theo pulls away to let me go. 'Please, Dot.'

I can't believe I'm doing this. Am I doing this?

'*Now*, Dot.' Mags turns for the door, dragging me backwards urgently.

With one final look at the others, the last thing I see is Theo smiling sadly as I stumble over my own feet and let Mags lead me quickly away.

33

I've never slept for so long in my life.

Mags got me home. Being used to driving an automatic, she crunched the hell out of my poor Fiesta on every gear change, but I was in no fit state so there was little choice. Once we were back – and after the pair of us both finished bawling our eyes out – this time, she put *me* to bed, where I promptly went out like a light.

When I woke up, all I knew was that it was dark, my phone wasn't on the bedside table bedside me where I'd left it, and I was absolutely ravenous. So, I made my way groggily downstairs, where I found Mags and Pen in the middle of another Netflix binge.

'I can't find my phone.'

The pair of them look up, surprised as I take a tentative couple of steps into the room. None of it seems real, somehow. Am I dreaming?

'Sleeping Beauty awakes,' Penny grins.

Mags smiles up at me, waggling my phone in her hand. 'I've got it safe, don't worry. You needed rest, and we didn't want you checking it every five minutes.'

Well, there's a role reversal. I have to laugh. 'Thanks, *Mom*.'

Mags winks at me. She seems so much more… herself.

'Is it Friday? Did I sleep all day?'

'Today too,' Penny nods. 'It's Saturday night.'

Woah. 'Seriously?'

'Seriously.'

I look around dozily for the missing member of our little group. 'Is Lisa on shift?'

Pen shakes her head. 'Took a few days off. She's just popped down the chippy. We ordered for you in case you woke up.'

God, Lisa. I know what she did at the house is part of her job and everything, and I suppose she sees it all the time, but still. Having to do that… and it not… working…

'Is she okay?'

'Lisa?' Penny turns to me, the light from the telly flickering across her face. 'Don't worry about her, she's doing just fine. Tired from what happened, that's all. We were all pretty wiped.'

When we left, it all looks so hopeless, but… maybe… was there a chance? 'I don't suppose…'

Might the ambulance crew have been able to… to do something?

'…Jackie?'

Mags looks away, biting her lip as Penny puts a reassuring arm around her and shakes her head. 'Sorry mate.'

I sigh deeply, dull tears threatening to spill again as my heart sinks into my stomach.

'She had a heart attack, mate. Might've even happened before she fell, Lisa reckons.'

Doesn't make me feel any less shit about it. I take a breath.

'What about the police? Did they—'

'It's all been taken care of,' Penny interrupts.

'But—'

'It's sorted,' Mags adds. 'This is exactly why we took your phone away. Becs and Rob—'

Becs? Since when did Mags start calling her that?

'—and Theo—'

My brain seizes. *Theo.*

'—and these guys all gave their statements, and—'

'Is Theo okay?' My chest tightens suddenly, and I reach in Mags' direction to take my phone back. 'Has he messaged—'

She snatches it away before I even get close. 'He's fine. But he wants you to rest.'

'Can't I just—'

'He's sorting stuff out,' Mags explains cryptically. 'He said you're to rest and not worry.'

I haven't heard him. In my head, I mean.

'Just one text, please?'

I'm scared I won't. I'm scared he's gone.

Mags shakes her head sternly, tucking the phone out of sight. 'Nope. He made me promise. *Rest*.'

Penny leans over to her. 'And chips.'

'Right. Chips,' Mags corrects herself, 'then rest. Priest's orders.'

Penny shakes her head. 'Vicar's orders.'

Mags shrugs, eyes back on the telly. 'Same difference.'

So, unhappily, that's what I do: after Lisa gets back with a bag crammed with bundles of chips, fish for the girls, pie for her, chicken for me; once she's finished hugging me practically to death, I eat. Then I rest.

The next time I wake up, it's because Mags is prodding me.

'Come on, you. We can't be late first day back.'

My brain isn't ready to deal with this yet. 'What?'

'Work. It's Monday morning, you dozy mare. Come on, get *up*.'

She yanks the covers away from me with force.

'I've got a meeting with Izzy Ramsay at half-nine, and you're not making me late,' she threatens. 'If you're not ready in twenty minutes, I'm going without you.'

So up I get.

I get ready in a daze, I walk with Mags to the station in a daze, I sit on the train in a daze. That sets the tone as I muddle through the rest of my day, never entirely sure if everything going on around me is actually real, or if I'm still asleep and dreaming. Mags comes back from her meeting excited and nervous, hoping to hear more before the end of the day; Pat's a mysterious no-show, Bonnie and the others cheerily swapping theories about her absence; and although the others have dealt with most of the files left on our desks last week, I'm grateful for some long dictations that still need doing so I can put in my earphones and keep my brain distracted.

Well. Mostly.

In the moments I can't keep it busy, I think about Jackie.

Late afternoon, Mags has been called back upstairs again, and alone in our pod, I think about Jackie.

About how I can't quite believe she's gone. Even though, with what I do, I know nobody ever *really* goes, it doesn't make their leaving any easier. Every time her image flashes inside my mind, I can't help but replay what happened, wondering what I could've done differently, if I could've changed the outcome.

Could I have saved her?

After every thought of Jackie comes the guilt. I don't think it matters how many people tell me it's not my fault; I'll always believe it. How do I live with that? How do I—

STOP IT.

It's *him*.

He's there.

SEE YOU SOON.

Oh. Oh, thank *god*.

LOVE YOU.

I've managed to get through the whole day without crying, but that might just set me off. Thankfully, Mags reappears just in time to interrupt me, her expression shellshocked as she drops into her seat.

'Well?'

She breathes out deeply. 'Well.'

When she doesn't go on straightaway, I give her a gentle nudge. '*Well?*'

Mags turns to me slowly. 'You want the good news?'

Uh-oh.

She grins. 'Or the other good news?'

I remember how to breathe. 'Mate, right now I'll take all the good news I can get.'

'They've offered me a job in Technology. An apprenticeship.'

Yes. At least one good thing's come out of the last week of shite.

'They'll sponsor my training, and I can progress further once I'm qualified.'

God, I'm so proud of her. As I reach over and hug her tightly, my eyes well up for a happy reason for the first time in what feels like forever. 'Oh mate, that's amazing.'

'I start in the new year. I can't…' she shakes her head. 'I can't believe it.'

'Believe it,' I tell her firmly as I pull back. 'You've earned this. You deserve it. Now just don't fuck it up, all right?'

Mags laughs. 'Thanks, Dot. You want the other good news?'

'God, please.'

'He's being charged.'

My eyes widen. 'Dickhead Scumbag?'

She nods. 'Well, they've passed it to CPS, anyway. The Officer in Charge called while I was upstairs. She couldn't give me details, but whatever else the police found was enough to turn it over to them pretty much straightaway.'

'Wow.' So bad people don't *always* get away with shitty stuff all the time. Who knew.

'If CPS charge him, he'll be remanded in custody. Could be months before it goes to court, of course,' she adds ruefully, 'but at least he'll be locked up.'

'Good. I hope he gets the crap kicked out of him in there.'

Honestly, I hope a lot worse happens to him in there because the bastard deserves everything he gets, but you're not supposed to wish things like that on people. So I keep the thought to myself.

Mags sighs. 'I just... I'm not exactly looking forward to giving evidence in court.'

'If they've got that much evidence,' I point out hopefully, 'you might not have to. He might plead guilty.'

'Maybe.' She doesn't sound convinced. 'But if I have to—'

'If you have to,' I remind her, taking her hand, 'I'll be there to hold your hand, right?'

She smiles back, tearing up. 'Right.'

And I suppose I might have to as well. But we'll jump off that particularly heinous bridge when we get to it. If we get to it.

'At least you can get the rest of your bed back soon.'

'That'd be nice. You snore like a fucking freight train.'

'Do not,' she laughs back. 'You ready to go? It's almost five.'

'Just need to shut down.'

'Hurry up then.' Mags nods as I start closing programmes, then looks up and hesitates, leaning over to me. 'Think you've got a visitor.'

'Ladies.'

It's Rebecca.

'I'll meet you in Reception.' Mags jumps up, grabbing her stuff before turning to Rebecca. 'See you tomorrow, Big Boss.'

Rebecca shakes her head. 'Not for long,' she teases gently. 'Traitor.'

Mags winks as she disappears around the corner, leaving Rebecca to perch on the edge of our pod. She waits as Bonnie and a couple of others wander past towards the exit, leaving only Stephen and a couple of other diehard fee earners dotted about in the quiet office, then looks at me steadily.

'I didn't get chance to thank you.'

I force a weak joke. 'For trashing your house?'

Rebecca ignores it. 'For helping my family. For *saving* my family.'

I shrug awkwardly. People don't usually thank me for doing... you know what. 'It wasn't just me. It was all of us.'

Including Jackie, I think dully.

Rebecca shrugs. 'We helped. But you did all the hard work.'

I don't know what to say to that. 'You're welcome, I suppose.'

She smiles back at me knowingly. 'Is it too late to ask another favour?'

I fail to hold back a snort. 'I don't think I'm over the last one yet.'

'Hmm. Well, Pat's handed in her notice.'

I look up at her, startled.

'And her GP's signed her off sick until it's up. I'd like you to step in.'

Oh. Shit. 'I remember you suggested that last time the job was available.'

'I remember you told me I could, and I quote, stick that idea up my arse.'

Hmm. That does sound like something I'd say.

'My answer still stands.'

'It'd be a big pay jump,' Rebecca explains. 'And a signing bonus. Lisa told me how desperate you've been to rent your own place. You could afford it on a team leader salary.'

My own place.

And no more needing my spooky cash in hand side hustle to save for it.

Tempting.

'Can I think about it?'

She frowns, and I can almost see the cogs turning as she comes up with a rebuttal. Such a lawyer. 'Tell you what. Agree to do it on a trial period, while she's signed off sick. Get a feel for it, see how you get on.'

I laugh. 'You mean get used to the pay rise and then I'm stuck with it?'

'You see. That's why I need you to do it.'

'Because I'm desperate for cash?'

Rebecca shakes her head. 'Because you're not an idiot, and you can see through everyone's bullshit. Even mine.'

That might be the nicest thing she's ever said to me.

'I'll think about it.'

'Good.' She stands up, pleased with a semi-result. 'Let me know in the morning. You can start straightaway.'

No pressure.

'Oh, and Dot?'

I look back at her as I put my coat on. 'Hmm?'

'It's Becs,' she replies over her shoulder as she heads back across the office.

Blimey. I'm in the Becs club. She must really want me to take that job.

I try to start a mental list of pros and cons as the lift takes me downstairs, but I've too few working braincells to manage it. As promised, Mags is waiting for me in Reception, and clocks my dazed expression as soon as I step out.

'Everything okay?'

I shrug, still feeling blindsided. 'Weird day.'

'You can say that again.'

We stop at the reception desk together. Phil's been covering, but now it's closed for the day, dark and empty but for some bundles of flowers people have laid. Jackie was incredibly well-loved, and word got around fast this morning.

'I can't believe she's really gone.' I fight back tears again.

'I know. It won't be the same without her.'

Mags puts an arm around me, peering closely at my face.

'She knew what she was getting into, you know. We all did.'

'Did you? Really?' I shake my head. Even I didn't, not really, and I'm supposed to be the experienced one. 'I should never have let you do it. Any of you.'

'And then what would've happened? Something even worse,' she reminds me sharply, 'and you know it. We all went into it with our eyes open. Maybe we were stupid to. But you beat the thing, didn't you, and I don't think that would've happened if we hadn't all been there to give you what you needed.'

I close my eyes, the tears finally falling.

'Even though you did all the hard work.'

I laugh bitterly. 'You sound like Rebecca.'

'She's a smart lady. You should listen to her.'

'Hmm,' I murmur dubiously.

'So was Jackie. And she wouldn't want you blaming yourself.'

Her words sting. I know she's probably right. But it's a lot easier said than done.

'Anyway,' Mags goes on abruptly, nudging me away from the empty desk and down toward the front doors, 'I have a present for you.'

She hands me my phone.

'That's it? My phone?' I frown. 'No chocolate at least?'

'That's not your present.' Mags shakes her head, pushing me through the frosted doors, the cold air enveloping us as we step out into the dark afternoon. '*That*'s your present.'

She nods across the road, and my heart leaps into my mouth.

Leaning on the office building opposite is a handsome, dark-haired figure in a thick winter jacket.

As Theo spots us, he smiles broadly at me, dodging through a break in the traffic to head towards us, and I remember his voice earlier.

SEE YOU SOON.

'Now, what was it you said?' Mags ponders. 'You've earned this. You deserve this. Now just don't fuck it up, all right?'

I can barely breathe as Theo ducks around a car parked in front of us and stops inches away from me.

'Hey you.'

'Hey.' My squeak barely registers as a sound.

He turns quickly to Mags. 'Sorry. Thanks, Mags, for looking after her. For everything.'

'You're welcome, Father,' Mags grins, then leans close to me. 'I won't wait up.'

As she trots away into the chilly evening, waving back as she heads for the station, Theo shrugs apologetically.

'I'm sorry for all the cloak and dagger stuff. I just… I needed to sort some things out, and I was worried but I couldn't be there with you and do that at the same time, and Mags was staying with you anyway, so…'

'I heard you. Earlier.'

'Oh, yeah, sorry about that.' Theo frowns sheepishly. 'I know you don't like me going in there, and I didn't mean to, really, but I could hear you and you were so upset and I just wanted—'

'I thought I might never hear you again,' I interrupt him. 'I thought you might be—'

He looks at me carefully as I stop myself. 'What?'

I can't meet his eyes. 'Gone.'

'From you?' Theo laughs gently, finally stepping close enough to pull me into his arms and hold me tightly against him. 'Don't be daft.'

He's here. He's really here. I'm not asleep, I'm not dreaming, this is actually happening. We're here, together; we made it. We made it to *after*.

It's about us now.

'I have a present for you.'

I laugh, face buried in his jacket. 'Is it chocolate?'

'Afraid not.'

Theo nudges me away gently, freeing up his jacket enough to unzip it and pull something small out of the inside pocket, which he pushes into my hands.

I look at it.

It's the photo. The photo of us.

'That night, when I was… when that thing was…' He struggles to say it out loud. 'When you stayed with me. I heard every word, you know. Every word you said. That's how I held on.'

He pulls me close again, planting a kiss on the top of my head.

'I knew you'd come for me.'

That's it. I can't fight it anymore. It's Sob City, population: Me. I bury my head against his chest in an effort to stem the tide, and that's when I realise something's different.

The shirt I'm wrecking with my tears isn't black. It's blue.

And it's not even a shirt; it's just a top. A smooth, cotton Henley with little buttons at the top, no collar.

No clerical collar.

My tears halt in shock as I lean back to look up at him. 'Did they sack you?'

'Of course not,' he laughs throatily, and it might be the most beautiful sound I've ever heard. 'They weren't thrilled. But no. Still a Vicar.'

He hesitates, and I frown questioningly.

'Technically.'

I forget how to breathe again. 'Technically?'

'I've taken a sabbatical. Three months, plus another month

or so of holiday they owe me from the last few years. While I… think about things.'

I can barely contain myself. While he thinks about things? What things does he have to think about?

Am I one of them?

'What things?'

'Ah, well. That's the other part of your present. If you want it.'

My smirk escapes before I can stop it.

'Not *that*,' he grins back. 'I'm still technically a Vicar, remember? But I thought you might want an apprentice.'

He's lost me. 'An apprentice?'

'You know. To help you fight ghostly crime.'

An apprentice?

'And to help me… figure things out,' he adds shyly. 'You know. With this whole… medium thing. If I should be doing it, or should I go back to the Church, or what.'

Awwww. He's lovely.

He's the loveliest, most gorgeous, sweetest, bravest man I've ever known.

I reach up and put my arms around his neck. 'An apprentice, eh?'

Theo smiles – that *damn* smile, gets me every time – and pulls me closer. 'If you'll have me.'

'I can't pay you.'

His eyes sparkle. 'I'm sure we can come to some arrangement.'

I repeat his words back to him, feigning outrage. 'You're still a Vicar, remember?'

'Only technically,' he reminds me breathily, his face an inch from mine.

I smile back up at him. 'I can work with that.'

As Theo kisses me, the cold November chill and bustling city centre crowds fade around us, as we disappear into our shared

little world and my heart bursts with light.
Yeah, I can work with that.

THE END

Printed in Great Britain
by Amazon